JULIETTE MEAD

Healing Flynn

HarperCollins*Publishers*

This novel is entirely a work of fiction.
The names, characters and incidents portrayed in it are
the work of the author's imagination. Any resemblance to
actual persons, living or dead, events or localities is
entirely coincidental.

HarperCollins*Publishers*
77–85 Fulham Palace Road,
Hammersmith, London W6 8JB

www.harpercollins.co.uk

Published by HarperCollins*Publishers* 2003
1 3 5 7 9 8 6 4 2

Nothing (from *A Chorus Line*) Words by Edward Kleban,
music by Marvin Hamlisch © 1975 Red Bullet Music
and Wren Music Co Inc, USA
(50%) Chappell Morris Ltd, London W6 8BS. Reproduced
by permission of International Music Publications Ltd.
All Rights Reserved.

Lines from *The Once and Future King* by T H White reproduced
by permission of HarperCollins Ltd.

A catalogue record for this book
is available from the British Library

ISBN 0 00 716387 8

Typeset in Sabon by Palimpsest Book Production Limited,
Polmont, Stirlingshire

Printed and bound in Great Britain by
Creative Print and Design, Ebbw Vale, Wales

HEALING FLYNN

Juliette Mead was born in 1960. After pursuing a career in finance in London, New York and Dallas, she switched careers to become a headhunter, which inspired her first work of fiction. She now lives in Wiltshire with her husband and four children, and has written five successful novels.

For my sisters Kathryn and Christine
and in memory of my friend, the writer Janos Nyiri.
I am grateful to and for them.

'When nothing seems to help, I go and look at a stonecutter hammering away at his rock perhaps a hundred times without so much as a crack showing in it. Yet at the hundred-and-first blow it will split in two, and I know that it was not so much the blow that did it, but all that had gone before.'

Jacob Riis

PROLOGUE
April 2000

George glanced round the table at the faces of his colleagues. God only knew what they were thinking, if they were thinking at all. It didn't look like they gave a damn about the poker game. If he closed his eyes and blocked out their listless expressions and the brown, plastic-covered benches lining the walls, he could almost imagine himself at home. If he shut out the background noise of the telly and the Abba song playing tinnily on a small radio, ignored the ever-present mechanical thrum, the sour milk odour that hung in the room and the saltiness in the clammy air, he could pretend he was sitting round the kitchen table with his family rather than killing time in the platform rec. room.

'Rec. room' was a flattering description of his environment. There was not a great deal of recreation to be had on Astra Four, an installation platform which scrambled a hundred feet above the North Sea like a giant Meccano set. The room was little more than a vast Portakabin pegged onto the topside structure of the platform. At one end a cluster of men were idly watching a football match. The green baize table that dominated the room had long since been deserted, and only a handful of off-duty workers still lounged on the benches, their faces tinged an unearthly grey-blue by the overhead strip-lighting. George, the Norwegian and three others were playing poker at the far end. Behind them stood a solitary bookcase with a small selection of tattered paperbacks slung on its shelves. It was said that five or six years earlier somebody had actually started to read one of them, but this, as George delighted in pointing out, was only a rumour. He turned the radio down as the sonorous litany of the shipping forecast began: '*Viking North Utsire, variable five or six, occasionally seven. Rain later. Mainly moderate. South Utsire Forties. Northwesterly backing easterly six or seven, perhaps gale eight later. Moving east and losing its identity. Cromarty Forth . . .*'

The youngest of the players tipped his chair back and scratched an armpit as he studied his cards. 'So long as they say all the names in the right order, you know nothing bad's going to happen.' Getting no reaction, he added, 'That's what my mam says, like.' He instantly regretted the impulsive sharing of this information.

George opened one eye and growled, 'Your mam some kind of meteorological expert then, Micky? Psychic, is she?' Having let the youngster know that by citing a supposedly higher authority – and of all higher authorities, a mother – he had breached the pecking order of the rig, George slapped him on the back benevolently. 'Piss or arse off the pot, lad.'

'I'll raise you a quid.'

Howls of derision met the boy's hesitant bid. George raised his eyebrows at the others round the table with a God-help-us expression and pulled the tab off a can of Coke. Alcohol was forbidden on the platform, but George didn't care: he had given up the booze years ago, and swore he'd never missed it. 'Now if my old lady was here . . .'

'If your old lady was here, we wouldn't be playing for money, we'd be playing strip poker. And praying –' Bengt Usily teased in his humourless, singsong voice – 'praying she'd lose.' The big Norwegian engineer glanced quickly at George to check his comment had been taken in good humour.

2

George's wife Mary was the pin-up of Astra Four's WRQ, the accommodation module that these men called home during their two-week stints on the rig. George had a ten-by-eight of Mary in a bikini pinned to the wall above his bunk, and every morning and every night he secretly kissed his finger and placed it on her lips. Unknown to George, so did several of his colleagues once George had left the quarters.

'In your dreams, Useless. In your dreams. Tomorrow night you and the boys'll still be on this scrap-heap and me an' Mary'll be . . .' George wrapped his arms around his chest and mugged for them with an exaggerated wink.

They played another four desultory hands before it was broadly acknowledged that George had won more than enough for one night, particularly given that his winnings would not be wisely invested in shore-leave alcohol but squandered on flowers for his wife. Two of the men headed straight for the WRQ but George and the Norwegian took Micky for a late night walkabout to greet those friends remaining on shift. George wanted to be sure that the new lad was seen to be firmly under his protection before he went to shore.

In the engine room beneath the derrick, two night-shift operators stared at the control monitors with glazed eyes. A production engineer was sitting with them, his feet up on the desk; for half an hour he had been engrossed in the specifications of a software upgrade in a computer magazine. He scratched his head, rolled up the magazine and thumped his nearest colleague on the shoulder. 'I'm off for a crap then,' he announced. 'I won't hurry back, so keep an eye on things.'

'Like we give a shite,' one muttered after the door had closed heavily behind the engineer. 'Expect he wants us to wipe his bloody arse for him.'

'Typical engineer, taking a computer manual to the bog.'

The two men were secretly relieved to be on duty with the graduate; his senior rank relieved them of responsibility, and complaining about him helped to pass the tedium of the graveyard shift. As they speculated on the engineer's sexual orientation, a tiny red light flashed intermittently on the control panel behind them.

It was a little after midnight. Astra Four soared above the water, seemingly a hundred glittering, swaying cranes linked together by gantries and open walkways. It had the feel of a deserted sports stadium, vast yet insubstantial. The North Sea slapped and wrestled with the giant legs of the platform as they sank four hundred feet beneath the surface of the choppy water. Dense fog loitered below the integral deck before curling like incense up through the metal grid and caressing the feet of the three men. The fog permitted the moon to shine a ghostly beam across the water like a broad path, and it struck George that this was a magical place to be on a magical late April night. Something about the place, something ethereal about the shape and feel of it, reminded George of the castles in the stories he occasionally read to his little daughter. The notion of Astra Four as a fairy-tale castle, wanting only a princess, was not something he'd share with the lads. He turned the collar of his yellow waterproof jacket up against the wind and squinted west towards the invisible coast, some 240 kilometres away. 'You got a girl back home, then, Micky?'

The roustabout prayed the murkiness of the night sky would cover his instant flush. 'No one special,' he admitted. 'Not one in particular, like.'

'Get yourself one sharp. Good-looking bloke like you, you should be able to find someone worth settling for.' George grunted and jerked his thumb at the Norwegian. 'Else you'll be ending up like Useless here, all alone in your empty bed at night.'

'Leave him alone, Grandad. He's got all the time in the world.' Bengt peered into the gloom beyond the artificial light. 'Anything special planned with Mary?'

4

George would have liked to confide in Bengt, to tell the gentle blond giant that he and Mary had a few hitches in what he might delicately have termed 'the bedroom department'. If they had been alone, if the boy hadn't been standing there, George might have mentioned that Mary had read a leaflet distributed by the company about the potential effects of stress on the libido of offshore workers, and had jokingly threatened that if he didn't see the doctor soon, then she would. That, or find someone else to warm her up at night.

'Just the usual,' he replied with a broad grin.

'The usual's good,' Usily affirmed. 'I could do with a bit of the usual myself.'

Micky laughed too loudly in attempted camaraderie. He stopped abruptly as George gave him a warning glance.

'Get some kip, lad.' Having dismissed Micky, George watched him descend towards the lower deck. He spat over the side of the gantry. 'He's only a kid,' he said under his breath to Bengt, 'shouldn't even be on a bloody rig.' He shouted into the night, 'Hey, Micky: don't lose your wages on the cards to those bastards! The money's the only thing that makes this job worth doing. Blow it and what the hell are you here for?' His final words were swallowed by the rising wind.

George and Bengt stood in silence, shoulder to shoulder, and watched the fog drift. George turned as heavy footsteps pounded along the walkway towards them.

'Hey, Usily, I've been looking all over for you.' The flustered junior engineer turned up the collar of his windcheater. 'The deputy OIM wants you in the engine room.'

'Why, he is lonely or something?' Bengt asked, with a broad grin to George.

'There's some connection problem between one of the ventilation ducts and the water deluge system.'

'What problem?'

'Some malfunction. It's dripping; that's all I know. The OIM wants you to take a look.'

'Can it wait till morning?'

'Maybe it can, but he can't. Probably needs a bloody good kicking.'

Usily faced George with feigned bewilderment. 'Does he mean the ventilation duct or the OIM?'

George saluted the Norwegian. 'Give them both a seeing to, Useless. I'll see you in a fortnight.'

George gazed up towards the gloomy face of heaven. No visible moon now, just the stars glittering down on the fretwork of Astra Four. George could do without the moon, he could happily live under the stars forever; under the stars with Mary. He could do without the sea and all; he had never liked being surrounded by water. Didn't even like getting wet, which made his career choice downright daft, he knew, but thirty-six was far too old to be having second thoughts about careers: trying a change would be dafter still. He'd like to take her off to the Highlands and lie on a hillside under a blanket all night, just counting the stars till morning. Funny how he never had a problem getting aroused by the mere thought of Mary when she wasn't there. He could just picture it, his head cushioned on the rounded pillow of her white belly, her strong legs entwined loosely with his, at once eager and compliant . . .

Except that in real life, Mary would never leave the kids. It was Malcolm's birthday the day after tomorrow. The new bike, Mary had told him, was hidden in the shed under a sheet, and George was to fit the trainer wheels the instant he got home. That, and install the new drum in the old washing machine, and regrout the bathroom tiles, and a host of other chores he knew his wife would have waiting for him. Certain that he was indispensable, and moved by the sudden wave of elation that that knowledge brought him, George did a little jig on the gantry, the steel-capped toes and heels of his boots clattering on the metal walkway as he danced.

A thin, high-pitched wail whistled through the damp air. On

6

the deck below Micky still lingered with two other roustabouts. All froze and looked up. With one hand raised in a salute that seemed part surrender, the other clamped round his throat, George whispered, 'It's a leak. It's a fucking gas leak.' He grabbed the metal railing and flung his voice into the wind, directly towards Micky. 'Get to the muster point now! *Now*, damn you!'

The gas alert sounded, keening into the night. At the far end of the platform, above the engine room, there was the muffled boom of a small explosion. It sounded blanketed. That's as it should be, George thought dispassionately; containable, all systems in place, Astra was a zero-incident platform. He knew he shouldn't be thinking at all, he should be moving safely but surely along the now flashing protected escape routes towards the emergency muster point. Standard assembly procedures. No sign of fire or smoke. It was contained; it had been controlled. Follow the drill. Any minute now they'd operate the deluge system. Everyone around him was moving, their expressions ranging from bovine stupidity through irritation to naked fear. All three were mistakes, George knew. His first personal golden rule was, Be Sceptical. His second was, But Don't Be Frightened. Fear plus an incident, even a minor incident, made an easy little equation that resulted in greatly increased danger and risk of death. Switch off and do what you have been trained to do. Don't think, just move. Follow the instructions on the PA system. Except there weren't any.

The force of the second explosion threw George fifteen feet and onto his stomach. He was not aware of pain, only of an icy sensation in his legs and an avalanche of black smoke consuming one end of the platform and barrelling towards him faster than anything he had seen in the simulated safety drills. Somebody dragged him back onto his feet and hurled him towards the edge of the platform. No sign of fire; not on the rig, not on the water, yet men were already plunging recklessly into the freezing North Sea. Through the ballooning smoke George could dimly make out Astra's two loyal support vessels, *Nepenthe* and *The Odyssey*, keeping watch some fifty metres off. The standby vessels' fire crews were scrambling on the deck, hoisting their great sea-serpent hoses in the direction of Astra Four. It was all right. There'd be a hell of an investigation, and a hell of a price to pay by whoever was responsible, and there'd be an almighty cost in shutting down operations, but it was all right. Tomorrow he'd be home and Useless would be in charge. Useless was a safe pair of hands; nothing went wrong on his watch.

Clinging to the edge, wondering why the life had emptied out of his legs, George saw men leap into the billowing black smoke and prepared to follow them. Then he saw the fire shoot straight up into the sky, so ravenous that for a moment it sucked the light out of the heavens. He watched the water ignite. Is that it, then? Wish I had a double whisky now. Jump. How am I going to fit the wheels by Friday? Just jump. What'd I look like if I got burned? Can't get burned – she'd hook up with bloody Useless. Useless. God help us. This was really going to fuck up Malcolm's birthday, no mistake. Go ahead and jump towards the stars, you dumb bastard, into that great shimmering white light. As he heaved his numbed lower body onto the edge of the railing, it comforted George that *Nepenthe*'s roving searchlights had personally picked him out.

ONE

The downpour set in just as Madeline Light arrived at Aberdeen airport. A sodden Allied Petroleum Company representative was waiting to meet her, looking simultaneously officious and exhausted as he riffled through the disintegrating pages of information on his clipboard.

'Dr Light? Stuart Mitchell, APC Human Resources. I've got a driver waiting to take us to the heliport.' He hurried her through the driving rain towards the car park. 'We've had a PR disaster here,' he continued grimly, then flinched. 'Sorry. Bad choice of words. It's been a long night. There's been a total balls-up on the communications side. Some of the press are already here, just local boys, but the nationals are bound to be on their way. There are a few reporters at the hospital and a telly crew going offshore, spewing garbage about lessons that should have been learnt from Piper Alpha. Some families know, some don't, our systems have gone haywire – Excuse me.' When he spoke curtly into his mobile phone, Madeline saw that his hand was shaking. 'She is, yes. We're on our way.

'To be perfectly frank we can't track who knows and who doesn't. We're trying to handle Coastguard teams, corporate teams, police teams, accident investigation teams, OSD teams. It's a living nightmare.'

Madeline jogged to keep up with his long strides and pushed back the heavy dark hair that the wind kept lashing against her face. She spoke in a raspy voice, surprisingly deep given her slight frame. 'What's the level of casualty and injury?'

'No final figures yet. Search and rescue is continuing.'

Once in the car he mopped his face, turned to Madeline and sighed. 'Right. Facts. The primary blast fire has been contained but part of the platform is still burning. The accommodation quarters weren't affected, thank God. The other two counsellors are on site, as far as I know. Somebody else was meeting them.'

'The level of casualty?' Madeline prompted gently.

'Latest figures were sixteen confirmed dead and twenty-seven unaccounted for.' Madeline could feel his flesh shudder as he sat beside her in the back of the car. When she lightly covered his hand with hers he jumped as if her touch were electric. 'I'm sorry.' He cleared his throat repeatedly. 'I'm so sorry. I haven't been involved in anything like this before. It's just, well, you know. A bit of a shock. You must do this all the time. I guess you're used to it.'

'Of course it's a shock. It must be harrowing for you.' Her green eyes met his steadily but her heart was pounding erratically, as it always did in critical incidents. Yes, she had done it before. She'd been handling public and private trauma for nearly eight years. She'd covered train crashes and fires, air incidents, all manner of disasters, yet each one had always felt like the first time. Used to it? Never. No one got used to it. She would be steady once she was properly on the job and could take control, try to help someone. 'Where do you want me to go?'

Stuart Mitchell stared at his notes without being able to read a word. 'They want you out on *Nepenthe*, one of the SBVs.'

'*Nepenthe*?'

'One of the standby vessels. The pilots couldn't risk using the platform helideck at all, so everything's been run from the two support boats. The fog's been so heavy it would have been hellish even without the smoke. Jesus.' He covered his face with his hands and pressed his fingers hard into his temples. 'OK. Nearly there now.'

'The survivors . . . any details of their injuries?'

Mitchell's left hand now gripped his right wrist in an attempt to still or disguise the compulsive tremor. 'We're talking everything. The works.'

Madeline looked away through the car window. Burns, then. Smoke inhalation; possibly fractures; most of all, shock. She remembered the drill, although it was over a year since she had been briefed as a human 'standby vessel' for APC Petroleum, and she had never been physically offshore. Everything would have been arranged to shelter the Operation Installation Manager and let him get on with recovering his men. Her job was to provide support for the living, even if that support was simply her intimacy with disaster.

The heliport was humming as crews loaded and unloaded passengers. The red, blue and orange crisis lights of various emergency services flashed intermittently across the compound.

'Are you coming to *Nepenthe*?' Madeline asked as she waited beside Mitchell.

'No, but you'll have some sort of company escort. The other two therapists must be on the boat by now.'

Madeline was concerned by the man's visible state of shock. 'Where do you go from here?'

'Back to the hospital. Get on the phone to the next of kin. Find a minute to sink a treble whisky,' Mitchell said with a joyless smile. 'Then find myself another job. I'm not cut out for this. I haven't the guts.' His mobile bleeped again. 'Christ . . . yes – I'll be there in ten minutes, tops. Hold on. I'm just delivering Dr Light for transport to *Nepenthe*.' Covering the phone he nudged her in the direction of the passport control booth. '. . . No, keep the families *away* from the hospital, for

Christ's sake . . . Gordon's setting up a relatives' reception centre at the Thistle Hotel.'

'Dr Light? Flynn Brennan. APC Petroleum.'

Madeline turned. A tall man in a brown leather jacket had materialised from nowhere. He tapped his mobile phone to his forehead and spoke with a lilting Irish accent. 'Cursed things. Designed to keep people in touch and they have precisely the opposite effect.'

Flynn cupped his hand under her elbow, leading her towards the checkpoint. His extraordinary height raised her elbow near level with her shoulder and reminded her of walking with her father when she was a little girl. Flynn held his passport out above her head as they were peremptorily waved through the checkpoint. 'You've been offshore before?' Madeline shook her head. 'Nothing to it,' he continued reassuringly.

In the transportation room a small, wiry man with a face like a Jack Russell stood tapping his foot in front of a large TV screen. 'I know you're all itching to get out there and get to work, but my job is to brief you on the helicopter drill. You need to listen carefully.'

The video began to roll as the safety instructor talked. Madeline felt her mouth dry and her palms turn clammy as she watched footage of a transport helicopter slamming into the sea and flipping over. The monotonous voice of the video narrator told them what steps to take in the event of plummeting into the ocean at high speed.

'After a crash like that you'd have no more than four minutes tops to survive in the water,' the instructor added, 'so after the film I'll distribute coldwater survival immersion suits, boots and vests.' He craned his neck and addressed Madeline at the back. 'We're not going to have anything your size, Miss, but we'll kit you out as best we can. Right. Next . . .'

Madeline struggled to concentrate on the information, praying she would be able to remember it, praying she wouldn't

12

need to, and all the time thinking, *What the hell am I doing here? Why have I volunteered to be in this situation when I could be home in bed with Patrick? I need my head examined.* She envied Flynn Brennan's composure; he seemed preoccupied by the duffel bag at his feet, but squeezed her shoulder in response to her nervous smile.

'Two last points,' the instructor barked. 'First, you won't be able to hear anyone on the helicopter. The pilot can talk to you through your headsets, but you can't talk back. *Don't take them off.* One, you'll lose contact with the pilot. Two, your eardrums might burst. Next, you taller blokes, remember we've a bugger of a wind tonight, strong enough to push the rotor blades below six feet, so crouch on approach if you want to avoid decapitation.' A couple of passengers smiled uncomfortably at the brusque warning.

The orange boiler suit swamped Madeline, making her feel clumsy and inept as Flynn shepherded her up the flimsy steps of the waiting helicopter. Seated, she hauled the heavy safety harness over her shoulders and up between her legs.

The pilot's voice crackled through their headphones. 'We've been cleared for departure. It'll take about ninety minutes to get out to the ship. It's been very choppy, but the wind's dropping a little now: it shouldn't be too bad. You'll see the fire on Astra Four well before we get there.'

Madeline stared out of the small porthole window, watching the new day break over the North Sea, imagining the wives widowed, children fatherless. At least sixteen men dead. And death, as she knew better than most, was far from the end of a disaster.

They came to rest bumpily on the deck of *Nepenthe*, less than eighty metres away from Astra Four. One end of the platform was still burning, the shattered turret of the derrick lurching crazily above the water. Huge searchlights splashed pools of silver across the sea as lifeboats bobbed on the surface, their divers sporadically flipping backwards into the water. Madeline saw a huddled row of uniformly yellow backs facing the platform. The watchers did not turn to acknowledge the arrival of the helicopter; their eyes were fixed on the water. No one had been brought back alive for the past hour.

Madeline waited patiently as Flynn approached a couple of Portuguese crew members, but their command of English was too scanty to help. In growing frustration he grabbed the arm of a passing uniformed officer. 'Who's in charge here?'

'The OIM, but he's up to his neck. The master was here a second ago, Captain Barton. What do you need?'

'I'm with APC and this is Dr Light. You're expecting her.'

The young man searched his clipboard in confusion. 'Dr Light . . . No, I don't have you down. What are you, paramedic?'

Madeline could see the impatience on her escort's face. 'I'm a therapist with the psychological trauma team,' she explained. 'There should be three of us on site.'

'I don't have you down,' he tapped his list, 'so you're not meant to be here.'

'For Christ's sake, man, check again.' The Irishman spoke distractedly, staring at the remains of Astra Four.

'Look, I'm co-ordinating the investigation teams, not medical, but I'm certain counsellors are assembling at the debriefing reception centre back at the heliport.'

Madeline looked from one man to the other. 'OK,' she said calmly, 'then I'll just go back.'

The junior officer shook his head. 'It isn't that simple.' With evident relief he hailed an approaching burly figure. 'They've sent one of the trauma counsellors over, sir.'

Captain Barton, his face streaked with black and his hair plastered to his head, closed his eyes for a second, as if in hope that Madeline and Flynn might have vanished when he reopened them. A deep frown corrugated his brow. 'Right,' he addressed them briskly. 'That's an error. We don't have the space or the facilities for you to see anyone here. We've

14

been working flat-out to evacuate the men back to shore for critical incident debriefing. That was my top priority.'

'I understand. I'll go back now,' Madeline repeated.

Behind them the helicopter that had delivered them had already been reloaded and was being cleared for take-off. 'I can't send you back now. We've got five full flights scheduled.'

'What are the latest casualty figures?' Madeline asked.

'Twenty-one dead. That we've recovered.' He nodded towards a tarpaulin tent at the far end of *Nepenthe*. 'The bodies are in there. With the pathologists. My . . . I . . .' The captain stared blankly past them, swallowing hard. 'The medical team are working on some minor injuries we haven't transported back yet, but they'll have to take priority over you. Eighteen men are still missing.' Swinging back towards his junior, Captain Barton began to snap orders. 'Take them to my quarters, Merrick, then get onto Control in Aberdeen and tell them they've fucked up. I'll get you both on the transportation list, but in the meantime sit tight and try to keep out of the way.' Above their heads a television crew circled. Captain Barton watched them with narrowed eyes. 'Bastards.' The big man gripped Madeline's shoulder, tears clearing ghostly tracks down his dirt-streaked cheeks. 'It could have been worse, you know; it could have been worse. The system worked. As far as any system works.'

Merrick motioned them to follow as the captain swung away, wiping his face with the back of his fist.

In the captain's quarters, Madeline untied the belt of her life-vest and sat still while Flynn prowled around the cramped cabin, repeatedly scraping his dark hair back with one hand. She had the feeling that they had met somewhere before. 'Have you been with APC a long time, Flynn?' she asked.

He lit a cigarette and dragged sharply, not looking at her. 'No. But I've worked in plenty of situations like this before.' The wall of his back let Madeline know he had no wish to

15

pursue the conversation, and she did not press him. She was accustomed to silence.

After a few minutes of pacing, he swung round to face her. 'This is ridiculous. They'll be spitting blood at the heliport. You sit tight – I'll go back and see if I can hurry up transportation.'

Madeline welcomed his initiative, but she also wanted to get on with the task ahead, not be left alone in the cabin. 'I'll come with you.'

It was clear her escort did not approve of her decision, but he swung his bag over his shoulder with a determined expression and pushed open the heavy door. 'After you.'

On deck the air was thick, the sweet tang of sweat faintly detectable beneath the fumes of smoke. Only the flashes of yellow worn by the watching men and the blue tarpaulin of the makeshift morgue broke the monotonous grey of the ship and surrounding sea. Fire crews were now returning to *Nepenthe*, helicopters continued to land, and in the ensuing cloak of confusion no one took any notice of Madeline and Flynn.

She heard him curse under his breath. 'Wait here,' he ordered.

Madeline's eyes followed him as he walked purposefully along the deck, carrying his body lightly, like an athlete. He seemed in no hurry to find the captain. She saw him set down his bag at the loneliest end of the ship, in the shadow of the mortuary tent, and bend to remove something from it. A phone, she thought; he'd be calling debriefing. Her gaze shifted to the nameless and faceless men hunched at the side of the ship, watching a trail of smoke coiling mournfully up into the eerily lit dawn sky. Madeline saw a couple of the men turn in Flynn's direction, their expressions blank and incurious, and followed their gaze. He was screwing a camera zoom into position. He raised the camera and began to shoot the crippled structure of Astra Four. Sensing that something was wrong, Madeline began to move towards him.

16

'What the *fuck* are you doing?' a voice roared. Madeline watched Flynn raise both hands in the air defensively, letting the camera swing from its strap as Captain Barton grabbed him by the front of his jacket and hauled him away from the side of the ship. 'You're not from Human Resources, are you, you bastard? You're from the fucking press . . .'

Madeline moved closer and saw Flynn nod, one hand shielding his camera as the captain hissed his accusation with loathing. 'I've a mind to throw you overboard. If I told any one of these men the scum you are, they'd do the job for me.' With an expression of utter contempt he spat in the photographer's face.

Madeline felt angry herself. The man had used her as his ticket onto *Nepenthe*, wilfully implicating her in his masquerade, as the captain's next words confirmed.

'Is the woman you brought with you press as well?'

Flynn's eyes briefly met Madeline's over the captain's shoulder. 'No. She's legit.'

'Captain Barton?' Madeline asked quietly. 'Is there something I can do to help?'

The captain's head hung low, swinging from side to side with the weary bellicosity of an old bull confronting a matador. 'If the police didn't have better things to do here, I'd have him arrested. Merrick!' he bellowed to his third mate, pulling himself ramrod straight. 'Get over here! This –' Barton's lips twisted in a snarl – '*bastard* is not authorised to be here. He's a press photographer. That makes him first fucking priority off my ship, you understand? *First*. Don't let him out of your sight. If he touches that camera, chuck him over.'

Barton took Madeline by the elbow and pulled her away, breathing heavily. 'I've got twenty-one men lying dead not fifteen feet from here, and I have to deal with a prick like that. I know them. All of them. Good men, doing a sodding thankless job. We're busting our arses trying to find the other eighteen, so we don't have to tell their wives and their mothers

17

and their children that they're still out *there*,' he jabbed a finger in the direction of the Astra Four, 'in *that*. And that scum thinks he can bluff his way onto my ship and –'

'I'm sorry. He said he was APC,' Madeline said. 'I believed him.'

'I'd like to get hold of the moron who checked his passport – probably says "press" all over it. Bloody *Irish* passport, too, I'll bet. His accent's thick enough.'

Madeline looked back over her shoulder to where Flynn waited under Merrick's guard, still standing tall in the persistent drizzle. What enabled a human being to act like that, she wondered. What professional motive was strong enough to insulate him from any element of fellow feeling for those suffering around him? What had dragged *him* from his safe warm bed at this ungodly hour?

Barton sighed heavily. 'At least he let me lose my rag. Someone was going to get it in the neck, so I'm glad it was him . . . I lost control,' the captain whispered in disbelief. 'I never normally lose my grip, but I keep thinking about Mary. You see, Doctor . . .'

'Madeline.'

'My sister . . . my little sister Mary, her husband . . . Will you see her, on the mainland? Madeline? You'll look after our Mary?'

'Yes,' she said firmly, 'I'll see her. I'll make sure I see her. We'll look after her, I promise you.'

'Mary Reagan.'

'Mary Reagan. I'll remember. Captain Barton, while I'm waiting, does it make sense for me to talk to the men you still have here?'

Trickles of rain ran down her forehead, and the oversized protective clothing made her look barely more than a child, yet there was a dogged determination in her white face and a stubbornness about her jaw that made Barton trust her. He nodded. 'Come with me.'

18

He led her downstairs and opened the door of a narrow galley where a handful of men waited. Most stared bleakly into space. Only one of them, barely more than a boy himself, was weeping openly, his face buried in his hands. As the door closed behind her, Madeline sat down beside him. It was always like this, a fine balance between being present and not intruding. Her first trainer had told her to imagine that she was picking up a stranger in a bar: *Just start talking*.

'Hello. My name's Madeline.' She laid a hand lightly on his shoulder, but did not speak again until his sobs had steadied to an occasional choking gasp. 'How are you feeling?' she asked quietly.

'I want to go home,' the boy whispered.

'That's being arranged. It won't be long now, not much longer. Is there anything you need while we're waiting?'

'D'you know what happened?' another man asked sharply. 'How many are . . . gone? No one's told us anything.'

'I'm sorry, I don't have reliable information about the dead.' Madeline did not know if the figure of twenty-one would increase, and was unwilling to pass on an estimate that might prove optimistic, but the sooner the survivors heard and used the word 'dead', the better. The man who had asked the question tipped his head back against the wall with his eyes closed. The shivering boy slumped against Madeline's side, moaning in his throat. 'What's your name?' Madeline asked.

'Micky.'

'How old are you, Micky?'

'Nineteen.'

'Micky,' she continued quietly, turning to face him and drawing his eyes into hers with the intimacy of her gaze, 'what happened to you tonight?'

'Where's George?' the boy whimpered. 'Is George all right?'

'I'll find out as soon as I can. What happened on the platform tonight?' Madeline asked again, one hand steady on his shoulder. 'Can you tell me where you were?'

19

Micky stared at her, his reddened, pale blue eyes fixed on hers. 'Don't know what happened. I just need to go home. . . . I've only been here a week. A *week*. I was going to bed and I saw George, up on the gantry, dancing like he was mad or something.' He choked. 'Took care of me, George did, showed me the ropes, like. He's not dead, is he?'

'I don't know, Micky. He sounds like a good friend, George.'

'Yeah. He's not dead, is he? He can't be dead.' Micky swallowed. 'He looked a right prat.'

'You saw George dancing . . . Did you go to bed then?'

'No,' the boy shuddered. 'I heard this noise, like an animal, like a sick horse, maybe. I looked up 'cause I thought it was George pratting about, and he was there, above me, waving like everything was fine.'

'Waving, like everything was fine,' Madeline repeated softly.

'But it wasn't fine. There was this blow-out. I ran with everyone else. Just ran.' Micky began to gulp for air, his body collapsing against Madeline's. 'He was fucking dancing,' Micky whispered. '*Dancing*.'

By the time Madeline and the remaining five men were brought back on deck, the rain was no more than a fine mist. Captain Barton stood to one side with Flynn as a helicopter descended clumsily onto the pad. Flynn hoisted his duffel bag. The captain took three long strides down the deck but stopped abruptly outside the temporary morgue. Swinging back to Flynn he taunted bitterly, 'Seeing you're so curious, maybe you'd like a good, long look before you go? If you've the stomach for it. Maybe then you'll understand what this is all about.'

Madeline did not know if she was acting from a desire to shield the survivors from a vision they did not need to see, or an urge to stand between the captain and the photographer, or whether she was in some macabre way testing her own resolve to look at the reality of death, but she found herself

20

following Flynn as he stepped past the two uniformed police standing guard at the tent and lifted the flap of blue tarpaulin. As he opened it the wind whipped through the tunnel, making the plastic sides suck and snap as if they were gasping for breath, yet the air inside remained suffocatingly close. The stench of burnt flesh and rasping, iron odour of blood nearly overwhelmed Madeline, and she went no further than the doorway.

Outside the tent, the rhythmic thwup of the helicopter's rotary blades and dim moan of the coastguards' alarms continued, but inside it was eerily muted. Two rows of corpses were lined along the deck, draped in white sheeting prior to being body-bagged. Flynn breathed heavily through his mouth as he walked slowly down one row and back up the other. Most of the faces were unmarked, their skin almost as colourless as the sheets that shrouded them, a chalky pallor that darkened to blue-grey under and around the eye sockets, mouth and down the neck, where the flesh was swollen and bloated. Madeline had seen enough fatalities to guess the primary cause of death. The smell which still rose from their clothes and grated against the lining of her nose lingered from the fumes which had swollen their airways, causing near instantaneous suffocation.

She saw Flynn stop abruptly as he reached the final three bodies. They looked as if they had come from an altogether different incident. What little skin remained bore no resemblance to human skin. It was either charred into patches of black leather or had been neatly flayed away, exposing raw flesh beneath. The photographer gazed down at the last corpse. Only one side of the face was identifiable as human at all; the other side gaped from eye socket to jawbone.

'Had enough, then?' Barton was breathing through his mouth as he stood beside Madeline at the entrance to the tent.

Flynn did not reply. He seemed transfixed by the figure at

21

his feet. Madeline shuddered as she saw a strange, secretive smile spread hesitantly across his face. A moment later Flynn dropped to his knees beside the body, wrenched back the sheeting and pulled the torso into his arms. '*Erik*,' he whispered urgently, then shouted the name, again and again, as the two policemen attempted to haul him off.

'You crazy fucker – is this your idea of a joke?'

Madeline's hand tightened on the captain's arm instinctively as Flynn wrestled with the officers, his eyes locked on the face of the dead man. He *knows* him, she thought. Lord, the shock of it . . . the pain . . . She forced herself to look again at the figure now at Flynn's feet. She saw the crumpled body of a middle-aged man lying in a foetal position. Scraps of blackened skin peeled off his shoulders and chest like bark, fluttering against the raw flesh like tatters of cloth. One of his arms lay outside the sheeting, twisted, broken at an acute angle, as black and burnt as a branch from a bonfire. It might crumble to dust if you touched it.

Captain Barton shook off Madeline's restraining hand and seized the photographer so violently that Flynn's neck-strap broke and the camera skidded across the slick floor. 'You know who that is, you sad bastard? Know him, do you? That's my sister Mary's husband. He and the other two were eaten alive by a fireball. *We watched it happen*. He went up like a torch and there wasn't a damn thing we could do about it. Lay one more finger on George and I swear to God I'll kill you with my bare hands.' The captain pushed past Madeline, ripping down the tarpaulin door as he left.

One of the policemen looked at Flynn with a glimmer of compassion discernible beneath his professional mask. 'You all right, mate? You look like you've seen a ghost.'

Flynn did not reply. His eyes remained on the face of the derrickman.

Madeline, Micky and five other survivors took their seats on

22

the helicopter. Flynn, his face ashen, was the last to board. As he moved to sit behind Madeline, he paused and his eyes locked onto hers. She had the distinct impression that he was glad she was there. She turned away towards the window. As the helicopter lifted bumpily from *Nepenthe*, Madeline watched the smoke still drifting lazily around one end of the middle deck of Astra Four. The blue tarpaulin frame was being dismantled and the bodies of the dead were being loaded onto stretchers for the journey home. Never in her life had Madeline felt so tired.

TWO

Although it was still early in the morning, the sun was beating down on her head, burning the back of her bare neck. It suffused the surrounding fields with golden light, sharpening the acid yellow of the rape flowers as her feet pounded down the drive away from the farmhouse. Bloated bumblebees droned in a cloud above a bamboo wigwam smothered in sweet peas, and their heady scent and the rich, warm smell of the hay harvest mingled with the stink of the rape and made her head spin. She had to get away from the house, but the faster she ran, the closer the house loomed over her shoulder. A family of ducks on the little river that ran alongside the farm were scared into flight as somewhere close a tractor engine kicked into life and somebody started to scream . . .

Chilly with sweat, her heart thumping, Madeline woke to the familiar droning vibration of the drill rising up through the floorboards from Patrick's studio. She breathed in deeply, smelling only the pungent aroma of newly brewed coffee, and stretched as she gazed out over the Thames through the glass wall opposite the bed. Without raising her neck from the pillow she could see Tower Bridge dominating the jagged skyline of the City on the opposite bank. The sight steadied her at once. It was a world away from the farm in Somerset.

Patrick grumbled that he'd never come to terms with the floor-to-ceiling window. Eight years earlier, as a condition of co-habitation, Madeline had demanded a civilised bathroom, basic refurbishment of the bedroom and floor-to-ceiling glass replacing the existing brick wall: she had craved a panoramic urban view. Patrick still claimed the window inhibited him, not that it stopped him frequently walking around stark naked. The rest of the flat had been left much as it was, with rough floorboards randomly covered by moth-eaten Persian carpets, ramshackle furnishings squirrelled during a lifetime's wanderings, a functioning if primitive kitchen, and a rickety, vertigo-inducing staircase that plummeted down to Patrick's studio. He hated the coy gentrification of the area, and regularly threatened that if just one more of the few original riverside warehouses was reconstituted as Liquorice Landings or Coriander Condos, he'd sell up and head straight back through the Mont Blanc tunnel to Italy.

Patrick Matthews had bought the lower half of the then near-derelict wharf in 1982 with the proceeds of his first, surprisingly lucrative, London exhibition. Pietrasanta, a town forever dependent on the marble quarries of the Carrara district, had at that time been his home for some fifteen years. Fifteen years of trying to be Italian, conducting two turbulent love affairs with two equally turbulent women, and of sculpting to growing critical acclaim but limited commercial success. It had taken a further seven years, a second acrimonious divorce and three more promising shows before Patrick had loaded up his van with as much marble as its suspension could support, driven through the tunnel, and taken shelter in Blake's Wharf in the winter of 1989.

For two years he had squatted, only a curtain demarcating bedroom from makeshift bathroom, and worked every waking moment, turning his face resolutely away from society, especially of the female variety, until one crisp autumn morning a prospective client had visited the studio with

Madeline Light in tow. Unlike most visitors to the studio, she had not flattered him; he had felt as much the focus of her cool, measured appraisal as his sculpture. He would have willingly sworn lifelong service to her merely for the pleasure of looking at her eyes and luminescent skin, the colour of heavy cream. But when Madeline observed how different it must be to sculpt pieces destined to stand in the diluted light of England rather than beneath a bleaching Mediterranean sun, Patrick had privately offered his heart, knowing she would be as sensitive to his personal constraints as his professional ones. He had tossed aside his self-enforced celibacy and set about courting the self-contained young woman. Eight months later, her agreement to share his home had completed his new, happy and resolutely unturbulent life.

When Madeline had dressed she joined Patrick at the vast oak table that dominated the living area.

'Hello, darling. You didn't get much sleep last night, did you?' she asked, towelling her hair roughly.

He shrugged as he lifted the coffee cup to his lips. Madeline let the towel drop around her shoulders as she looked at his hands. They were strong, workman's hands, with one or two pale gashes drawn on the backs of each. That morning they were heavily speckled with white stone dust.

'I wanted to clear the decks. Did I wake you?'

She took his hand in hers and turned it over. With a fingertip she delicately traced the longest and faintest scar, which ran from his palm some four inches up his wrist, paying testimony to youthful inexperience with a chisel. She held it to her lips for a moment as she considered telling Patrick about her dream.

'No. I slept like a baby.'

'Why do people say that? Babies don't sleep more than two hours at a stretch.'

'But when they do, they sleep deeply.' Madeline dropped his hand and sat next to him. 'Innocently. No bad dreams. That's the theory at least. Personally, I think babies *do* have bad dreams.'

'Do *you* still have bad dreams, baby?' Patrick studied her face tenderly.

Madeline paused before reaching for a piece of cold toast. 'You really have to get more sleep,' she said. 'You're working too hard and not sleeping enough.'

'You mean, for a man of my advanced years.' Patrick laughed but there was an edge to the chuckle.

Madeline wished she'd sounded less like a nanny and more like a lover. 'Is there anything . . . anything *bothering* you?' she asked. 'Have I pissed you off in some way? Or is it work?'

'You? Of course not.' His voice was gruff with love. 'I'm just preoccupied with Basil.'

He waved the coffee pot over her cup, but Madeline glanced at her watch and shook her head. Patrick was a touch over-sensitive about his age, she thought. Being nearly fifty-five wasn't that bad. God, there were days when she looked forward to being fifty-five, felt fifty-five might herald her golden years. She'd be free to work and nothing but; released from the expectations that came with being an attractive, 'younger' woman. At least friends would stop asking if Patrick wasn't just a *tad* old for her. When she was fifty-five and he was seventy-one, nobody would give a damn about their age-gap.

Patrick watched her apply a slick of lip gloss, enjoying the intense concentration on her face as she looked in the mirror. Madeline was one of the very few women he had ever met who was entirely without vanity. He knew this cosmetic application to be merely professional preparation, her final piece of armour before she stepped out to face the world. He addressed her reflection: 'You look beautiful.'

'It's too red. I look like a tart.'

'Nothing wrong with tarts. . . .' As she shrugged into a

jacket, he glanced up at her from under bushy eyebrows. 'You haven't forgotten Michael and Lydia are coming tonight, have you?'

Madeline's wince confirmed that she had. 'I have a late client but I'll be home by – oh, eight? I'll warn Michael if I see him in the office.'

'In other words, you'd like me to knock something up for dinner.'

'You're ten times the cook that I am.' Patrick smiled, shaking his head as she offered, 'Or I could pick up a curry on my way home.'

'Have you ever in your life cooked a meal?' Madeline's utter lack of domesticity was another of the things he loved about her.

'I have a vast repertoire of gourmet dishes. I've cooked enough macaroni cheese to feed an army. I'm a dab hand at Pot Noodle. Dead Man's Leg . . .'

'Dead Man's Leg, hmm?' Patrick folded his hands on the top of his head, covering the few strands of grey hair that remained, and leant back in his chair. 'I'll sort something out.'

'What time's your meeting this afternoon?'

'Three o'clock. The whole team's coming. Maybe even the cardinal.'

'Wow. The big guns. You're honoured.'

'I'm entitled. They greatly admire the "spirituality" of my work.' He pressed his hands together in a mocking imitation of the monsignor who had commissioned him to carve the memorial bust of Cardinal Basil Hume for Westminster Cathedral and was coming to give final approval of the plaster cast before sculpting could begin.

'Bet they wouldn't admire the spirituality of your *life* if they knew anything about it.'

'That's why I don't want you around.'

'I'd be the soul of discretion.'

'Maybe, but the sight of us brazenly cohabiting, you looking like a tart . . .'

'They still think you're devout?'

'You bet,' Patrick confirmed. 'My devotion is not in question. I may have confessed to a few lapses in the ardour of my Catholicism –'

'Lapses? More like *co*llapses. *Pro*lapses.' She grinned at him. 'And when do I get to see it?'

'Tonight. If today goes well. If they like it.' He picked up the newspaper. 'Pick up some wine, OK? The cupboard's bare.'

As Madeline walked down Mill Street towards the bus stop she felt a pang of guilt towards Patrick. For the past three months, ever since the Astra Four disaster, she'd been too busy for more than a quick mutual update on work. Their timing was terrible. For the next month or two, as her schedule lightened, Patrick would retreat into the solitude he required at this stage in a commission; he would be so drained by the physical effort of it she'd be lucky if he even acknowledged her.

Had she rebuffed him too curtly the night before, by saying she was too tired to make love? Was that why he'd left their bedroom? It had been the truth: only a longing for sleep had prevented her from returning his advances. She had known that he needed her emotional engagement even more than he needed her physically, but she had not been able to muster the energy to offer it. Madeline occasionally stepped up the tempo of her affection, demonstrating a fiercer passion than she felt in deference to Patrick's pride, but last night she had lain beside him, aching for sleep, and stubbornly ignored his restless turning and twisting. Even when he had risen and retreated to the studio, she had not asked what troubled him. The commission, she'd told herself; understandably, he was preoccupied with the commission.

Yet as she walked to the bus in the sharp light of that July morning, Madeline had an intuition that there was something that Patrick *knew*, something he wanted to tell her but wasn't able to say, and for once she hadn't been able to ask the right question. She had always respected his privacy, as he did hers; it was a bond between them. Too many couples confused having no secrets with honesty. But because Patrick demanded so little of her, it was all too easy to take his intimate presence in her life for granted, and now, as often before, she wondered if she really knew him at all. She had jumped to a series of conclusions about what might be on his mind – her rejection of him sexually, his age, the challenge of the commission – and by choosing to voice the last had allowed him to confirm her suggestion, a lazy slip she would never allow herself to make with a client. And she had been cowardly about his – very pertinent – question about her bad dreams. Tonight, they'd talk, Madeline promised herself; before he got too stuck into the Cardinal. Tonight or tomorrow night, or certainly the night after . . . Right now, she had to prepare herself for Mary Reagan. Strictly, she should not have been seeing Mary at all. Her duties towards the survivors and bereaved of the Astra Four disaster had officially ended with arranging ongoing local counselling. But Madeline did not find it easy to turn away anyone in need. It gave her life a purpose.

On the other side of the Thames, in the no-man's-land where Chelsea surrenders reluctantly to Fulham, Georgia Brennan also woke up late and alone. Stopping first at her nine-year-old son's bedroom she hauled the duvet off Oliver and flung open the curtains, then rapped twice on her daughter's door before opening it.

'Beth. You'll be late for school.'

One slim white arm emerged from under the covers and fumbled for the clock. Two seconds later, a tousled fair head shot from under the duvet. 'Christ, Mum,' Beth whined, 'why didn't you wake me earlier? I told you I had to wash my hair!'

'You're old enough to set your own alarm, Beth. I'm your mother, not your keeper.'

'You know how important today is.'

'So shoot me. You think I've been lying in bed for half an hour thinking, shall I wake Beth up? Nah, why bother? I'll paint my nails till it's too late for her to wash her hair, so she goes to the auditions looking like a greasy hag. . . .'

Mother and daughter faced each other, hands on hips, remarkably alike: two soft, pale English roses, even if one was a little more full-blown than the other. Georgia smiled at the mirror reflection of her physical past, as Beth glared at her physical future. The knowledge of how mortified Beth would be if she thought she would end up looking exactly like her made Georgia grin. '*Move it*. Get your skates on and leap in the shower. You can help yourself to my incredibly expensive new shampoo.' As Beth ran from the room her mother began to pull bits of school uniform out of the wardrobe and drawers and toss them onto her daughter's bed.

Back in the kitchen, Georgia turned on Radio Four, switched on the kettle, and shoved butter and marmalade on the table before padding barefoot down the corridor to the darkroom. She tapped at the door, resenting the fact that there were two rooms in her own house she was forbidden to enter without knocking. It wouldn't be long before she lost open access to Oliver's, too. 'Flynn? I'm doing poached eggs for Ol. D'you want some?'

'Maybe later,' her husband called back distractedly.

Georgia paused with her temple resting against the door. These days Flynn was no more predictable than Beth, but couldn't be exonerated on the plea of surging adolescent hormones. Just a few months ago – well, maybe a year ago – Flynn would have flung open the darkroom door and pulled her onto the old sofa for a long good-morning kiss, Georgia pretending to struggle, protesting that they had to get the children ready for school, loving the feel of his grip on her shoulders. But for the past few months – months? It felt like years – Flynn had barely touched her.

'Fine,' she snapped. 'If you want them later you can make them yourself.'

The two children happily engaged in sibling bickering while Georgia sat on a stool examining her left foot with an expression near distress. She was obsessed with her feet. They were perfectly normal feet, did the job they were intended to do and did not cause her pain. They were even attractive, she acknowledged, so long as she looked down at them. That was precisely her concern, precisely why she sometimes caught herself unconsciously touching them, checking the abrasive patches on her heels and the leathery thickness of her soles. However many pedicures she had, however much she laboured to keep them smooth and elegant, however cared-for her feet seemed from above, appearances were deceiving. Her soles betrayed her.

'Don't bring any of your gross little oiks back this afternoon, Ol. Martin's coming to work on our project.'

'My friends aren't gross, they're cool, and Martin Garfield's a creep. And everyone knows he's gay.'

'How would *you* know, you little toad? You don't even know what gay means.'

'Who's gay? And in what manner, gay?' Flynn ambled into the kitchen and kissed both his children. 'Is this Martin a particularly cheerful lad, with a song in his heart and a spring in his step, or is he –' Flynn dropped his voice to a whisper, cranked his Irish accent up a notch or two and glanced furtively around the room – 'a rampant *homosexual*?'

'Oh, *Dad* –' Beth dragged the word out to three syllables – '*please*.'

Georgia surrounded her son with eggs, toast, marmalade, juice and tea, leaving the space in front of her husband conspicuously empty. Immediately disgusted by her childish display of pique, and knowing Flynn wouldn't even have registered it, she poured him a cup of coffee and a glass of juice before returning to the high stool to begin a minute examination of her right foot. 'Aren't you going to eat any-thing, Beth?'

Rolling her eyes, Beth sighed heavily. 'I've told you, Mum: I'm on a *diet*.'

'Dieting's not a social activity, Beth. You don't do it just because all your friends are doing it,' Georgia observed without looking up. 'You only diet if you need to. And you don't.'

'*You're* not eating anything; why should I?'

Georgia, who was on one of her impulsive and generally short-lived crash diets, shrugged. 'I'm not hungry.'

'Neither am I.'

'Liar,' Oliver chipped in. 'You're always stuffing your fat face when no one's looking.'

'At least I don't look like a weasel-faced rat's bum.'

'Christ.' The muttered exclamation was not provoked by the children; Georgia's inspection had moved up her legs. She flexed one knee a few times, watching the skin just above her kneecap turn crêpey as her knee straightened, then tauten again as she bent it. She made a mental note never to wear short skirts in public again. Raising her heels to the top rung of the stool in the hope that gravity would succeed where the gym had failed, she returned her attention to her children's nutrition. 'If you ate a proper breakfast, Beth, you wouldn't be craving junk food by break.'

Flynn opened the newspaper. 'Leave the girl alone, Georgia. She looks grand. Always has. Missing breakfast now and again won't kill her.' He grabbed the remote to the small television that sat on the worktop. Georgia's jaw tightened. The Brennans had four television sets dotted around their terraced house; at least one of them was on if Flynn was home. At least two, if either of the children were there as well.

Half watching the screen, half reading the newspaper, Flynn addressed his son. 'So what have you got on at school today?'

'We're finishing off our project on Native American Indians. Today's the best bit. Today we get to name everybody.'

33

'Name everybody? Like how?' his father prompted.

'You know, like Dances With Wolves.'

'Olly, don't speak with your mouth full.'

'Now various appropriate names for your mother spring to mind,' Flynn teased.

'She Who Nags Round The Clock?' Beth offered, standing in front of the mirror, pulling her blonde hair off her face, then dropping it back into what she hoped was an artlessly abandoned look.

'OK, Beth,' Georgia said. 'From now on I'll call you Stands With A Mirror.'

'I don't think the nagging thing's fair to Mum,' Oliver said loyally. 'I think we should call her She Who Cooks Breakfast.'

'Oh.' Georgia knew he had spoken without a trace of malice, which made it far, far worse. 'Thanks, Ol.'

Oliver grinned and went for a second hole in one. 'Beth can be She Who Fancies Poofy Gay Boy Martin Garfield – Fat Chance.'

Beth's face first blanched then hardened as she leant over her father, her arms entwined around his neck. 'I've got one for you, Ol: how about, He Who Won't *Ever* Get Picked For Any Football Team On Earth In A Million Years.'

As Oliver's bravado collapsed Flynn clapped his hands for their attention. 'Right, you rabble; what about me then?'

In the silence that followed he looked expectantly at his children. Finally Georgia answered. 'I guess they don't know you well enough to reply. He Who's Never At Home? He Who Lives Abroad? The Bloke In The Darkroom?'

'Ah, I get it,' Flynn said slowly. 'He Who Earns His Family's Daily Crust.'

'At his family's daily expense,' Georgia countered, slamming the fridge door.

'It's only a joke, Mum,' Beth said nervously.

A car horn tooted jauntily outside.

'There's Suzie. Hurry, kids – don't keep her waiting.' Georgia shepherded them through the hall and down the path. 'Good luck with the audition, Bethie – I'll keep everything crossed.'

Georgia remained barefoot on the pavement long after Suzie had pulled away and turned the corner. It wasn't as if Flynn had said anything terrible, not that morning; it was simply the aggression she heard couched in his voice as he played at being a normal dad enjoying a normal family breakfast. She heard it even if the children didn't, and Georgia suspected that the children felt the tension between them as keenly as she did. Beth in particular was increasingly jumpy in her parents' joint company. Fine, she thought, chewing her lip, he's pissed off about being out of work for so long; fine, I understand that, but it's time to grow up and face facts. She should go back in and tell him he had to pull himself together. Or she could go back in, apologise for her short fuse and start the morning all over again. What she could not do was pretend that everything was 'normal', because nothing had been 'normal' for months.

With her arms folded tightly over her chest, Georgia tried to pinpoint when things had gone wrong between her and Flynn, tried to fix the exact day when the lion of a man whose love she had never doubted had become a stranger. There had always been something mercurial about Flynn, a chameleon quality that helped him to fade in and out of different environments; it made him a natural at his work. But recently something else had emerged. Something seemed to move across his face, a taut, imprisoned bitterness she did not recognise. She wanted to believe it was all down to Astra Four, that it was since he'd returned from photographing the explosion three months ago that he'd seemed at war with the world. It had been a bad gig, was all he'd said; one he should never have taken on, but with commissions drying up and the piggy bank near empty . . . He'd refused to discuss anything about it and had walked out of the house when she kept pressing him.

But it wasn't just since Astra Four. Georgia fought the gnawing recognition that he had been at war, at least with her, for months before the platform had blown. It had always been difficult for her to know when to keep her distance from Flynn, but she had learnt when to look away, when to leave the room, when to give him space. They had coped, somehow, given each other a wide berth when tempers were short. But now something else seemed to be at work; the signals she had learnt to recognise in Flynn were crossed. Her eyes misty with tears, Georgia shivered at the side of the road. *But we used to be so happy together; we were happy, we were once so very happy . . .*

When she returned to the kitchen, Flynn was watching footage from the Kosovo-Albanian refugee camps. Georgia stared blankly at the screen. 'I'm surprised you're not there.'

'You know perfectly well why I'm not there.' His eyes remained fixed on the television. 'You grounded me.'

Georgia held her tongue, but it was deeply unjust of Flynn to blame her for his lack of work. The three picture editors with whom he worked most closely had each, with varying degrees of tact, implied that his recent work had something missing. The bluntest – the one Flynn trusted the most – had said his work was shite and to sort out his head before he'd give him carte blanche on foreign assignments. As Georgia knew better than anyone, Flynn did his best work only when that carte blanche was held tight in his fist.

Stiffening her resolve, Georgia switched the set to mute and sat down at the table, willing him to talk to her. Her husband continued to watch the silent screen. The camera had zoomed in on a small family group in the crowd of refugees; a squatting young woman, rocking rhythmically back and forth on her heels, was weeping to the incongruous radio accompaniment of Sue McGregor discussing the weather. On each side of the Albanian woman stood two skinny children, loosely holding onto their mother's torn clothing, their eyes vacant, mouths hanging open.

'They blew it there,' Flynn muttered, pointing to an old man at the far edge of the frame. 'They should have focused on him, not the mother.'

Georgia was compelled to look again. He was right; he was normally right when it came to dramatic images. That was what had first brought them together: Flynn's visual genius. Fifteen years ago she'd been a junior news editor on the foreign desk at the BBC. Flynn had strolled in with one of their correspondents, helped himself to one of her cigarettes and flirted with her for twenty minutes. The second they'd left for a boozy lunch she'd hotfooted it to the research library, pulled up every photograph of Flynn's they had on file and surrendered her heart. It had been that simple. She'd barely slept until she'd engineered to meet him again; then hardly slept until after they were married. There had been many years of married life when Flynn's photographs had moved her to tears and straight into bed with him. It had often appalled her that his ability to capture suffering left her erotically charged. Just listening to him talk about a frame could still lift the hairs on her neck.

'What do you think, George? What do you think about that shot?'

'I don't agree. The mother's good.' She didn't think so at all, but at least he was asking her opinion; dissension might hold his attention. 'Mothers and children are the most reliable way to achieve the greatest empathy in the shortest amount of time.'

Flynn snorted. 'That's a cliché. The shot's a cliché, George. You've lost your touch.' He paused: one; two; three beats. 'Mothers are always a cliché.'

Apart from Sue McGregor, the kitchen was silent for several minutes.

'I'm beginning to hate your work, Flynn.'

'I hate lots of people's work, but seeing as I don't have to do it, I try not to let it worry me.'

'Things could change, you know; we could change our lives. We don't have to live in this, in this –' Georgia tried to sound reasonable and keep her voice steady, but she couldn't cushion the brittle edge in it – 'this *rut*. Maybe I should go back to work. Maybe I'd get my touch back.' And maybe, she continued silently, maybe I'd get *you* back. She waited for some reaction but he neither replied nor looked at her. 'Do I bore you, or something? Ever since you came back from Astra Four, you've been so cold. I don't understand. What have I done? We have to talk. Don't we?' She moved next to him and laid a hand tentatively on his forearm, feeling the muscle harden under her touch. 'I'm trying to *help*, Flynn. If something's bothering you, I'm here to help you talk it through. If you'd let me. And if *I'm* the thing that's bothering you . . .' She could not allow herself to complete the thought. 'Listen, darling, you know all I want –'

'Yes, I know all you want. All you want is for me to turn into some declawed, castrated pussycat and ponce round Westminster Green fawning over MPs. Taking their portraits for the profile section of the Sundays.'

'I've never wanted that!' She was stung by his accusation. 'That's so unfair. And it's unfair of you to be a bastard at home and then do the high-minded, "Which of earth's hell-holes shall I honour with my presence next?" shit –'

'That shit happens to be my job.' Flynn looked at her with a coldness that made her stop breathing. She lowered her eyes to the table.

'OK, OK,' she began again, telling herself it was good that he was talking, however unpleasantly, anything to lance the boil of his anger, 'let's talk about your job. I know how good you are at it, really, *rarely*, good, and how much it means. To you. To me. To us. How important it is. But what's going on?' Georgia raised her eyes. 'You've moped around at home

38

for half a year. You've been turned down on the last three assignments you've suggested. You've done nothing at all since Astra Four . . .'

'It's grand of you to point out my career's in free-fall. Just in case I'd forgotten.'

'I'm not trying to rub your nose in it. I don't care if you work or not, I just want to know what's going on. Don't you realise how much you've changed? I'm trying to understand, that's all. I don't know if you even *want* to work. Sometimes I wonder if the only reason you work is to get away from home.'

'If that's what I wanted, trust me, I wouldn't need an excuse.'

Georgia bit her lip, tears beginning to well in her blue eyes. 'Don't you love me any more, Flynn? Don't you care how much it hurts when you shut me out like this?'

'Don't be childish. If you need people to tell you they love you all day and every day, then go and get a job. Go work for some worthy cause. Battersea Dogs Home. Do whatever it takes.'

'I wasn't serious about getting a job; a job doesn't matter –'

'No? Well, mine matters to me.' Flynn's chair scraped the tiles as he rose angrily.

'Then what the hell is stopping you from doing your god-damn all-important job?' Georgia also stood, not knowing whether she did so in order to be better able to confront him, or to have the chance to walk out before he did for once. 'I've never questioned your work, never complained about your being on the road for weeks – months – at a time. I've always been so *proud* of what you do. All I ask is that we talk about it.'

'That is precisely what I don't want to do.'

'Why? Because I wouldn't understand?'

'Maybe. Maybe I don't want you to understand. Maybe I don't want you to be part of it.'

'Because I'm not up to it? You think your work's too noble, too glorious for me to understand?'

'Glorious?' he smiled oddly. 'Glorious? No. I don't think that.'

'Yes you do. Nothing matters to you the way work does. Not me, not the children. Is that why you're behaving so oddly, being so touchy?' Georgia gripped the edge of the table, hearing herself rant but unable to stop the accusations spilling from her lips. 'Are you some kind of risk junkie, starved of your fix? Don't you ever think about the children, what it means to them when you're on assignment? All it means to them is that you're *somewhere else*. They're the most important thing in the world, *they're* where your responsibilities lie, but you're too pig-headed to realise what it is you're throwing away. I know you're a great photographer, outstanding, but you're wrong if you think you're going to get some kind of immortality from photographs. The only crack at immortality you've got is Beth and Ollie.'

Flynn began to walk out of the room, but stopped in the doorway with his back to her. 'Don't lecture me about my responsibilities, Georgia, and never lecture me about the children.'

'You take it for granted I'll deal with the children, the house, the bills . . .'

Flynn paced slowly back towards her. 'You really drew the short straw in life, didn't you, darling? You suffer when I'm here and you suffer when I'm not. Let's look at all this stuff you deal with, shall we?' His voice was silky with menace as he picked up the post Georgia had brought in and thrown on the table. '*Gardens Illustrated*. That's an essential, seeing as all we've got is a graveyard for two rusty bicycles. Barclaycard – Mrs Georgia Brennan. *Reader's Digest* sweepstake, for Mrs Georgia Brennan again. . . . Lloyds Bank – aha! *Mr* And Mrs F. M. Brennan. The school, Mrs Georgia Brennan. A parcel,

Mrs Georgia Brennan. I'll open it, shall I, so you can witness me taking domestic responsibility . . .'

Georgia tensed as he ripped open the box. He lifted out a jar labelled 'Gardener's Miracle Whip' and theatrically held it up for inspection, twisting it this way and that. 'What kind of miracle does it perform, sweetheart? You morph into Capability Brown?'

'Stop it, Flynn. It's for my feet.'

'Your *feet*. Of course. How could I have forgotten your feet? Let's see what other goodies we've got in here . . .' With his eyes shut, he plunged his hand into the box and extracted a mysterious bubble-wrapped object. 'I'll be damned. A giant terracotta egg cup. For an ostrich egg?' He studied it with genuine bewilderment before Georgia said sullenly, 'It's a watering can.'

With intense deliberation Flynn unfolded the note that accompanied the order and read aloud: 'Original medieval design pottery watering can, hand-crafted by Precious Tools Ltd. Water is released when the thumbhole is uncovered. Twenty-one pounds ninety-nine.'

He walked to the sink and filled it. Keeping his thumb over the hole he held it high, released a trickle of water then pressed his thumb quickly back over. 'On. Off. On. Off. But this is brilliant. A work of engineering genius. How did those pig-ignorant thirteenth-century peasants come up with something so sophisticated? Must be an Irish design. Thirteenth-century *Irish* peasants knew a thing or two . . .'

'I get the message.'

'Do you, darling?' Something dangerous stirred under the flippancy in his voice. 'Do you?' Georgia flinched as the pseudo-medieval watering pot hurtled over her head and smashed against the opposite wall.

'Twenty-one pounds and ninety-nine pence,' he said softly as she began to cry, 'twenty-one pounds and ninety-nine pence. I don't think you get the message at all.'

THREE

After the client had left, Madeline sat at her office desk writing. When she had first qualified as a therapist she had made meticulous notes after each session. Now she tended to record no more than the date and a shorthand list of apparently unconnected words to remind her of her personal reaction to each session.

'*Stupid. Worthless. No time for her. Bored,*' she wrote. When her client had talked about having sex with strangers when she was too high or too drunk or simply too bored to know what she was doing, that had been her instinctive reaction: that this was a woman she would have no time for if they met outside of the therapy room. Marking that response, she wondered if that was how her client felt about herself. Far from condemning her, Madeline had to use her own feelings to explore her client's. Her shifting feelings provided a valuable map to the progression of each client's treatment: they acted as signposts. Sometimes her instinctive response caught her by surprise, pointing her back down the same path to recover her steps, or sending her veering off at an acute angle. These signposts were not always reliable – they were indicators, not certainties – but she had to record them to ensure she did not let her client, any client, down. Madeline doodled around the last word to emphasise her frustration then picked up the phone.

'Jillian? It's Madeline.'

'Hello there,' her supervisor replied, 'that must have been telepathy. I was just thinking about you. How are you?'

'Fine . . .'

Jillian Ashcroft tutted sternly. 'You know what I feel about the word fine, Madeline.'

'I'm allowed to say it even if clients aren't.'

'But you *are* my client, Madeline.'

Madeline laughed. 'Touché. OK, I'm not "fine". I'm exhausted. There's been a ton of new follow-through on Astra Four, which is why I haven't been able to see you . . . I don't suppose there's any chance of meeting tomorrow?'

'Is something in particular bothering you? You sound a little—'

'I just need to sound off.'

'That's what I'm here for, Madeline. I'm free at one forty-five, is that OK?'

'You know what I feel about the word "OK", Jillian . . .'

Both women were smiling as they hung up.

The evening sun streamed in through the window onto her desk; it was already half-past seven. Madeline doubted she'd make it home before Michael and his wife arrived for dinner. Her hand was on the doorknob when the answer machine picked up a call.

'Damn!' her mother's voice cursed. 'I've missed you again. Listen, darling, it's me. Just calling to say I'm settling in, the condo's great, bang next door to Pat's, and we're having such fun . . . It's like we were back at school again, you know, younger than springtime . . . I might do this every year. The Canadian owners want to swap for at least three months annually so they can really "do" Europe . . . Pat calls them snowbirds because they only winter in Florida. I can't tell you how much I love driving their vast car about! Now to business: I've got my fingers crossed it's pouring in London and you'll feel so jealous of me soaking up the Florida sunshine that you'll have to nip over for a week or so . . . I know, I *know*, you have "client commitments", it's just that I miss you already.'

Madeline leant against the doorframe, listening with enjoyment. It wouldn't have made any difference if she had picked up the receiver. Her mother would barely have paused for breath anyway, but she would certainly have stayed on the phone for longer. 'Which reminds me, I met a wonderful man last night, a widower of *course* . . .'

Her mother Rachel's mercurial brain and the series of seemingly random connections it made were one of the world's great mysteries, Madeline thought, and could have kept twenty neurological researchers occupied for a lifetime.

'He's a Yank, quite a bit older than me – well, aren't they all, darling, given the way I knocked ten years off my age last birthday – but *très distingué* and quite charming. He called this morning and wants to take me to the yacht club for dinner next week. Should I go, do you think, or might that look too eager? Maybe I should play hard-to-get, hmm, what do you think?'

'I think you should play hard-to-get, Mum. Why break the pattern of a lifetime?' Madeline addressed her empty office.

'I know what you're thinking, Maddie, you're thinking I'm a silly old bag and it's high time I grew up. You were always mature for your age; I remember your first headmistress saying so. You were what? Seven – eight? The idea of you being *mature*. Anyway, this is just to say I'm thinking about you and you have to call me OK, darling? I worry about you, especially at this time of year. Always at this time of year. Let me know you're OK. At least send me an e-mail care of Pat. She says you have her address and she's teaching me how to use it. And they say you can't teach an old dog new tricks!' That wonderful, rippling laugh. 'Bye for now. Hope all's going well and you don't have any real crazies. Kisses to you and Patrick from your silly old mother.'

Thinking of her far-from-silly mother made Madeline smile as she walked down the stairs. She'd been delighted when her godmother Patricia Patterson – an American her mother had known since schooldays – had masterminded a five-month exchange between Rachel and her neighbours on the Gulf coast of Florida. A change of scene would do her mother the world of good, even though it was hard to have her so far away. Especially at this time of year. She switched on the alarm and was double-locking the front door behind her when a voice made her jump.

'Dr Light! What an unexpected pleasure!'

A tall figure loomed in the shadow of the next doorway. The man dropped his cigarette and ground it out as Madeline asked curtly, 'What are you doing here?'

'Now is that any way to greet an old compadre? Or have you forgotten me?' He clicked his heels and made a short bow. 'Flynn –'

'I remember you, Mr Brennan,' Madeline interrupted. 'APC Human Resources, isn't that correct?'

'I was hoping you wouldn't hold that against me.'

'Is there a reason for this impromptu visit?'

'Sheer coincidence. Do you believe in fate, Doctor?'

'No. I don't.' Except that, try as she might, she was destined to be late for dinner. Flynn followed her as she began to walk down the street. Despite his height, she thought, the man had a trick of disappearing into his surroundings, some predator's instinct that enabled him to catch his prey offguard, long before he had been scented. 'You seem to make a habit of materialising from nowhere.'

'Personally, I am a great believer in fate.'

'How did you find my office?'

'Jesus, sweetheart, it doesn't take Sherlock Holmes to track you down: you're in the phone book.'

Madeline halted and Flynn flung up his hands. 'Don't glare at me like that, you'll frighten the horses.' He regarded her with open appreciation. 'Now that's what I call a disconcerting pair of baby blues. No, green. I didn't get a good look at you last time we met.'

'Whereas I got a very good look at you.' Madeline registered the physical pull of the man alongside a feeling of territorial invasion. She took a step backwards and said coolly, 'You'll have to excuse me, but I really am in a hurry.'

'Surely you won't turn away a troubled soul, Dr Light. Surely you can spare me ten minutes?'

'For what?'

'Professional advice.'

Over the preceding three months Madeline had often found her thoughts drifting back to the photographer who had used her to con his way onto *Nepenthe* only to be visibly knocked backwards by what he saw in the mortuary tent. She had been angry that he had trespassed on the private, delicate pain of others, but that anger had been softened by compassion for his evident distress. Most of all she had been curious. She had not expected his eventual reappearance, but neither was she now surprised by it. Yet her pulse quickened.

'I see. Mr Brennan, I practise psychotherapy between ten a.m. and six p.m. Clients are generally referred to me for an initial assessment and then, if appropriate, we set a schedule of regular appointments. For which they pay.'

Brennan looked wounded. 'But that's precisely why I'm here – to become a regular, paying client and make an appointment.'

She raised her eyebrows. 'Then I suggest you ring the number which you no doubt also found in the phone book and make one.'

He grinned. 'To be honest, I don't believe I need therapy. Not as such. I had more of an MOT in mind. How about a quick jar at the pub on the corner?'

'Thank you, Mr Brennan, but no. As I said, I'm pressed for time.'

'Flynn.'

Madeline raised her chin and looked at him with the steady gaze that had unsettled many before. 'All right. Flynn. First, Flynn, you have to make an appointment. Secondly, I'm not sure that I have time to take on any new clients at the moment. Thirdly, I doubt very much that it's appropriate for me to see you, even if I did have space in my schedule.'

'Appropriate? Come on, Doc! Live dangerously; throw away the rule book! Are you always this tight-arsed?'

Madeline peered past him, waving down a passing taxi, then turned back to address him one more time. 'You can phone me tomorrow. But I am late for an appointment and – to be blunt – I'm finding your facetiousness extremely trying. Could you please move out of my way?'

He stepped aside with a strange look and Madeline strode down the street, leaving him calling after her. 'You don't understand . . .'

'Damn right,' Madeline muttered under her breath, 'and I'm not sure that I care to.'

Behind her, Flynn cupped his hands around his mouth and shouted, 'If you won't see me, I'll . . . I'll kill myself.' Several passers-by stopped and stared curiously.

'Oh *please*.' Madeline paused, her hand on the taxi door, then swung back to face him, now furious. 'A man who cons his way onto a helicopter, despite the fact that there are men who have been killed and maimed, a man who impersonates a *human resources* representative of all things, in order to photograph the aftermath of an explosion surreptitiously, doesn't leap up and spontaneously *top* himself because an unknown therapist won't talk to him.'

She wrenched open the taxi door, but as she did so she glimpsed the stricken expression on Flynn's face. It recalled the unearthly desperation that had possessed him when he saw the corpse of George Reagan. Compassion immediately dissolved her anger. 'Look, if you genuinely want to discuss therapeutic options, please call me tomorrow morning.'

Flynn had a foot on the step of the cab, holding the door open. 'I'm sorry,' he said slowly. 'I'm not normally such an utter arse.' He closed his eyes and passed his hand over them with a sigh. 'This isn't a situation I know . . .' He opened his eyes and held her gaze. 'Say you'll see me tomorrow. Any time. Day or night.' He reached a hand towards her. 'Please. I told myself I'd set it up tonight or not at all.'

Madeline studied the wearied lines and kind creases of his face. Some instinct that he was not as he seemed sparked her engagement if not her trust; there was something hauntingly familiar about his face. Swayed by her own curiosity, Madeline relented.

'Come at ten tomorrow morning. But I have to warn you, I doubt I'll be able to take you on as a client, even if you were able to convince me that is what you want and need. I should at least be able to refer you to someone suitable.'

'I can be very convincing.'

'I have no doubt of that, but my concern is ethical. The first time we met was under circumstances that make trust difficult to establish.'

'I'd trust you with my life.'

'The therapeutic process requires mutual trust. I have to be certain that I am able to trust *you*. Goodnight.'

'Patrick?' she called as she entered the deserted flat.

'Hey . . . we're down here.'

Madeline kicked off her shoes before descending the internal steps to the studio. Once Patrick had given up the romantic fancy of having his stone delivered by boat, the riverside hatches had been sliced into huge windows that flooded the internal studio with light. An entire wall of the room was now dedicated to official and private photographs of the late

48

Basil Hume, alongside some two dozen sketches that Patrick had made of different angles of the cardinal's head. On an adjoining shelf stood five small clay maquettes. Michael and Lydia Whitchurch were standing in the open doorway to the external yard, admiring the plaster-cast bust of Hume that was to be painstakingly translated into marble.

Michael Whitchurch had been Madeline's tutorial partner at university. They had drifted apart for several years until, much to their mutual surprise, they had met at a lecture at the Tavistock Institute and discovered they were both in the process of qualifying as psychotherapists. Six years later, the availability of a small suite in Madeline's office building had coincided with Michael's decision to move his therapy practice from Edinburgh to London, and ever since they had been the closest of friends as well as co-tenants. Madeline trusted Michael's wisdom as she trusted Jillian's; barring his inability to deal with the tedium of office administration – specifically never buying filter papers for the coffee percolator, which she attributed to genetic Scottish frugality – she did not fault him personally or professionally. His wife Lydia, a tiny and elegant Parisienne, was the icing on the Whitchurch cake. Madeline liked her immensely and Patrick adored her.

'Sorry I'm late.' Madeline flung one arm round her colleague and the other around Lydia before kissing Patrick's cheek. She approached the Cardinal on his waist-high turntable and could not resist trailing her fingers over his lower face. 'Wonderful. I see what you mean about his lower lip.'

'Were you held up by a client?'

'Not exactly, more waylaid.'

'At the off-licence?' Patrick directed a slow wink at their guests.

'At the what?' Madeline clapped her hand to her head. 'Jesus Christ. I completely forgot the wine.'

Patrick nudged Michael. 'What d'you think? A screw loose?'

'The whole toolbox I'd say.'

'Ignore them, Madeline.' Lydia Whitchurch intervened in

the clipped French accent she retained despite twenty years in England. 'Patrick met us carrying a case of wine. There is enough to sink a large boat.'

'You would have loved the procession,' Patrick said an hour later as he carved the veal. 'The Catholic Church at full throttle. There I was, scraping and bowing, doffing my cap and wringing my hands like a medieval stone-carver . . . which is what I am, as far as they're concerned.'

'Who turned up?'

'There was enough black flapping about for a murder of crows. Let me see. Hume's successor, His Eminence Cardinal John Patrick McClonagh; the cathedral architect, the commissioning monsignor and the Director of Works.'

Michael whistled. 'Holy Mother of God.'

'Not in person, no, but she was definitely there in spirit.'

'You will not believe what Leo said to me last night about the Virgin birth. We *must* move the children to a good Catholic school . . .'

Two separate conversations developed over dinner. Lydia and Patrick analysed the complex risk-return ratio of a Catholic education; Michael and Madeline talked work.

'I need to sound you out on something, Michael.' Madeline quietly recounted her second encounter with Flynn Brennan.

'Tricky call. Not the best way to kick off a therapeutic relationship.'

'You can say that again.'

'I remember you describing this bloke looking at the body on the ship. You said you were *certain* there was something else going on with him; something apart from Astra Four.'

'Yes. His reaction intrigued me. A tenderness passed across his face when he looked at the body. Maybe not tenderness; maybe relief.'

'What's his story? What was the trauma trigger?'

'I haven't heard it. It may not even be trauma-related.'

'So you see him tomorrow, get a feel for him, judge whether he's bullshitting you and why. See if you can set aside the initial duplicity. If you can't, then refer him.'

Madeline nodded slowly. 'I don't know why, but this man feels dangerous to me.'

'So? What's wrong with a little danger?' Michael took her hand across the table, concerned by the change in her expression. 'Are you sure you're all right, hen?'

'I'm tired, that's all.' She gave his hand a squeeze in return. 'I've been backed into a couple of client situations against my will . . .'

Michael feigned amazement. 'And you don't *like* that? Oops. Better back off fast if you're not completely running the show . . .'

'Hey; don't go there.' Madeline held up both hands with a laugh. '*That* stuff I know about. It's just been a long day. It started badly and finished worse.'

'Thanks. Next time you invite us to dinner I'll remember to say no . . .'

Michael wasn't a trauma specialist. If he had a therapeutic bent it was in the spiritual field. He did not adhere to any one school of psychotherapy but embraced them all, believing predominantly in the power of love, whether human or divine. Madeline would have valued more of his opinion on both Flynn Brennan and Mary Reagan, but the dinner table was too public a place. Besides, she felt too tired. She wanted to talk about holidays, the new exhibition at the Tate, the cricket season, even mortgage rates – anything but herself. She made a dismissive gesture. 'I'm all right, Michael. Forget it. If I have a problem, I'll come to you first, believe me.'

'You'll go to him first about what?' Patrick asked.

'An issue with a client.'

'Which client?'

Madeline smiled archly. 'Wouldn't you like to know?'

'Sphinx,' he whispered. After eight years Patrick understood that, for his sake and hers, not to mention the client's, she could not bring work home to him.

Madeline shifted to face Lydia. 'When are you going to bring the children over? It's been so long. I thought we could get a boat on the Thames, while the weather's good; take a picnic. Tell me what they're up to.'

Lydia needed little encouragement to talk about her four children. As she recounted their small sporting and academic triumphs, her voice rang with an almost unholy pride. She stopped abruptly, embarrassed. 'What a bore mothers are. How is *your* mother, Madeline? Is she enjoying Florida?'

'Loving it. She's already got a date at the yacht club.' Madeline rose to clear the plates, gesturing to Lydia and Patrick to stay, but accepting Michael's help. She dumped the plates on the draining board and swung round to face him. 'You've told Lydia about me, haven't you?'

'What? What about you?'

'You know what I'm talking about.'

'Lydia's not an idiot.'

'I know Lydia's not an idiot. Why did she suddenly stop talking about the children?'

'She worries she boasts too much. Maddie . . . hen.' Michael folded his arms around her. 'Fifteen years ago, I went to a wedding . . .'

'Don't. Not now. I'm too tired.'

'You're over-loading like a circuit board. I can feel it.'

'Are you two bringing the cheese or *making* it?' Patrick shouted from the living room. 'Grab a bottle of red too, OK . . . ?'

When they reappeared, Patrick was lighting Lydia's cigarette. 'You know, you don't have to sneak off to the kitchen to discuss clients; we won't spill any secrets.'

'For once we weren't talking shop.' Michael helped himself to a wedge of Brie but kept his eyes on Madeline. 'We were talking about weddings.'

52

'The Barretts?' Lydia said. 'Yes, darling, do tell them about the Barretts' wedding; it was extraordinary.'

'Some good friends of ours were married last weekend in sort of a humanist celebration. The groom made a cracking speech. He's very interested in Buddhism; I have a feeling you met him last –'

'Tell them about the ghosts,' Lydia urged.

'I will if you give me a chance! So in his speech he pointed out the distinction between the cultural, ah, *spiritual*, if you like, makeup of those raised in the Eastern tradition and us in the West. It struck me that the concept could be useful in general psychotherapy. And I'm sure it has resonance for post-traumatic therapy.' Michael held Madeline's gaze for a moment before he continued. 'In the Eastern tradition, individuals are so deeply embedded, so tightly wrapped in a blanket woven from family, social community, cultural identity, that they lose track of their uniqueness: they search for a route to their *unique* identity. Whereas we in the West –' Madeline leant forward. '– for us it's the mirror opposite. From birth we are taught to be individual, self-sufficient and independent. We're not "attached" to our mothers' lives so much as temporarily recipients of their services. What do we teach a nine-year-old? Stand up for yourself. Fight your own fights. Don't come running to me if you trip on those shoelaces. Take responsibility for your own belongings.' Michael's eyes were drawn back to his wife's face. 'It's not that we're bad parents; not that we're mean, or unloving. It's just part of our societal structure. We are constantly reminded that we are above all *alone* in life; responsible for ourselves and nothing but. There's an absence of integration, a disconnection from everything and everyone else. Mark, the groom, said that Eastern Buddhists describe the West as the realm of the hungry ghosts.'

Patrick grunted. 'Sounds like a crap wedding speech.'

Michael shrugged. 'He believes marriage is the one chance we Westerners have of truly integrating.'

'Well.' Patrick reached for Madeline's hand. 'We're perfectly well integrated without doing the official bit.'

'Don't you two ever think of marrying?'

'My track record's not impressive, Lydia. You know I was married twice before I met Madeline.'

'Third time lucky?' Michael said. 'You can but try.'

Madeline laughed and again threw up both hands in a back-off gesture. 'No way! Frankly, my mother's more likely to marry again than Patrick is. I wouldn't be a bit surprised if she comes back from Florida engaged.'

When their guests had left they took the remains of the Barolo and sat on their 'terrace', the rough, concreted slab that held the Thames back from the studio. Madeline leant back between Patrick's bony knees with her eyes closed and her face tipped up towards the stars.

'You should have seen them, Maddie, after they'd paraded around the yard and the studio. Six inches of stone dust like a frieze on their hems.' Stop drivelling, Patrick instructed himself as Madeline remained silent. Don't bore her. 'I know what you're thinking,' he murmured, smoothing her dark hair.

'How do you know what I'm thinking?' she grumbled. 'I'm a sphinx, remember? You're never supposed to know what I'm thinking. I might not even be thinking at all.'

'You're never not thinking. Besides, your chin's sticking out. You're definitely thinking about something and I've got a pretty good idea what it is.'

Madeline smiled as she tucked her chin back towards her chest. So he thought she was preoccupied with the notion of their getting married. She wasn't; she was debating whether she'd made a mistake agreeing to see Flynn Brennan. She twisted into Patrick's arms. 'So – what *do* you think about it, then? Marriage?'

Patrick considered the night sky. What he thought was

that marriage was a waste of time in ninety-nine per cent of cases. Not that it did actual harm; it just didn't do any good. Patrick had known romantic obsession to turn every ordinary, mundane domestic activity into a state of bliss. He had been close to physical rapture washing the dishes with his first wife, mesmerised by the tiny, rainbow soap bubbles creeping up her forearms . . . In the early days of the marriage. But women, and men, although Patrick laid most of the blame at the female door, wilfully deceived themselves with impossible expectations once marriage was added to the romantic equation. Two women had mistakenly invested such expectations in him, loaded all their eggs into one frail basket, closed their eyes and pushed off from the bank, all for the assumed lifelong devotion of one ordinary, mortal male. And he *had* been devoted; in those early days; in his youth; initially. To both of them. The weight of investment on one side of the scale was so enormous and the pay-off on the other so pathetically small, disappointment was the certain outcome. The key was not to have huge, impossible expectations, not to invest your partner with every imagined virtue, not to think that love had some special, sacred meaning, and never to abandon your other resources, but always to balance love with work, the joy of sheer hard work.

After a pause, he said simply, 'Marriage works for some people. Maybe if you're good at it, as I'm sure your mother was, you should just plunge in again and again.'

'But you wouldn't plunge in again?'

'I wasn't good at it. You put your hand in the fire once, you learn not to do it again. I was fool enough to get burned twice before I learnt my lesson. I've made all the marriage proposals I'm going to make.'

Madeline smiled to herself. 'But if someone were to propose to you?'

'Nobody's ever proposed to me. Not seriously.'

55

Madeline pressed her head back into the hollow of his shoulder.

'Nobody except me.'

'Nobody except you,' he echoed slowly. 'Nobody except you.'

FOUR

By ten-twenty the next morning Flynn Brennan still hadn't turned up and Madeline was kicking herself. She knew precisely what she wanted to say to him. The hitch was that he wasn't going to give her the satisfaction of showing, which made her an idiot, not only to waste her time expecting him, but to waste it further by planning what she'd say when he eventually tipped up. By ten thirty-five her thoughts were only of his well-being. Had her condemnation of his conduct on Astra Four been too harsh? Had she failed to extend to him the basic compassion that anyone deserved?

There was a sharp rap on her door. It inched open and Flynn's face appeared around it wearing a sheepish grin. 'I'm in the doghouse, aren't I?'

'No, not at all.' Madeline was relieved, but as if an inner warning had been triggered, she was immediately on guard. *Hold it right there, chum; don't think you can get round me because you have crinkly eyes that you can crease up at will: I'm not going to play that kind of game.* She knew that it wasn't uncommon for traumatised clients to deliberately or unwittingly act in such a way as to put their therapists' backs up, in order to claim that the therapist was unwilling or unable to help them. No presumption was ever warranted in the treatment of the potentially traumatised, and she'd already made several.

Madeline mentally erased the slate. 'I can still give you twenty-five minutes. Have a seat.'

'Here? Opposite the desk? Or do I lie on the couch?'

'Wherever you feel comfortable.' Madeline was curious where he would choose to sit, although his comfort was not her objective. Post-traumatic therapy rarely involved feeling comfortable: safe, definitely: comfortable, very rarely. Some clients at once flung themselves, near prostrate, on the sofa; others chose the smallest, hardest chair in the room. Wherever her clients sat, Madeline always kept her back to the window, away from the light.

Flynn looked around before selecting a large, easy chair and stretching out in it, one foot resting on his knee. 'So. Where do we begin?'

'This is a preliminary assessment.' *It may not be a beginning at all*, she cautioned herself. 'Tell me what it is that you are hoping to achieve in coming here.'

'Personal fulfilment, profound joy and the Holy Grail.'

'That's ambitious.' Madeline smiled. 'Tell me what made you come last night? Why me, why then?'

'I liked the look of you. You've got awful pretty eyes. Do you need those glasses, by the way? You weren't wearing them in Scotland. I was thinking maybe they're a prop to make you look more academic, not so good-looking?'

She returned his gaze steadily. Her glasses were only for reading and working at the computer screen, but now she was disinclined to take them off.

'I'll take that as a no. Right: bottom line, I don't know any other therapists.'

'What did your GP feel about it?'

'I didn't ask my GP. Come to think of it, I don't *have* a GP.' He treated her to the lop-sided grin again, shovelling his hair back with a hand. 'Besides, like I told you, I believe in fate.

We were fated to meet again. Meant for each other. We'd been brought together for a purpose.'

'If not entirely by fate.' Madeline's mind was racing, marshalling the entire therapeutic weaponry she had acquired over eight years of experience. When in session with a client, she was always aware of the several different levels on which her mind operated: her primary, intellectual response to what the client said; the instinctive, intuitive effect it had on her; the physical, near chemical gut changes that occurred in both the client and Madeline herself, and finally the moments of complete departure from the client when she might find herself thinking, *what'll I have for lunch?* Or, *I mustn't forget the dry-cleaner.* Instances of drifting away from the client could tell her as much about the underlying therapeutic connection as anything that was actually said.

Already she was listening intently to her inner voice: *Does he know why he's here? He's flirting. To get me to like him, or to stop me from liking him, knowing it will put my back up? He knows I don't like facetiousness, so he lays it on thick. I'd enjoy this if he wasn't a client; I'd enjoy taking him on. He's big, strong; maybe a bully. But scared of being here. For all the bravado, he's scared. OK.*

'Let me start by explaining how I work.' Madeline pushed her glasses onto the top of her head, keeping her eyes on his. 'First of all, I am not a general psychotherapist. I work exclusively in the field of post-traumatic stress. Which casts a pretty wide net. All the people I see have had an experience – possibly one event, possibly a series of events – often life-threatening, that has affected them psychologically in such a way as to persistently interrupt what they consider a "normal" life.'

Flynn waved a hand. 'I know all this, Doc. I've read up on PTSD. I know that's what you do. I didn't think you flew out to *Nepenthe* to treat agoraphobics.'

Madeline kept her face impassive. She tended to avoid using the label post-traumatic stress disorder; the condition wore so many changing faces it could prove a distraction to dwell on what matched the blueprint and what did not. 'Exactly what does the term PTSD mean to you?'

'Poor Terrified Sod's Disorder. Classic journo's syndrome.'

She met his self-deprecating look with a smile. 'OK. As you may have read, PTSD is a catch-all label for a collection of different psychological and physiological conditions. Often the boundaries between a sufferer's inner and outer worlds seem to shift; sometimes to shatter completely. Some of my colleagues would disagree, but I feel it is a disorder only in that its symptoms disrupt "normal" life. It is a natural reaction to extreme stress.'

'That's a comfort.'

'What is common to all my clients is that the work we do together is not intended to be long term, unlike most branches of general psychotherapy or psychoanalysis. Depending on the nature of the client's needs, I would not expect to work with them for more than six months. Two to three months would be average. In certain cases, I might see a client for only a few sessions, over a matter of weeks.'

'I understand. Fast turnover. First in, first out. Sound business practice.'

Madeline could see he was watching and listening to her acutely. He sat very still, with his eyes fixed on hers, barely blinking. She contemplated mirroring his flippancy but continued to play it dead straight to see if he would follow suit. 'I set a limited time horizon because research has shown that the syndrome is either relieved – by which I mean symptoms disappear – within that time, or the treatment isn't helping and continuation does not improve chances of recovery.' Madeline paused, aware of sounding overly formal; his deliberate levity was making her feel pompous. 'Let's put it another way: I believe in being economical. If I can help you, let's roll up our sleeves and get on with it.'

Flynn visibly relaxed. 'Three months,' he mused. 'About a

hundred days, hmm? OK. That's good. And if the treatment doesn't work?'

'We will consider alternatives together.'

'You'll do me just fine.'

Madeline leant forward. 'It's important you understand that if I feel I can't help you, or if the difficulties you are experiencing are not post-traumatic, I will recommend someone better suited to you. I certainly won't let you waste your time.' A ghost of a smile flickered over her lips. 'Or mine.'

'What made you get into PTSD?'

'May I ask why you want to know?'

'Occupational habit. I'm used to checking credentials.'

'I specialise in trauma from personal interest,' she replied simply. 'As far as my credentials go, I qualified eight years ago and have spent almost all of that time working with trauma, whether individual or critical incidents involving numbers of people.'

'Give me some examples.'

'We're here to talk about *you*,' Madeline reminded Flynn gently. 'What it is that has made *you* decide to get help at this time, and what it is you need help with.'

'Assuming,' Flynn drawled, 'that I want to be helped.'

'You're right. As you came to find me last night, and returned this morning, I did make that assumption,' Madeline replied. 'I'll try not to make any others. Could you give me some brief biographical details?'

'Got your notebook handy?'

'That won't be necessary.' As she leant back in her chair and crossed her legs, Madeline saw his gaze flick to her knee. She was fully on her guard and would have to keep on the qui vive, which was clearly a state he was accustomed to.

'Right you are. Name, Flynn Michael Brennan. Date of birth, 14 April 1959, which makes me forty-one. That's where you make the note, "suffering from conventional mid-life crisis".' He flashed his teeth at her. 'Nationality, British by

61

papers, Irish by descent. Marital status, married. For, let me see . . . fourteen years and all to the same woman. Georgia. Progeny: two; one of each sex, Beth and Oliver. Sexual orientation: heterosexual. Profession: some say newsgatherer, others photojournalist. I prefer photographer. Specialisation: war. Qualifications: virtually zero. References: few and far between. And none of them good. Will that do you?'

'Tell me about your original family.'

Flynn leant back in the chair, stretching his legs out. The room suddenly seemed small to Madeline, too small to contain him. 'Jesus now, you're not going to ask me whether I was untimely ripped from my mother's womb, or bottle-fed, or deprived of chocolate? You're not going to blame my poor old mother for all my problems?'

Madeline allowed her impatience to show a little. 'Flynn, we're a little pressed for time here. Tell me where you grew up, about your family background. You said you were British; I had . . . *assumed* you were Irish.'

'Now whatever might lead ya to think that?' he asked in heavy brogue. His gaze settled on a spot behind her head. As he talked about his childhood, Madeline measured every non-verbal signal: the rhythm of his breathing, the manner in which he sighed, the way even a sigh could tilt upwards at the end in a question mark, his eye movements, the way he stretched or eased a different muscle in his body, shifted in his seat, the speed and rhythm of his blinking all told her something about his inner world.

'. . . and this unholy accent grew in him, a bastard thing – a road map of everywhere he'd ever lived or wanted to live. My dad wanted so badly to be Irish, but it made no difference to the natives. They always saw him as a blow-in.'

'Are you close to him?'

'Not any more. He's dead.'

'Your mother?'

'A good Suffolk girl who spent the best part of her life trying

62

to thrash the Irish out of my dad. He didn't want that to happen to me and my brother, so he sent us to a boarding school in Limerick. Which gave us nothing but a one-hundred-per-cent Irish Catholic view of destiny.'

'Tell me about that. What is an Irish Catholic view of destiny?'

'It's not complicated. Nothing Catholic is. You're born facing one direction so that's the way you're going to go. Just keep going.' He shrugged. 'Personally, I couldn't give a fuck about the Hibernian soul, but I can still tell one or two.'

'One or two?'

'Limericks. Would you like to hear one of my own compositions?' He did not wait for Madeline's response. 'There was a young doctor called Light, Blessed with great sense and insight. All her clients were sad, Or mysteriously mad: They couldn't tell wrong quite from right.'

Madeline smoothed an eyebrow thoughtfully. *Gamester. He kept falling back on humour to avoid addressing why he was sitting there in her room. Most of her clients were only too eager to tell their stories once they'd struggled to the stage of sitting opposite her. Yet again he'd fired her curiosity. Which did he think he was – sad, mad or helplessly amoral?* 'You are aware that I am not a medical doctor, merely an academic one?'

'I guessed that, but therapist didn't scan and I didn't think you'd like to be called a psycho.' This time he waited for a reaction but Madeline did not indulge him with so much as a flicker of an eyelash. 'All right, it needs work, I'll grant you that. I'd like to get plight in there. And perhaps tight . . .' His voice drawled suggestively to a close.

'Try an alternative rhyme . . .' She was curious to see if he would go for 'fight'. Everything about him was combative.

'Alternative, ummhmm – I've got it! Night! We could work on this together, we'd make a grand team: On a foggy and dark April night, A therapist flew into sight. She crossed the

North Sea, Then met terrible me – Now that was a Godawful plight!'

Madeline tugged slightly at the neck of her shirt with one hand, running the chain of her necklace through her fingers. 'You found that night on *Nepenthe* a Godawful plight?' she asked.

'Oh, let's stay with the poetry.'

'I'd like to stay on *Nepenthe*.'

'Sooner you than me. Let's be poets.'

'I'd like to know more about your siblings.'

'Look, I don't want to be rude, but you're doing it again.' He looked up at the ceiling and said in a bored tone, 'I had a perfectly normal, ordinary childhood. Why do you have to know all this stuff, Doc? Is it rule one in the manual?'

'I'd rather you called me Madeline.' Madeline felt a fizz of irritation; she took more pride than she would readily admit in her reputation as a maverick. She was not accustomed to being branded a textbook slave. She considered how to answer his question and chose to use his professional idiom rather than her own. 'I'm trying to see what's in the background before we focus on you. To put you in context.'

'Very smart. Respect the space around a person – don't go in too close or you'll end up with everything out of proportion – huge noses and bulging eyes. The only hitch,' Flynn drawled, 'is that I'm not comfortable on this side of the camera.'

'I'd like to come back to that thought. If, that is, we decide to continue.'

'Meaning?'

'Meaning there are a few things that remain to be resolved before we can establish an ongoing working relationship. One is whether we will be able to establish a basis of trust between us, whether I am the right person to help you. The key thing is what's brought you here. Now; today. You said you've read up on PTSD; do you recognise any symptoms in yourself?'

Flynn shifted in his chair. 'My wife . . .'

'Georgia?'

'Yes.' He looked suddenly ashamed. 'My marriage is shite. I don't know why, but I know I do it – I make it shite. I can't seem to help it. I find myself hurting her.'

'Hurting her in what way?'

Flynn shook his head. 'Not hitting her. I'd never touch her, not like that. Just being a bastard. Something comes over me; she becomes someone I don't know. Someone I don't like.'

Or he becomes someone he doesn't know, someone he doesn't like, Madeline thought as Flynn searched for the words to continue.

'It isn't Georgia's fault. Sometimes, recently, I feel a rage come down and I don't know why. It isn't anything she's said, more that she's there at all. Sometimes I have to get out of the house. Like she's hanging around me and she should be someplace else; I should be someplace else. But it isn't Georgia's fault,' he repeated. 'She keeps wanting to talk. I can't talk to her, she's not part of it. This isn't about Georgia. It's about work. She doesn't know that part of me. She shouldn't carry that . . .'

'What is it she shouldn't carry?'

Flynn shrugged. 'I've seen stuff she doesn't need to know. She's always wanted to "talk" when I get back from an assignment. It took her years to learn that was the last thing I needed.'

'Why is that?'

'Nothing's as bad as being badgered about what happened, how you "feel" about it. When you come back from a bad place, you don't want to remember it, and even if you did, there's no way to explain what it was like to somebody else. Not even your wife. I don't want her to become part of it. She and the children should be something apart. But before, it never used to make me angry with her. Now it makes me mad. And sometimes . . . sometimes, since Astra Four, I look

65

at them and I don't feel anything. D'you understand? I look at my family and I don't feel anything at all.'

'That must be very difficult for you.' Madeline watched him as he tossed a pack of cigarettes from hand to hand. From behind her back the persistent sounds of the street rose up through the muggy air: the muted grumble of traffic; the hurried clattering of high-heeled feet up the steps next door; a front door slamming.

'I've been having trouble falling asleep. For years, now I think of it. Sometimes I can't go to sleep without the light on. Like a little kid.'

'How does the light help?'

'I hear too much in the dark. I lie there waiting for something to happen. I've tried jogging, coming home so tired I'm on my knees; it gets me out of the house but it doesn't help me sleep. There are times when I panic for no reason at all – not when I'm working, when I've got a reason to panic, but when I'm doing nothing. And recently I've spent a lot of time doing nothing. I can't work. Or rather,' he corrected himself dryly, finally raising his eyes back to hers, 'I can't *get* work. Is that problems enough for you?'

He'd hit four major PTSD symptoms: disturbed sleep; panic attacks; sudden rage; and dissociation – the lack of connection with others, an inability to feel. 'I'd say that's more than problems enough, Flynn. All these symptoms, sudden temper, the feeling of estrangement, loss of control, are normal. They indicate to me that you are perfectly sane. One of the brain's functions is to protect itself when it has been profoundly shocked, and all these feelings are there for a purpose: to protect you. But,' Madeline added gently, 'they can be pretty unbearable to live with.'

Flynn looked relieved. 'Right. So all we have to settle is your basis of trust thing. I'm certain you're the right person. As for trust, like I said last night, I'd trust you with my life.'

'I'm glad.' *Even if his trust had been offered a little too easily.*

Madeline's tone was contemplative as she felt her way gingerly ahead, her fingers still on the chain around her neck. 'What if I had questioned you that night – morning – on *Nepenthe*, when we first met? Checked up that you really were with APC?'

'You didn't.'

'If I had?'

'I'd have been buggered,' he acknowledged simply, 'but it would have been a relief. I tipped up at the heliport thinking I'd have a go blagging my way out to the platform, pretty certain I'd be seen off sharp. Hoping I would be.'

'You didn't want to go out to *Nepenthe*?'

'No. I was just doing a friend a favour, an editor I know. He couldn't find anyone else willing to go in the middle of the night. That shows you my career's been a bit down in the dumps . . . it was a gobshite job. But it was a *job*. Overhearing you and that APC bloke presented an opportunity. I took it.'

'What made you take the opportunity?'

'The job,' he repeated. 'Fate. That's what I do. I told you. Take opportunities. Go in the direction I'm heading. Bad judgement. I don't know, call it whatever you like. I'm glad my shot got the *Guardian* front page because I'm glad that offshore safety systems will get reviewed again.' Flynn rolled his eyes and groaned. 'I don't know if that's true. I don't know if I give a shite about offshore safety systems. Ambulance-chasing isn't my normal line of work. Like I told you, I do conflicts. War.'

Madeline waited for him to elaborate but he sat silently opposite her with his arms folded stubbornly across his chest. 'How did you feel that night on the standby vessel? What did you see exactly?'

He looked away from her, staring intently at the blank wall for a moment or two with his head tilted to one side. When he spoke his voice was firm but flat. 'I saw the bloke you were with, the man in the suit, and knew he was an HR guy because he had cheap shoes: if he'd been anyone important they'd have been better. I saw you. I saw your jeans were frayed across the knee and that you had been in a hurry to get there because your hair was half scrunched up with a funny blue thing. I saw you were beautiful . . .' Flynn's eyes flicked to her face and immediately away with a shyness that Madeline did not expect. He cleared his throat. '. . . I saw you were frightened. First in the transportation room, again on the helicopter. I heard it in your voice, but when you walked to the helicopter there was a swing in your step, and it was light, too, despite the boots, so I thought, she's frightened, but she's exhilarated at the same time; stronger than she looks. I saw the blank in the eyes of the men watching from the side of the ship, and the captain, how he'd cut himself shaving that morning, you could see it under the grime on his face, and you could see he was frightened too, and the third mate, Merrick, had a safety pin in place of a button on his jacket. He covered it up with one hand so the captain wouldn't see, as if the captain would have given a fuck that night. Everyone, everyone on that ship stank of sweat.'

'You're very observant.' *So he sees, she thought, he sees, he hears, he's alert to everything around him. But what does he feel?*

'Occupational necessity.'

Madeline knew she had broken several of her most precious guidelines: she had allowed herself to be bullied into seeing him; she had tolerated his being late, and she had now let him go on well over the remaining allotted time. She would be at least an hour late for Jillian. 'We have to finish shortly, but one last question. Why have you chosen therapy now? Can you think of anything that might have triggered your decision?'

Flynn looked at her steadily, without blinking, and then fixed his eyes on the ceiling above her head. 'Not a clue.'

'Nothing at all?' Madeline asked.

'Well, there's one thing, but I don't want to make too

much of it. I don't want you to think I'm raving bonkers or anything.'

'Why would anyone think you are raving bonkers?'

Flynn moved uneasily, flexing one leg. 'I saw a friend of mine on that ship.'

'A friend?'

'A journalist. A bloke I knew back in Rwanda.'

'How did you feel when you saw him?'

'I don't know. Strange, I suppose. I don't really remember how I felt.'

On the street outside a dog barked; there was a rapid scuffle of toenails on the pavement, an urgent whistle, the shout of 'Max . . . *Max*!' Flynn did not seem to hear; he kept his gaze on Madeline.

'I'd like to know how you felt when you saw him.'

'A wee bit upset.'

'Why did you feel upset?'

He gave her a twisted smile. 'You're thinking I resented the competition, aren't you? It wasn't that. I like competition . . .'

Madeline returned him swiftly to the ship. 'But seeing this particular journalist on *Nepenthe* disturbed you in some way?'

'It disturbed me, yes.' He seemed to shudder minutely, so momentarily that Madeline was uncertain whether she had seen him tremble or whether her vision had blurred for an instant. He uncrossed his legs and studied the floor between his feet for a moment before raising his eyes to her face. 'There was one peculiar thing about it, Madeline; one thing that really got to me. I hadn't seen Erik for six years, not since May 1994. That was the last time I'd seen him. In Rwanda. And he was stone dead.'

FIVE

Jillian Ashcroft finished watering the plants and flinched as she eased herself into the recliner. The conservatory was awash with light, crammed with tropical blooms and flamboyantly decorated in the violent colours that helped to transport Jillian into a Gauguin painting. She massaged her birdlike hands before pressing her fingertips against her temples where her white hair was beginning to thin. For some time she sat with her eyes closed, inhaling the almost hallucinatory scent of trachelospermum while the sun made splashes of red, violet and green dance brightly against her eyelids.

Jillian had been relieved when Madeline called to say she would be an hour later than planned. It had given her more of a breathing space between seeing the orthopedic consultant and seeing Madeline; time to put her feet up and prepare. The nature of Madeline's work meant that she was less able to keep to a regular schedule than were the other therapists who made up Jillian's client list, yet it made rigorous supervision all the more important. Jillian's role was to act as a sounding board and dumping ground to her clients, and therapists like Madeline who daily relived the trauma of others needed the most resilient of sounding boards and most liberal of dumping

70

grounds. Jillian was feeling neither resilient nor liberal that afternoon, she was too annoyed by the decision that she could not avoid surgery, yet she was looking forward to seeing Madeline. Her sessions with the younger woman always challenged her and gave her a surge of energy. Jillian both admired Madeline and was very fond of her; she allowed herself the private indulgence of thinking of her as the daughter she had never had.

By the time the doorbell rang she was able to rise easily, and paused only to smooth her hair in front of the hall mirror. She returned Madeline's embrace and waved aside her apologies before laying both hands firmly on her shoulders.

'Let me have a good look at you.' Jillian was struck once again by the younger woman's beauty. Madeline's looks were not scene-stealing; she would not be the first woman to catch the eye in a crowded room, but when her eyes were downcast the pallor of her skin, straight dark hair and delicacy of feature brought to mind a Da Vinci Madonna. The heat of that afternoon had put colour high in her cheeks and made her green eyes all the more startling. She looked a little thinner than she had a month ago, a little paler, and her cheeks were a fraction too hollowed, but Jillian put that down to the workload of Astra Four. 'You look surprisingly well.'

Madeline tipped her head slightly to one side with a broad smile. 'Do I? That's good to hear. I wish I could say the same for you, Jillian. You're looking tired.'

'I'm not,' Jillian said stoutly as she led Madeline down the narrow corridor to a room at the back of the house. 'I'm merely looking my age. I'm fit as a fiddle. I've simply spent too long cooped up inside working and not taken the benefit of all this good weather.'

Unlike her conservatory, Jillian's consulting room was furnished simply with a richly coloured Persian rug, two arm-chairs and one small sofa. Apart from the ink drawing of two heads in profile, one male, one female, which sat above

71

the sofa, the room was featureless, yet it did not feel clinically professional or bleak. It was designed as a simple shelter for whatever happened within. The wide window offered a vista onto the rolling hills that surrounded Jillian's cottage and extended the boundaries of the room into the world outside.

As Madeline sat at one end of the sofa, tucking her legs beneath her and began to talk about Mary Reagan, widow of the derrickman George, Jillian leant back in her chair. She recalled that Mary had two small children and that her brother, the captain of *Nepenthe*, had witnessed the moment of George's death.

'You said you'd arranged for her to see a local grief counsellor before you left Scotland?'

'Yes, Angus McIntosh. But she phoned a few days ago and asked to see me in London.' Jillian listened without comment as Madeline talked through her professional and personal reluctance to see Mary, and what their most recent session had revealed. 'For three months before the explosion she had been having an affair with another man on the rig; a Norwegian.'

'What happened to him?'

'He came through it without a scratch.'

'Christ.' Jillian grimaced.

Madeline smiled wanly. 'That's precisely the word Mary keeps using. She's devout Church of Scotland. As she sees it, twenty-six men died as punishment for her infidelity and she'll burn eternally. As her husband did. She says she can't go back to the church: I think she's looking for the authority of psychotherapy to understudy for the authority of religion.' Jillian had been seeing Madeline long enough to know her antipathy towards organised religion; she would not appreciate her work being put in the same light. 'How do feel about being a surrogate minister?'

'Like an unholy one.' They both smiled. 'She's back in Angus's hands. I don't have time, Jillian. All day yesterday, after seeing her, I felt resentful. Put-upon.'

'By Mary?'

'Mary . . . the follow-through on Astra Four. Guilty about other clients I've been short-changing. I don't have time,' Madeline repeated.

'How many regular clients are you seeing now?'

'Fourteen. Possibly fifteen. There's someone I'm considering taking on.'

'And you're still running the combat veterans' weekly group?'

'Yes, but that's shared with Jack Zabinsky. I don't carry that alone.' Madeline fell silent.

Jillian had heard the strain in Madeline's voice and considered her carefully. Madeline's general ability to stay in close contact with her own feelings during client sessions greatly reduced the legwork needed in supervision, but that afternoon the young woman seemed less emotionally articulate than normal. 'Fourteen post-traumatic clients plus the group and your critical incident work add up to a demanding schedule,' Jillian said slowly, as she thought, but not overly demanding for a therapist of Madeline's emotional stamina. 'How are *you* managing with all of this?'

Madeline looked up as if surprised by the question. 'Astra Four blew a hole clean through my diary.'

The phrase rippled through Jillian like an electrical charge. 'That's a very explosive image.'

Madeline shrugged.

However natural it was to use explosive imagery to express feelings about disasters, Jillian was certain there was something more there, something Madeline needed to explore. 'How does it feel to have a hole blown through your diary?'

Madeline stared out through the wide window, deep in thought as Jillian waited patiently. 'Not good,' she finally replied, 'because I know I'm normally able to hold things together objectively, however deeply they affect me.'

Jillian nodded. One of the skills she most respected in

Madeline's approach to her clients was her ability to work within the cipher of objectivity. It was a tough skill, and one Jillian herself found difficult to master, especially with Madeline; her affection for Madeline had occasionally hampered their work together. A therapist needed to engage utterly and completely on every level with her client, but also, for her own sanity, had to be able to close the file at the end of the session and go home. Madeline generally handled this better than most, but Jillian had often asked herself if the closing down was too absolute, if Madeline left herself nothing to take home. She had the sense that she needed to tread carefully.

'I wonder if Astra Four threatened your sense of control because you identified with the fear of the men on the rig. Perhaps your misreading of the photographer – accepting he was from Human Resources –' Jillian leant forward – 'your own fear of betrayal, your personal vulnerability in that situation, out there in the elements of sea and wind and rain, made you identify more strongly with the victims of Astra Four than those of previous critical incidents?' She saw a sudden tightness set about Madeline's eyes as she ventured, 'Enough to leave you with a lingering sense that a hole has been blown through your life . . .'

'I said a hole had been blown through my diary.' Madeline again turned her gaze away from Jillian to the window. 'Not my life. I don't need to discuss this, Jillian. I'd rather talk about A.D. She's made enormous progress over the past five weeks . . .'

Madeline spoke rapidly and with increasing animation about a client towards whom she could feel protective. As she listened to her describing the progress of her sessions with a woman who had been repeatedly raped and battered by her husband, Jillian watched her searchingly.

'. . . I feel immensely proud of her,' Madeline concluded.

'Justifiably. It's wonderful to witness that kind of recovery,' Jillian affirmed. She waited, watching Madeline drag one fingernail slowly along the arm of the sofa, and was conscious of the dull, smouldering burn in her hip joint.

'I'm sorry. I didn't come here to review the work with A.D.,' Madeline confessed suddenly. 'When I called yesterday I just wanted to see you. I felt so tired and worn out : . . But right after I'd made the appointment something else happened, and that's all I've been thinking about. A potential new client.'

'Tell me.'

'The photographer on *Nepenthe* – the man I misread, as you so aptly put it – turned up on my doorstep last night, asking to see me.' Madeline smiled slightly at the surprise on Jillian's face. 'I didn't want to, but he persuaded me to see him this morning. That's why I was late.'

'That must have been interesting.' Jillian had never regarded Madeline as a malleable character, yet both George Reagan's widow and the photographer had been able to persuade her to meet. She remembered how angry Madeline had been with the rogue photographer during their first supervisory session after her return from Astra Four.

'He arrived forty minutes late and played games for half the session.'

'What kind of games?'

Madeline made a dismissive gesture. 'Telling me I had nice eyes, that sort of thing.'

'Well?' Jillian leant forward. 'You do.' Madeline was too clever to be thrown by such a simple distancing device. Jillian often warned her students that therapeutic years were the opposite of dog years; it took seven years of qualified practice to equate to one year of experience. By this rule Madeline was a relative beginner in the field. Yet Jillian also believed that the gift of instinct could make up for a decade of experience, and she was certain Madeline had that gift. 'What bothers you about his behaviour?'

'On *Nepenthe* I trusted him completely. I was frightened, but I looked at him and thought, it will be all right because this man is with me. This man. Then I discovered he was using me as his ticket to sell a story . . . and three months later he's on my doorstep asking for my help. I don't think I can trust him again.'

'Do you feel this is another sham? That he doesn't need your therapeutic support?' Madeline was an attractive woman. It wasn't unheard of for people to meet therapists socially and attempt to establish a personal relationship under the auspices of seeking therapy. Deeply erroneous, Jillian thought, to see therapy as a short-cut to romance, but not unknown.

'No,' Madeline said with conviction. 'I told you about his reaction on *Nepenthe* when he looked at one of the bodies. What he *saw* was a friend of his. A friend who'd been dead for six years. He wasn't acting. I was there. I saw his reaction. I'm certain he had some form of memory intrusion.'

Jillian's chin rested on her thumb, her index finger closing her mouth as she listened. 'Have you agreed to take him on?'

'Not yet. I agreed to see him again. I'm pretty sure I'll take him on.'

'Madeline, dear girl,' the endearment slipped from Jillian's lips without her catching it, 'can you identify what it was that made you trust him, this man above others, that let you feel safe in a very insecure environment?'

'I felt I'd met him before.' Madeline shook her head slightly, the awakening of understanding on her face. 'I *recognised* him. Not visual recognition exactly, but that sense you have when you pass someone on the down escalator as you're going up, and know you *know* them. But you don't. You turn back to look again; there's that uncanny moment of transfer, that certainty: he's one of *them*; he's one of *us*.' Madeline's hands were clasped against her breast. 'I can't explain it. But that's why I was so angry. I saw what he was, I recognised it. I recognised something in him and he flung it back in my face. Maybe my vanity was punctured. My vanity in my intuition.'

'Maybe your intuition was right: he's come back. It's no

crime to be proud of intuition,' Jillian said softly, with a smile that lit her pale, lined face. 'Not so long as you're fully aware it may be fallible. I doubt you were wrong in this instance. You've been forced to question your intuitive judgement and re-examine yourself. That's not easy. Never forget Jung: "Only what the doctor can put right in himself can he put right in the patient; it is his own hurt that gives the measure of his power to heal."'

'Perhaps that's the key,' Madeline said slowly, testing the water, 'perhaps his issues are all about trust. It isn't about my inability to trust him. Perhaps I feel that so keenly because he isn't able to trust *me*; maybe he can't trust anyone. There's something I'm not seeing, something butterfly-light just in the air above me, like the fluff of a dandelion clock.' She shook her head in frustration. 'Something's gone. Something's missing.'

Jillian sat motionless with her hands in her lap but her skin prickled. There was Madeline talking about holes again, another reference to central emptiness – did she recognise it in this man or in herself? She listened intently as Madeline filled in his family background and work, and the split life he led between work and home.

'Certain people elect to put their lives regularly at risk: emergency service workers, the military, the police. Perhaps he is a man who exists by surviving crises, exposing himself to danger as a way of proving, to himself or others, that he can cope and not fall apart.'

'Again and again and again?'

'Again and again and again. That's what we all do, isn't it, Madeline? Whatever it is that we do, we do it again and again and again. The notion of a divided life is intriguing. I've come across people who work like that, who lead two distinct lives . . . are in effect two people.' And many of them are therapists, Jillian thought to herself, pausing as she considered how far she could afford to direct Madeline's thoughts, and deciding that Madeline would make the connection herself.

77

'This man might spend ten days in a war zone and come home to find himself totally absorbed in the price of carrots. It functions as an escape; a kind of inner emigration.'

'Or the reverse,' Madeline said quickly. 'The inner emigration might be *into* the war zone, away from the family, the home, the domestic. I have an instinct that this man is fundamentally drawn to the wreckage.'

A shadow of concern must have skimmed across Jillian's face, because Madeline immediately sat up and shook her finger at her supervisor. 'Don't look so worried. I've already registered that – the parallel between his work and mine. I worked through that on the train coming here. But I don't see myself as a constant witness of wreckage; I see myself as a witness of recovery. He doesn't have that privilege.'

Madeline had taken hold of a thread of perception that bound her directly to her client – for Jillian was now certain that the photographer would become a client. 'I have a feeling we're going to need a name, Madeline.'

Madeline nodded. 'F.B. Call him F.B.'

Jillian embraced Madeline as they stood in the doorway and walked her to the waiting taxi. 'Madeline? Don't underestimate the impact of the explosion on Astra Four. You need to take care of yourself in the midst of all this turbulence. You, as well as your diary, have been stretched thin.'

She watched the taxi pull away and tilted her face up to the sun, letting it warm her. There were times when Jillian regretted that she had agreed to act as Madeline's supervisor. There were times when she wished they could simply be friends, when she would not be obliged to monitor the advice she gave and withheld. She would have liked to have told Madeline about the growing discomfort her hip gave her and to have looked to Madeline as a friend. Yet these momentary reflections only served to remind her of her duty towards the younger woman. Something, although she could not see what that something might be, something about Astra Four had opened a direct path to the centre of Madeline's own experience.

Madeline waited for the train with a sense of foreboding. She took a seat in the middle carriage, up against the window hoping for any faint breath of air she might catch in that humid summer. She was long accustomed to the vague feeling of dread and the slight tightening in her chest whenever she travelled by rail. For ten years, it seemed, she had been getting on that train, and there was no way, apparently, that she could stop the journey.

Back at Blake's Wharf that evening she headed straight for the shower. Blown a hole. So what? It wasn't a strange choice of words. Hole, whole. Holy, holiness, unholy. Wholeness; vaginal; blew, blow . . . blow-jobs. Or wholesome? Damn it. Damn Jillian and her pedantry about words. Now she wasn't going to be able to get the damn phrase out of her head. Which was precisely why clever old Jillian had flagged it.

Patrick was working in the yard, wearing only a pair of baggy khaki shorts and a pair of dust goggles clamped to the top of his sunburnt bald head. He was slick with sweat. From the first-floor window Madeline watched him for a few minutes as he prowled around the marble block which was destined to become the bust of Cardinal Hume. It was now in place on a waist-high turntable near the door into the studio. His shoeless, bony feet were entirely white, so that when he stopped moving he looked like a sculpture himself. His face twisted into a scowl; he circled the turntable like a cat attempting to entrap a particularly troublesome mouse. At the back of his leg a vein stood out; it bulged and twisted and meandered like the Niger on a relief map of Africa, a tell-tale sign of the hard physical labour involved in his work. Madeline observed him tenderly. He could pass for a man ten years younger, and had the strength and stamina of a thirty-five-year-old. His back was tanned and broad, only the grizzling of the hairs across his shoulders showing his age: his arms remained muscular, his calves as tight and elegant as a dancer's. Madeline smiled as she imagined his reaction to her admiration.

She recognised the signs that he was moving into what she privately considered the ugly stage of a commission, the hundred days of solitude. The thought took her back to Flynn: a hundred days, he'd said; a hundred days of therapy . . . Their projects shared a parallel timetable. The marble block clearly did not meet with Patrick's approval. No block chosen by somebody else ever did meet Patrick's approval. For a day or two he would best be avoided entirely. The cathedral architect, the monsignor who had awarded the commission, the stoneyard that had supplied the block, Patrick's part-time apprentice Ed, the power-tool manufacturer, whichever God was responsible for the poor quality of English sunlight, his two ex-wives, as well as Madeline herself might all be held responsible for an entire panoply of misfortunes sent to try him: the inferior raw material on which he was expected to work miracles; the crippling disadvantage of having to work from photographs rather than a living, breathing model; the staggering effrontery of the Catholic Church and its benefactors not to pay him a full commercial rate for what was set to be a bitch of a commission . . . The only thing that shielded Cardinal Hume himself from Patrick's ire was his demise, and if Patrick's antipathy towards the four-square block deepened, even death might not provide adequate protection.

Luckily for all concerned, this aggressive state should last no more than forty-eight hours, by which time Patrick would – Madeline prayed – be reconciled to his block, might even begin to point out its hidden virtues and grudgingly acknowledge how seductively the pale grey vein meandered through the white marble. He would then stop talking altogether during the most physical stage of the work, the four to five days it would take to shear planes off the block and arrive at the essential geometric form of a human bust, in preparation for eight to nine weeks of carving. By then, Patrick might be disgruntled, and almost certainly exhausted, but he would also be working at a level of absorption that excluded everyone except his subject. Basil Hume was destined to enter the intimate space of their relationship far more than previous partners ever had. All this Madeline foresaw and accepted; two years earlier Patrick's efforts had been dedicated to a life-size, full-body limestone study of a reclining footballer's wife. If Patrick's obsession with her scrawny right flank had not perturbed Madeline, his devotion to Cardinal Hume was unlikely to either.

She leant far out of the window and gave a low wolf-whistle. Patrick looked up with a grimace. 'Chuck me a towel, Maddie.'

He rubbed it vigorously over the back of his neck and dragged it quickly under his armpits. When Madeline joined him in the yard he jerked his thumb at the block.

'I told them I was happy to source it myself. I *said* I was happy to go to Carrara myself and find something suitable, something of sufficient *quality* to pay tribute to the eminence of the subject. No, no, they said. Fear not. All in hand. Trust in the Almighty.' Patrick tossed the towel on the ground and kicked it. 'Arses. Pompous arses who haven't a clue what's involved here. I'd talked to them about the base of the bust, the idea of leaving something raw so we'd have a sense of origin, where the block came from, a sign of what the stone originally *was*, some integrity, maybe just to leave some excrescence around the base, so that the polished, reflective surfaces could *leap* out of the rough stone,' he thundered around the block, loose-cannoned, gesturing at it with disgust, 'and they send me *that*. Why would anyone want to see the origin of *that*? Where's the heart of *that*? A bland lump of shit. Might as well carve him in shit. Shit might have more character now I think of it. Shit might have more rhythm than *that*. Shit at least has *origin*.'

81

'Why not look at it in the morning,' Madeline suggested soothingly. 'After all, it's a while since you've worked marble –'

'Meaning?' Patrick demanded. 'Meaning I'd forget what marble's about? Twenty-two years of living next door to marble quarries and working it every day, and you think I don't know a good block from a piece of shit, hmm?'

'*Meaning* come inside, have a drink and look at it tomorrow. I'm hungry; shall I fix us something?'

Patrick shrugged and turned to go into the studio with an almost feminine flounce of his head. Madeline stood still, her hands on her hips and a smile on her face. A moment later Patrick was back facing her, framed by the doorway. When he flung his arm round her shoulder and pulled her into his side her face was pressed against his breast. Madeline was not short, but Patrick was a giant of a man, a great, strong, grumpy embracing giant, and he dwarfed her.

While Madeline hunkered down in front of the fridge searching for cold cuts and lumps of cheese, Patrick stood before his Hume wall. Every inch of plaster from waist height was covered with photographs and sketches of the cardinal. Below the photographs hung some of Patrick's tools, a varied array of hammers, dummies and tungsten chisels. His expression now calm and thoughtful, lost in contemplation, Patrick gazed at the central ten-by-eight photograph and slowly rubbed his thumb along the cardinal's bottom lip, as tenderly as if it were a lover's. The upper lip had barely an indentation, but the lower lip was swollen like a plump segment of tangerine, finely cracked with pith-like traces of skin, near bursting with voluptuousness. Hume's eyes, too closely placed for classical proportion, were keenly focused on something behind and above Patrick's left shoulder; his brows bristled with long white hairs that interrupted the two-dimensional line of the eye. A large, bony nose, flattened at the tip; slack neck; powerfully moulded, sticking-out ears; boyish, bristly white hair, stiff as a fox terrier's coat. The sculptor leaned close to his subject, his face bare inches from the photograph, his eyes roving hungrily over the minute facial details that were already as familiar and beloved to him as Madeline's. If only Hume could stand before him, in the flesh, so he could inhale the intelligent goodness of the man's face. But he could imagine it. 'Fantastic,' he muttered to himself. 'Bloody beautiful.'

After consuming half a pound of cheddar, a bowl of salad and a bottle of red wine, Patrick had mellowed enough to discuss the dignitaries of Westminster Cathedral without spitting. Fingers entwined behind his head, he leant back with his eyes closed. 'It's a great commission,' he said slowly, 'I know that. It isn't that they're only paying me ten grand when it should be double that to justify the time and work involved. I understand the delicacy,' he opened one eye at Madeline with a hint of a smile, 'of the Church's position, not wanting to be seen to be squandering money, even if the money is specifically donated by some rich bastard hoping to oil his sanctimonious path to heaven.'

'So if it isn't the money, what is it?'

'It's the time. I can't afford to give this more than three months. I want to do my best,' Patrick said simply. 'But I have to make a living. I can't spend three to four months working for ten grand.'

'You certainly *can*; it's more a question of whether you will. My hunch,' she added with an intimate smile, 'is that you will if you need to.'

For some time there was silence between them. Madeline left the table and stretched out on the battered chaise-longue. She lay with one arm flung up over her head, half-shielding her face, her eyes closed. Patrick pulled a drawing pad towards him and sketched her for ten minutes. Neither spoke as he recorded her Odalisque form. She'd make a beautiful corpse, he thought. Near perfect. He wondered what fortified her calm; few women had that quality of emotional continence. Such control she had, such inner rhythm, and no need to shove it in your face. What a piece of work.

Long after Patrick had gone back to the yard to pace around his block, Madeline remained motionless. I was talking about my *diary*, she repeated furiously to herself. I was only talking about my goddamn diary.

SIX

Georgia Brennan stuffed the tell-tale Peter Jones carrier bag behind the sofa. She hadn't meant to buy more fabric, she'd popped in for a cheese grater, but the store was cunningly designed so that even the most innocent mission led her through – at least *near* – the fabric hall, a Vanity Fair of temptation to which Georgia succumbed once every month or so. She had a chest packed with metres of floral chintz, rich, dark brocades, Madras cotton checks and velvety chenilles, all irresistible, all destined to play some crucial role in her interior design plans once she got around to redecorating the house. If they ever had the money to do so. If she ever found a decent, inexpensive upholsterer, or someone who could make curtains. In other words, she had a not-so-secret-as-she-liked-to-think addiction to material, and her serial acquisitions were likely to remain in the blanket box for ever. That morning she had spotted the forest-green hessian and impulsively bought twelve metres for the ragged old sofa in Flynn's darkroom. If he wouldn't let her replace it altogether, he might be talked into having it re-covered.

Having hidden her latest indulgence she sat on the floor with a bottle of wine and Beth's old school reports spread round her in an arc. Beth was in her room with her friend

Emily. Georgia had asked the two girls if they wanted to come down and join her, but Beth had given her a look that said the idea of spending an hour chatting with her mother was significantly less appealing than repetitive bouts of colonic irrigation. Olly was on the computer, supposedly doing his geography homework but probably playing a football game. Georgia had pulled out her daughter's reports because she was worried about Beth's academic progress – or rather, the lack of anything that could be described as progress. And because Flynn might walk in any minute and she needed to discuss Beth with him. These days she felt she was walking on glass with Flynn and had lost the confidence to raise domestic subjects directly; he had abandoned even the pretence of listening to her. Fearing she was failing as a wife, she was determined to be a good mother. Beth was running so fast from childhood that you couldn't see her for dust, and Olly had what – three, maybe four years left? Fifteen hundred days left to prove herself a good mother.

But Georgia, in her own opinion, was not a good mother. Georgia no longer thought she was a good anything. There was a time when she had known herself to be a good TV news editor. Not only a good one, but a necessarily tough one, which was perhaps the same thing. Ten years earlier she had been able to give the flak and take the flak, able to choreograph reporters' lives, able to bully – tactfully – a reluctant old warhorse into covering a court case in Hull. She'd been clever enough to deal out stories to the deserving without pissing off the youngster with untested potential. She'd been good at her job, damn good, and a good chum, and a good daughter, but all these roles had somehow slipped away from her. She had slid seamlessly from girlfriend to wife, and when Beth had arrived on the scene Georgia had willingly given up work. The dual role of wife and mother left precious little time to be a good daughter. Besides, her parents tended to avoid her when Flynn was around. They had never established a rapport with Flynn; they considered his career unsuitable and Georgia had given up trying to persuade them that she supported him one hundred per cent. She couldn't convince Flynn himself of that and saw no point in duplicating the effort.

So, if she was not a good mother – and Georgia was canny enough to recognise that most people who knew her would say that she was first and foremost an exemplary mother – why was it that she found herself thinking increasingly about having another baby? There was the age thing of course; the 'age thing' crept into most of her conscious thoughts. Only a week ago she'd nearly crashed the car on spotting what she thought was a white hair in the rear-view mirror. But if she were honest, she didn't want to go back to the exhausting days of nappy-changing and lonely nights of pacing the corridor, however much she longed to have a pair of eyes that looked for her alone. A voice inside her whispered: did she want to have another baby in the hope it would bind Flynn more closely to her? Did she want to shove something under Flynn's nose, which she couldn't do with a nine-year-old, let alone a thirteen-year-old – and say, *there*, that's you and me, together, got it? Did she have any right to want a baby, for that? So she could use it as a battering ram to knock down the wall that had sprung up between her and her husband? And what if she had a baby, selfishly, and Flynn left her anyway? What if she couldn't make everything in the garden rosy again?

So much of Georgia's life depended on the what-ifs: What if Beth gets into drugs? What if she's stupid? What if Ol smashes his skull in a rugby match? What if Beth gets pregnant at sixteen? There had been many nights when Flynn was on assignment that she had trembled with fear for her husband and her children; when she had occupied a very different world from his, a wholly female world. She had often felt a pang of guilt that she did not care more about the terrible things going on in the world, no more than a jerk on her heart strings when the next Red Cross appeal landed on her doorstep with its inevitable tragic photographs. And then Flynn would come home and she'd draw him in through the front door and want to lock it behind him, close up the curtains, pull everything within her own four walls, forget how fragile her happiness was and hold on tight. But what if the loving net she had tried to weave around her family snagged and ripped apart and failed to draw them in safely at the end of the day?

And what if Flynn leaves me? She felt her heart flutter with panic at the thought. She'd call Mark. Mark had always wanted her. Mark had loved her. Mark had wanted to marry her. Fifteen years ago he'd wanted to marry her, and he'd said so again, just that April, over coffee, when Flynn was in Scotland for Astra Four. Thinking about her ex-boyfriend, catching herself pocketing some juvenile, idiotic, get-out-of-marriage-free card, only made Georgia focus on Flynn. Whatever happened, she didn't love Mark. He gave her no more security than the blanket box full of fabrics. She only wanted Flynn. It's all about love, she told herself fiercely. It's about whether I can hold on to enough love to weather whatever it is that's happening to us. She knew the threat of cession; she felt Flynn closing her down. It was difficult to love absolutely in such a vacuum, but she was not going to give up. However much she was kept in the dark. The night before – his sweat, the violence of his dreams . . . in the light of the bedside lamp she had watched spasms seizing his face for fifteen minutes. She did not know why Flynn would no longer sleep in the dark. She did not know what preyed on his mind. She did not know whether he loved her. She did not even know if he'd come back that night.

When she agreed to take Flynn on Madeline had known that it was going to be a delicate and tricky relationship; she had seen his capacity for taking three steps forward and four back. She had decided to schedule him after Alexandra; balancing her most rewarding client with the one she expected to be most demanding would strengthen her. The practicalities had been settled: they would meet each Monday, Wednesday and Friday at 5.00 p.m. He'd asked for her home number but she had not given it; when he'd questioned why she imposed so many rules, she'd told him bluntly, 'You'll simply have to take my word for it. You know how to take pictures; I know how to handle trauma therapy.' She had given him a messaging service to call if he needed to speak to her outside of sessions.

From the moment he had entered her room the following Monday and thrown himself in the furthest chair Madeline had been aware of his psychological as well as physical distance from her.

'How are you feeling about embarking on therapy?'

He shrugged and crossed his arms. 'I haven't thought about it.'

'What have you been thinking about?'

'Nothing much.'

'I've been thinking about something you said during our first session. I was very struck by the experience of seeing your colleague on *Nepenthe*. It must have been terrifying.' Flynn nodded curtly. 'Have you seen him again?'

'No.'

'I'd like to hear about what happened to you that night.'

'Which night?'

Madeline paused. He was stubborn and immutable opposite her, a great brutish force. 'The night on *Nepenthe*,' she persisted.

'It's nothing to do with that. It's not about the night on Astra Four.'

'Which night is it about?'

'Nothing. No night. It's just about work.'

'Tell me about your work.'

Flynn closed his eyes, his brow furrowing. 'I take pictures. Tends to be big-event stuff that your man calls me in for: war, famine, drought, plague . . . you know. The devil's work.

That's my spec-i-al-i-ty. I take pictures of people, living and dead. Generally not very chirpy ones. Most of the time I'm commissioned. I'm lucky; a few editors I know let me pick my own assignments, but sometimes I work speculatively. If it's any good I send them to the papers, or a magazine, and they pay me. That's it.'

The devil's work, Madeline thought. *Interesting phrase.* 'But you haven't been working recently, is that right? Not since Astra Four, I think you told me.'

His eyes narrowed. 'That's right.'

'Do you like your work?'

'It's a job. Do you like yours?'

'Yes.'

'That's nice for you.'

'Do you find your work satisfying?'

'It isn't a reaction I've consciously had, no.'

'Tell me how you felt the first time you were in a war zone.'

A slow smile spread across his face. 'What makes you smile?' Madeline asked, a little sharply.

'I liked the way you asked. It reminded me of a song – from that old musical, you know? About the drama students. *Chorus Line*. That's it. "And I reached right down to the bottom of my soul, to see how an ice-cream felt . . .".' Flynn had a beautiful voice, strong, well pitched and resonant. He mimed an actor, intense with concentration, struggling to identify with an ice-cream. 'And all the wannabes say "I feel cold!" "I feel like vanilla!" "Ooo, I'm melting!" And the one poor honest lassie sings, "And I felt nothing. Simply nothing. Really nothing."'

'Is that what you felt? Nothing?' Flynn did not reply. He looked away from her.

'The first time you saw death, professionally,' Madeline persisted, 'that first job, first assignment, first war.'

'If we're going to talk about death, you'll have to show

90

me your credentials first, Doc. Have *you* ever seen death?'
Madeline met his gaze without answering. 'Well of course you
have. I'm an eejut. So tell me; what did *you* feel?'

Madeline waited several beats, weighing up how much of
herself to offer. She could not establish a precedent whereby
he felt entitled to ask her questions and divert therapy into
a social dialogue, but she needed to establish a connection. 'I
found it very shocking,' she said. 'What about you?'

'I wasn't shocked. That's what I was there for. To make sure
other people saw it and knew it had happened.'

Ah: the eyes of the world. 'Did you want to look?'

'Of course. That's what the camera's for.'

'How did you look?'

'I don't know what you mean.'

'I don't know anything about photography. Explain the
process to me.'

'Point and click. That's it.'

Her generous mouth tightened fractionally. 'Oh, come on,
Flynn; help me here. Did you walk around the body first or
start taking pictures right away, or squat down, or what?'

'I don't remember.'

Most of Madeline's clients talked like a bursting dam.
Something very powerful had brought Flynn to her, but he
used either smart-arsed flippancy or stonewalled her questions.
She would have to assume a more forceful approach with him
than she generally adopted. 'Where were you?'

Flynn shrugged.

'Who was with you?'

'I told you I don't remember!' Flynn rose to his feet and
pulled a pack of cigarettes out of his pocket. 'What is this,'
he growled, 'a court martial?'

'Does it feel like one?'

He prowled the confined space, dragging deeply on his
cigarette. 'Look. I'm just a photographer . . .'

Madeline had closed the window before he arrived to shut

out the noise from the street, but the room was airless and his constant pacing heightened the closeness. As she opened it the noises of the street immediately invaded the room. 'I'm afraid you can't smoke here. Would you mind putting that out?'

He glared at her. 'You're kidding me, right?'

Fine, Madeline thought. *So you feign indifference to the first time you saw death, but care mightily about my taking away your cigarette.*

'No, I'm not kidding you. Different people use this room all day. I don't allow any of them to smoke.' Flynn chucked the cigarette out the window with no regard for anyone passing below. 'You were saying, you're just a photographer . . . How do you take your pictures?'

'I walk around the bodies, if they're dead. Several times. I take a lot of shots.' He spoke very slowly, as if she were a foreigner or an idiot, spitting out the final consonant of each word. 'I squat down; I step back. I go close again. It's my job.'

'And you did your job that first time, walking round the dead?'

'Yes. It was quiet. They were safely dead. I mean, there were no bullets flying around. Sometimes you don't have the leisure to circle the bodies.'

'But the first time you did?'

'I suppose so.'

'You remember it?'

He grinned lopsidedly and said in a cod French accent, ' "Ah yes. I remember it well." I was twenty-one. Three protesters had been shot dead by the military police on a street in Algiers. I was there with two veteran correspondents.'

'How did you feel?'

'Curious . . . fascinated. Then disgusted. I shot my film, walked twenty yards down the road and threw up.'

'Why did you walk away?'

'I didn't want the others to see me puke my guts.'

92

'Tell me about those three bodies.'

Flynn pulled a straight-backed chair only six inches from her knees and straddled it. Madeline registered that he was far too close for comfort but she did not comment. She was curious as to why he wanted to be physically close to her; it could be an act of intimidation or a desire for intimacy. Either implied a need for physical or emotional connection.

He licked his lips. 'Let me tell you a story I heard from a doctor in Sarajevo. I can't swear to the veracity of it, but it rings true to me. A certain lady journalist I'm much too gentlemanly to name came to visit the Bjelave kindergarten, up above the Kosevo hospital, and asked if there were any children. "No, not any more." "Raped women?" "No." "Well, traumatised soldiers, then?" "No, this is the home of seventy chronic schizophrenics." "No story there then", said her ladyship, and called off her cameras.'

Again he'd side-stepped a question about his personal experience in favour of a general debate. 'What do you feel about that?' Madeline asked when it was clear he was not going to continue.

'It's the name of the game now. Do you know how many members of the media accompanied NATO forces when they entered Kosovo after the bombing campaign?'

'No.'

'Would you like to try to guess?'

Madeline shook her head. The tempo of his voice had changed again; his speech rattled like machine-gun fire.

'Two thousand seven hundred. Compared to a total of twenty-eight thousand NATO troops. Nearly ten per cent. And you can imagine the number of military press officers needed to control the pack. We're talking about conflict fought by *battalions* of press officers.'

'Were you there?'

'For a bit. We were just circus dogs, dancing for one government or another.'

Madeline was simultaneously fascinated and repelled. He was near enough for her to see close up the stubble which gave his jaw a bluish tinge and the two pale scars on his face, one above his eyebrow, another at his hairline. He leant so close that she could feel the faint push of his breath warm on her cheek. A squeal of brakes made her eyes flick towards the window before she turned back to him. 'Is that why you no longer find your work satisfying?'

'I fucking love it,' he murmured. 'Every single goddamned minute of it.' Before Madeline could register what he was doing, he kissed her on the mouth.

When Georgia heard the front door open and close she sat still, her face turned towards the door. He walked in, heavier yet handsomer than when she'd married him, with the same broad-shouldered carriage and animal grace. Georgia caught her breath at the sight of him, at the way his teeth flashed at her in a smile that made her feel simultaneously elated and frightened that he would bite her.

'Hey, good-lookin'.'

'Hey, handsome,' she replied with relief.

Flynn nudged the pile of papers with his foot. 'What's all this?'

'Oh, I was just looking through Beth's school reports, trying to gather ammunition. . . .'

'For what?'

'I had a call from Mrs Hembry – I mean, *we* had a call from Mrs Hembry. Beth's work's dropped off this term, apparently; she's not keeping up. She raised the possibility that Beth might have to repeat the year.'

'What does Beth have to say about it?'

'She doesn't know. She's upstairs with Emily.'

Flynn flicked through his daughter's last report. 'A "C" average. Looks all right to me. Don't sweat it. School doesn't mean shite in the big scheme of things.'

'I agree, but I don't think we can afford to let *her* feel school doesn't matter. She's capable of much more. She needs motivating.'

'She's thirteen, Georgia. *Thirteen*. So she gets a shitty grade in History. So what?'

'What if they made her repeat the year – how would that affect her socially? She'll get a complex; she'll lose her friends. I mean, *why* isn't she trying harder? I think we've got to consider this carefully . . .'

'She's a kid.' Flynn dropped the report back onto the floor. 'Childhood isn't something to dissect; it's just something to get on with.'

'But what if there's something going on we don't know about? What if she's being bullied? What if she's involved with some boy? Or drugs?'

Flynn lit a cigarette and drew deeply on it. 'And what if the sky falls, chicken-licken?' He looked at his wife's forlorn expression and nudged the pile of school reports with his foot. 'I'll have a word with her later. Maybe tomorrow. I'm going to grab a shower while you put this garbage where it belongs and forget about it.'

She was still sitting on the floor when he came back down wearing a broad grin. 'The girls are watching a movie on Sky.'

'I know. They asked.'

'They're watching *Eyes Wide Shut*.'

'Jesus! They promised me it was a PG!'

'That's the problem with parental guidance. You can't trust the kids to ask for it.'

'I'll go and turn it off.'

'Leave it. Sex won't hurt them.'

'Is Ol watching too?'

'No; he's on the computer.'

'I hope he's doing his homework . . .'

Flynn held out his hands and dragged her to her feet and

onto his lap on the sofa. 'You worry too much. Have I ever told you what the Fulani say about worry?'

'The Fulani? No . . .' The hand on the back of her neck soothed her as she curled into his shoulder. 'Tell me.'

'The Fulani are cattle herdsmen by tradition. They have a variation on the creation story that would appeal to you.' Georgia pressed her mouth to the base of his throat, feeling his steady pulse through her lips. Her friend Suzie complained that marriage had made her husband boring. Suzie swore that passion and sexual intimacy could not survive the habitual, tedious grind of married life, that she and Roger now knew each other far too well to be genuinely interested in each other. Georgia had disagreed, but she had not explained why. She had not told Suzie that each time Flynn touched her she felt she might explode with the charge he lit. As she listened to him it occurred to her that Suzie was on the right track. Perhaps she did not know Flynn well enough; perhaps lack of knowledge was a good thing.

'The Fulani believe the world began as a drop of milk, which I suppose is a natural deduction for a cowherd. God descended from on high and from milk he created stone. From stone, iron. From iron, fire. From fire, water, and from water, air.' As he spoke, Flynn twisted a lock of her fine blonde hair round his finger. 'From the five essential elements God created man. But the people became too proud, so God created blindness to humble the people. When blindness became too proud, He created sleep, and sleep defeated blindness.' Flynn stopped.

'And when sleep became too proud?' Georgia asked curiously.

Her tone reminded him of Beth when he used to tell her bedtime stories. 'Well, when sleep became too proud, God created worry. And worry defeated sleep.'

'It's a good story,' she murmured throatily, nuzzling his neck. 'But it would have been quicker to tell me to stop worrying.'

'Quicker, but not as much fun. Now *that's* the stuff schools should be teaching in religious studies, not making the poor kids compare and contrast the gospels.'

Georgia twisted in his arm to face him. 'Flynn . . . about sleep. Worry defeating sleep.'

'Hmm?'

'I never wake up with you sleeping beside me any more. I wake up, and either you've gone or you're having a nightmare. Last night you thrashed around all night. Sweat was pouring off you.'

'It was?' His voice was expressionless.

'The bed was *soaked*. I thought you were dying.'

'I can sleep in the dark room if you want.'

'I'm not complaining. I'm worried.'

Flynn waved a hand. 'Don't worry about me.'

'There's something you're not telling me. I can feel it, I watch you when you're asleep. Sometimes I think you must be awake. Your eyes are open, but you're *not there* . . . And I worry, I do worry, I can't help it, it's like there's something in you –' she groped for an image – 'like an ingrown toenail –'

'There you go again, banging on about your feet. Leave it be. There's nothing wrong with me.'

'If you don't share worries, problems, they fester . . .'

'Georgia,' there was now an unmistakable warning in Flynn's voice, 'I'm dealing with it, OK? Drop it.'

For a moment Georgia was silent as she wrestled with whether to confront him. It's all about love, she reminded herself. 'No. I'm not going to drop it,' she said in a low voice. 'I want to talk about you. Your problems.'

'My problems?' Flynn echoed with deliberate lightness. 'Now there's a pleasant topic for a family evening. . . . Just forget it.'

Georgia, who had so often looked away or left the room, decided it was time to be brave. Whether it was the bottle of wine or his unexpected tenderness towards her, or the fear of what he might say, something gave her courage. Courage had always been about fear management for Georgia; she had to use fear because she couldn't not feel it.

'What's going on with you? I don't care what it is. Even if you're seeing someone else. I just need to know.'

Flynn rose so suddenly he tipped her off his lap. Since leaving the therapist's office he had been trying to decide whether to tell Georgia about it or not. He wanted to keep Madeline private, but he felt as if he had a flashing red beacon on top of his head, a warning to all that he was – different. 'D'you mean an affair? Is that what you think? No. I'm seeing someone else, but it's not an affair. I'm seeing a therapist.'

'You're *what?*' Georgia's eyes widened.

'What was it in that statement that you couldn't understand?' Flynn asked coolly.

'No, I mean . . . *God*. I'm delighted. It's a bit of a surprise, out of the blue. But a good surprise.' Georgia stood up shakily. 'I think I could use a drink. Do you want a drink?' Georgia poured two large shots of whisky and passed him a glass. 'I'm glad . . . so glad you decided to get help. I just thought you might have mentioned it first. But that doesn't matter. When did this start?'

'I don't want the Spanish Inquisition.'

'You're seeing a therapist, and I can't even ask how long you've been doing it?'

'Two or three times.'

'Who is he?'

'A Dr Light. Good name, hmm? Beats Dr Dark.'

'Tell me about him.'

'There's nothing to tell.'

'Can I meet him? Can I come with you sometime?'

'No.' He refilled his glass and headed for the door. '*The Times* called about some old prints I need to look over. I'll be in the dark room.'

'Wait – that reminds me. I want to show you something.'

Georgia heaved the green hessian from behind the sofa. 'What do you think?' Flynn stared at the material. 'Don't you think it's great? I got it for you. You know – for your sofa. To cover up all those old stains . . .'

'I have to get on . . .'

'What about dinner?'

He waved his glass. 'This'll do me.'

Georgia could not resist more questions as he reached the door: 'Is he young, old? I've always been curious about what actually happens in therapy . . .' Her index fingers drew little hooks around the word. 'Do you talk about work, or about everything? Do you talk about us . . . me? It's fine if you do. I expect you have to. Even if you slag me off, whatever, it's fine. I'm just curious.'

Flynn shook his head slightly. 'I haven't even mentioned you.'

Georgia heard the door to the darkroom open and slam. Therapy. Good. So she'd pushed a little too hard when he'd opened the door a crack, that was why he'd slammed it in her face. OK. One step at a time. She went into the kitchen, put away the supper she'd prepared and began to do the washing up. As she plunged her hands into the soapy water she was reminded of the second time she had met Flynn. She had bullied the BBC foreign correspondent into inviting them both to dinner, and had been pumping her host for background information when Flynn strolled into the room and filled it. He had accepted a beer, unslung his camera and begun to take photographs of Georgia, of their host, his wife, who was increasingly distracted as she tried to cook around the growing crowd in her kitchen – while at the same time telling a wild story with a strange half-smile on his face that had made Georgia wonder if there were any truth in it at all. And all the time taking pictures like he was drawing breath, rolls and rolls of film . . . She had fallen in love, as naturally as breathing and with as little conscious volition. Infatuation had put her into a fugue state; she remembered no one else at the table. Later she had volunteered to do the washing up with Flynn simply so that she could stand close to him over a dirty sink; soap bubbles had floated about the scummy water and gleamed like a million iridescent crystals on his forearms. When he said good night Flynn had taken her phone number, brushed her lips with his and told her he'd see her the next day. Over the following months Georgia had carefully piled stone after stone of expectation on top of this glittering, ephemeral foundation.

So Beth had been conceived a little earlier than might have been ideal, but Flynn had been delighted. And maybe their marriage had taken some knocks – that wasn't surprising, given the nature of Flynn's work; but at last he had had the sense to call in Dr Light, a professional fixer, to repair any damage in the construction.

When his father came into his bedroom and sat down on the bed, Oliver kept his eyes on the computer screen. 'Hi, Dad.'

'Your mother wants to know if you've finished your homework.'

'Sort of . . .'

'What was it?'

'Boring. Drawing a stupid map. Did you hear about Chelsea's new manager? Raniani or something. Bet he's rubbish.'

'What are you playing?'

'A game Mum gave me. She said it would help my geography . . .' Flynn leant over his son's shoulder. 'See? You get these clues, and you have to solve the crime and track down the villain . . . I'm looking for this guy, the clue said he'd been asking about the great apes. I've got an idea where he's gone.' Oliver clicked on the icon of a plane and a list of world destinations appeared on the screen. Flynn watched as his son double clicked on Rwanda. Blink. Blink, blink . . . the plane passed slowly across a map of the world to Africa. 'Kigali,' an

American voice intoned melodically, 'land of lush vegetation and home of the great apes . . .'

'Yesss!' Oliver crowed. 'I've got him!'

Flynn stood silently above his son for a few minutes until Oliver had the evil criminal behind bars and had been promoted from rookie to sleuth. He laid a hand on Oliver's shoulder. 'Turn it off now, Ol. It's late.'

SEVEN

In the privacy of the darkroom Flynn threw himself on the threadbare, deep-seated red sofa as the room dissolved around him. The room was his lair and sanctuary. For the past year he'd had little work to do, since his regular commissioning editors had dropped him, but he retreated there more than ever. Georgia rarely entered it; he had told her not to plump up the flattened cushions, not to wipe down the worktop. He had no inclination to cover up the stains on his sofa. He did not want even the dust disturbed.

He lay in the dark remembering how cold Madeline's lips had felt against his. Her hands had remained clasped in her lap but she had pressed her shoulder blades hard against the back of her chair and said, *Don't do that again.* He had remained leaning towards her, unable to sit straight, glad that he'd kissed her, ashamed that he'd kissed her, without the slightest idea why he had kissed her. Her voice had been icy and furious. *Let me make it crystal clear,* she'd said. *You talk, I listen. You don't do anything else. Anything else you do – kiss me, smoke, pace the room, anything – is simply a reflection of your desire to run away.*

Then he'd been able to pull back. He'd told her she was full of crap, that he smoked because he'd smoked for twenty years, that he'd kissed her because she was a beautiful woman and maybe that was a habit too. Her eyes had flashed in response. He could feel the heat lifting off him even now, hours later, on the other side of London. He could feel the chill as her voice sliced into him, each word swinging sharp and straight and clean: *If you are looking for a smoke, or a beautiful woman, or any other kind of crutch that lets you bury your problems in a dark corner, go somewhere else and find someone else.*

He hadn't been able to speak: the notion of being cast adrift from her and left alone had felt like a strong hand clamped round his throat. Later she'd given him her word that she would not get fed up and end it, told him that when the time came to end their sessions they would work through it together. She had held his gaze firmly in hers and her low voice had reeled him back in. *Whatever defences you've used before, whatever habits you have relied on are clearly not working or you wouldn't be here.* She had let him know without any possibility of confusion that they had hard work to do together and he had felt grateful. He had the sense that her arms were about him, holding him up, and he wanted to know everything about her – who she was, what made her able to stand beside him and see what he saw. Sometimes, he had admitted, he looked in the mirror and did not know who looked back; he woke up in bed not knowing who he was. He needed to be certain of Madeline but she would not even tell him how old she was. *Old enough.* That was all she'd said.

Now he lay flat on his back and was immersed in the mist around *Nepenthe*, smoke filling his lungs. He felt his pulse quicken and heard his blood pounding in his head. He felt the sting as Madeline's hair lashed across his eye and smelt the heady, spicy smell of her perfume – roses, roses, and deeper notes of something more pungent, more sexual, something darker than he had ever scented on Georgia. As soon as he had seen her Flynn had known that there was within Madeline something that corresponded to his hidden heart. He had wanted to kiss her to see how she would taste and

103

how she would respond; her utter lack of physical response had pleased him. Perhaps because she didn't care.

Flynn knew that Georgia cared; she cared about the state of the world and she cared about him and she cared about making everything better, and when she couldn't make it better she would at least strive to make it look better. He thought with remorse about Georgia, how lonely he had made her and how needlessly cruel he had been in telling her he had not mentioned her to Madeline, when much of their last session had been spent discussing Georgia. He had tried to describe how good things had been between them but had not been able to find the words. There was so much that he was able to describe minutely – such as the night on *Nepenthe* nearly five months ago, the time in Kigali with Erik six years before that – without quite remembering being there. When it came to Georgia, he could remember how good it had once felt between them but he could not describe it in words. He had only been able to say that he'd once known something grand in his wife but had lost sight of it somewhere along the road.

Flynn was all too aware of cruelty within himself. He wanted Madeline to feel as he did when he left her room, to be unable to return to her orderly, he suspected, and very private life. He needed her to feel as raw and exposed as he did. He wanted one person – not Georgia, never Georgia – to share what he felt alone in the dark. Thinking about the therapist took away his sweats and bad dreams; thinking about her let him feel he could stop pretending. Thinking about her brought his strength back. Forty-eight hours. Forty-eight hours until he would see her again and smell the scent of roses as he entered that private space. He rose with leaden legs and went into the kitchen looking for his wife. Without speaking he took Georgia's face between his large hands, kissed her slowly and powerfully on the mouth and felt her melt into him with instant gratitude. Shame near broke his heart.

*　　*　　*

104

The Bar Espana had been holding its space for twenty years, jamming both its elbows into the ribs of its increasingly fashionable neighbours on the little square behind Madeline's Clerkenwell office. The management's only concession to refurbishment had been to install a double row of rustic tiles around the dingy walls, but the basement bar remained as unassuming inside as it was without: dimly lit, resolutely brown and rarely more than half occupied. At six o'clock on a Thursday Madeline had her choice of tables. As she sat in a corner waiting for Michael, Madeline wondered how she would have felt had a stranger at a party, with no warning or invitation, kissed her in the way that Flynn had done the day before. She would have dismissed him as a stupid, self-destructive bully and walked away. Was that how Flynn saw himself, or wanted to be seen? Was that why he had cloaked his aggression and helplessness in what should have been the most tender of all human gestures? Again he'd set her up: three times he'd caught her completely off guard. It had taken Madeline twenty-four hours to steady herself and marshal her thoughts.

Generally Madeline's clients willingly submitted to an unequal relationship in which she held superior authority and status; that was part of the contract. Her side of the bargain was to use that power only to foster their recovery. If she had withdrawn from him he could have rejected her as weak; had she shown hostility it would have reinforced his fight instincts. I will not be manipulated by him, she had told herself fiercely; I will take back control. She took a paper napkin from the beaker, smoothed it flat then folded it carefully, turning it over and over again and pressing heavily on each crease. Was I so shocked because of what he did, because of the way he did it . . . or because some part of me liked it? She still could not answer her own question. She closed her eyes, arched her neck and tried to get a breeze from the limp fan.

Michael clattered down the steps with his tie askew and

his limbs flying, as if he had not yet learnt how best to control them.

'Hen, I'm sorry – total insurrection on the home front . . . it's Lydia's bridge night and the children have revolted against the au pair who's screaming blue murder down the phone. She's a seventeen-year-old Serbian and scares the shit out of us. Have you ordered a bottle? I need one all to myself.'

'If you want to get home that's fine – really.'

'Home? Last place I want to be. No. I told Vlatka very firmly that I had a practice meeting which couldn't be rescheduled and was bound to drag on for hours. She can tie the kids down in front of the telly. It won't do them any harm.' Michael turned to face the morose-looking waiter behind the bar. 'A bottle of your finest house red, Diego, a pack of Marlboro and don't spare the horses . . .'

'Does Lydia know you're smoking again?'

Michael took a small breath spray from his jacket pocket and waggled it triumphantly before tucking it back with a broad smile. 'Of course she does. The woman knows everything. She knows I know she knows I know she knows, and she's longing for me to crack. But I won't. Now . . . first business, hen, then pleasure.'

'Business' – that Michael's solicitor was sorting out the extension of the lease, that Madeline had booked the inspection from the fire department and that Michael would, he swore, remember to buy coffee filter papers the following morning – took precisely ten minutes and two cigarettes to settle. Throughout those ten minutes Madeline considered telling Michael what had happened in the session with Flynn. No, she thought: I know what he'll say and it's Jillian I should talk to. I can hold this together. Self-medicate. That's what therapists do all the time. Not necessarily in the rule book, but I can handle it.

'D'you want to hear some really juicy gossip? A little bird told me there's been an almighty fracas at the Institute –'

'Michael,' Madeline twisted the bottle of wine by the neck and stared at the label, 'I need a second opinion on a client.'

'I thought you'd never ask. I *love* giving second opinions.' Michael clapped his hands as if to rub them together, but stopped suddenly. 'It's the photographer, isn't it? The one from Astra Four.'

'How did you know?'

'I don't know. I just knew.'

Madeline nodded. 'He has classic PTSD symptoms. Memory disturbance, dissociation, personality swings. Flashbacks. Something happened to him in Rwanda; a friend of his died there.' She looked up at Michael's open and earnest face, still uncertain of what she would say. 'He's very difficult to work with. Sometimes arrogant; sometimes he throws himself wide open. Cynical, but in the way that only an idealist can be. I'm worried.'

'About his stability?'

Madeline bit her lower lip as she shook her head. 'Worried I can't handle him. He flouts every boundary control, breaches every possible limit.'

Michael settled into his role, looking the part. 'Give me an example.'

'OK. In the middle of our last session he ... well ... he kissed me.'

Michael raised his eyebrows. 'What do you mean, he kissed you?'

'He kissed me. Hard. On the mouth.'

'Tongue?'

Madeline jerked her head angrily. 'For God's sake, Michael, *tongue*? I don't know. I think so. Yes. Maybe for a second his tongue was on my lips.'

'Bloody hell. That's a boundary violation if ever I heard one.'

Madeline picked up an olive but dropped it back into the bowl. 'I had a rush of complete panic.'

Michael whistled through his teeth. 'I bloody bet you did. What happened next?'

'I read him the riot act.'

'And got him back on track?'

'I suppose . . . I kept thinking, this is way out of hand. I felt so exposed. And furious he'd put me in that position. I tried to understand how exposed he might feel, how isolated.' Madeline rested her elbows on the table and held her face between her hands in a way that pulled her eyes up like a cat's. 'He began to talk about his wife, his work, wanting to care about them both again. He said he wanted to trust himself to do things well.'

'All credit to you, Maddie. You got him back. It unsettled you, understandably, but you coped with it. Better than I would have done. If one particular lady client of mine did that to me I'd be a puddle on the floor . . .' One shot from Madeline's eyes let him know this was not the time for levity. 'OK. Bottom line, as the song says, a kiss is just a kiss. Focus on what was behind it.'

'I *think* –' Madeline began hesitantly but as she talked her voice strengthened – 'it was the only way he saw of making a connection. His estrangement is not only from his wife and work, but from everything in his world. He's all about confrontation. He engineers a situation where he's got nothing to lose and nothing to win. He claims he doesn't care about his wife, doesn't care about his work, but everything about him shouts that he cares a great deal. Kissing me was his way of making a connection.' Madeline reached across the table and shook a cigarette out of the packet. 'Don't you dare say a word. Not one word to anyone.'

'About what? I didn't see anything. . .' Michael leant forward to light it.

Madeline inhaled, wrinkled her nose slightly and stroked the burning tip against the ashtray. 'He asked me if I'd just get fed up and end it. It was like a kick in the stomach, a flash recognition that he's terrified of being abandoned.' She dragged deeply and let the smoke drift slowly from the corner of her mouth, looking at Michael all the time. 'Am I conning myself, trying to rationalise all this?'

Michael emptied the bottle into her glass and waved for another.

'I don't think getting pissed is going to help me much.'

'Who said it's for you, hen? Have you talked this through with Jillian yet?' She shook her head. 'Well, you're going to need to do that, OK? So long as you talk it through with her, then I can tell you what I think as your chum.'

'And as my chum,' Madeline asked slowly, 'you think . . . ?'

'We all stretch a little on boundary issues, don't we? Why is busting them wide so important for him? Important for you? Maybe it's worth stretching the rules: see what happens, see if there's a gap in his defences . . . You don't have to live by the book.' Michael leant forward and picked up a glass in each hand, his cigarette bobbing between his lips as he talked. 'Watch.' He put one glass solidly in the centre of the table. 'That's safe, isn't it? It's safe, but it isn't interesting.' He took the other glass and balanced it precariously half over the edge of the table. 'Now *that's* what I call an interesting situation.'

'For you or the glass?' Madeline smiled and immediately moved it a couple of inches back. 'I won't risk you smashing up the Espana's glasses for the sake of some misguided metaphor. And I'm not inclined to risk smashing up my clients. But I get the point, OK? Maybe I do lead them – carefully – right to the edge . . .'

'Because?' Michael prompted.

'Because acceptance is the only way forward. But I can't give them a hefty shove in the back.'

'That's what he's trying to do to you, Maddie; you have to stay less frightened of what's on the other side of the drop than he is.'

'Yes.' Madeline slipped her hand under her shirt and rubbed

her palm back and forth over her shoulder. 'He drains me, Michael. I've never felt so depleted by a client.'

'Then you've got to work out why. What is it about him that taps into you and drains everything out?'

Over Michael's shoulder Madeline saw Jack Zabinsky stoop as he came down the steps, peering into the gloom, and stubbed out her cigarette. He had a narrow, clever face and stiff black hair that shot off his forehead. It lent him a permanently surprised expression which sat at odds with his world-weary manner.

'Thought I'd find you two here,' Jack growled as he dumped his briefcase on the floor and loosened his tie. 'Can you give me one reason to patronise this place? It's a miracle they can still afford the rent.'

'They can't.' Madeline moved along the leather banquette to make room for him. 'Michael subsidises them just to piss you off.'

Jack glanced from one to the other. 'I get the feeling I've interrupted something here. Are you two having a *liaison dangereuse*? Is that why you choose this dump, because no one in their right mind would set foot in it?' Jack put his feet up on a chair. 'You know, Madeline, if you had an affair with me I'd show you a better time. Dinner at the Caprice; a suite at the Ritz. Play your cards right and you're onto a winner.' He commandeered Madeline's glass and grimaced. 'Better wine, too.'

'I'll add you to the list, OK, Jack? When I'm through with Michael.'

'The offer's only good for another month, sweetface, then I'll have to move on. You can't keep an engine running without a foot on the gas, know what I mean?'

Jack wasn't the only one at the Espana who wondered exactly what was between Madeline and Michael. Diego, from his haven behind the bar, had seen how displeased Michael had looked at the American's arrival, and decided not to offer him a clean glass.

'We were having a serious discussion about a client, Jack, before we were so rudely interrupted –'

'Hey, all work and no play makes Mike a damn dull boy, you hear what I'm saying, Madeline? Therapy schmerapy. Always remember clients are just using us like a drunk uses a lamppost.'

An expat New Yorker, Jack talked as if he were Humphrey Bogart spouting lines from a B-movie script. Despite the fact that he was cynical, arrogant, hyperactive and opinionated, Madeline couldn't help liking him. He was one of the very best therapists she knew.

'Look. I'm sorry about kissing you last time.'

'I'd like to come back to your kissing me . . .'

'Good.' Flynn grinned. 'Does that mean I can come back to it, too? Sorry, I'm sorry. I'll shut up and keep my hands to myself. It'll remind me of piano lessons as a boy.'

'Flynn, I'd like to talk about Erik.' Madeline watched a muscle in his cheek clench and unclench.

'Did you see "Who Wants To Be A Millionaire" the other night?'

His evasiveness was about as subtle as one of Patrick's tungsten hammers. 'No.'

'My kids are addicted to it. This woman goes through the first few questions, answers the name of your man on "EastEnders" and other shite. Goes fifty-fifty on who discovered penicillin and phones a friend who tells her William Wyler directed *Ben Hur*. By now she's up to sixty thousand quid, right, and then comes the twister: Belgrade is the capital of which country?' He couldn't sit still. Madeline watched him as he pushed his hair back with both hands, gesticulating constantly as he talked, shifting his watch up and down his wrist. He pulled a pack of cigarettes from an inside pocket and had one half out before he caught the look on her face. Flynn tossed the pack on her desk. 'Have 'em. I'd hate for you to think they were a crutch or anything. So. *Belgrade is the capital of which country?* I thought, that's a wee bit tricky: if she says the Yugoslav Republic, are they going to take the sixty grand away because she didn't say Serbia, or the Former Yugoslav Republic? But no: you know, it's a multiple choice deal. The jerk gives her four possible answers: Russia, Korea, Yugoslavia, Latvia. The woman breaks out in a visible sweat. She asks the audience, who splits its vote between Latvia and Yugoslavia. Three per cent go for Korea. She decides to retire with the money.'

'How did you feel watching that?'

'How did I feel?' he repeated. 'Like a champion arse. I mean, we're talking about a country we've been *at war* with. We sent an *army* out there not much more than a year ago, paid for by the people in that audience. The names of these places have been plastered across our newspapers and television screens for years, and for what? She couldn't have told you which fucking *continent* Rwanda was on.'

'You seem angry about that.' Madeline was used to stating the obvious.

Flynn was on his feet. 'Angry? It makes me fucking furious. I mean, what am I doing? Who am I taking pictures for?'

'Tell me who you take them for.'

'Well, not that cow apparently.' He leant his back to the wall with his shoulders hunched. He kept his deep-set eyes on her while he thought and offered grudgingly, 'For myself, I suppose. I just want to be there.'

'So why does it bother you what some woman thinks? She doesn't choose to be there.'

He drew his hand wearily over his eyes, shaking his head. 'It's not right. All those dead, Madeline. All those dead. You'd think there'd been enough bodies to scratch the name of Belgrade on her consciousness. At the least, she should have been interested. The dead have never lost their fascination for me . . .' His mouth twisted in an odd grimace.

'. . . Or do I mean that I have never lost my fascination with them?'

'Did that fascination lead you to become a war photographer?'

'I'm not that much of a pariah.' His expression shifted from resignation to suspicion. 'I know what you're doing. You want me to set myself up as some sort of idealistic hero, but I won't fall for it. Look,' he hunched forward, conviction as clear on his face as a preacher's, 'I used to be a complete believer in multilateral action on a massive scale. When I was young I thought that if people saw those ripped-apart bodies, the orphaned kids, the wrecked homes, the grinding, sheer awful fucking misery of it, the loss of anything that you or I would see as the bare bones of human dignity, if people saw all *that*, they would do anything to get those images off their TV screens, off the front page. But we don't. We don't want to do anything. We don't want to pay for it financially, and we don't want to pay for it with our own boys' lives. Ivoirians, sure. By all means bung in the good old Gurkhas, no problem. Americans even – Christ knows there are enough of them to spare. But let's keep European casualties at a minimum and for God's sake, *no Brits*.' Flynn again ran his hands through his shaggy hair. 'No. There's a simple way to forget about the poor bastards of the world: switch the TV to Who Wants To Be A Million-fuckin'-aire.'

'I'm hearing that you feel what you do is pointless.'

'Wrong. I'm saying I do it for me.'

'Why, Flynn? What is it that happens when you're there?'

'*I* see it. At least *I* see it. It isn't a noble thing. I don't have some great white banner of truth unfurling about my head. It's just an urge.' He lowered his eyes and plucked at the stitching on the front of his jacket. His voice was steadier. 'I don't want to sit dangling my toes in the Kensington Round Pond letting other people tell me what's happening in the world. I want to see it for myself.'

113

'Why?'

'I don't know; it just beats scooting up a tree and howling about how pointless life is . . . but each time I have to ask myself, have I been effective? And each time the answer's a deafening *No*. Pictures of suffering don't bring in peace-keeping forces. When we do get involved, we get involved for economic reasons.'

'Who's we?' Madeline was trying to plot a pattern in his adopted misanthropy. She was certain, despite his verbal denial, that his initial professional motivation had been idealistic, but something had happened to make him lose that connection.

He swung his arm in a broad, dismissive gesture. 'NATO, the UN, England, whoever you like. Kosovo was a humanitarian action, right? We got involved. No real economic motive, but a hundred thousand refugees are crossing the border every day, right, fleeing for their lives. Terrified. Hopeless. We're there to help. To put an end to it.'

'We?'

'NATO, the UN, England,' Flynn repeated impatiently, his eyes dark as he crossed to stand at the window. 'In Rwanda, more than eight hundred thousand people were slaughtered *in a hundred days*. Not by land mines or machine guns or airborne missiles but by machetes. That's hard work, killing someone with a machete. Ask a butcher how much time and muscle it takes to carve up a cow, and that'll give you an idea of what's involved.' Flynn's breathing had become rapid and shallow. She waited silently as he again brought his distress under control. 'So . . . eight thousand people a day, on average. Over a hundred days. And we stood back. Why?'

'Why do you think?' A hundred days. He'd locked onto it as the probable duration of his sessions with her. The same time it would take Patrick to complete his commission. The time it took to enact a genocide.

'Too distant. Too culturally remote. Maybe we think – that's just the way Africa works, the "natives" are like that.

114

Just another scrap between tribes. Let them sort out their own shit. But above all, not enough economic interest.'

'But you were there, Flynn?' She looked at him in profile as he stood on guard at the window, the muscle in his cheek flexing constantly. He looked fearful of what might appear on the street below.

'For a bit. "A lesson we'll never forget", some arse politician said later. What pure shite. You think the human race gradually *learns* to be civilised? Generation by generation? Bollocks. We're no more humane now than we were fifty years ago, or a hundred. Three hundred. We've just become a little more fastidious about how we kill. Keep it all at arm's length.'

Madeline jotted the word 'Rwanda' on the pad in front of her. She wondered how many times Flynn Brennan had made this speech and to what audience – his picture editors, fellow journalists, his wife? It was too generalised, too impersonal, despite the tension in his voice. 'Your work doesn't permit you to keep at arm's length; quite the opposite. Your work is extremely dangerous. Why do *you* intervene?'

'I get paid to. Don't make the mistake of thinking I'm some kind of hero.'

'I don't.' Madeline replied instantly. He flashed her a quick, appreciative grin, but she kept pushing him down the trail. 'Tell me what you've got against heroes.'

'They don't exist. Sometimes I lie awake at night trying to think of one, honest-to-God hero. Sometimes there are people – the guy on *The Herald of Free Enterprise* – the human bridge. I guess I'd call him a hero. Can I remember his name? No. And he probably wouldn't want me to. Others?' He gave a theatrical shrug. 'I can't even find one in fiction. Not even Shakespeare created one credible, true hero. I don't see them in the media. You see awful nice fellers and smart fuckers and guys firing on nothing but adrenalin; there are plenty of brave souls, but they're not heroes. It's just the job. We're professionals. Soldiers protect or kill – or both. Politicians negotiate.

115

Doctors put people back together. I take pictures –' he leant forward, pointing his finger – 'and *you* listen. Therapists do nothing but listen and . . .' He stopped mid-stream but she waited impassively, knowing he was longing for her to fill the gap. He gave a slight, dismissive wave with one hand before continuing, 'I guess you're trying to put people back together too. But you still make your living out of misery and hell – and probably earn a fuck of a lot more than the soldiers or doctors or poor arse-licking press corps do. It's all work. Nothing but work.'

Madeline did not resent the accusation levied at her own profession; it was one she had often heard, but as she had told Jillian, she believed that her work was grounded in recovery, not suffering, even when her underlying faith in justice and humanity had been most severely stretched. She asked an open question to discover if his own faith had been similarly strained.

'Faith? Ahhh, you want to talk about *God*?' Madeline did not reply. If he wanted to talk about God, she certainly wouldn't stop him. 'Faith,' he scoffed. 'Like somebody once said, there are no atheists in foxholes. I've had moments of devout faith. They only last till the shelling stops.'

'Tell me more about that.'

'If you're out in the open under a few MiG fighters, you believe in God as much as you believe in the hand at the end of your arm. You pray damn hard it's going to stay there. Sometimes I've believed in a kind of warped divine justice. Sometimes I've thought, yes, there is a God, *yes*, the cholera epidemic in the camps after the genocide was God's swift and terrible answer to the Hutus – sometimes you've got to have the walls of Jericho come tumblin' down, got to have the devastating flood, the wipe-out of Gomorrah . . . But other times there's jack shit. The walls of Jericho don't come tumblin' down.' Flynn sat back down on the edge of his chair, leaning forward, his hands clenched in a double fist. His conviction made him convincing, Madeline thought; he would

116

have made a powerful preacher. 'When half the world believed in God he popped up everywhere, sticking his great hooter into everybody's business and whipping out tricks like rabbits from a conjuror's hat. The parting of the Red Sea, poor old Lot's wife – what the hell did she do to deserve that, if he wasn't just showing off? Since when was curiosity a crime? Now, when it's really time for a bit of sleight of hand, a little bit of magic to convince the atheists, what does God do? Does he stick his head over the parapet? Does he fuck.'

Madeline was listening acutely while Flynn sat slumped, apparently depleted by the verdict he had released on God, government and the gutless. The effort of sharing his weariness and despair left her bruised.

'I'm interested in what you say. The first time you came to see me, when we met on the street outside, you told me you were a believer in destiny. Several times since you have said you believed in fate.'

'If I did, it was only to persuade you to see me. I don't wear a white suit or carry a rabbit's foot or any of that bollocks. I have my rules – like you – my rituals, but they're practical ones. If I'm working in sniper territory, I might pull a pair of tights over the lens cap, or use an old tin to lengthen the lens.'

'You'll have to explain that.'

'Survival skills. Camera lenses, glasses, binoculars, the human face all catch the light, show up in the dark.' He mimed aiming a gun, swinging it from side to side, seeking a target and settling on her. 'They attract the sniper towards you. So I try to cover up. It's a precaution, that's all. I don't think a bunny's foot is going to save me when my time comes. I just hope I'll go with good grace, not whimpering that I haven't seen enough of the party. But I don't go looking for a bullet.'

'You wear protection?'

'A condom, generally.'

Thank God he had a sense of humour. Outwardly Madeline barely smiled.

117

'All right, I get the message; no jokes. I wear a flak jacket, when I can, if it's not going to slow me down. You have to give yourself a chance. My eyes are my best defence. I count on them to tell me when something's going down, give me the signal.'

Appropriate, for a photographer. 'What other signals do you rely on?'

'The people you're with, other journalists, local intelligence . . . If you know them, that is. New guys are the worst. They can get you shot at a checkpoint just by the way they look at the guy with the gun.'

'That must be a tense moment,' Madeline said, deliberately bland.

'Tense? Jesus, woman. You want to crap yourself. At a checkpoint the other journos are more dangerous than the boys with the big guns. At least they're the devil you know. You can spot the types; your basic, automaton soldier; the rebel fighter who barely knows who his leader is any more; the guy who's out of his brains on drugs or booze. But when the bloke sitting next to you is an unknown quantity and your life depends on his understanding the rules, *then* your guts turn inside out.'

Madeline wanted to ask about Erik again, but she couldn't afford to be clumsy so near the end of the session. 'How do you feel about your media colleagues?'

Flynn squinted at the ceiling. 'Ninety per cent of them are decent. The only ones I've got no time for are the correspondents who award themselves the Oscars of war reporting.' Flynn stood up, imaginary mike in hand, and slid one hand over his heart between the buttons of his shirt before beginning to speak in an awful parody. '"I don't know quite how to tell you what I saw this Friday morning . . . *clear your throat* . . . this Good Friday morning . . . but lest we forget, I will try . . ." D'you ever hear them say, "I was that scared, I crapped myself"? Because we all do.' He winked at her.

'What is it exactly that offends you?'

'Either they're spouting crap, in which case they shouldn't be doing the job, or their feelings are genuine. In which case they shouldn't be doing the job.'

'And you, Flynn. Do you feel that you should be doing the job?'

'Me? I'm cut out for it.' He laid his right hand over his heart. 'I am what is known in the trade as a remorseless seeker after truth.'

Madeline looked at him piercingly. 'I'm sorry? What did you say?'

'I said I was a relentless seeker after truth.'

'That's what I thought you'd said. It's an interesting phrase.'

And a remorseless seeker after truth was an even more interesting one.

EIGHT

After he had left, she sat at her desk while the light gradually faded. It was barely the end of summer; autumn was still some weeks away. The room was warm, the air fresh, yet throughout the session she had had a sense of a mist in the atmosphere between them that had reminded her of being on *Nepenthe*.

She had liked listening to him talk about his work; she shared some of his yen for an Old Testament-style God; she had liked him for the first time. Now uncertainty hung in the air like a fog and made the skin on her arms ripple with goose-bumps. There was something in Flynn that reminded her of a child's fear, both of being seen through and not being seen through enough. She remembered what she had once been told by a Royal Marine she had debriefed: 'in a true war story nothing is ever absolutely true'. To begin the journey she had to move Flynn off the soap-box polemic and onto his personal experience, but she could sense that in some way, for Flynn, things were no longer as they seemed. The fog was thick, there was no clarity, no focus, no way through the confusion; right and wrong had intermingled; everything swirled into ambiguity.

She chewed her pencil and stared at the word on the notepad in front of her. *Rwanda*. For all his mouth, she suspected that the way through to Flynn was through his eyes: his best defence, he'd said. She jotted down the date and added several words – *kiss, camera, sight*, then in a leap of conscious association, *camera obscura* and finally, *the realm of the hungry ghosts*.

When Patrick came home from a recce to the British Museum, Madeline was sitting on the sofa nursing a glass of wine. His mind was full of the classical busts he had seen and he was eager to return to Basil Hume, but the melancholy in Madeline's face made him linger.

She patted the cushion next to her. 'Can I ask you a question?'

'Anything, so long as you don't bank on my giving the correct answer.'

'Do you think Shakespeare ever depicted a real hero?'

Patrick shrugged. 'I've some dim memory of a couple of plays from school . . .'

'Name one true hero.'

'I can't think, offhand.'

'There aren't any, are there? None in *Lear*, none in *Hamlet*, none in *Macbeth*, none in *Antony and Cleopatra*,' Madeline said. 'I mean, he sometimes gives us crackingly good, semi-heroic figures – an Antony, a Hector, a Henry the Fifth, but fundamentally they're great soldiers. Not heroes . . .' she finished sadly.

'What's put this in your head, Maddie?'

'Something a client said. I have a feeling he's searching for the heroic in life. In himself. I've been trying to come up with an example to see if it works for him. It's made my head hurt.'

Patrick held her head between his hands and pressed her temples with the pad of his callused thumbs. 'Maybe Shakespeare didn't believe in heroes.'

'Do you?' Madeline asked.

121

'I think Hume was a hero. He had a hero's face. That's good enough for me.'

Madeline smiled. 'You're besotted.'

'Of course I am. I always am, aren't I? If the piece is to be any good. You can't work on a subject that intimately and not fall in love.' He began to massage Madeline's head, tapping sharply and pressing down hard so that she'd feel it right to the soles of her feet. Madeline purred. Hume could wait. 'Even if I did believe in heroes, I'm not sure I'd like to meet one in the flesh.'

'Why not? I would.'

'That's because you're not scared of difficult people. I have a hunch heroes are difficult. Great to sculpt; good to know that there are some at large in the world, but not necessarily the types I want to bump into on holiday. There's plenty of room for heroes in the world – God knows we need them – but there have got to be some of us who just sit on the side and clap as the heroes parade past . . . Personally I'd rather be a clapper.'

'Or a sculptor.'

'Same thing. It's about celebrating others.'

His humility touched her but she questioned his reasoning. Sculpting was a highly creative process. To her mind, Patrick didn't merely celebrate heroes: he created them.

'Don't give me that look . . .'

'What look?' Madeline asked innocently.

'That look that says I don't believe you. That *therapist* look.'

'I always believe my clients. Just not you.' Madeline cuffed him lightly. 'Why are you doing so little in wood these days?'

'Right now I'm happier with stone. I find it more challenging.'

Not long after they'd become a couple he'd taken her to Rome to see Michelangelo's *I Servi* and she had asked him if, when he sculpted, he felt as if he was releasing each figure from the prison of the stone. He'd told her the notion was a bit of a myth; that, whether a sculptor worked in stone or clay or wood, it was the same process of imposing one's notion of the subject onto the raw material. You had to respect the material, he'd said, always respect it if you're going to work with it at all, but you can't be in awe of it. She had often thought of his words when in session, where she tried so hard not to impose her notions on her client, even when she felt she had nothing but a bare wire armature before her.

'Why more challenging?' she asked. 'Because it's more permanent?'

'Go look in any old church you like, anywhere in the world; take a look at the headless busts and fractured Pietas,' he said lightly, 'and then tell me how permanent those stone monuments are.'

'That's so terribly sad.'

'Nothing's permanent, Maddie darling. Nothing lasts for ever, not the good work and –' his melancholic expression changed to a smile – 'thank *God*, not the bad. Even marble's deceptive; it's surprisingly fragile. Needs to be treated gently if you're not to ruin it.'

'Have you ever ruined a piece?'

'Not for a long time. I'm too cautious. Bit by bit, slowly, slowly, you take it away. Or slowly build it up. It's the same process.'

'Is it?' Madeline smoothed the deep crow's feet that stretched to Patrick's temple. 'Is it?'

Flynn's right ankle was crossed over his left knee. His foot jiggled sporadically.

'My wife thinks I'm a toenail.'

Madeline could not suppress a smile at the incongruity of the image. 'A toenail? Do you know why she might think that?'

'It's her way of telling me I'm a pain in the arse.' He leant forward. 'Within that world view, I'm an ingrown toenail. She says I'm festering.'

'It's a provocative image.'

'She thinks I spend too much time in my darkroom.'

'Do you?'

'Maybe.' He stretched his arms over his head, flexing his hands. 'Georgia's obsessed with feet. Feet and fabric. She's got crates of the stuff . . . thinks I don't know . . .'

They had been meeting for several weeks, and Madeline was now accustomed to the rhythm and pattern of his speech. As he talked about Georgia he tilted his head to one side, his gaze as usual on something behind Madeline's head. '. . . I catch her looking at them as if they weren't hers. I can't for the life of me understand what she's so worked up about . . . They function, they don't hurt, they're perfectly normal, honest-to-God feet, but they drive her nuts.' He flashed the grin which lit up his otherwise restive face.

'What makes you smile?' Madeline asked, struck by the physical energy he exuded in even so fleeting a gesture.

'She'd die of shame if she knew I was telling you about her feet. Now me, I count on mine. You have to, in my business: you count on them to get you out of trouble fast. Maybe Georgia's too used to having her feet under a desk. She wants things to work and look pretty at the same time.' He shrugged. 'She's bound to be disappointed.'

'Do you think Georgia feels disappointed?'

'To be sure she does; she's too clever not to be. We can all keep the surface looking nice and pretty, whether it's our marriages or our careers, or our godforsaken feet. But we've got the callouses, haven't we, Madeline? The stuff the camera can't see – the ugly truth.' He gave her one direct, conspiratorial glance, then his eyes were back searching the corners of the room. 'The only way to keep your hands clean is to keep them shoved in your pockets. I don't hold with that.'

'So what do you do, Flynn?'

124

'I get my hands dirty. Only Georgia thinks I don't get them dirty enough, or don't get stuck into the "right" kind of dirt. She thinks I don't bother with the house, or the kids, or all that. But this is bollocks. I've not come to you for marriage guidance.'

Madeline nodded once, but now that Flynn had voluntarily raised the subject of his family relationships she was not going to let him dodge away from it.

'Do *you* think that you get stuck into the dirt of family life – the house, your children?'

'When I'm about I do,' he said, 'but I don't sweat over their every cough and cold, and I don't lie awake at night wondering if they're going to have happy marriages.' It was a curious conjunction, health and marital contentment, but Flynn plunged ahead too fast for Madeline to check him. 'I love my children,' he said, 'and I love my wife. But they don't know what's going on in the world.' Flynn had been talking about nothing of real consequence, or rather, anything but himself, for the first ten to fifteen minutes of the session. Chit-chat about Tony Blair, a bit of bluff about war photography, but only the bare bones he offered at drinks parties.

'What is going on in your world, Flynn, that your wife and children don't know about?'

'My kids don't know what Rwanda's about. They barely know where it is.'

'What *is* Rwanda about?'

At once Madeline felt a chill fall, felt Flynn leave her and the space between them stretch. He fixed his eyes on the ceiling at a corner of the room, not shiftily, but it was enough for Madeline to recognise that Rwanda was his private territory, that whatever he claimed, he did not wish others to enter his knowledge of the place. 'Rwanda was about hell. But that's not what Oliver thinks. He's nine, right? A clever boy, a real smart lad. He wants to play football or computer games, not study an atlas or read a book. So his clever, conscientious mother buys "geography" computer games. With the result

125

that he knows one thing about Rwanda. You know what that is?'

Madeline shook her head.

'Blink, blink, blink. Kigali, Home of the Great Apes,' he recited portentously in an American accent. As Madeline met his gaze, her face blank, he prompted, 'You recognise it, don't you? "Where in the World is Carmen Sandiego?" Computer game?'

'No.'

'You must have heard of it . . .'

Madeline again shook her head.

Flynn's eyes narrowed. 'It means nothing to you, does it? You've spent all this time refusing to tell me anything about yourself, but you've just blown your cover. Well, I've got you now . . . I know something about you, Doctor Light, I know something about you for a *fact*.'

Madeline smiled. It was good to see Flynn's journalistic, investigative instinct to the fore. 'You've caught me red-handed. I don't play computer games.' She relaxed back in her chair, letting herself enjoy being teased. 'So? Educate me.'

Flynn took his time. 'Carmen's the criminal mastermind behind a ruthless band of international villains. It's the detective's mission to track down her evil henchmen all over the world – Mad Jack Jenkins, Carlos the Butcher . . .' he waved his hand vaguely, '. . . their criminal aliases escape me.'

'And? What does it have to do with Rwanda?'

'Nothing.' His eyes twinkled, the grin was back on his face as he watched her reaction.

Madeline's playfulness dissolved at the silkiness in his voice. 'Flynn, what are we doing here, playing charades? Because if so, I'm losing the thread. You'll have to help me.'

'It's a computer game.'

'So you said. What does it have to do with Rwanda?' The days were growing shorter. Dusk was already on the horizon. Madeline glanced at the window with a presentiment

126

of trouble. He'd been circling closer to dangerous ground, dancing skittishly around Rwanda.

'Nothing.' Flynn crossed his arms with the laid-back composure of a cat that's certain the mouse is cornered. 'But now I know two things about you. You know nothing about computer games, which I might have guessed at . . . but that also tells me you don't have children.'

The blood drained from Madeline's face. For a second or two, she closed her eyes before saying in a fierce, low voice, 'You're wrong. I have a child.'

Madeline consciously lowered her jaw and filled her lungs. 'Let me make something perfectly clear,' she said. 'Something I've said before. We're not here to play games. It's a waste of time and money. If you want to play games, go and play somewhere else. It's entirely your choice. If you choose to continue, then do me the favour of not making assumptions about me and I will show you the same courtesy. Whether I have children or not is irrelevant. It does not concern the problems you are dealing with, however much you wish to avoid them.'

Flynn held his hands up in a gesture of genuine and disarming remorse. 'I'm sorry. Truly. I didn't mean to tread on your toes. I'll bet you're too good a mother to let your kid play computer games. I bet you're a wonderful mother. I'm a clumsy fucker sometimes . . . It was only meant as a joke. I'd kill for a smoke. Can I? No. There you go then. Right. I was trying to get at name associations, you know? This game, this stupid game my son was playing, says, "Kigali, home of the great apes". You know, Dian Fossey, all that malarkey. Like saying, Nuremberg, famed for its wood-carvers, or Hiroshima, native home of the rare blah-blah-blah orchid . . .' His voice died away as he met her eyes. 'You haven't forgiven me, have you?'

Flynn stretched one hand out to her, palm down, in penitence. Madeline stared at his hand without comment. 'Smack it if you like. It would make me feel a lot better.'

'I'm not here to make you feel better,' Madeline stated. 'I

think you're doing all you can to avoid feeling a lot worse. I understand that, but it's time we got moving. What does Kigali mean to *you*, Flynn?'

Madeline listened as he continued, but another part of her raced along a different and murky route. *How could I let it go like that? How could I? I want to cut this session short; get out of here.* Her stomach clenched and knotted. Madeline struggled to focus on Flynn, what he was saying and what he was not saying.

'If a country, a town, a region, are indelibly branded by the events that happen there, if they *absorb* the memory of past actions and events – like the theory behind homeopathic medicines, that somehow the water *takes on* the memory of one tiny particle of the stuff – then it stands to reason that people do, too. Kigali was a *tiny* bit of my life. I absorbed it. However diluted, I cannot get rid of it. I believed that I wanted to see things, needed to see the world as it really is, but maybe, after all, it's better not to. Maybe it's better to have an easy life, take the low road. Otherwise, it's a lifelong infection, really. And there's no end value in seeing it. If nothing changes, if Vietnam goes into Cambodia and Korea into Bosnia, Rwanda, Kosovo then what is the point? They're permanently damaged places.'

'Do you feel permanently damaged by them, Flynn?'

'Of course I'm damaged.' Flynn stood up and reached for the cigarettes he had tossed on her desk when he arrived; he shoved them in his pocket and walked to the window. 'I'd like to meet a man who isn't damaged by seeing that shit, because he can't be human. Any of us can do the adrenalin run, get through the hell of it, make a living, laugh and joke about it even, but you don't come through undamaged.'

'How were you damaged?' He closed his eyes and scratched his head, looking pained – *by the banality of her question, or the difficulty in answering it?* 'Are you able to tell me,' Madeline continued, 'what happened to you in Rwanda?'

'Nothing. My friend Erik was killed. That was all.'

128

NINE

Two days later Flynn stood motionless, leaning heavily on the window sill, staring out across the greyness of Clerkenwell Road. 'Erik was killed. That was all,' he repeated. 'Erik and up to a million others. It was no big deal for me personally.'

'He was your friend. Why wasn't his death a big deal for you?'

Flynn hunched his shoulders. 'Erik wasn't a friend. Erik was just a fellow journalist, working for AP. He was a good guy, good at his job. He was there doing a job, like me. I didn't really know him. We weren't a team or anything like that.'

Why did he feel so isolated? Why did his every comment make her feel so isolated? We weren't a team. 'Tell me Erik's story.'

'I can't. It's his story, right?'

'Then tell me what you know about him.'

'Like I said, I didn't know him well; not well enough to trust him. We bumped into each other in Kigali. He was a young guy, ten years younger than me. A Dutchman. A madman.' Flynn smiled oddly. 'Crazy red hair. There were hardly any Western journalists about, and the few who were there weren't doing well. It was tough to get local material, hard to get in, hard

129

to find local fixers, good information, hard to get leads, to get connected to either the government troops or the RPF. The local media, those few who hadn't got out before the massacres started, were having a better time of it, understandably: they were trusted more than we were. Or maybe they weren't. But we were rank outsiders, Erik and I. We sort of hooked up to find the story.'

Madeline watched a vein pulse below Flynn's jawbone. She had witnessed the unfolding of the trauma narrative many times, and something in Flynn's manner did not ring true to her. He was too calm, too verbally composed. 'Did you and Erik find a story?'

'There wasn't anything you could call a "story". It was a mad place, a mad time. Mad. Everyone was terrified. Things were crazy there. You didn't know who to trust. Nobody wanted to admit they were scared; we were just trying to stay sane, think logically. Like there was anything logical about Kigali.'

For a couple of minutes neither of them spoke. Madeline tried to pick through the phrases that kept recurring – trust, or the lack of it; madness; fear. She needed to trace back the skeins of his memory one by one to find where they had unravelled. She waited, knowing that Flynn did not like silences, and certainly not silences that left his fear twirling in the air like a corpse from a gibbet. Flynn exhaled deeply and began again. 'Media guys who follow wars round the world . . . we see ourselves like gladiators, the ultimate hard men. We'd rather order a round of Babycham down the boozer than admit to feeling fucked. But we were. Except for Erik.'

'How did Erik react?'

'He was punch-drunk, longing to get stuck in. Tutsi refugees were fleeing the city in droves, when they felt safe enough to try to get out or desperate enough to risk a run. I heard a story from one of the few blokes I trusted. There was a family of women and children hiding in Kigali who were going to make a break – head out to take refuge with some priest in Gitarama. I thought about it. Whether to go look for them alone or take Erik. I should have gone alone. I didn't owe Erik any favours. Maybe I was frightened of going alone, maybe I wanted his company, maybe I told myself I was giving him a break. I don't know why I went or why I took him with me. Maybe I was fed up with sitting in a shite hotel scared shitless, with my thumb stuck up my arse, my head clogged with the noise and the reeking stench of the place. It wasn't my kind of story – it wasn't a "photo opportunity".' His voice dripped with derision as he remained at the window, one hand on the blinds. 'Naturally Erik wanted to come. We managed to get a few UNAMIR blokes to escort us to where the family were hiding. They'd already left. We went after them. It was lunatic . . .' Flynn sighed heavily.

When he resumed his voice was leaden, as if he had formed the words a hundred times. 'But we went. I blagged my way into borrowing a Land-Rover from the UNAMIR boys. We headed out on the Gitarama road. Erik couldn't stop talking. It made me want to punch him.' Before he continued, Flynn took several heavy breaths, his nostrils flaring. 'Maybe three miles out of town we hit a road block. The Tutsi family could never have passed it, so why should we? Erik was too damn curious: he wanted to check the mood, try and work out if they'd turned them back to Kigali or whacked them then and there. *He wanted to see what would happen.* Normally, I'm OK at checkpoints. I can hack it.' He turned his head to look at Madeline. 'It's like school, you know?'

'In what way, like school?'

'Like being sent to your housemaster. Catholic schools – third rate Irish ones most of all – are an excellent training ground for freelance correspondents. You learn how to keep your eyes down without looking too evasive, too humble, too guilty; you can't show fear and you can't ask for trouble. Ingratiate yourself, but not so far as you'll stand out. They teach you to endure anything without cringing. But at that roadblock I was fucked with fear. I was shitting myself that Erik would cause a scene and blurt out something about the refugees. I said we were going to Gitarama to meet up with press colleagues at the UN station. There was the usual palaver about who we knew in Kigali, who we knew in Gitarama, who from UNAMIR. Lots of questions, taking passports. I handed over some booze, some smokes. I never dreamt they'd let us through. But I was wrong . . . partly wrong. In the end they took a dislike to my cameras. They took them and sent me back to Kigali. They let Erik through. He went on. I went back. The next day I heard that the party of women and kids had been ambushed. Erik had caught up with them. He was machetéd alongside the women and children.'

Madeline sat across from Flynn, erased by the emptiness in his voice; she wanted to sink her head into her hands with the pity of it. 'But you weren't there, Flynn?'

He shook his head. 'No. I was in Kigali.'

'How did you get back, the three miles back to town?'

'I don't remember.' Up went his shoulders. 'Walked, I imagine.'

'And Erik took the Land-Rover?'

'I shouldn't have let him go. He didn't have anyone but me to tell him what to do.'

'Did you tell him?'

'Of course I did!' Flynn cried. 'I told him not to go, but his blood was up – he was on a story, had a green light. I told him he should *never* be on his own. He asked me if I'd ever been on my own.'

'And you said?'

'The truth. Not that we had much time to talk; the soldiers were antsy, wanted us gone one way or another. We'd never considered the possibility that they might let one of us go and send the other back. I should have covered that before we got to the road block.'

132

'You said you told him the truth?'

'*Yes*,' he reiterated. 'I said I'd been on my own a lot, but not until I'd been in the field far longer than him. Besides, I'm a different type from Erik; I'd have had a better chance. Erik was the kind with an aura about him. When you clock that, whether the guy's a journalist or an aid worker or a soldier, when you see that kind of goodness, real courage, you know one thing for certain: they'll be the first to get whacked. They're always the first to get whacked. And you know what that says about me, that I've survived so long?'

'What does it say about you?'

He tried a lop-sided smile. 'It says, goodness, courage . . . big zero.' He was holding the blinds open with two fingers, craning his neck to look out.

Madeline's mouth twisted as she pressed her lips together with a tiny shake of her dark head. 'That's not what I sense in you, Flynn. Not what I hear. What I hear is that you're an old hand at this. As you told me, you're not going to go looking for a bullet. You are an experienced professional and understand risk; Erik didn't.'

'It wasn't a calculated decision not to go – *I would have gone*; I got turned back. But I handed him the story; I arranged the transport and I let him go on without me. I said, I said – I think I said – suit yourself . . . And I *knew* – you're right – I *knew* the risks.' The blinds shut with a snap.

Back seated, Flynn was bent over, holding himself. Madeline's knuckles turned white as she gripped the arms of her chair to stop herself moving to him. She had never before felt such a strong desire to comfort a client physically. She ached with his pain and guilt, but she had heard the gaps in his story clearly, and had to help him retrace his steps, back down the via dolorosa, walking beside him, as soon as he felt safe enough to resume the journey.

'How did you feel at the checkpoint, when you parted from Erik?'

133

'That it wasn't a risk worth taking.' Flynn's eyes turned mean and angry. 'But I've had it up to the gills with editors who say, *no story's worth a life*. They say it all right, but they don't mean it. They like sounding dramatic, but some of those bastards would kill their own reporters with their bare hands, if it would guarantee a story. When you're at the checkpoint, trying to make that decision, and they're nursing a hangover at their desk, tucking into egg sandwiches, you know in their guts they *want* you to go, whatever shite they're made to say. That's one reason I went freelance. I don't want to have to deal with that. Sure, they don't want the responsibility for your death, but they want that story like they want nothing else. And they're right to feel that, whatever effluence they spout. *No story's worth a life*. Fuck. This was a story that had already raked in hundreds of thousands of lives. If it's not worth a life, then it's not worth a leg, or an arm, or a foot, or your fucking sanity. It's not even worth your time. Of *course* it's worth a life.

'You look at how we live here, under the thumb of the safety brigade: locks on windows, child-proofed in case the little devils try to hurl themselves to their deaths; not being allowed to stand on the open platform of a bus. And so the likes of Erik go trooping off to blackest Africa – to the sodding heart of darkness my *arse* – to find out what they're made of, bone and gristle or *pulp*, because they want to know how they are going to deal with it. It's bloody hard here in England to take responsibility for your own life . . .' Flynn's gaze scanned the room, the calm, white order of it, the pot plant on the near-empty bookcase, the regimental order of Madeline's almost bare desk, his eyes finally settling on Madeline's pale face.

Madeline's chin lifted. *So many unseen dangers lurking round corners; such fragility, for all of us, children most of all . . . She could hear Patrick's gruff voice in her ear. Nothing lasts for ever, Maddie, not the good and not the bad . . . But why did Flynn need to seek out more and more risk? Why was he so hungry for responsibility? It was Flynn, not Erik, who was motivated by wanting to know how he was going to deal with it, whether he'd pass the test. Again and again. As he'd said, he barely knew Erik. That was why Flynn had chosen this life, the reason why he spurned any suggestion of heroic or noble motive. He was driven to test himself again and again because he did not believe he deserved to pass. And this time he had failed.*

Flynn continued to tick off society's restrictions on his fingers. 'You can't smoke, you can't drink, you can't move without somebody checking the ground under your feet . . . At least when I'm working I'm free to make my own decisions. In some way I must have wanted Erik to share what I saw and feel the way I feel. I led him there.'

'What did you want him to share?'

'The freedom, the thrill of it; the proof that you can get through. Christ.'

'You tried to stop him.'

'Oh yes, I tried to stop him,' Flynn said with heavy sarcasm, 'but inside I willed him to go through, just like the editors do. Because I couldn't. And if I had . . .'

'What would have happened if you had?'

'Maybe I'd have died, too, but it would have been better than this.'

'Why would it have been better than this?'

Flynn was on his feet. 'Will you stop repeating what I say, for the love of Jesus?' he shouted. 'Tell me what you *think*. Tell me I'm a prize arse, a piece of cowardly shite, but don't parrot my words back at me! You know nothing about it. You don't know what it's like being in a place like that.'

'You're right. I don't. Tell me what it's like.'

Flynn held one hand over his eyes. 'It tires you to the bone. I'm still tired six years later.'

'Can you tell me how you felt as you walked back to Kigali? What was it – three miles? At night?'

'I didn't walk. I drove.'

'How did you get a car?'

Flynn blinked several times. 'I told you.' He spoke very slowly, very patiently, as if talking to a particularly slow-witted child. 'I'd got hold of a UNAMIR Land-Rover.'

'Yes, you did say that. And you drove it back to Kigali?' *Erik had taken the Land-Rover.*

'Yes.'

'From the checkpoint, after you left Erik?'

'Yes, goddamn it!'

'How did you feel driving back?' Madeline felt her capacities expand as his orderly narrative began to fall apart; her compassion, her detective intuition; her empathy; her curiosity. Flynn hadn't been lying before; Flynn simply did not know the truth. He could not locate the right memory file.

Flynn grunted. 'I was just fucked off they hadn't let me through. I was angry. I should have tried to bypass the road block, approach from the other side, but I didn't want to get lost in the dark and I was sure there'd be other blocks up. I didn't even try. I drove back thinking about a girl, not just any girl, trying to think of the perfect girl. Maybe a girl like you.' Madeline grew increasingly uncomfortable under his bleak scrutiny. 'I didn't think about Rwanda. I didn't want to think about who else I was going to come across before I made it back to the hotel. I tried to imagine the perfect girl, the perfect line of poetry, the perfect image, the perfect photograph, the perfect bit of Bach. Most of all, the perfect girl. I didn't think about Erik.'

'When did you learn what had happened to him?'

'The next morning. From another journo.'

'Do you remember how they told you? What they said?'

'Yep. The guy was white as paper, shaking like a leaf. He

said, "Flynn, you know that Dutchman you were hanging around with? He's dead."'

'How did you feel?'

His hooded grey eyes turned on her without emotion. 'How did I feel?'

'Yes.'

'I felt nothing. I wasn't surprised. Like I told you, death was all he had coming to him. Do you want to know about death, Madeline? Do you want to know what it looks like?'

The sensors on Madeline's skin rose, set it tingling, her heart pounding. *He wants to scare me off the trail,* she thought, *to scare me off because he can't afford my compassion. He wants to keep his guilt. He is so deeply attached to it.*

'I want to know how it looks to you,' she replied levelly.

'It's curious.' Flynn's voice dipped to a soft lament. 'Sometimes death gives something extra. I've seen girls look far more beautiful dead than they were alive. Sometimes it erases everything. I saw a kid in Bosnia who'd been battered to death with a rifle butt. When his mother picked him up, you could see that every bone in his face had been smashed. The skin round his skull was the only thing holding it together. His head rattled and flopped about on his neck like a deflated football, just a smash of bones wrapped up in skin . . .' He stopped abruptly, searching her face. 'Are you getting off on this? Do you give a shit – or is all this like sitting down in your front room to watch a horror film? Why trauma when you could be listening to old farts nursing their Oedipal complexes?'

'You'd be surprised how interesting some of those Oedipal old farts are.'

His appreciative smile broke the exhausted set of his face.

Again he was challenging her, again turning the tables and kicking the whole board over like a child that knows he's losing the game. Madeline could feel her skin turning clammy as she struggled to find clear air. 'Go back to Erik. Back to the checkpoint. Tell me how it feels when you're under real threat.'

'I told you, checkpoints are normally OK. There are rules. It's when you're out in the open, crouching in the bushes with piss running down your legs and into your boots, that's when you're witless with fear. You freeze for a second – who're you going to be, if they bother to ask you, or give you a chance to tell them? In most places there isn't a safe answer. You don't want to be French, you don't want to be British, and Christ knows you don't want to be American . . . You don't want to be press, you don't want to be military, you don't even want to be an aid worker . . . You don't want to be white and you can't afford to be black . . . That's when you feel things go wrong.'

'So what are you, Flynn? In that situation?'

'Invisible,' he said dryly. 'Like I said, I try to take myself back to school. Be a grey man; an accidental bystander. That way smart kids have of looking when they know they're in trouble. Keep your eyes down, your expression blank and pray to God you can shuffle away.'

'Is that how you felt leaving the checkpoint on the road to Gitarama?'

'No. I was too angry. And the soldiers were clowns. The last tattered remnants of FAR, the government army, waving their RPGs around like they were off to a fancy-dress party . . .'

'So you turned back . . .'

'Damn right I did. You'd turn back too if you'd the barrel of an AK47 four inches deep in your gut. And they'd taken my cameras; there wasn't much I could do without them. There wasn't a whole lot of purpose in arguing.'

He'd said that the lead he was following, the refugee family, wasn't his sort of story; wasn't a photo opportunity. So why were the cameras a factor? 'Did you care about losing your cameras?'

Flynn grinned. 'I've had so many cameras taken away from me I can barely get insurance. I was more pissed off by losing my wallet and wasting time chit-chatting to the bastards. And I didn't fancy having to walk three miles back in the dark not knowing how many members of the Interhamwe I was going to bump into.'

Madeline frowned. His tone had again shifted into flippant reflection. The moment of terror at the checkpoint had become no more than a waste of time and the vehicle had disappeared again . . . 'Excuse me, Flynn; I'm confused. Did you return to Kigali on foot or in the Land-Rover?'

Flynn stiffened. 'Erik took the Land-Rover. Maybe I got a lift with one of the soldiers. I don't remember. Maybe I walked.'

'It would have been a very long and difficult walk, wouldn't it?' Flynn shrugged. 'What concerned you about losing your wallet? Was it the money?'

'I was glad they took the money. I wanted them to have the money. They might have killed me if they hadn't found any.'

'So was it credit cards? Photographs? What?'

'I don't keep real photos in that wallet. I don't ever take real photos with me on assignment. I have some dummies.'

'Why?'

A smile flickered across his face. 'I had a real mean bitch of a picture editor once, when I was starting out. A gorgeous girl, but cold as an iceberg and twice as deadly. I carry round photos of her.'

'Explain.'

'It's a trick a veteran newsman taught me. If you get taken hostage, the first thing they look for is personal photos, so they've got something to hold over you. You know, they can hold the picture up and say, do you ever want to see your wife again? Well, if they hold up pictures of Stella, it wouldn't bother me one iota if I never laid eyes on the bitch.'

Madeline smiled. 'Have you ever been taken hostage?'

'No. But I like to be prepared.'

'But you *were* annoyed they'd taken your wallet?'

'Yes, it's the principle of the thing. You've got to hold

onto your self-respect somehow; you can't bend over and meekly present your arse. Though in their shoes, I'd probably do the same thing, and in mine, they'd feel annoyed, too. That's human nature.' Flynn sat still, his arms folded across his chest.

She was struck by his implied identification with the perpetrators. 'When you heard that Erik had been killed, were you able to put yourself in their shoes, to identify with them?'

Flynn looked stubborn. 'The soldiers at that roadblock weren't the ones who killed Erik.'

'Do you know that for certain?'

'Yes.'

'How do you know that?'

His shoulders rose marginally. 'I just do. Someone must have told me. They weren't FAR.'

'How did you feel about the people who had killed your friend?'

'I wanted to kill them,' Flynn said simply.

'Did you go to the place where Erik had been killed, after you'd heard what had happened?'

Flynn looked away over his right shoulder. Madeline could see his face working in profile, his brows drawing in to create a furrow. He swallowed several times before answering her. 'No. No . . . Yes, I think I did. I don't remember going, but I must have, because I see it all the time.'

'What do you see?'

'Where he was, the way he looked. I see a clearing, just off the road. I hear him calling . . . I can't do anything to help.' His words were thickening, his speech slurring as if he were slightly drunk. The muscle in his left cheek began to twitch.

'When do you see this, Flynn?'

'When I think about him. When I'm asleep. It's a dream I sometimes have. When I'm awake I try not to think about it.'

'But you dream about it?'

'Not like a normal dream. More like a scene in a film I've watched a lot. A movie in my head.'

'Do you have these dreams often?'

'It's not "these" dreams. Just the one.'

The mere reference to the dream had triggered physical sensations over which Flynn had no control. Beads of sweat had broken out on his forehead. Madeline was tempted to overrun the session and ask him to relate the dream, but she was wary of the force of his reaction and did not want to enter this new zone without having sufficient time to allow him to recover. She felt confused. He had narrated the circumstances that led to Erik's death with an air of rehearsed detachment, had trotted through the logical legitimacy of his anger and fear as if emotionally anaesthetised, and offered self-justifying factors only to dismantle them without any signs of physical distress, yet the merest suggestion of what he had seen the following day and how it had haunted his dreams had dulled the drug and left him raw. His eyes were narrowed, his breathing had become shallow and the tendons in his neck stood taut. 'Flynn,' Madeline asked softly, probing like a surgeon with a scalpel, 'do you have this dream about Erik often?'

He seemed unable to answer; his teeth were clenched, the muscle pulsing more quickly above his jawbone. 'No.' The contradiction came immediately in a groan of pain: '*Yes*. When I came back from Rwanda, yes, I dreamt about Erik a lot. Working made the dream go away. Somehow, now, I don't know why, it's started coming back.'

'Frequently?'

'Once or twice a week since Astra Four. More often, the past month or so. Since I started seeing you.'

'We need to stop in a few minutes. I'd like to come back to this dream the next time we meet.'

Flynn's face slackened with relief. 'So, Madeline, tell me: are we making any progress, you and me?'

His question took her by surprise. She had stopped herself

asking what was known in the trade as a 'doorknob' question, one that opened new territory when there wasn't time to cover it, when the client's hand was virtually on the door. Now he'd turned the tables on her. She had never had a client ask that question so early in therapy, certainly never after such a heightened moment, and never at the end of a session.

'Yes,' Madeline replied carefully, 'I think we are making progress, moving steadily . . . What do you think?'

'I think a rocking horse moves steadily,' he stood up, shrugging one arm into his leather jacket, 'but that doesn't mean it's going anywhere.'

TEN

'It's stupid not to use Ed. He wants the work. You trust him.'

'Don't start at me, Madeline. I'm worn out.'

He looked it. He looked old. The sheer physical effort involved in the preliminary shaping of the marble block drained Patrick of his surplus energy but it also emptied him creatively. Increasingly he had relied on his assistant Ed to take on the hard grind of preparatory work, but he was too proprietary about this piece to share the burden. Although Madeline generally empathised with his absorption, indeed envied how purely and single-mindedly focused he could be on one sole creative effort, at that moment she resented it. She found herself preoccupied by Flynn, who belonged in the sanctuary of her therapy room, not in her living room. She didn't have the energy to mother Patrick, and would have liked to have been alone thinking about the living, rather than a dead cardinal. She laid her hand over Patrick's roughened one.

'So. How's Basil?'

'Bloody hard work, mean old bugger. I'm not near him; still taking the planes off the block.'

Which only made her think about Flynn again. 'That's precisely what Ed should be doing.'

'I'm not such an old crock that I can't handle a power tool.' Patrick groaned, his joints aching. 'Or maybe I am.'

'Why have Ed at all if you won't use him? You've said before that planing takes your focus off the real work.' Patrick pulled his hand away from hers. 'Fine. If you want to break your back, go ahead. Just don't whinge to me about it.'

Patrick stomped heavily out of the room. Moments later Madeline heard the shower running.

Sod it, she thought. She wasn't angry with Patrick. So who am I angry with?, she asked herself in the gloom of the living room, lit only by the moon's full beam and the reflected light from the north side of the Thames bouncing off the water. She could not escape the tight, constricted feeling in her chest, the surge of debilitating panic that struck her whenever she thought of Flynn. She knew Flynn was shackled by over-powering anger and fear, knew the guilt he bore for leaving Erik at the checkpoint. Flynn was now struggling to live within a diminished life. In his company she had felt her perception dim and fade. His memory was wreathed in a permanent fog of confusion, the intermingling of right and wrong, action and inaction, desire and dread, to the point where he did not know what had happened on the road to Gitarama; he did not even know if he had driven the Land-Rover back to Kigali.

Again she returned to the moment Flynn had kissed her. He had kissed her to provoke a connection, to trample roughshod on both her professional and personal boundaries: but why? Because he was ashamed that he had allowed himself to be turned back at a very tangible boundary – the road block on the way to Gitarama? Because, feeling under the power of others – herself, the soldiers at the road block – he had had to believe he could wrench back control? Because, by making her reel with vulnerability, he could distance himself from his own? Madeline considered all these angles, but she did not know why she felt as she did. She did not know why

144

she felt so depleted and she did not know if she could muster the strength to help him as he needed.

She wanted Flynn there in the comforting, ambiguous darkness, sitting beside her. She wanted to hear his voice and she wanted to talk to him, to tell him how *she* felt, in the conviction that he would understand her, and, with one long arm thrown across her shoulders, he would dismiss the darkness and make her laugh again . . . Had there been no professional connection between them, she could imagine their sitting up all night, drinking red wine, talking until the cafés opened for breakfast. She could not resist the fantasy in private. What if they'd never met on *Nepenthe*, if he'd never approached her as a therapist, but they had met at a party, been introduced by Patrick – not Patrick, by Michael, perhaps, Michael had a broad circle of friends – who was to say what might have developed between them? What if she had been able to welcome his kiss and respond to it, admit that she was strongly attracted to him . . . How many nights might have been filled until those cafés opened?

One indulgence in fantasy, one stolen treat . . . With a sense of shame at how readily she had drifted down the path of illicit sexual fantasy, Madeline slammed down the lid of the chocolate box. Clients often fell in love in therapy; it was understandable, sharing such intense, high-level intimacy with another soul, and nothing, no external intrusion – not so much as a telephone ring – to interrupt it. Madeline had been powerfully attracted to countless clients, women as well as men, knowing it had nothing to do with 'normal' relationships. She did not know Flynn as a man, not as she knew Patrick, and she never would. She *did* know that if it was, well, perhaps unfortunate that she was sexually attracted to this client, as she had not been to others, it was not a problem so long as she remained vigilant and did not let desire distort her professional filter.

The guilt she felt was manageable, too. Like Flynn's, her own sense of guilt could be turned to positive advantage: it was a sign of her psyche trying to draw a useful lesson from potential disaster, trying to find a place to register the experience and file it away for future reference, to recover a sense of self-control. Madeline was good at managing her memory files: they were dense and complicated and she worked ceaselessly to keep them in order.

It was improper for a supervisor to attempt to set the agenda, but Jillian felt impatient, a sense of discomfort that she drew from Madeline. For the best part of an hour the younger woman had recounted what had occurred in her sessions with the photographer; they had discussed the inconsistencies in his story and behaviour without Jillian having any grasp on Madeline's personal response. She shifted in her chair. Aware that time was limited and also that she would not see her for several weeks, Jillian repeated her original question with greater emphasis.

'Madeline, how are you *personally* finding these sessions?'

'Difficult.' Madeline tossed her hair back as if it annoyed her. 'He unsettles many things I thought I'd resolved. Doubts about my work, why I'm doing it. Concerns about family and personal relationships – what I feel about Patrick . . . Mainly work. He gets too close.'

'Physically too close?'

'Well . . . maybe, a bit, yes . . .' Madeline edged along the sofa, trying to get comfortable. 'But that's not it. I feel he's invading me. I don't know if I can deal with that feeling.'

Under threat, Madeline had thrown up her own defensive shield. Her face turned towards the window; the light glinted against the small opal dangling from her right ear.

'He implied that I'm getting some sort of voyeuristic kick out of trauma work. Maybe I do get a kick out of it.'

'So you should,' Jillian asserted. 'I'm sure he gets a kick out of his work, too. Both your professions risk the charge of

146

voyeurism – and risk vicarious traumatisation. But everybody should get a kick out of a job well done.'

'And how should they feel about a job done badly?'

'Do you feel your work with F.B. is going badly?'

'No. It's been all uphill for the past month, but he's beginning to feel safe. Safer. He's talking about Rwanda.'

'Is it difficult to hear?'

'No. But I'm confused by my reaction to his grief, the sense that he desperately needs . . .' Madeline leant forward, her shoulders hunched. 'I wanted to lay my hand on his cheek, touch his hair; anything to let him know that I was there.'

'He knows you're there.'

Madeline gave a tiny shrug. 'I don't know if I'm enough.' Jillian studied her intelligent, searching face as Madeline struggled to find the words. 'Why him? What is it about him that makes me want to protect him so much? Why should I want to touch him, more than any other client?'

'Have you touched him?'

'Of course not. But why do I want to? I'm attracted to him, I'm not bothered by that, but this was something else, not exactly sexual . . . but not strictly therapeutic either,' Madeline admitted. 'I wanted to take his pain away quickly,' she snapped her fingers, 'just like that.'

Jillian sat listening, her hands folded in her lap, waiting, with some degree of impatience, for Madeline to voice what was quite evident to her: this client, more than any other, was hauling Madeline unconsciously into her own past and feelings, and her heart ached for him as it did for herself. She knew it was her job as supervisor to lead Madeline consciously into those feelings. At the same time she had to safeguard the interests of the client; self-doubt might, she considered, turn out to be a positive state for Madeline, in that it might stretch her as a therapist, but it was of no use at all to him. Madeline looked utterly wretched. Her pallor and the strain evident on her face concerned Jillian greatly. More so when Madeline

147

added, almost as an afterthought, 'I've been thinking about referring him to someone else.'

Madeline had never suggested referring any of her clients before. Jillian became conscious of the burning pain in her hip and felt irritated by the frailty that old age was rudely foisting upon her. And as she did so, she pulled herself up sharp. Madeline's loss of self-confidence was infectious.

'I'm struggling with it,' Madeline continued. 'Early on he asked me what would happen if I just got fed up and ended it. I don't want to confirm his fears, but I have to be certain that I'm the right person to take him through this – for his sake. Not my own.'

'*Do* you feel fed up, and want to end it?'

'No,' Madeline said, her face wonderfully stern in the certainty of her statement, 'absolutely not.' She looked past Jillian through the window and out to the open fields beyond. She seemed lost in a reverie for a moment or two, then turned back with a frown. 'He feels he abandoned Erik; he fears abandonment, and, knowing that, I am determined not to let him down. But is that itself more dangerous for him?'

Is your desire to be omnipotent more dangerous for you than anything else? Jillian asked silently, but only said, 'You need to think very carefully about this.' *As I do*, she thought, *as I do*. Jillian could not sanction therapeutic abuse by not intervening, but she trusted Madeline instinctively, with her whole heart. She tried to find a way to caution her without undermining her further. 'You may want to think back through the rules of the therapeutic engagement. There are rules you cannot go beyond, which are there for your protection as well as his, as you know well. I do not, at this stage, know whether those rules are in jeopardy.' Her heart flooded with compassion for the struggling woman opposite her, and she reached for the right words and direction. 'I have never for a moment doubted your integrity; but integrity isn't about omnipotence, Madeline; your strength has always lain in your capacity to trust, to trust yourself as well as others. If you feel that has been injured, or blocked in some way, that could be dangerous for you as well as for him. Only you can answer that question.'

'I'll think about that. Thank you, Jillian,' Madeline said simply. She unfolded herself from the sofa and smiled. 'Is the same time next week good for you?'

Jillian pushed herself to her feet with a slight wince. 'I should have mentioned this earlier, but I'm afraid I won't be around for the next two to three weeks.'

'Are you going somewhere nice?'

'If only. I have to have an operation on my hip, very minor, quite routine.' Jillian rubbed her left hip ruefully. 'Too much gardening, I expect.' She saw the flicker of concern in the younger woman's eyes.

'Then I'll bring flowers,' Madeline said quickly. 'You need to tell me where and when, Jillian. It matters to me.'

Madeline stood at her office window, looking out over Clerkenwell Road. It was half-past five on a late October afternoon, but there was no sign of Flynn. She sat down at her desk, switched the phone back on and used the unexpected free time to scan through her e-mails. Most were routine, a request from an A&E conference organiser asking her to submit an outline of her introductory lecture on post-traumatic care, one from Jack Zabinsky about their last combat veterans' group meeting in his regular stream-of-consciousness style, post-scripted, as they always were, with a flirtatious invitation to dinner . . . another message from her mother Rachel, asking if Madeline could be persuaded to snatch a few days in the Florida sunshine. Her attention was momentarily distracted by the sound of a car back-firing in the street outside and a dog barking nervously in response. She dimly heard the repetitive, reluctant rrnn-rrnn-rrnn of a car engine trying to choke into life. Madeline dialled her mother's Florida number.

'Morning, Mum.'

149

'Darling! What's wrong?' The instant delight in Rachel Light's voice was at once replaced with anxiety.

'Nothing's wrong, everything's fine. Do I never call you unless something's wrong?' Madeline held the phone in the crook of her neck as she typed a short reply to Jack.

'Not often,' Rachel replied matter-of-factly. 'Certainly not on a weekday afternoon.'

'That makes me sound terrible . . . like a foul-weather daughter. The truth is I've been stood up by a client, Patrick's obsessed with his current commission, I'm feeling miserable, and, most of all, I'm missing you . . .' Her voice caught and cracked.

'*Darling* . . . you need to get away from your office. Call a friend. Go see a movie. Make Patrick take you to Paris – at least take you dancing for a night.'

'Yeah, you're right. That *is* what I need to do.' Madeline tapped a pencil against the edge of her desk, thinking, *but Patrick doesn't want to go dancing, and I don't know who to call.* Most of her old girlfriends had either given up on her after she'd cancelled a date for the fifth time in a row – due to work, always due to work – or were too absorbed in their own family lives. 'But really I just want to see you.'

'Does that mean you'll pop over? Just for a bit? Maybe for Christmas?'

'I'd like to, Mum, but I'm not sure St Pete Beach is Patrick's sort of place.'

'Rubbish!' Madeline smiled at her mother's snort of indignation. 'There's a world-class art gallery here – the biggest collection of Picasso in the world. Or is it Dali? I don't know. Who cares? Just come.'

'I'll tell him.'

'I'll phone him and tell him myself.'

'You do that; just get your facts straight. How's Patricia?'

Rachel sighed. 'You know, up and down. Some nights she

gets out her condolence letters and reads them all over again. It's nearly two years since Jim died.'

'It takes time, Mum, lots of time . . . I'm sure it helps having you there.'

'I hope so.'

'Maybe I *will* come out at Christmas. Get my bikini out of cold storage; I could use a week lounging on the beach. And I'd love to see Patricia. I haven't seen her since Jim's funeral.'

'She'd adore it. She always says your letter was the biggest comfort of all.'

Madeline rubbed her eyes with her free hand. She couldn't stand to hear her mother's proud, loving tone any longer. 'OK, Mum, I'll try, I promise. I've got to go – my client's arrived, but I'll call soon about Christmas, OK?'

'I love you, darling . . .'

'As I love you. Give Patricia a big hug from me . . . tell her to send me an e-mail sometime.'

It was six o'clock, but there was no sign of Flynn. It was far from the first time that a client had failed to turn up for a scheduled appointment, and generally Madeline waited to see if they would appear on the following session and how they explained the no-show. Perhaps he was fed up with riding the rocking horse and had simply decided not to come any more. She ignored the instant punch of loss that this possibility provoked and dialled his number. The phone was answered by a breathless female voice.

'Hello. Could I speak to Flynn Brennan?'

'I'm afraid he's not here. Can I take a message?'

Madeline hesitated. 'My name is Madeline Light. I wonder if you could ask him to call me when he has a moment?'

For a few seconds there was silence on the other end of the line. Madeline could almost hear the other woman's brain working.

'Madeline Light? As in Dr Light?'

'Yes, that's right.'

151

'Flynn's therapist?'

'Yes. Could you ask him to give me a call?'

'This is his wife, Dr Light. Georgia. I, uh . . .' Madeline heard a nervous laugh. 'It's good to hear you. Good to know you actually exist! You are a *real* therapist, aren't you?'

'Yes, I am.'

'Sorry. I must sound a total twit.' Georgia's voice lowered conspiratorially. 'I'm relieved, that's all. Just a bit surprised. Flynn never said you were a woman. In my mind's eye I'd pictured an old man with wire-rimmed glasses and a beard.'

'That's all right. Could you –'

'I'm so glad he's coming to see you, getting help. And I'm glad to have a chance for a private word, actually. I want you to know I *really* support his having therapy, I'm right behind it all the way. If there's anything I can do . . .'

'Mrs Brennan, if you'd be good enough to just pass on the message.'

'Of course I will, but I thought he was with you. He left at – oh, about four? Said he was going to see his therapist.'

'Perhaps he was held up. Just let him know I called.'

'Do you think he's OK?'

Madeline heard the concern in Georgia's voice, and it flashed through her mind that most, if not all of Georgia's married life must have been spent in a state of fear for her husband's safety. She withdrew as gently as she could. 'I'm sure he was simply delayed.'

'But do you think he's OK, in himself?'

'Believe me I understand your concern, Mrs Brennan, but I'm unable to discuss a client with a third party.'

'Third party? I *am* his *wife*.' There was a slight pause before Georgia said flatly, 'It isn't easy for any of us you know. The children, me . . . it affects all of us.'

'I understand,' Madeline repeated in a softer voice. 'If you feel it would help, I can willingly give you a number to call for counselling, though obviously I can't see you myself.'

152

'OK,' Georgia replied. 'I'll think about that. I'll let Flynn know you called.'

While sympathetic to Georgia's feelings, Madeline was glad to get her off the phone. Anything Georgia said would reveal nothing about Flynn, but a great deal about his wife, and that information might taint Madeline's judgement.

She was still reluctant to leave her room and go home. She began to type the introduction to the lecture she was due to give to an assembly of A&E staff:

'The typical reaction to a life-threatening experience is a mixture of distress, anxiety and fear, and is characteristic of the basic survival instinct. These emotions enhance an individual's memory of the traumatic incident, and so help in the recognition and avoidance of similarly dangerous situations in the future. However, in a significant minority of individuals, this natural reaction to trauma becomes uncontrollably and disastrously intensified, resulting in the disorder, PTSD. Its symptoms are diverse; a complex mixture of psychological and physiological processes are involved . . .'

Was Flynn OK in himself? No; he wasn't OK in himself. Poor Georgia, to be sitting at home waiting for such a long time, not knowing where he was or when he'd come home. Madeline felt her heart leap as she began to type faster.

'Lethal threat has a powerful impact on body chemistry. To understand the physiology of mammalian arousal during stress is to begin mobilising the mind in pursuit of recovery. PTSD sufferers are likely to have two alternate behavioural responses to those they encounter: to overreact and intimidate, or to shut down and freeze.'

When Madeline later pulled the front door of the building closed and locked it, she paused to look around, half-expecting to see Flynn loitering in a doorway. He was not there.

Two hours earlier, Flynn had been parked opposite her office with the engine running. He had seen Madeline standing at

153

the window, and for a second felt he could catch the scent of her on the late afternoon air. It had lifted the hairs on the back of his neck. When she had moved out of sight he turned off the ignition, searching for the courage to go into her room and face her. *None but the brave*, he thought, *none but the brave, none but the brave deserve the fair* . . . He could not muster the courage he needed. His hand was back on the key ready to drive home when there was an explosion somewhere on the street behind him. The sudden report had him instantly flinging his arms over his head and smashing his forehead against the steering wheel. For several minutes he cowered, frozen, feeling the blood trickling down his face and tasting it, thick and salty at the corner of his mouth. Eyes shut tight, he heard the sound of wailing, screams of fear rising and falling and someone calling his name; then loud, disconnected yelling, the frenzy of dogs barking. All the dogs of London were howling, but no one else seemed to hear them. Slowly he pulled himself upright. Who have I become, he asked himself, trembling in the stationary car. *What* have I become? A man who leaps out of his skin when a child's party popper goes off? Dies of fright in a summer thunderstorm, and nearly pisses himself when a door slams? Overcome with whinnying, snickering panic when a car backfires in an ordinary London street?

Wiping the blood off his face with his sleeve, Flynn tried to start the car, barely able to grasp the key. The engine spluttered and choked. Three times he tried, saying *steady, steady* to himself, knowing he was flooding the battery, knowing it wasn't ever going to start again, feeling sweat – or blood – trickling down the back of his neck and seeping forward, round his collarbone and pooling over his chest. *Steady, steady*, he muttered in a growl. He ripped the key out of the ignition, flung open the door and booted it shut behind him, then strode down the street with his hands thrust deep in his pockets and his shoulders hunched.

He did not want to talk about Rwanda to Madeline. He did

not want to talk about Rwanda to anyone. He could feel the truth of it sitting in his mouth, sour and corrosive. It was *his* war, and he was jealous and possessive about it. Damn well *his* war. And his dreams were part of it, and he wasn't going to share it, wasn't going to talk about his dreams either, not to her, however fine and strong she was. He walked quickly, in a state of vigilance, glancing over his shoulder and all around him, scanning the people heading for home, ready to swing at anyone who so much as looked at him. Swing at them? He could have shot them all, the smartly suited men on their way home from work, the bored shopkeepers pulling down their security grilles. Against what – robbery? The theft of a bunch of bananas and the odd bottle of gin? What would they say about Rwanda? A few desultory shakes of the head, the assumption of a deeply troubled, *deeply* compassionate expression – *ah yes; terrible, that, wasn't it, simply dreadful. So many innocent people brutally butchered. Apparently it's all ethnic, you know? Thank God it's not like that here . . .*

Bastards. He could have mown them all down with an automatic machine gun, blasted them to hell with an RPG, right there on Clerkenwell Road. And his own kind, the print journalists who thought the war still belonged to them. *Their* war? It was like when he was a boy following Ipswich. Some bastards who'd watched with him had switched sides when their team got kicked out of the Cup and now got all worked up about somebody else's team. *His* team. It made him want to shout – but they're *my* bloody team. I'm the real supporter, not you. I wouldn't abandon them when they started to lose; with them for ever, I am. He could feel proprietary about anything, even a disease: *my* dad had cancer; I know all about *cancer*, watched him die of it. You can't tell me anything about cancer.

Flynn stopped and stood with his back to a pub wall, trying to steady his heartbeat. A bustling, middle-aged woman halted three yards away from him with a concerned expression on her face. She seemed about to address him but then walked

155

hurriedly away, staring fixedly at the pavement. It made Flynn grin. You're all right, dear, get on with your life. Don't go looking for trouble where you're not wanted. But everyone was looking at him. He could feel their eyes: cold; judgemental; recriminatory. Why didn't they have the guts to come out with it and ask him straight up? Just ask him why he'd let Erik go to his death and done nothing to stop it? And seeing as he'd done nothing to stop it then, why couldn't he shut up now and carry on, white-knuckled maybe, but just carry on? Why did his head keep banging on asking him why? What wouldn't he give to swap a large part of his brain for an ounce more backbone, a thicker spinal cord, which was all that was needed when you came right down to it . . .

He went into the empty pub and ordered a double Scotch.

'Been in a fight, mate? I hope the other bloke looks worse than you.'

Flynn stared at the bartender aggressively.

'Suit yourself.' The man shoved the glass towards him. 'I couldn't give a monkey's, so long as you don't put off the punters.'

Flynn set his glass down at a secluded corner table and went to the Gents. Glancing in the mirror, he prodded the shallow three-inch gash above his eyebrow with a finger, splashed his face with cold water and shook his head like a dog. Drops of water beaded his face and hair as he stared at his reflection. Who am I? What have I become?

Sitting back at the table, Flynn felt fear screaming up behind him, the paralysing fear one feels on catching sight in the rear-view mirror of an oncoming car travelling far too fast. He was helpless to halt it and had no time to get out of the way. He simply saw it coming, an instant-impact crush of fear that made his heart stop. In the flash before collision he thought calmly and quietly: I am going mad. That's it. I am simply going mad. That's all it is. I am sitting here in a soulless, empty pub somewhere between Islington and Clerkenwell, going mad. It is not my war. It was not my war. I am not in Africa. I am not in a Land-Rover. I am not in danger. I never was. I do not deserve to feel frightened. *Bang* – the fear slammed back into him from behind.

Four teenagers came into the pub, the three young men vying with each other to impress a doe-eyed girl as skinny as a toothpick. Flynn carried a second double Scotch back to his corner and stared into the glass before drinking urgently, using the whisky like a blunt instrument. Ah Nepenthe, he thought, the mythical opiate that cured grief and heartbreak. Come find me, Nepenthe, come have a drink with me and rescue me. Don't leave me here all on my own. That's what he called Madeline in the privacy of his heart: Nepenthe. Nepenthe.

ELEVEN

'Darling?' Georgia's voice called from the kitchen when he arrived home at eight o'clock. 'I didn't hear the car . . . *Jesus Christ!* What happened to your head?'

Flynn fingered his temple. 'That? I had engine trouble. Went to look under the bonnet and cracked myself on the head. It's nothing. A graze.' He bent to kiss Oliver and Beth as they sat at the kitchen table staring at him. 'I had to leave the car. I guess auto-mechanics isn't my strongest suit.'

Georgia didn't comment. Several times, coming back from assignments, Flynn had described how he'd had to climb under an utterly trashed jeep or truck and nurse it back to life because nobody else was capable. Georgia looked at him as he perched on a high stool between the children. There was something incredibly male about him, the gash on his forehead, the well lived-in face, his lean, muscular thighs straining tight against his jeans. She looked away, limp with desire.

'So, fruit of my loins, how did your days go? Don't give me any of the bad stuff: I only want to hear good news.'

'That'll be a short conversation.'

'You clearly managed to drag yourself out of bed and get to school on time. That's a triumph in my book.' Beth bore his teasing sullenly. 'Uh-ho; do I detect that "life's so serious" expression?'

'It isn't *all* one big joke, Dad.' Beth's hair swung down over her face in a curtain.

Georgia mouthed at Flynn, gesturing as if she were playing charades, then drew one finger slowly across her throat.

Olly looked from his father to his mother and back again. 'Mum's trying to tell you they put up the cast list for *Romeo and Juliet*. Martin Garfield's Romeo, the big poof, but Beth only got the nanny.'

Beth gave her brother a lingering and poisonous look.

'The nurse? But the nurse is a far better role than Juliet,' Flynn assured his daughter.

'That's just what I said,' agreed Georgia.

'How can you say that?' Beth raised a tear-stained face. 'It's a *horrible* role and I'm not going to do it. I'd rather not be in the play at all. Everybody just laughs at you. And she's fat,' she spat the word with disgust, 'the nurse is *always* fat. Even in *Shakespeare in Love*, she's a dumpy little fatso.'

'That's probably why they chose you.'

'That's enough, Oliver!' Flynn barked as Beth's fork flew past him heading for her brother. 'Beth. If you really want to act, the nurse is a much more demanding role to cut your teeth on. You should be flattered. Your teacher must think you've the talent to pull it off.'

'No she doesn't!' Beth shouted as her chair scraped along the tiled floor. 'She thinks I'm fat, that's all – *everyone* does! Because I am!' Beth fled the kitchen, her feet pounding up the stairs and along the corridor above them.

Flynn raised his eyebrows questioningly.

'Don't go,' Georgia advised. 'She's burning up with hurt. Give her a bit of privacy, time to settle herself. D'you want a drink?'

'What do you fancy?'

'A kiss hello for starters.' The accommodation of her wish provoked groans of disgust from their son and a remembrance of contentment in Georgia. She knew how hard he was trying to make everything normal and familial, and she kissed him back with gratitude as well as love. She could taste the Scotch on him. So he hadn't kept his appointment with the therapist, but however he'd spent the past four hours it had restored him to his old self. 'And a gin and tonic would make everything perfect.'

Flynn flicked on the television while he fixed Georgia's drink and poured himself a slug of whisky.

'Can I watch telly, Mum?'

'Have you done your homework?'

'No.'

'Then no, you can't watch telly.'

'But it's easy. It'll only take me ten minutes.'

'What is your homework, Ol?'

'R.E. We have to write one page saying why we believe in the after-life.'

'That's a hefty assignment.'

'But I'm going to say I *don't* believe in it,' Oliver chirruped with a grin. 'Easy-peasy lemon-squeezy.'

'You still have to explain why,' Georgia warned. 'I want to see it before there's any chance of telly.'

When Oliver was safely out of the room, Flynn put his feet up on the kitchen table. 'I can't believe the crap they make these kids do.'

'I don't know . . . it's not such a bad theme.'

'He's not even ten, George. He doesn't need to think about dying.'

It was on the tip of her tongue to ask why, in that case, Flynn encouraged his children to watch grisly news footage over their bangers and mash, but she wanted to wrap Flynn's easy mood in cotton wool.

Stirring the sauce for the chicken and keeping her eyes on the pot, she asked as casually as she could, 'How was your therapy session?'

Flynn turned up the volume on the television. 'Not so good.'

Georgia's teeth tugged at her bottom lip. That's OK, she told herself sternly. It's his business. 'Why was that?'

'Because I didn't go. I played truant.'

'Oh. Really? Why?' Inwardly she didn't care why; she simply thanked God he'd told her the truth.

'I bumped into a mate. Went to the pub. Probably did me much more good.'

Georgia felt a flash of skittish relief. He was right; it had clearly done him good. Maybe that was what he needed, not therapy, but normal engagements with old friends. 'Who was it?' she asked.

Flynn stared fixedly at the TV screen. 'Adrian,' he grunted.

'Adrian?'

'You don't know him. Works for Reuters.'

'Adrian Horwood?' Georgia swung round. 'But of course I know him. He used to be with ITN, didn't he?'

'Maybe. I don't know.'

Georgia resumed her stirring. 'Your therapist called here looking for you.'

'Did she?'

'Yes. She sounded nice.'

'She is nice.'

'It's funny, because somehow I had the idea she was a man.'

'You didn't get that idea from me.'

'No . . .' She remembered the conversation clearly. She had assumed the therapist was male and Flynn had not corrected her. 'It's just funny you didn't mention it.'

'George.' When she turned nervously, picking up on the slight touch of menace in his voice, she saw that Flynn's mouth was twisted into a smile, one eyebrow quirked knowingly. 'Why do you think I didn't tell you?'

'Because you thought I'd be jealous.' She laughed. 'But now

I *know* it's a woman, and that you didn't want me to know that, now I feel *more* jealous.'

'No need. She looks like the back end of a bus.'

'Really?' Georgia's voice fizzed with relief.

'It's not charitable of you to sound so pleased about it.'

Georgia flushed. 'I'm not. It's just funny. She sounded so . . . nice.'

'Well, she can be "nice" and still look like the back end of a bus.'

'You're going to keep going to see her, though, aren't you?'

'If it makes you happy.'

'It does. You know what, darling, why don't you go up and have a soak in the bath – you've got half an hour or so before dinner's ready.'

'That'd be grand. I might just take another dram up with me . . .'

'I could bring mine and join you,' Georgia offered, but Flynn had already left the room.

Maybe it was all going to be all right, Georgia thought. Maybe it was already all right, if she'd just stop looking for trouble. Maybe, if she stopped asking herself whether Flynn loved her, and thought only about him, concentrated on looking after him as well as she could, they'd make it work again. Georgia gripped the edge of the counter, closed her eyes and prayed, ferociously but inarticulately; she could not go beyond *Please God help him, help me, keep us safe . . .* She put a bottle of Sancerre in the fridge, poured herself another G & T and carried it upstairs.

The bathroom was full of steam. Flynn lay back in the bath with his feet resting on top of the taps so that his head was near submerged, the water lapping around his ears. His eyes were closed. Georgia sat on the loo watching him, then, with the smile of someone with a secret too delicious not to share, she stripped off her clothes and wrapped a towel around her. It

162

was several years since they'd shared a bath, even longer since they'd made love in one. He looked so peaceful. Gorgeous. She held her breath as she edged closer on silent feet, letting the towel slip low over one breast. 'Flynn,' she whispered. He could not hear her. She stretched out an arm and gently tugged his big toe. Flynn's eyes flew open, the look in them wild; half the bath water emptied on the floor over Georgia's feet as he rose from the water with a roar in one seamless movement. 'Jesus Christ what the *fuck* are you doing?'

'God . . . God, I'm sorry – I didn't mean . . .' Georgia was frozen by his rage. She shrugged helplessly.

Flynn was panting. His eyes narrowed. 'Don't *ever* do that again. Don't *ever* sneak up on me like that. You nearly gave me a heart attack.' He clapped his hand over his chest. 'I'm not sure you didn't, it's pumping so damn hard. Jesus Christ, woman.' He slumped back down in the water.

'Sorry,' Georgia said in a flat voice. 'I didn't mean to frighten you, I just wanted you to make room.' With her feet in a puddle of water, Georgia clutched the towel more closely around her as Flynn stared at her with a hollow glare.

He snorted heavily then pulled his knees up. 'What are you waiting for, then? If you want a bath, get in.'

Georgia climbed into the bath, her heart racing as fast as his. She sat with her back to him, without speaking, hugging her knees tight, tears trickling silently down her face. After a moment Flynn reached for the soap and began to sponge her shoulders with one hand, the other holding her hair clear. Slowly Georgia relaxed, slowly she leant back against him and his hands moved forward over her breasts. As her head arched back against his chest, the base of her spine was pressed hard against his groin and she could feel his erection. Twisting round in his arms, Georgia kissed his chest with a series of butterfly kisses and gazed at him, her eyes cloudy with need.

Flynn took a long swallow of whisky, feeling panic bubble within him. He desired his wife; there had never been a moment in his life since meeting Georgia when he had not found her beautiful, but he could feel the pull of her dragging him physically away from his thoughts and he was not ready to leave the place where he had been. He loved her. She was beautiful, inviting and warm, yet the thought of making love to her made him feel nauseous. When she had had her back to him he had desired her; now he found the slickness of her hair against his cheek unpleasant, the faint astringent smell of it suddenly distasteful. He pushed her away from him and stood up, grabbing a towel off the rail. 'I'll just check on Ol,' he said in a tone of such apology that Georgia knew he would not return.

'Is it me?' she asked in a small voice.

'No, lovely. I just want to check on the kids.'

It wasn't anything to do with Georgia that night. It was the process, the certain anticipation of the slippery, sticky slickness of sex that made his stomach lurch into his mouth. It made him think of blood.

She stayed in the bath staring at the taps while he rubbed himself dry and pulled on a pair of jeans. His leaving made the level drop and she turned on the tap, wanting the water hot enough to scald.

'How's your essay going?' Flynn lay down on the bed next to his son's outstretched form. 'Has it ever occurred to you, Ol, why we bought that desk over there?'

Oliver chewed his pencil. 'I think better lying down.'

'That's all right then. So tell me about the after-life.'

Oliver rolled onto his back and rested his head on his hands. 'You remember when we went to Granda's funeral?'

'I do.'

'And the vicar –'

'The priest, yes . . .'

'He said it wasn't really goodbye, because all the dead people we love are just waiting for us? And he said the soul was stronger than the body, right?'

'Right.'

'So think about it, Dad.'

Flynn was thinking about it. He was remembering what the priest had said at his father's wake, that the moment of death must be a grand thing, a release from worldly pain and a grandstand ticket into a world of joy. That there would be a veritable quickening of the metaphysical pulse at the very moment of death, a quickening of the pulse in anticipation of meeting those you had loved who had passed on ahead. He remembered the pleasantries of his father's former patients, and the small queue of Irish family, each saying exactly the same words as their turn came: *I'm sorry for your trouble*. Flynn had stopped listening to Oliver. He was thinking about what quickening the anticipation of meeting Erik would have on him. Not his father. Erik.

'Dad? Think about it. People have been on earth for – I don't know – a zillion years? Imagine all those billions and trillions of ghosts. Don't you think, even if lots of them are stupid, there must have been a few who were smart? You know, ghosts like Einstein and Winston Churchill and Pythagoras and James Bond.'

Flynn smiled at the ceiling. 'I agree. There must be some super-smart fellas flying about heaven.'

'Exactly. So doesn't it strike you as odd,' Oliver's eyes gleamed with satisfaction at the power of his own rational deduction, 'that not even *one* of all those brilliant ghosts has been smart enough to find a way of letting the people *on earth* know for a fact that there's life after death? Like Einstein. He discovered everything. You'd think he'd have been able to work out a way to tell us that it's all OK; that when you're done down there, everything's fine here. D'you see what I mean?'

'I do, Ol, but maybe our brains don't work in the same way in heaven as they do on earth. That's the point, maybe: in heaven there's no need, no motivation, to communicate. Maybe the way we'll think is utterly different.'

165

Oliver wagged his finger knowingly. 'But that's not what the priest said. He said the soul was stronger and better than the body, didn't he?'

'Yes.'

'And if there is a God, and he's sitting up there with all the most brilliant ghosts who ever died, you'd think he'd want someone to have a proper conversation with, so he wouldn't take away their brains completely.'

'It sounds like a good essay, Ol.'

'It *is* a good essay. So you know what I think? I don't think there is an after-life. And *so* –' his voice ringing with confidence, he gave a secretive smile and laid his head close to Flynn's – 'I don't believe in God at all.'

Oliver turned his head to look at his father for approval. 'Dad? Dad? It's OK, Dad, I *do* believe in God. I will if you want me to, I'll write something else, I can do it differently if you want . . .'

Georgia was still in the bath, routinely letting warm water out and topping it up with hot, when Oliver's frightened face peeped round the door. 'Mum? Something's wrong with Dad. He's crying.'

Patrick loved the place but to Madeline it seemed incomplete. He'd asked her to accompany him to Westminster Cathedral so that he could take another look at the chapel of St Gregory and St Augustine where Hume's bust was destined to sit in perpetuity. It had been a gesture on Patrick's part, a means of including her in the process, and this effort to draw her into his solitary creative life had touched her. But as soon as they entered the cathedral she felt uncomfortable. It felt at once airy and oddly subterranean. Patrick had told her it was stylistically Byzantine and she had imagined a heavily worked, ornate building, covered with gold. Instead it had a strangely interrupted atmosphere, as if the builders had nipped out on their lunch break and would be back to resume work any minute. Some chapels *had* been elaborately mosaicked, positively dripping with gold, but the mosaics ended abruptly, leaving the dark brick arches of the ceiling naked. The stained glass in the main windows had both the translucence of jelly and the vivid, unnatural colours of sweet papers, but coming in from the mid-morning autumnal sunshine the deep gloom of the cathedral made her feel cold.

Patrick dipped his fingers in holy water and crossed himself. He glanced sideways at Madeline. 'Old habits die hard,' he muttered. 'Come and see the chapel.' They leant over the railings, looking at the cardinal's grave; two fading bunches of flowers stood at his head and his feet. The chapel glittered with decoration in every colour, every marble, every stone on earth, bejewelled with lashings of gold. Patrick sighed heavily. It was clear he did not admire it. Madeline fleetingly touched his cheek.

'Go look at Eric Gill's Stations of the Cross. You'll like them – just walk round and see all fourteen. There you go. Start there.' He pointed to a carving mounted on the wall.

Madeline nodded and moved away from him. She raised her eyes to look at the plaque, read the narrative inscription, 'Jesus fails for the second time', and walked on. A few paces further on, she stopped dead and retraced her steps to read it again. 'Jesus falls for a second time', she read clearly. If that didn't constitute a visionary Freudian slip, she thought grimly, nothing did. The church was gradually filling with people of every description – tramps, a young woman so brilliantly dressed she made Madeline think of a butterfly, businessmen, housewives – all gradually taking their places, some at the back, some at the front, some sitting quietly in side chapels. As Madeline wandered she felt like a spy, or a tourist – a blow-in, as Flynn had described his father – and wondered how many of the casual congregation might share the sentiment.

When the choir began to intone a Latin chant she walked back to the chapel of St Gregory and St Augustine. Patrick was on his knees, his head buried in his hands. Madeline had never seen him pray before. She felt wretched as she watched him. He seemed at home in the inner life of the cathedral in a way that she could never be, and she wondered if she knew him at all. As the rhythmic, rolling murmur of the Mass filled her head she stepped away with a sense of foreboding. She moved to the next-door chapel to wait for him, sat down on the solitary wooden bench at the back and closed her eyes.

When she opened them a middle-aged couple, obviously American, were sitting beside her, holding hands. The woman smiled at her before raising her gaze back to her husband's face. Feeling intrusive, Madeline lowered her eyes. After another five minutes the couple rose, genuflected, nodded pleasantly to Madeline and left the chapel. Madeline continued to watch them surreptitiously, moving to the altar end of the little chapel to keep them in view. At the end of the nave the woman went up on tiptoe and whispered to her companion; he inclined his head and kissed the top of hers. Madeline watched as the woman fell to her knees and began to crawl, inch by inch, down the nave towards the main altar. Nobody else looked at her. Nobody else seemed to find her behaviour strange.

Madeline sat down again at the back of the chapel. The couple had left a sheet of paper on the pew where they had been sitting, covered with graceful, cursive script. Madeline picked it up curiously:

'But it shall come to pass, if thou wilt not hearken unto the voice of the Lord thy God, to observe to do all his commandments and statutes which I command thee this day, that all these curses shall come upon thee and overtake thee . . . The Lord shalt send upon thee cursing, vexation and rebuke, in all that thou settest thy hand unto for to do, until thou be destroyed, and until thou perish quickly; because of the wickedness of thy doings, whereby thou hast forsaken me.'

What outrageous wickedness, Madeline thought indignantly. How can intelligent people even read this twaddle, let alone copy it out and carry it around? But as she read on to the end of the passage she felt a deep internal chill:

'The Lord shall smite thee with madness, and blindness, and astonishment of heart: And thou shalt grope at noonday as the blind gropeth in darkness, and thou shalt not prosper in thy ways: and thou shalt be only oppressed and spoiled evermore, and no man shall save thee.'

She looked for the American couple. She wanted to give it back to them, tell them to throw it away at once and convince them that guilt, whatever their reason for it, did not have to be borne in this way. She could not see them anywhere. *The Lord shall smite thee with madness, and blindness, and astonishment of heart*. Her thoughts turned to Flynn and the unbearable burden of responsibility he carried. All right, God, you win, she said bitterly to herself. You don't want me to save him; you want to do it all by yourself, to make him believe in you. I'll light a candle to help him on his way, and you on yours. She rummaged in her handbag looking for her wallet. With her face set like stone and eyes flashing with indignation she left the chapel and found Patrick, hands thrust deep in his pockets, gazing at one of Gill's Stations of the Cross.

'What do they charge to light a candle in this place?' she whispered furiously.

Patrick raised his eyebrows. 'You're not . . . ?'

'I am, yes, but I've lost my purse. Give me the money and don't say a word about it. I want to get the hell out of here. I just have to do this first.'

'I don't know the current rate, but anyway I left my wallet in the car.' He took her by the elbow and moved towards the door, but Madeline resisted. 'OK, OK . . . just do it. If you light

169

one to St Anthony, he won't mind. He's the patron saint of lost things.'

'Lost things?'

'Lost anything. Lost causes, lost faith . . . lost purses.'

For a moment Madeline considered, then looked back at the chapel where she had been sitting. The nomination read, 'The chapel of St Patrick and the saints of Ireland'. She shook her head. 'No. It has to be that chapel.'

Patrick looked at her in bewilderment; he wondered if she were ill. That, or the subject of divine intervention. 'Go ahead and do it. You won't burn in hell, I promise.'

Madeline also wondered if she were ill. Or mad. Or blind. She walked purposefully back to the chapel, pulled out one of the long candles and lit it. She waited until the flame burned strongly then returned to Patrick with a faintly embarrassed smile.

He flung his arm around her shoulders. 'That was a tender thought from a non-believer. Lord knows I need all the intercession I can get.' Madeline barely heard him. Outside, she looked in vain for the American couple and described the wife's behaviour to Patrick. 'Why would she do that? Why would she crawl on her knees like that?'

They strolled towards Birdcage Walk. 'It was probably a penance. She was seeking forgiveness.'

'What could a sweet, middle-aged American woman, clearly in love with her husband, have possibly done to make her grovel the length of Westminster Cathedral?'

'What makes you so sure they were married?'

'They were so loving. Intimate.'

'My guess is that he's brought his mistress to London on a business trip. Either she's a Catholic, or they both are. They can't go to mass in Boise, Idaho: the priest and congregation would be scandalised. So they pop in here, during an illicit holiday. She confesses to some anonymous, foreign priest, makes penance, and by now they are probably back in their

170

junior suite at the –' he glanced at the name emblazoned above the building they were passing – 'St James Court Hotel, ready to peel off their spanking new Burberry macs, climb into bed and screw the living daylights out of each other.'

Madeline grinned at the image he conjured. 'I hope they enjoy it. I hope they *really* enjoy it.'

'Oh, they won't – not for more than five minutes anyway. She'll know she wasn't absolved because she didn't properly repent. If you're only halfway sorry, you don't get any long term relief. But they'll like that, because guilt is the worst thing anyone – at least any Catholic – can lose. Guilt's the most valuable thing of all.'

Madeline halted in the street. 'Why do you say that?'

'Because most people I know cling to guilt so tightly, they must think it's very precious. Isn't that one of the problems for you therapists? If you cure clients of all their problems, everything that's caused them to feel guilty or bad in the past, what are they left with? Who are they, in fact, when you take all that away from them?'

'Psychotherapy doesn't aim to do that,' Madeline snapped. 'It's quite the opposite. When you shear all that marble off the block to turn it into Basil Hume, it's still solid stone in the end, isn't it?'

'Not really. It's a block of stone on which I have imposed my notions. It isn't just a stone any more and it isn't Basil Hume either. It's my idea of Basil Hume. Isn't that what you do with your clients?'

The idea that Patrick might think that was what she did horrified her. She shook her head. Patrick leant on the roof of the beat-up old American station-wagon he had imported years ago as the ideal vehicle for carrying blocks of stone.

'Fine. If that isn't what you do with your clients, then don't do it to that poor American couple. You have no idea who they are. Maybe people walking past us say to each other – what's that beautiful young woman doing with that old derelict? It

171

can't be money, he clearly hasn't got any, judging from his clothes and heap of a car. So what's she into him for?' He gave her a sad smile. 'I'll tell you what they think. They think I'm your poor old dad, and you, like a dutiful daughter, are taking me out for a spot of lunch before depositing me back at the nursing home.'

Madeline shoved him roughly against the car and kissed him hard and long on the mouth. 'That'll teach them to jump to conclusions,' she said, pulling open the driver's door. 'Now get in the car and drive me to work, Pop.'

TWELVE

'Does this ever make you feel like a hooker?' Flynn handed over the roll of six twenty-pound notes he'd had in his hand as he opened her office door. 'You know, getting paid in advance for services about to be rendered.'

Madeline put the money in her desk drawer with a restrained smile. 'It doesn't, no. But you're not the first person to suggest that.'

'You should count them; I'm paying you for the session I missed too.'

'I can see that. Thank you.'

'You're cheap . . . I like that in a woman.'

Madeline folded her hands and looked at him steadily, not showing her irritation that he had effortlessly back-tracked into provocation and innuendo despite the ground they had covered in the preceding weeks. 'How have you been?'

'Just grand; now how's yourself?' When she did not reply he continued, 'Aren't you going to ask me why I stood you up on Wednesday?'

'You're welcome to tell me; it's up to you.' *Come on, come on, Flynn! Let's get going!*

He looked at her accusingly. 'You called my wife.'

173

'Yes I did.' *Why did I call?* she asked herself. *Because I was worried about you.*

Flynn's shoulders slouched. He hadn't bothered to take off his jacket and was unshaven. He looked surly and ill-tempered. 'I'd told her I was seeing a therapist, but I hadn't told her you were a woman.'

'Was there a reason for not telling her?'

Flynn stared straight up at the ceiling above him, then dropped his head and began to massage the back of his neck with both hands. 'She gets jealous.'

Madeline felt the short distance between them lengthen rapidly. 'If you don't want me to call you at home, I apologise,' Madeline said evenly. 'I was concerned. I didn't know if you were late, or if something had prevented you from keeping the appointment.' *That's not why he's angry with me*, Madeline thought; *it isn't because of Georgia, but he's certainly angry.* 'Why does Georgia get jealous?'

'Now let me see . . .' Flynn crossed his leg and tapped his bottom lip in a parody of somebody pondering a difficult question. Madeline registered an immediate desire to slap him for re-erecting the old walls and swinging from sleaze to aggression.

'Maybe I've given her cause to be jealous, could that be it?'

'Have you given her cause to be jealous?'

'Have you given her cause to be jealous?' he mimicked, in a high, sing-song voice. 'How the hell do I know? I'm not inside her head. It's just words, anyway. I don't trust words. Words are a load of crap. People come up with these supposedly significant phrases like "the sound of one hand clapping"; well, what the fuck does that mean? I'll tell you what it means. Jack-shit.' Barely two long strides took him to the boundary of her consulting room, dramatising his sense of entrapment. 'I don't want to talk about whether or not somebody else, some third person, my wife for example, might or might not be justified in feeling some minute, inner inklings of jealousy. I don't care if she does. I don't care if she doesn't. I don't think we need words to say anything other than the elemental stuff: I'm hungry; will you give me that loaf of bread? Now *that's* a real question. I need money; give it to me. Get me a doctor. Do you want to fuck?'

Madeline remained outwardly impassive but she was listening acutely to Flynn, questioning her reactions to his aggression, tuning in to get a clearer reception of the responses she used like a medic's stethoscope. He was telling her he didn't like words; words were her medium. He did not trust it; he did not trust her. *OK, Flynn. Go ahead and provoke me. Because I can give it right back.* She realised that anger had wiped out the distance between them.

'When you say, do you want to fuck, how do you want me to react?'

Back came the lazy, lop-sided grin. 'Listen. I think you are gorgeous. I'm fair dying to make love to you. See? I can say it. I'd like you to be straight for once. I'd like you to say, "Sure, Flynn, let's have a shag, but see you make it a good one." If you can't see your way round that, then say, "If it's all the same to you, I'd rather not; you're not my type." Just tell the truth.'

'And whatever I told you, you'd accept that as the truth? Words are a load of crap, aren't they? How would you know whether or not to trust the veracity of a verbal expression of my feelings?'

His smile twitched. 'You're not just a pretty face, are you, Madeline? You don't have to tell me whether you'd like to have sex with me or not. I can see perfectly well that you fancy me a wee bit but you don't want to have sex with me.'

'Then there's no need for us to discuss it further.'

'I don't want to discuss it; I want you to admit it.'

'Why?'

He cupped both hands to his heart. 'Because then I'd know you cared . . .'

'I care about you as my client. I care very much about helping you to face what is making your life so difficult.'

'But that's where you're wrong. I work by putting things I can't help and can't change behind me and getting to grips with what's in front of me. What I'm already facing. Like you. You are here in front of me. I've put plenty of stuff behind me in the past. I know how to cope with past shit; I'm an expert. Bury it. That's the first lesson you learn in my job. And it works.'

'Except that it isn't working for you any longer or you wouldn't be here,' Madeline said sharply. Flynn's eyes strayed around the room, everywhere but on her face.

'Let's get *going* with this, Flynn. Let's get moving. You're sitting on the rocking horse, not me.'

She was happy for the silence to continue. Silence did not discomfort Madeline, because, more than Flynn realised, he continued to talk without speaking. He picked at the rough cuticle on a finger of his left hand before replying in a voice that was now steady if distracted.

'I told Georgia she didn't have to feel jealous because you looked like the back end of a bus. I said it because Georgia wants us back the way we used to be. So do I. If I tell her about this, about you, if she knows . . . I won't ever be able to put it back in the box. Because we'll all know. It's the same reason I don't want to talk to her when I come back from an assignment. It's better to keep things separate. It's no big deal.'

'I'm getting the feeling that keeping these two sides of yourself separate – the family, your relationship with your wife versus your work, and your feelings about that, and your sessions here with me – *is* a big deal for you, Flynn. It must take a great deal of stamina to keep them separate.'

He flinched. 'OK. You told me to get going, so let's do it. You said you wanted me to tell you about my dreams. Remember I told you I only ever had one dream and it was always pretty much the same?'

'Yes.'

'The other night I had a new dream. I was standing with some other people . . . three men, I think. I don't know where I was and I don't think it matters. Nothing happened. Nobody spoke. There was nothing going on. Then my eyes started bleeding. Not like they were damaged. It was as if they were tearing, but tears of blood. At first, it was just one or two drops from the corner of one eye. I put my hand up, thinking it was odd to be crying when there was nothing to cry for . . . I saw the blood on my hand. Then the other eye started. And then they sort of – seeped blood.' As he recounted the dream, Flynn acted it out, putting his knuckle first to his right eye, and then his left. 'And that was it,' he said with a shrug of finality. 'Like I said, it was nothing much.'

A phrase coiled and twisted like a vapour inside Madeline's head: *The Lord shall smite thee with madness, and blindness, and astonishment of heart* . . .

He sighed heavily. 'It was slow, so slow . . . It went on forever.'

'Tell me about the other people there.'

Flynn shook his head. 'There were two or three blokes, but I never really looked at them. I didn't know them.'

'They were strangers?'

'Not exactly. It seemed natural that they were there.' Flynn's brow pulled down into a heavy scowl. 'But I was damned if they'd see my eyes leaking blood. When I wiped them, I turned my back to hide it.'

'And did they see?'

'No.'

Madeline leant back deep in her chair, twisting a pencil between her fingers. 'I think it's a fascinating dream, Flynn.'

'You don't think it's sick? You don't think I'm mad?'

'No, I don't. Do you?'

He shrugged noncommittally. 'My eyes matter a lot to me. I rely on them. Why wasn't I bothered about it?'

177

'You could see perfectly well; you knew they weren't damaged. I have the feeling you were acting rationally within the dream, knowing what was happening to you and simply concerned to keep it private.'

Again he gave a lazy smile, the corners of his eyes crinkling into deep crows' feet. 'So tell me what it means then, Doc; spill the beans. I've read up on Freud.'

Madeline returned Flynn's smile. 'Freud wasn't all that hot on dreams; read Jung if you want the really meaty stuff. And even Jung – though this is just between you and me, and don't repeat it or I'll probably get struck off the register for heresy – even Jung was a little too prescriptive in my view. I'm no hot-shot on dreams. I can't tell you what it means, only you can do that. But I have the impression it is a restorative dream, in its own way. I'm interested about the other people, who they might be.'

'I think they are watchers. I think they are witnesses.'

'In what way are they witnesses?' Madeline did not want to suggest anything to Flynn's now open mind. The word 'watchers' had brought the image of the yellow-jacketed men on Astra Four flooding back to hers. She considered whether the dream might have emerged from his unconscious as a product of entering therapy, whether she herself was the unknown witness to his pain. He wanted to let her know that he was hurt, that what he had seen had hurt him, yet he was not quite ready for her to look at him full on; he'd had to turn away, to put it behind him. She felt a surge of excitement; at last she felt she stood right beside him. 'What are *they* watching, if they are not watching your eyes bleed?'

Flynn shook his head slowly. 'I think they must be media. There's something about the way they're standing there watching that makes me think of the fringe element.'

'What do you mean by the fringe element?'

'My type of journalism attracts the fringe element. They're that fraction removed from society . . . And they like it like

178

that. People ever on the outside struggling to get in, knowing they can't. People for whom something in their lives has gone horribly wrong. People looking for a home. I'm not saying all the men and women who cover war are like that, but there's a type – the fringe element; there's nothing else I can call it. Things have gone wrong for them, somewhere, and they wander around trying to put it right. It may be nothing more serious than a broken home, or shite parents, but there's . . . a code between them. They recognise each other.' As his voice trailed away, Flynn closed his eyes.

Madeline's skin had turned icy as she listened to his description. He had not made any connection between the watchers in his dream and herself, but she had. While his eyes were closed she leant towards him, trying to absorb the hurt and fear of shame that he bore; she could smell it on him, taste it on her tongue. 'Open your eyes, Flynn.' She spoke rapidly and with conviction. 'You're not sick. You're hurt. In my experience of working with people who have suffered trauma, dreams try to express what we cannot express in words, the things that are simply unspeakable. They also attempt to restore what has been ravaged in your waking life. I think you should continue to think about this dream, and we will continue to talk about it, but I am curious about the dream that *does* concern Erik. Perhaps there is a connection between them.'

Flynn studied her face without speaking. Then he said softly, with wonder, 'Your face just changed.'

'Would you describe your recurrent dream to me?'

'The look in your eyes has turned so gentle. You're glowing.'

'Tell me about Erik, Flynn.'

'You *do* fancy me, don't you? You do right now, right this minute. Why? You didn't before, not ten minutes ago, but you do now. I can see it.'

Madeline had not been aware of desire for him; she had been conscious of a feeling of love stretching from her heart to his.

She chose each word carefully. 'What *I* see is that whenever anything gets painful or difficult for you, you run away. You try to switch the focus to me. It's you we're here to talk about.' Immediately his expression turned bleak. 'You cannot avoid this, Flynn. We need to talk about Erik.'

'Which one of us is doing the running away, Madeline? Me from Erik, or you from the fact that we're attracted to each other? Let me ask you: what would happen if I get up and come over there and kiss you again? Kiss you properly? What would *you* feel? If you tell me, I won't do it. I promise you. If you won't tell me, I won't make any promises at all.'

She kept her voice free of the tension she felt. 'I don't negotiate like that, Flynn. If you feel unable to talk to me without approaching me sexually, then I must refer you to another therapist.'

'No!' Flynn said sharply. 'I don't want another therapist. I can't start this over again.'

'Would you tell me about the Erik dream?' She tried to steer him back on track.

'No. I don't even know that it *is* about Erik,' Flynn growled. 'I don't know what it's about and I'm not ready to talk about it.'

He'd walked out twenty minutes before the end of the session. After he left Madeline did not feel ready to go home. She called Jack Zabinsky to take him up on his offer of a drink, knowing it would only fan the flames of his ridiculous infatuation. Jack was in session. She called Michael, but he had left for the day. In dire need of distraction, with nothing but her computer and work to distract her, she scrolled down her incoming e-mails. Work. Work. Nothing but work. Patricia Patterson. Madeline smiled. Patricia's e-mail would be full of Florida; pool gossip, beach trips and dinners at the yacht club. It was exactly the release she needed. She clicked open the e-mail:

'My dear Madeline,
Your mother and I were up half the night talking about
you. I guess you know how much she wants you to tie the
knot with this sculptor of yours. I was thinking about you
for the rest of the night, and I want to give you my two
cents' worth.

It's two years since my beloved Jim passed away, after
forty-two years of very happily married life. I won't write
how lonely widowhood is, but I wanted to tell you what
losing him made me realise. When I met Jim we were both
starting out and full of ideas about how our future should
be. We agreed on pretty much everything: that God
willing, if He blessed us, we'd have two boys and a little
girl. We chose their names, we even settled on a family
home some five miles away from where we lived then, one
we'd want to live in if we could ever afford it, and agreed
with that family we'd need a big ol' Buick, but maybe one
day, when we were old, we'd treat ourselves to a Cadillac
– Jim set his sights on a gold one! What I'm trying to say
is that what brought us together was all the hopes and
plans we shared, and could look forward to fulfilling.

Of course, not everything worked out like we'd
planned. As you know, we have two terrific sons, but
we never were able to have that little girl. I don't feel
bad about that, and as the years passed it seemed like
we'd always wanted just our boys. We never bought that
house in Connecticut, but we had a real good marriage.
We had our fights, just like everyone, but what held us
together was all those shared memories, the way we had
the same view of all the little things that had happened
to us, whether they were happy memories or sad ones,
the triumphs and failures of two ordinary lives, woven
together. Even things we disagreed about at the time –
well, after some five years we had the same version of
it. Even memories that strictly belonged to only one of

us became held in common, and over time we could tell each other's stories, in the same way, with the same jokes, whether or not we'd even been present. I guess that's what marriage means, sharing everything, and it just doesn't matter a damn whether your memories are what really happened or not, so long as you have the same general idea of them.

I didn't know any of this until Jim passed away and I was all alone. That's when I realised that, without Jim, I didn't have a past. There's no one I can share it with and no one to tell me if what I recall is right. The way our boys remember things is different. And that's when I started thinking about you. You're still young. So many memories are still ahead of you, yours for the taking, and you need to fill the photo album in your mind with somebody you love. Tell yourself nothing matters just so long as you can share everything, and share yourself with someone you really love. We don't get long in this life, so gather happy memories like you're gathering in a harvest.

I hope you'll join us here for a Florida Christmas, and come bringing your sculptor with you.

With all my love, dear girl,
Patricia.'

Madeline printed off the e-mail. When she re-read it on the bus home, tears poured down her face.

THIRTEEN

Madeline sat next to the hospital bed clutching a large bouquet of flowers and studied her friend's face with concern. The papery skin was mapped with a fine tracery of broken red veins and wrinkles that Madeline had never before noticed. Jillian looked far too frail. A cannula was taped to the back of her hand to feed fluid into the vein; it gave Madeline the uneasy and wholly irrational feeling that the sac of clear liquid was the only thing keeping Jillian alive. Each time one of her hands plucked fitfully at the bed sheet, Madeline thought she might be waking up, but for the past half-hour Jillian had not opened her eyes.

'Is there somewhere I can find a vase?' she whispered to a nurse standing on one leg at the station next to Jillian's bed. 'If I can find a vase for these, I'll leave and come back to see Mrs Ashcroft later . . .'

'Look in the scrub room; there may be one left.' The nurse glanced at her watch. 'But you can't see Jillian later: visiting hours stop in ten minutes.'

'Madeline?' Jillian did not open her eyes but spoke in a cracked yet still authoritative voice. 'You're to sit down and see *Mrs Ashcroft* now.'

'Now, now, Jillian.' The nurse busied herself at her patient's bedside, straightening the sheets and taking Jillian's wrist between firm fingers to check her pulse.

Jillian snatched her hand away and opened her eyes. 'Why don't *you* go and find the vase and let me talk to my guest. For as long as she's able to stay.'

The nurse put her hands on her hips. 'Family only after four o'clock. Is this lady family?'

'Yes,' Jillian and Madeline replied in one voice.

Jillian's eyes followed the nurse as she crossed the ward, holding the bouquet in front of her as if it were a toxic substance. 'What wonderfully hot colours. How well you know me, Madeline, and how dear of you to come.'

Madeline tipped her head towards the retreating nurse. 'Seems a bit of a dragon.'

'She is. How long have you been here?'

Madeline sat down and held Jillian's free hand in hers. The back of her hand was splotched with age spots, and Madeline could feel heavy calluses on the cushions of the palm. 'About three minutes. I just arrived as you woke up. So. How are you feeling?'

'Stupefied with boredom. My hip hurts like hell; worse than it ever did before, and this one's plastic. So what's that about?' She smiled at Madeline. 'Pull your chair closer. My throat hurts, too, so if you're here as a visitor, you'll have to entertain me, and if you're here for supervision, you'll have to do all the talking. Or I'll croak.'

'For God's sake don't croak, Jillian, whatever you do, don't croak! I need you.' Madeline squeezed her hand. 'But I'm here strictly as a visitor. Stuff supervision. Why didn't you tell me you were having a hip replacement?'

'Because it's too dull . . . Cheer me up and tell me what you've been up to.'

'OK; this will really make you jealous – it's been a non-stop party.' Madeline's eyes danced teasingly. 'I've just come back from a two-day seminar on positron emission tomography . . .'

184

'Oh, *God*,' Jillian groaned. 'Go on. I'm listening, if I have to . . .'

'I'm not quite so insensitive as to bang on about PET scanning . . . I'm here to see you – make sure you're OK.'

Jillian inched herself gingerly up the bed. 'I am absolutely one hundred per cent fine. Except that if I don't have a conversation that isn't about whether I "need the toilet", or tomorrow's "yummy" menu, I'll go mad.'

'How long are you stuck here?' Madeline glanced about the Lady Margaret Cooper ward. The windows were sealed shut and the room was hot despite the autumnal snap in the air outside. The air inside bore an odorous melange of boiled cabbage, warmed-up curries and Heinz tomato soup. The lift had smelt worse: piss and stale cigarette smoke. In the bed across from Jillian's an old woman lay propped up on a pillow, staring at a black and soundless television screen through eyes that teared constantly.

'If I'm a *very* good girl, I'll be out by the weekend. I'm told my consultant's coming round this evening. I have to convince him I'll be able to cope at home alone.'

'You don't have to; you're welcome to come and stay with Patrick and me. The guest room's on the ground floor. Patrick's home all day; I'd be around a lot of the time, too.'

'That is a very sweet offer, but it's out of the question. You know I won't intrude on you like that.'

'I'd enjoy it,' Madeline said simply. 'I could boss you around. It would stop you being able to lecture me.'

Jillian smiled. 'That's another reason why I won't take you up on it. I at least want to be able to sit in my conservatory if I can't get out in the garden. If needs must, my niece Anna will come to stay for a few days.'

'You must loathe being out of sight of a green field or garden.'

'Pass me that glass, would you?'

185

Jillian watched Madeline turn sideways, and knew she was trying not to look too closely at the tubes that hung behind the bed. Her eyes scanned the collection of needles, cardboard urine bottles and swabs that littered the bedside table. Something in Madeline's physical bearing had shifted. There was a new vulnerability about her; she held herself tenderly, as one does nursing a broken arm. She hates hospitals even more than I do, Jillian thought as she took the glass.

'I wish you could meet my consultant. He's extremely handsome.'

'You can't be feeling that bad if you've got the hots for your consultant.'

'Oh, he's not really my type.' Jillian handed Madeline the glass and lay back with her eyes closed. 'I was looking at him yesterday and thinking he might be yours.'

'Oh yes? Tell me more.'

'He has a very intelligent face. Tall, fine-boned . . . elegant.'

'Fair or dark?'

'Golden.' A smile hovered mischievously about Jillian's thin lips. 'Like the sun busting through the clouds.'

Madeline burst out laughing. 'You *have* got the hots for him! Good. He doesn't sound my type at all.'

'Tell me about your type.'

'Oh, large; dark; moody. Gloomy, even.'

'Is Patrick your type?' Jillian had never met Madeline's partner, although she felt she knew him well. When Madeline did not reply, Jillian glanced up to see her lost in thought. She had thought it impossible for Madeline's face, normally so mobile, so fluid and communicative, to be expressionless. 'Is Patrick your type?' she repeated.

'Oh yes, yes he is,' Madeline said too patly. 'He's certainly large, moody . . . and gloomy. Right now he's definitely gloomy. He's so absorbed in the Hume commission I feel a bit cut off from him. In fact I almost dread going home these days. I find myself lingering in the office, looking for

186

something to do.' Madeline's gaze wandered about the ward before she turned back with a bright smile. 'What shall I bring you tomorrow? Grapes? The papers?'

Jillian pulled the *Guardian* from under the sheets. 'That's one thing they provide. At a cost. No. Tell me more about Patrick's work. I'm interested.' If Madeline felt better able to talk about her private life now they were outside her consulting room, Jillian did not want to lose the connection, however tired she felt.

'He's about halfway through. The further in he gets, the harder the work, the less of him there is left over.' Madeline leant over to look at the newspaper open on Jillian's lap. The front-page photograph was of a black soldier running for cover.

'Of all journalists I think I admire photographers the most,' Jillian mused. 'They always have to be where the fighting is fiercest.'

Madeline smiled broadly. 'It's no good trying to sound innocent, Jillian. If you want to ask about Flynn, go right ahead.'

'Good, because I do.' *So he was Flynn now; not F.B.* How are the sessions going?'

'Unpredictable. I don't know which direction he's going to come from next. He jumps — well, he reminds me of a chess knight.' Madeline plucked at the edge of her shirt, worrying a stray thread of cotton. A wistful smile played fleetingly across her lips. 'I was always rotten at chess; I always forgot about the damn knights, pouncing from nowhere when your back's turned. I spend too much time thinking about him. It takes me a long time to wind down after seeing Flynn. A long time.'

'Madeline . . . is Flynn your type?'

'Yes and no. Once,' the blood rushed to Madeline's cheeks, 'I caught myself fantasising about him. Utterly silly stuff. You know: I'd be good for him, he'd be good for me . . .'

'Would you be good for each other?'

'Of course not. It's clearly erotic counter-transference.'

187

'You're sexually attracted to him?' First Flynn had made Madeline feel all depleted; now aroused?

Madeline shook her head.

Jillian could tell she was concealing something, and was instantly reminded of Winnicott's observation that, although an illicit secret might feel delicious, it was very hell to have it remain undiscovered. She could feel Madeline wavering on the edge. In some way Flynn had touched her, she was certain, touched her profoundly.

Lost in a reverie, Madeline lifted one hand and pressed her fingertips delicately along her lips, as if in unconscious answer to Jillian's unspoken question. *He's kissed her*, Jillian guessed at once; *my God: he's kissed her, and she is not willing to tell me.*

As Madeline's eyes lifted back to Jillian, she half rose from her chair in alarm. 'Jillian – what is it? Shall I call a nurse? You're in pain, aren't you? You've gone absolutely white.'

'No, I'm not in real pain, don't fuss. Far too many drugs for that. I was just reminded of something which worried me . . .'

Madeline bent quickly and pressed her lips to Jillian's cheek. 'You are not to worry about anything, all right? Promise. And absolutely not about me. Everything's fine with my clients. *All* of them. The important thing is that you get well.'

The swing doors of the ward flung open to admit a woman hopelessly trying to shepherd three scampering children clutching posies of flowers. 'Auntie Jill . . .'

Madeline stood shyly to one side just outside the family circle until Jillian had greeted her family. She made her goodbyes, and at the ward door turned back to look at her supervisor. One small child was perched on the edge of the bed in the crook of Jillian's arm, shredding Michaelmas daisies. The other two plundered a box of chocolates. The contentment on Jillian's face made Madeline both happy and envious.

'I'm inside a house,' Flynn repeated as she asked him to take her step by step through his recurrent dream for a second time that afternoon. 'Wind's ripping through the place and I'm frightened. It's not a safe place and I'm trying to shut whatever doors and windows I can find, pulling all the curtains tight as I move up through the building.'

'Can you tell me more about the house?'

'I don't know that it *is* a house. It's some sort of building, except that it feels so open and exposed. I don't have the impression of solid walls, more of a shell. Maybe it's been bombed – I don't have a clear picture.'

Madeline listened. What Flynn was describing followed the form of a dream that several clients had recounted to her, one that often presaged a key session. Flynn knew that he was opening up and losing his defences and he feared the wind that blew through him. He was trying to close up his house, a dream state of battening down the hatches and walling off the whole experience, but the walls themselves were too flimsy. It surprised Madeline that his face did not show the expected signs of resistance to opening up. Instead, his expression was one of naked fear as he told her: 'I can hear mortar shelling pretty close – *krumph*, doomdoomdoom – and I know the house isn't safe anymore.'

'It felt safe at first?'

'No. It never feels safe. Not from when the dream starts.'

'Then you hear mortar shelling?' He nodded. 'Do you know who is attacking you?'

'I have no idea. I don't think they are out to get me, personally, I just happen to be there. As I'm trying to leave I keep falling over things, tripping, there's stuff all over the floor . . .'

'What sort of stuff?'

'Rubble, bits of broken furniture, lumps of stone, plaster falling off the ceiling in chunks . . . I can barely see, it's so dark, and I'm frightened, too frightened to look close, but as I get to the door . . .' Flynn shook his head violently. 'I don't want to talk about this.'

189

Madeline listened to his breathing until he resumed with effort. 'OK. When I get to the door I stumble over something in the dark and pick it up. It's a child, a small child. I know it's my boy, Oliver. I'm surprised. I didn't know he was in the house. I don't see his face, but I know it's my son, I *feel* it's him.'

'How do you feel, when you find him?'

Flynn caught his breath as he searched for the right word. '*Annoyed.* Like, what the hell are you doing here?' but I don't think about it, I know we've got to get out fast. I pick him up and we're under attack, him and me. I'm just running, scared shitless, carrying Ol – then we're outside, I'm covered in plaster dust and there's mud everywhere, sticky black mud up to my knees so I can hardly walk, hardly hold onto the kid . . . I think I'm going to let him go . . .'

Madeline let Flynn sit with his head in his hands. *The image of Flynn covered in white dust brought Patrick to her mind; she saw Patrick stumbling from a bombed house.* Flynn's shoulders heaved sporadically, but when he eventually looked up his eyes were dry and staring through her to the window behind. 'I feel him slipping, you know, slipping down against my groin. I can't get a proper grip, I can only just keep him out of the mud, and the noise is louder, closer now . . . *krumph*, doomdoomdoom . . .'

His head sank back into his trembling hands. Madeline could feel the room darken; the air felt close and humid. Flynn met her eyes, his expression bleak and his voice jagged: 'I stagger into a clearing. Can't make it out. It's strange . . . Quiet suddenly. Dead quiet. It gives me a breathing space but I feel even more frightened. For a moment I don't see anything.' The words began to fall ever faster from his lips, like tears, as if telling the dream furiously might flood away the grime and the dirt and the hurt of it. 'My chest hurts so badly, I've been running so long, it's like my ribs're cracking. I'm holding onto Ol, at the edge of the clearing. When I turn around I see there are bodies all around us. And I think, so they're the ones they're after, not me . . . Bodies of women and children, African women, their blood running into the dirt in rivers . . . And there's a man. I see the man because his dick is sticking up in the air, straight up. Like a flagpole. There's not much else of him left. I don't want to look at him it's so – undignified.'

As he said the word, Flynn sat up straight and forced his shoulders back with effort, opening out his chest. Madeline was listening acutely, listening so hard that her head throbbed as his darkness washed over her. His eyes were glazed, fixed past her. 'Out of the blue, we get hit. I don't hear a sound but I know my boy's hit, I can feel bullets thudding into his body, one after another, a whole clip. He almost *shivers* into my bones, softens like melting butter. I realise I'm hit too, the bullets have passed through him into me. It feels real. It *is* real. It hurts like hell. I think, is this it? Am I dying here? Me and my son? I feel so much pain and I think, fuck, it's not supposed to be like this, it's not meant to hurt, everybody tells you that, and this hurts like shit. So I can't be dying. But I *know* I am about to die. I hear people calling me to come back, crying for help, but I can't help because I am dying and they don't understand. It's the real thing, do you understand? It's real. It isn't a dream. And then I wake up, or Georgia wakes me up, and I'm dripping with cold sweat.' *Just as you are now*, Madeline registered. 'I can still hear that deep crack, the thump, doomdoomdoom . . . But it's only the sound of my heart pounding in my eardrums. That's when I realise it's a dream.'

Flynn was silent.

'Is it always the same?'

'Exactly the same. Only the starting point changes. It's going back further each time. Now it starts in the house. Before, it started in the clearing.'

'Are you always carrying Oliver?'

He nodded.

'And the man, the man in the clearing . . .'

He nodded jerkily. 'Erik.'

'When do you know it's Erik?'

'Right away. Before I see him.'

Madeline was appalled but equally intrigued. PTSD dreams were generally not nightmares so much as confused flashbacks, or memory intrusions. Given that Flynn had not been physically present at Erik's death, it was unusual for the death 'scene' to haunt him so much more than the moment at the checkpoint, but this made the dream no less powerful and no less disturbing. *Had Flynn seen Erik as a younger version of himself, someone under his protection and tutelage? And so in the dream Flynn delivers his son to the scene of his execution? Or did the child represent Flynn's younger, more idealistic self – was it his idealism that had been butchered in the clearing?*

'Do you know this clearing? Is it familiar?'

Flynn shrugged. 'No. There's a sort of deep ravine, like a river bed, to one side.' He shook his head. 'I've told myself it's where Erik died.'

'Where Erik was murdered?'

'Yes.' Flynn drew strength from her deliberate correction. 'Yes, where Erik was murdered. I never saw it myself. I only see it in the dream.'

Once again, Flynn had confused what he had seen and what he imagined. He'd told her he'd visited the scene of Erik's death: now it was an imaginary place, firmly a fixture of his dream world. 'Tell me exactly what you see as you come into the clearing.'

Flynn closed his eyes and sighed. 'Trees. Eucalyptus. It's lush. I think it's a shelter. Safe. I've kind of stumbled in backwards. I've got my back to the clearing. I turn round slowly and see the bodies.' His neck was stretched taut, his Adam's apple rising and falling as if he were fighting a wave of nausea.

'Can you describe them?'

'They're cut up bad. Some have their limbs severed. One of

the women has her stomach slit from crotch to breastbone, guts spilling into the dirt. There are flies everywhere.'

'They are all dead?'

A shadow passed over Flynn's face. 'Except for one small boy. He's maybe three or four, but very small. He's squatting next to his dead mother.'

Madeline found herself fumbling with contradictory chords of emotion, aware of both tenderness towards Flynn and revulsion. 'Does the boy look at you?'

Flynn's mouth twisted into an ugly grimace. 'He's got his hand up to his mouth, he's – he's . . . I don't look at him because I see Erik.'

'You look at Erik?'

'I don't want to.'

'He's there amongst the heap of bodies and the flies?'

'To one side. On his back.'

'Do you notice anything else about him?'

'I told you. His dick is standing up like a flagpole.'

'What do you feel about that?'

He shrugged. 'It's good they didn't cut it off.'

'You said it was undignified.'

As she had expected, the flatness in Flynn's expression was at once replaced by cold anger. 'Damn right it's undignified. It's more than that – it's outrageous. *Obscene.* Is that a way for a man to die, with his cock in the air, a grin on his face and a great sucking hole in his chest?'

'Erik is smiling, in the dream?'

'It isn't a pleasant smile.'

'But you look at him?'

'Yes. That's when we get hit, out of the blue.' Flynn caught his breath sharply. 'Except that it's *not* out of the blue. I *know* it's not safe. I know we shouldn't be there. All the time, I have this dread. You don't walk into a place like that and stand gawping at the bodies, you get the hell out before it's too late.'

'Do you feel that *in the dream*? That you should leave?'

He shook his head, the hair falling over his eyes until he raked it back. 'I've no choice but to be there.'

Yet you've gone in backwards, Flynn; you've stumbled into it, trying to protect your child; Erik; yourself. Madeline spoke very gently: 'When you were at the checkpoint three miles outside Kigali, with Erik, you were not given a choice either.'

'No,' he corrected fiercely. 'I could have stopped him. I could have *made* him come back with me. I was the one who wanted to go on at first. Maybe I gave him the confidence to go on . . .' His voice tilted up questioningly.

'You didn't kill him, Flynn.'

'So why do I keep dreaming this?'

Madeline leant forward with her hands tightly clasped. 'Perhaps the dream recurs because you want to change the sequence of events; rewrite the story, change your memory. You want to be there with him. You are trying to alter the fact that you survived – by luck, by chance, by fate – and Erik did not.' She tried to help him understand how his healthy mind was straining to repair the rents that trauma had caused. 'With a dream like this one, call it a PTSD dream, or a memory intrusion, it repeats and repeats because your memory of the true events has been fractured. You *can't* make the necessary connection, you cannot absorb what happened to Erik after he left you, and what happened to you as a result of that. This is a terribly painful memory, too painful to approach consciously, so you revisit it in a dream world.' Her voice was low and intense and there was a look of certainty on her face as she assured him, 'But there are very positive aspects to this process, believe me. Little by little, you're trying to integrate a deeply traumatic experience and come to some way of handling your emotions, not be buried by them. A dream like this gives you some control back, where you feel you had none.'

Flynn did not look convinced; his expression shut down on her again. 'Have you ever had a dream like that, Madeline?'

'Not like that, no.' *As she denied it, Madeline could feel the morning sun on the back of her bare neck and the stench of summer rape and the sickening, headachy perfume of sweet peas invaded the room. Her own recurrent nightmare, the impossibility of her escape from the summer and the farmhouse looming ever closer, come back to haunt her.*

She turned her head quickly to the window. It was twilight, an autumn twilight, when for some twenty minutes day and night met graciously and companionably. It was her favourite time; her natural time. Steadied, she returned her full attention to Flynn.

'So explain why I die in it.'

'Do you die in it?'

'I'm about to die.'

'But do you die?'

'No. I just know I am dying.' Although Flynn fell silent, she could read some other train of thought on his face and waited. 'Sometimes, if it wasn't for the children and Georgia, leaving them alone, I wish I had died there with him. It would have been better. It might still. I carry a big life policy; Georgia and the kids would be OK. I'm not frightened of death.' He stood abruptly, hooking his jacket by a finger over his shoulder. 'Death's just a shadow at our heels; a lazy, reluctant bastard of a companion you don't much want hanging around your back, but you know he has to be there. He keeps his distance.' Flynn moved towards the door.

'Are you leaving?'

'Looks that way.'

'We have a little more time.'

'I'm done here, Madeline. I've told you my dream, which was what you wanted, so now I'll be off. I need a smoke.'

'Please sit down. I'd like to ask you a few more things.'

'Will you let me smoke?'

'No. It won't be long.' He shrugged into his jacket. 'How long did you spend in Rwanda during the genocide?'

Flynn stood warily with his hands thrust deep in his pockets, his shoulders hunched. 'Dunno. Five or six days in all? Not long. Some people were there for weeks. And some . . .'

She did not need him to finish the sentence. 'Flynn, I can see this is very hard for you. I can see how much it hurts. Please sit down. There's something else I need to ask.'

'No, Madeline. I won't sit down, thanks very much.' He stood with his feet apart, balanced and bristling with aggression. 'No, I won't sit down, and no, you *don't* know how hard it is for me and you *don't* know how much it hurts. I don't think you know what it's like to be responsible for someone's death; what it's like to be carrying that coffin and have some smart-arsed, poker-spined, platitudinous woman patronise you and politely request that you sit down so you don't puke your guts all over the floor of her pristine little office.'

Madeline felt as if he had struck her face with each phrase. 'I'm sorry you think I'm patronising you. It's not what I feel.'

He strode to her chair and grabbed the arms with both hands so that he loomed above her, six inches away from her face. 'What *do* you feel then, Madeline,' he began in a low voice. 'Do you think my immortal soul is damned? D'you feel contaminated – *infected* – simply by being near me? Is that why you don't want me to come near you? And don't tell me to sit back down so you can carry on with your circus, because maybe, if I am a good boy, then *maybe* you'll answer me, maybe, for a special treat we can go in the kitchen and have cookies and cocoa . . . Don't give me any more shite. Just answer me this: How do *you* feel about *me?*'

Madeline's teeth pulled once at her bottom lip as she made the decision to gamble. 'All right,' she said, nodding slowly, looking straight back at him. 'I have told you that these sessions are about what you feel, but as you so badly want to hear what *I* feel, here it is. I think you are so frightened that you don't know how to handle yourself, except by intimidating other people. You are horrified that I might actually like you when you don't feel worthy of being liked; that would make you feel even more guilty. I think you have become so deeply attached to your guilt and your pain, you are worried that nothing will be left of you without it. You are desperate to provoke me to the point where I tell you to get out, so you can feel it's OK to walk away from this pristine little office and close the door on all this. To put it behind you, as you are so very eager to do with your life. Shut out the past, even if it means shutting down your present and your future, your wife, your family, your work. And you know what, Flynn? You're absolutely right. You *can* walk away and never come back. I won't chase you.'

Madeline was breathing heavily, gripping the arms of her chair, the colour high in her cheeks but her eyes were fixed steadily on his. 'But this dream isn't going to go away, it's going to get stronger and more frequent, and Rwanda and Erik and your bleeding eyes aren't going to go away either. I'm not your problem, Flynn. You want me to dislike you? Well, I can certainly see the parts you hate in yourself. You're hurt; you want to hurt someone else. Understandable, but *none of that matters*. Every time we talk, every time we get closer to *you*, to what you are really feeling, you fling the whole thing out the window because you are frightened. You're right to say that you want to keep what happens in this room separate and private. You are right, because what happens in here is a difficult and painful effort, and requires absolute conviction on your part and mine. In this room the only thing that matters is, do you want my help or not? What matters is, do you want to go on living in this angry, terrified, disconnected hell that you have walked backwards into, or do you want to find a way out of it?'

Flynn took a step back. 'I'm sorry.' Madeline did not reply. He backed away from her until he reached his chair and sat leadenly, rubbing his hand back and forth across his eyes.

197

'You're right. That's why I didn't show up last time. I was too scared of being . . .' He leant forward, looking at the floor between his feet with his hands hanging slack between his knees. 'I feel dammed up, if you know what I mean. If I let the dam burst . . .'

'What will happen if you let the dam burst?'

'I don't know where the water will stop. I don't know if it'll find a level or I'll be engulfed. When I'm with you, when you're listening to me, I feel it's OK, that it's bearable. Then all of a sudden I feel the pressure building and I think, no – it's not, not bearable, it's not OK, because she doesn't know who I am or what I've done and what I'm responsible for. And then I feel the waters rising and I have to get the dam back in place *fast . . .*'

Madeline looked at his bowed head with great tenderness. 'It takes a great deal of courage to do what you are doing.'

'Now that's a shame, because courage is something I have in short supply.' He did not lift his head. 'I can do self-pity. If you're looking for sheer bloody-mindedness, I'll take a shot.'

'I think you have plenty of courage.'

'What was it you wanted to ask me back there, before I acted like a prize eejut?'

'I was thinking about the clearing . . . I wondered if you had photographed the location of Erik's death?'

'No. And I despise myself for that.'

'Why?'

'Because there's no point being somewhere with a camera if you are not prepared to use it. It's like I betrayed him twice. I should have recorded it, but it was too much for me.'

'You did record it, Flynn. Perhaps more profoundly than any scene you have ever photographed.' *He had recorded it and walled it off. It was a normal reaction – a sane reaction. People like Flynn, trauma survivors who were haunted by Flynn's type of dream, people who repressed automatically, tended to have thick boundaries and be the most naturally resilient to trauma. But once it took hold they had no way of letting it go. Which was why it was so hard for him to let that dam burst. Erik was there like an undertow, sucking at his heels.* She felt an intuition of which direction to take, if she could just reach out and hold it fast.

'I'd like to see some of your work.'

'Why?'

'I'd like to try to see exactly what you see when you look through the camera.'

'You would?' Flynn looked doubtful.

'Yes, if you're willing to let me.'

'Nobody sees what anybody else sees.'

'How do you mean?'

'We pass everything through our own personal filter.' He held his hands up to one eye, framing her between his fingers. 'When I do this,' he looked out from round his hands and then back, 'I'm looking at you. But what I see isn't what your husband or your child or your best friend sees. Think of the camera as a filter, except it's not the camera, that's only a prop, it's the photographer's interpretative filter – his imagination. Every person, every scene, every room even, has a voice, maybe raucous, maybe timid. That's what you have to find in the frame, but it's your own filter that tells you what sings and what screams. You, for example, sing.'

One corner of her mouth twitched in a brief smile. 'So you'll bring some pictures in one session?'

'Maybe I'll dig some up.'

FOURTEEN

Georgia cradled the phone between one hunched shoulder and her jaw as she rhythmically whisked the eggs and flour for batter. 'So what happened with the car?'

Suzie Bushell, her best friend, neighbour, confidante and cohort on the school run had already been on the phone for a good ten minutes. 'Oh, God – another seven-hundred-quid garage bill. It's the third time this year.'

'What did Roger say?'

'Roger said nothing. Because I didn't *tell* Roger I'd pranged it. I said someone must have driven into it overnight. He probably thinks it's you. Maybe I even encouraged that . . .'

Georgia laughed. 'Thanks a heap, Suze!'

'It's his fault for having such an expensive car. If he drove a normal one it wouldn't cost an arm and a leg to have the bumper fixed. Anyway, who cares about cars? It's not like he sleeps with it or anything – though sometimes I think he wants to. It gets a hell of a lot more bodywork than I do.'

'Rubbish. Roger adores you.'

'Yeah, well . . . sometimes I don't get that impression. Honestly, Georgia, Roger can be such a first-degree world-class rat . . .'

Georgia put down the whisk and hopped onto the kitchen

countertop as she listened to Suzie's regular diatribe. Suzie worked for an 'arriving' fashion designer whose ETA had long since come and gone, overseeing his finance department on a schedule that was part-time on paper and full-time in practice. She was paid a salary that would have looked stingy had it been doubled, and, as a result, in Suzie's mind, while she worked her arse off, her husband Roger: a, didn't consider her income worth acknowledging, therefore b, didn't value her work, and so c, was resentful that she couldn't run his house and home more efficiently when her 'hobby' left so much time on her hands.

'As it is, I'd be entirely buggered if you weren't doing the afternoon run. Whenever anything concerns the children, it's *me* that has to cancel meetings, drop everything and hare off to school. Last month when I was in Brighton the school nurse called Roger to say Luke had suspected appendicitis: did he rush down to the hospital? Did he hell. He called his mum and asked her to go. I wouldn't care if he'd been in the final stages of some massive hostile takeover, but he was having *lunch* . . .'

'Tell the school to call me. I'm normally about.'

'Thanks, hon. Really. I know I shouldn't rant. I *know* his job is demanding, but God, the way he goes on about it you'd think investment bankers were an endangered species. At least Flynn's job really *is* important.'

'Yeah. Oh, *Suzie* . . .' Georgia longed to confide and be comforted, but she could not betray Flynn by telling her friend how humiliated she had been by his sexual rejection and how frightened by his tears the week before.

'What?'

'I don't know how to help him, and it just makes me want to weep.'

'So the therapy thing isn't helping? Listen, Georgia, it takes time; I should know. I tried three therapists before I got anywhere. Flynn just has to keep at it and you have to bite down hard and bear it. He'll be OK. You both will. Christ, half the women in this street would cut off their right arms to have the kind of marriage you and Flynn have.'

'Used to have,' Georgia corrected forlornly. She trickled milk into the mixing bowl and flicked the whisk about half-heartedly. She could not tell Suzie the bargain that was beginning to form in her mind. There was only one thing left to do; make some sacrifice in exchange for Flynn's recovery. Have this. Take that. Take some precious thing away from her. Her looks? Her health? Her self-respect? All fine. Anything to swing the scales in Flynn's favour. But not the children. Anything but that. Maybe nothing she *chose* to offer would be enough. Even to herself she could not voice what she dreaded might be the necessary trade: that she would have to give up Flynn himself.

'I am trying, really I am, but he won't let me near him,' she said slowly, watching spots of batter splatter on the worktop as she tapped the whisk against the bowl. 'He doesn't want to sleep with me anymore. He grabs any excuse to sleep on the sofa. I keep telling myself this therapist will sort him out . . . but what if I'm part of the problem?'

'This is just ridiculous. It makes me furious he's putting you through all this.'

'He can't help it.'

'You know what? We should make a plan. One day, one day soon, before Christmas, we're going out to lunch. We'll get out of our skulls and forget about men and children and work and all of it. We're going to go out and have *fun*. Just the two of us. My treat. OK? Is it a deal?'

'Sounds great.' Georgia tried to sound enthusiastic when she felt nothing but bone tired. She wished Suzie could have presented a real, hardcore solution rather than another short-term fix that would be neither fix nor fun when she woke up with a hangover.

'Good. As soon as I've sorted out something for Ma . . .'
'How is she?'

'Oh God.' Suzie's voice emptied. 'It's so hard, so hard losing her this way. Seeing her . . . The home won't keep her; I can't look after her here . . .'

'You know if there's anything I can *ever* do – sit with her, take her out, bring you – or her – a bottle of gin, anything. Just say the word.'

'Forget it. You've got enough on your plate.' Suzie's answer sounded brusque but Georgia knew that her friend found it impossible to talk about her mother without weeping. 'Oh look, I can see your divine husband walking my rotten kids up the drive. He looks fine, George, really *happy*; he's grinning like a Cheshire cat.'

Oliver was the first to explode through the front door, satchel swinging. In his wake came Flynn, laden with plastic bags full of muddy sports kit, and Beth chewing the end of her ponytail.

'*Salve, mater obesa!*' Oliver said formally, bowing to his mother. 'I got an A in Latin today.'

'I don't know whether to thump you for the first bit or hug you for the second.' Georgia managed to land a kiss on his ear as he ducked his face away. 'And I bet that's not how Roman schoolboys addressed their mothers.'

'No, Dad taught me in the car. We talked Latin all the way home. He's brill at it.'

Flynn unloaded the bags on the kitchen table. 'What I suggested was "*mater pulchrissima*", Ol, if you remember, but you said that was too pukey.'

'Did you get the new gerbils, Mum?'

'Go up to your room and have a look.' When Oliver had left the kitchen, Georgia shrugged at Flynn and Beth. 'I had to. You know how upset he was about the last two.'

'He wasn't upset,' Beth stated. 'It's not like you can have a meaningful relationship with a hairy-tailed rat, for God's sake. Not even Ol can do that. You just spoil him.'

203

'Your mother spoils all of us,' Flynn said, 'not just Oliver.'

'Oh well,' Georgia said brightly, 'it isn't as if they cost an arm and a leg.'

'If they keep dying they will,' Beth pointed out. The way Ol looks after them they only live about two and a half minutes.'

'The first two got sick. That wasn't Oliver's fault.'

'What about the two he starved for three weeks? And the two the Bushells' cat ate when Ol left the window open and the lid off their cage?'

'We don't know for *certain* the cat ate them,' Georgia corrected her daughter.

'Oh sure, Mum, no evidence,' Beth scoffed, 'just that *disgusting* mangey slime-ball resting its huge gut on Ol's bed and bits of bloody entrails all over the carpet . . .'

Oliver reappeared with a small grey gerbil sitting on his shoulder and a pale brown one trembling in the cup of his hand.

'D'you like them, Ol?'

'They're *wicked*, Mum; really friendly. I've been trying to think of names for them.'

'Hmm . . . How about something Latin?' Georgia suggested. 'What's the Latin for gerbil?'

'*Foulus Ratus*,' Beth said immediately.

'Are they boys or girls?'

'Boys. I *think* the man said boys.'

'Maybe Caesar and Brutus?' Oliver mused out loud. 'What do you think, Dad?'

Flynn stared deeply into the beady eyes of the grey gerbil. 'How about Rigor –' he paused – 'and Mortis?'

Georgia swung towards the oven to hide her grin. 'OK, darlings – dinner in an hour, homework first.'

When the children had gone, Georgia draped her arms around Flynn's neck and ruffled her hand through his thick hair. 'I love you, I love you, I *love* you.'

'That's mighty kind of you, Ma'am,' he drawled in an atrocious American accent, flicking on the news at the same time.

Had she wanted him to say 'I love you too', however trite? Yes, she thought crossly, chopping imported rhubarb as if it had personally offended her. Just once in a while he might offer an endearment, let her know that he cared. She remembered how Flynn used to come back from an assignment, stride into the house and pick her up, holding her pressed hard against him without saying a single word, burying his face in her hair and inhaling the scent from her neck. Then she hadn't wanted any words at all.

'I'm thinking of going back to work.'

Georgia's guts twisted into a hard ball in the pit of her stomach. He'd raised it so casually, as if he were considering having the car serviced ahead of time. Five minutes ago she had felt so perfectly, foolishly happy; now she braced herself against reality.

'What do you think about that?'

Her back to him, Georgia closed her eyes momentarily, then resumed slicing the rhubarb into neat, two-inch chunks. 'Do I have any say in the matter?'

'That's why I just asked what you thought.'

'What's the assignment?'

'Sierra Leone. The government's increasing our military presence; there's bound to be some display of force, a bit of flag-waving.'

'Who offered it to you?'

'Ashley.'

Ashley was *Time*'s European director of photography; she was also the person who'd told Flynn eight months ago not to come back until he'd sorted himself out.

'Why you?'

'I know Freetown. Listen, Georgia: they've signed a ceasefire; it's not dangerous. As Ashley says, it's a chance for a quirky take on colonialism after ten years of civil war. It'll be perfectly safe.'

Georgia's hand shook so badly she was in danger of cutting herself. A place like Sierra Leone was never perfectly safe. You had to live on your wits in a place like that; nothing else counted a damn.

'Why Africa? If you have to go back to work, why Africa?'

'Come on! You know why Africa. Where d'you want me to work? Luxembourg? Stop asking stupid questions and tell me what you think.'

'OK.' Carefully she put the knife down and turned round to face him, holding onto the worktop behind her. 'I don't think it's a good idea. In fact, I think it's a bad idea. I don't think you're ready for it.'

Flynn's eyes narrowed. 'What makes you say that?'

'What does your therapist say?'

'She doesn't say anything. She listens. That's the point.'

Georgia felt rebuked. 'I see. And what do you tell her about going back to work that you don't tell me?'

Flynn sighed. 'George, if you're going to be so damn touchy, let's not discuss it at all.'

'No. I'm interested. Maybe you've given her a good argument, talked it through, and just presented it to me as a *fait accompli.*'

'I haven't even mentioned it to her.'

Georgia's relief was instantly replaced by shame. This therapist was meant to be helping Flynn; she couldn't feel jealous of what he told her and happy about what he didn't.

'Maybe you should,' she suggested, 'just to sound her out.'

Flynn made a dismissive gesture. 'It's not her job. Besides, you don't know what it's like in those sessions. She never says anything at all. She wouldn't be caught dead giving actual advice. If I said, it's raining, she'd probably say, what makes you think it's raining? And if I said, well, I'm soaked to the bone and there's water dripping off the end of my nose, she'd say, how does it feel to have water dripping off the end of your nose? And if I said, well, to be frank, it feels *wet*, she'd ask what "wet" feels like . . .'

Georgia laughed, her teeth catching her lower lip as Flynn parodied an intense, penetrating expression. 'Maybe you should try someone else, if she isn't helping.'

'I didn't say she wasn't helping.'

'You said you couldn't even talk to her about going back to work.'

'I said I hadn't, not that I couldn't.' He turned his attention back to the news.

Georgia squeezed orange juice over the rhubarb and banged the saucepan on the hob. How to get back to the *mater pulchrissima* – even the *mater obesa* – how to get back to that happy little domestic realm of toad-in-the-hole and fruit tart? How had they swung from haven to hostility in so short a time? She felt tears welling hotly in her eyes. Letting it drop would be cowardly. Flynn wasn't well; if Ol or Beth had been sick, she wouldn't have shrugged her shoulders and said, fine, go to school if that's what you want. She shouldn't bite down and bear it; she should turn and fight for him. 'So will you talk to her about it?' she persisted stubbornly.

'Maybe.'

'I understand she doesn't tell you what to do, but surely, on a matter like this, she'd have an opinion?'

'I'm certain she'd have an opinion. Whether she'd express it or not is a different matter.'

'Does it annoy you when she won't tell you what she thinks?'

'No, she doesn't annoy me.'

'Do you like her?'

Flynn rubbed his upper lip with a thumb contemplatively. 'I've never thought about whether I like her or not.'

'Give me a thumbnail sketch.'

207

Flynn smiled lazily. 'She looks fragile but is tough as old boots. A little scary.'

'She's old?'

'No, not old, not young. I don't know her age. She's old enough.'

'What *do* you know about her?'

'I know nothing about her. And I like it that way.'

'She sounded stiff on the phone. A bit pedantic.'

There was something in the slight yet sudden movement of Flynn's head – the way he looked away from her and seemed to leave the room – that alerted Georgia: her husband felt strongly towards this woman, whatever her age, whether he liked her or not. Without saying a word, Flynn had made it clear that she was prohibited the right to comment on Dr Light, that his relationship with her was exclusive. His expression had softened for an instant before he had firmly pulled down the visor that shut her out. Georgia felt stupefied by a confusion of reactions: what was it she had glimpsed on Flynn's face; what unfamiliar expression had flashed across his face when she had offered the suggestion that Dr Light was stiff and pedantic? Georgia searched for the word and felt stunned when it took shape in her head: *protective*. Flynn's instinctive reaction had been one of shielding Madeline Light from her. She recoiled as if she had been slapped.

'I thought you said she sounded nice when you spoke to her,' Flynn said. The rhubarb had been left to turn into a greenish-brown sludge. Georgia did not attempt to rescue it, just stood, stirring blindly, as resentment bubbled up inside her. She tipped the slimy mess into a pre-baked pastry case as Flynn walked up behind her and studied the tart.

'I don't think I can do this any more, Flynn.'

'Any more? You never could make puddings.'

In one fluid movement Georgia's hand swung back then forward in a perfect arc. He looked at her until she lowered her eyes, her cheeks even redder than the one she had struck. Georgia knelt to slide the tart into the oven.

'I'm sorry,' she said quietly, with the door still open and all the heat escaping.

'Forget it. I have.'

'I don't think you should. I think we have to talk it through.'

'You're like a scratched record, Georgia. How can I get it through your head that I don't *want* to talk about my therapy – or therapist – with you? It's something I'm dealing with; leave it be. The subject doesn't concern you.'

'But that's where you're wrong.' Bitterness rippled through Georgia's voice like a red standard. 'The subject *is* me. The subject is *us*. If you can't talk to me, if you have to shut me out of everything, then I think I am going to have to leave you. If I don't, I'm frightened I'll go mad. And I'll have to take the children with me.'

'Of *course* you should take the children,' Flynn said in a strangely pleasant tone, 'if you want to go.'

'I don't want to go. You're making me go.'

'I'm sorry, Georgia – you're confusing me. Did *I* strike *you*?'

His expression infuriated her. 'No, but there's some part of you that *wants* me to leave, that's shoving me out the door, and I don't know if I have the strength to fight back any longer. Oh *please*, Flynn, if you'd just try to understand how I feel. I feel so lonely.'

'Well you better get used to it. Most people do. It's part of growing up.'

Georgia gazed at him blankly. I've been lonely so long, she thought. I can barely remember a time when I was not lonely. 'Listen, Flynn – I'm not saying you're the bad guy and I'm the saint –'

'Good. That'd be like trying to distribute guilt between the Muslims and the Croats and the Serbs; who the hell started what in the thirties and forties.'

'That's precisely why I have to get out.'

'Because of former Yugoslavia?' Flynn raised an enquiring eyebrow.

'Because when our marriage is in real crisis,' she whispered, 'when I tell you I'm thinking of leaving and taking the children, you talk about Yugoslavia. Maybe it's a joke, maybe you're serious, but I don't want our family partitioned by Yugoslavia. Maybe that's how you see our relationship, but I don't. I don't know what to do but leave. I can't pretend everything's OK. I hate the idea of your going to Sierra Leone, but that doesn't make a jot of difference to you. I don't know why you bothered to ask me. You know who you remind me of, Flynn?'

'I can't wait to hear: I imagine it's a top-drawer, world-class, humdinger of a bastard. Milosevic? Ratko Mladic?'

Georgia flinched. 'You remind me of Suzie Bushell's mother.'

'Suzie Bushell's mother?'

'She has Alzheimer's,' Georgia replied flatly. 'She's in a nursing home. When Suzie goes to see her, she says sometimes she's there, and sometimes she's . . . not there. When she's not "there", Suzie holds her mother in her arms, and thinks, God, this is the body of someone I love dearly, but the person I know has *moved out* . . .'

Flynn's eyes darkened as they stared at each other. 'Poor Suzie,' he muttered.

'What's for supper, Mum?' Beth came into the kitchen and draped herself languidly over the back of a chair.

'Toad-in-the-hole and rhubarb tart.'

'God. School dinner. Can't we have chicken salad or something? Sometimes I don't know why I bother coming home.'

'You know what, Bethie? You don't have to,' Georgia snapped, brandishing a slotted spoon. 'Each member of this family, *each* of us, has a choice.'

'Georgia . . .'

The spoon clattered into the sink. 'And *my* choice is to go

210

to bed. Dinner's in the oven. None of you has to lift a finger. What a change.'

When Georgia had left, Beth walked over to her father and leant into his side like a cat. 'What was all that stressiness about, Dad?'

'She's tired, lovely, that's all.'

'She's probably menopausal. Most of my friends' mums are.'

'I don't think she's menopausal, Beth,' Flynn said firmly. 'I think she's angry. She's fed up with me.'

'Well *I* think you're wonderful. Everyone at school's jealous of me having such a cool dad. Martin says you're famous.'

'Does he now? Then your man Martin has a thing or two to learn about fame. Would you go and get your brother while I dish up?'

Several hours later, Flynn stood outside his bedroom door. Slowly he opened it. The room was dark. Georgia was asleep in bed, one clenched fist lying on top of the duvet, her forehead pulled into a tight frown. As he watched, she turned over; when she flung her hand behind her head the lines on her forehead vanished. She looked like a golden child, all tumbling fair curls and a pouting moue of a mouth, her beauty as alluring as it was the day he had seen her in Archie Gordon's kitchen. He drew a finger over her lips and in her sleep she clumsily batted his hand away, as if it were a fly. Flynn kissed her forehead and went downstairs to the darkroom. He lay fully dressed on the sofa and soon fell into a deep if troubled sleep.

Patrick bought blocks of stone simply because he liked them; over time, he would recognise the secret form within each block as it suggested its own destiny. For the time being, he was oblivious to all the patient monoliths that lined the yard: his heart and mind were focused solely on the work in progress. Had the monsignori of Westminster Cathedral

211

been present at Blake's Wharf that weekend afternoon, they might have withdrawn the commission. The atmosphere, and the sculptor's language, were distinctly unholy. Patrick sat on a stool studying the bust on its turntable. The grey vein which ran intricately through the white marble suggested the crease of experience in Hume's face. Patrick wore a dust-mask but had shoved the plastic-lensed goggles on top of his head; his face and body were coated with a film of white dust that made him look like a Titanic sculpture himself. The original plaster cast was beside him on a revolving stand, and he ran the flat of one hand tenderly over the bony bridge of the nose, pouched lower eyelids and sensual bottom lip of the Cardinal's face, lost in thought, before picking up his pointing instrument to take precise proportional measurements off the plaster bust. The physically shattering, maelstrom stage of the work was over; he had embarked on the long haul of turning the stone, by a near alchemical process, millimetre by millimetre, into the recognisable and living image of the late cardinal. He was completely unaware of Madeline's tentative approach from the kitchen.

'Is your back troubling you?'

'It's killing me,' he growled, 'fucking agony.'

'Why don't you stop and have lunch with me?'

'I want to get on. Scoot that stool over here, could you?'

Madeline watched him silently for a few moments. His union with the face before him was so exclusive that Madeline felt an ache of loneliness as she placed a cup of coffee on the ground beside him. The coffee had grown a skin and turned cold by the time Patrick noticed it; he only did so at all because he accidentally kicked it over.

FIFTEEN

'You know, when we started together, there was only one thing that I knew for absolute definite.'

'That you didn't want to be in this room with me?' Madeline teased, smiling warmly at the woman sitting opposite her. Alexandra grinned back and Madeline's heart skipped. When she had started seeing her at the beginning of the year she had barely dared to hope that one day she might see such a natural and confident response in the young woman. Now Madeline felt bereft at the imminent loss of her client's positive presence.

'I love this room. This room's –' Alexandra cocked her head on one side – 'home. That's it. No, Madeline, what I knew for a *fact* was that I would never let myself be with a man again. Never.'

'I have always remembered what you said in that first session last February. You said the only living souls you would ever trust were the woman who'd brought you into this world and the one you'd given birth to. And now . . .'

Alexandra ducked her head in acknowledgement. 'I know. It was always about trust, wasn't it?' Her warm smile turned shy and hesitant. 'I just wish there was something I could do for you, something I could give you to say thank you. I hate the idea of saying goodbye . . .'

'So do I,' Madeline said sincerely. 'But you've given me a great deal, Alexandra. I'm very happy for you.'

'You saved my life.'

'You saved your own life.'

'If anything went wrong, if I felt I couldn't handle something –'

'Call me. You're going to work well with Louisa; better than well, I think you'll get a great deal from each other – but you can always come back. I have the feeling that you won't, but the door will be open.'

'I'll always remember you.'

'As I will you. Particularly in the late afternoons. I will think of you at four o'clock for years to come.'

Madeline opened the door between her office and the little ante-room and was surprised to find Flynn waiting, ten minutes early, with a large leather case at his feet. When Alexandra hugged her impulsively he did not look away, as many would have done, but watched them with close interest. Madeline kissed Alexandra and watched her walk down the stairs before turning to Flynn: 'Could you give me ten minutes and I'll come and get you?'

When she eventually ushered him into the room he made the comment she had expected.

'I see some of your clients are allowed to touch you.'

Generally loathe even to acknowledge the existence of another client, let alone discuss them, this time Madeline felt Flynn needed reminding that there was an objective in sight. 'That was our final session. We were saying goodbye.'

'Ah. Then I have something to look forward to.'

'How have you been?'

'Good. Apart from a few skirmishes with Georgia. Have you ever seen *The New Yorker* cartoon of a husband and wife sitting at opposite ends of a sofa, divided by three UN peacekeepers? I'd kill for a copy.' He placed the leather case carefully on her desk and lifted a projector and three reels of slides out of it.

'I brought a range of work, covering various assignments. Do you want to see them in chronological order?'

Madeline was less interested in the photographs themselves than in the manner in which he chose to present them. Dealing with the tools of his trade, even his physical movements had gained sharper definition and become economical. 'Any order that makes sense to you.'

'Grand.' He considered the room and chose the wall opposite her desk. He moved a straight-backed chair into the middle of the room and dropped the blinds. 'You'll have to sit there if you want to see properly.'

Madeline acquiesced. She had not envisaged sitting in the dark staring at images projected on her wall, but she was curious to see what he did with a free rein. There was a professionalism about him which presented him in a new light, and she felt an anticipatory thrill as he sat behind her on the desk, next to the projector. He turned the lights out.

Four young girls, glasses in hand, stood in classic drinks-party poses, their slim necks elongated, pretty heads tilted to catch the conversation, cigarettes held loosely in manicured fingers. One bore her weight on one leg, her other hip jutting out like a filly's. Another looked into the camera with an expression that fell somewhere between distrust and disdain. The other two paid the photographer no regard. Although the image was black and white, Madeline felt the iridescent shades of the girls' cheap fashions. Their outlines were hazy, deliberately skewed; he had caught the women in motion and that lent a louche, intoxicated air to the scene. They instantly reminded Madeline of being in that sliver of time between girl-hood and womanhood. But there was something profoundly unstable about the scene, something that told Madeline this had been no ordinary social gathering. Gradually she took in the shattered window behind the women and the strange refraction of light from a large cracked mirror to their side. The longer she looked, the more uneasy she felt.

215

Flynn's disembodied voice came softly from behind her back: 'Where do you think this is?'

'A party,' Madeline began, 'but there's something about them, a sense of waiting . . .'

'It was taken in the lobby of the Hilton in Sarajevo. These girls were there twenty-four hours a day, working as trans-lators and fixers for the foreign press. They'd all lost family during the siege, had brothers and husbands and boyfriends dead, or at the front, all witnessed terrible things, but just look at them: clean and bright, glossy hair, high heels, lipstick, a little glamour . . . I was lucky with that one. It tells you – I hope it tells you – that the men and women trapped in those situations are just like us, having a drink in some flash new Notting Hill bar, except maybe they have more pride. More dignity.'

'Tell me how you took the picture; why you chose that particular angle.'

'This is one transient moment in those girls' lives, but there's so much going on outside the frame. You see the way Slavka is looking away? It leads your eye out, hints at other incidents, other potential photographs, so you know you're seeing just one frozen instant in a complete drama. That's why I love photography; it has the capacity to go beyond what looks like an innocent surface and suggest something else entirely . . . I don't want to shout, that window's been blown out by mortar shelling and there's a stack of AK47s behind that door. It's more a question of an impression, the suggestion of a secret, and, behind that, another impression . . . maybe another secret. I want you to look at these girls and recognise them.'

The projector clicked and before Madeline had looked enough the pretty young girls vanished to be replaced by a graveyard full of rough wooden crosses. Frame after frame flashed onto her white wall. A building shattered into jagged teeth. A woman filling a jug with milk. A child racing across a street with a small dog in her arms, the wall behind her pock-marked by bullets. An old man playing patience in front of a bombed-out tenement. He had turned her wall into a window, taking her into another reality. As she looked at each picture in turn, Madeline could hear the clink of glasses, the milk splashing, the puppy whimpering. The series formed a narrative rather than one iconic image; she could see that Flynn worked on the detail, burrowing closer and closer into his subject. Not one of the pictures was easy on the eye and their rapid succession made Madeline dizzy. Flynn paused on a portrait of a young man, not one but two machine-gun bandoliers slung across his chest, a handgun shoved into the waistband of his trousers, a scarf knotted jauntily round his head and a necklace of grenades running from his pocket. He was festooned as heavily as a macabre martial Christmas tree. His piratical grin and devilish air gave him the look of a child preparing for a fancy-dress party and belied the guerrilla pose.

'This is Mike, an American correspondent. Now *he's* definitely one of the fringe element I was telling you about. A grand feller . . . always straight up. A lot of people in these situations – correspondents, aid workers, mercenaries – want to take a peek over the extreme edge, a single hit of the action. They want to taste it on the tip of their tongue and then get the hell out. Mike knows all about the allure of violence. He understands that he has to be able to identify with the perpetrators of atrocity and not write them off as animals.'

'Explain that to me; how is Mike – or you – able to identify with perpetrators of atrocity?'

His reply came from the dark behind her. 'If you're going to photograph people, you've got to recognise the extremes of human nature and all that lies between. Killers are human too. If you don't acknowledge their humanity you don't have the right to judge them at all. We've all got the beast inside, hey, Madeline, struggling to get off the leash? It's only a question of what snaps the chains. Maybe they make a different

217

'choice . . .' Flynn's voice faltered and he cleared his throat. 'But the sensations they experience are the same ones we do. Now Mike, Mike feasts on the sensory . . .' Flynn laughed suddenly. 'And women too. He's probably had half the women in the international press corps.'

'What about you, Flynn? Do you have affairs on assignment?' Madeline wondered why she had asked the question. Did Flynn connect sex and violence? What was it like to *be* Flynn on assignment? *To be with him . . . She wanted to know about him sexually; what sort of women attracted him, how many women had he kissed, how many women had he made love to?*

'Not like Mike. Some mornings it was hard to believe the man could walk, let alone work. The girls call him "Woodja". You know: Woodja lend me fifty bucks? Woodja like to come to my room? Woodja like a fuck?' Flynn laughed again at the memory. 'He always makes it easy for them to say no . . . though not many do, according to Mike. He's always straight up about it.'

'And you, Flynn; how do you handle affairs?' Madeline was grateful for the dark, and Flynn's position behind her back. She was uncertain quite what expression lay in her eyes.

'It isn't a question of having "affairs". Sometimes, in those places, you need to fall on the floor and have grinding, teeth-to-teeth sex all night long. But it doesn't connect you with the woman; you might barely greet her the next day, or she you. It's only a release. An involuntary spasm. Fear's a grand aphrodisiac, you know; you want wipe-out sex to wipe it out. Better than yelling like a banshee.'

Madeline noted that he avoided the personal pronoun, distancing himself from what he presented as a common need. She thought about the moment he had kissed her in a new light. After a difficult session she had often wanted somebody to hold her, somebody to weep with, or fight with; anything was better than being alone. She could identify with

218

the yearning for wipe-out; to be able to erase everything but erotic connection.

The projector whirred and clicked again. 'OK; this is the last of the Bosnian pictures.' As he adjusted the focus, an image clarified on the wall. A small boy, so blonde that he at first appeared to be bald, leant against a white jeep in freshly laundered and neatly ironed T-shirt and shorts. Barely a square foot of metal on the car was not riddled with bullet holes. There was no glass – windscreen, windows and mirrors were gone. The driver's door was missing, the nearside wheel ripped to shredded rubber. On the driver's seat the head and upper torso of a Barbie doll lay beside a wooden duck. A pair of childish legs dangled from the top of the frame, only seen from the kneecaps down; the girl's shoes swung clear of her heels, only held on by the angle of her toes. One hand was just visible at the top of the frame, holding onto the edge of the open door.

Flynn did not need to caption the photograph. The little boy's penetrating frown, the absence of any adult or guardian, the wrecked toys; all narrated the story for him. The settings had been recorded with pitiless detail, but Flynn had dealt very tenderly with the faces of those whose lot it was to live there; he managed to channel all the sorrow and pity and anger he felt through the camera and out onto the wall of her office. It was almost embarrassing to look, but just as you were about to turn your head, they begged you not to look away.

With a sudden revelation, like the fingers of a sunburst penetrating cloud, Madeline saw that her previous interpretation of Flynn's work was misguided. In her ignorance she had assumed the camera to be part of Flynn's defensive system, an armour-plating that inured him from the suffering he witnessed. Staring at the little boy, she saw that the camera was an extension of Flynn's heart, allowing him to focus on his own empathy. He could never look away. She was again glad of the dark when she found her eyes swimming with tears, tears for Flynn as well as tears for the two children, and she listened to his steady voice.

'I try to remember that taking pictures can be an act of trespass; you can't go in and *pillage* the drawers of your subject. I try to respect that, not to raid for my own purposes, to prove *my* point. I shouldn't have a point at all. If they need a mask, if they wear a mask, like Slavka, like Mike, then the mask is the important thing; I don't want to strip that away. I need their help to know what is valuable, what is relevant to them in their particular position – you can't make assumptions, can't jump to conclusions about one particular memento or another . . . I try to think all that without losing sight of what I want the person looking at that photograph at their kitchen table to feel.'

'What is it you want them to feel?'

'Different things, but generally I want to upset them. I want them to forget about having the boiler serviced. I want them to feel something. Stop feeling nothing.'

'How would you feel if you had the sense that the people looking at your photographs feel nothing?'

In the dark his voice was intense, but deliberate. 'I used to feel angry with them. I wanted to drag them to look at what I'd seen . . . I don't feel that any more. If they don't feel able to face it, or can't be bothered to face it, my being angry won't make any difference. I learnt that from my father. He was always angry. Used to roar and pound the table all day, thump us, even the girls, just to make his point. The sort of Irishman who puts the B in bejasus . . . There was no harm in him, poor soul. He wasn't a violent man, but he was frustrated when people didn't see things the way he did, and more so when he couldn't persuade them. He wasn't a bad man, you understand, he was a dedicated doctor, but after that, and ten years of boarding school, my God, did I hate bullies . . . Anger doesn't persuade people of anything; it can't make them share your version of reality. So I stopped feeling angry. If people don't respond to my photographs, it doesn't change what I do. It's my job. It's what I'm good at.'

She thought how pervasively the photographer's shadowy presence marked his work, as if each photograph were stamped with a pale but distinct thumbprint. What Flynn termed his professional filter, his imagination, she thought of as his heart and mind. These pictures had been taken by his heart and mind as much as by the camera. *Madness and blindness and astonishment of heart.*

'I want to show you a few from another assignment . . .'

Madeline was wary of road-to-Damascus moments in therapy, but she had experienced, with other clients, two different states of comprehension that were near magical, and she felt one of them now with Flynn. She saw a door beginning to open that she had not realised was there; she had a clear view of the doorway even if she did not know what lay on the other side, and her blood seemed to double in volume, to surge through her, bringing renewed strength, as well as the courage and discipline necessary to help him. She needed that courage simply to be able to look closely at the images that followed.

Flynn told her he had taken the cycle at a Moldovan orphanage. Skeletal children with ancient faces lay curled on the stone floor; she could hear their animal whinnying, she could smell them, too, the reek of the forgotten. Babies, their cheeks and throats as loose as scrotal sacs, sat slumped against the bars of cage-like cots, staring sightlessly, eating their own faeces and vomit from the thin bedclothes. Scrawny adolescents, half adult, half infantile, licked the filthy floor. Madeline found her palm involuntarily pressed flat against her mouth.

'This time the media coverage had an effect. I'll show you part two.' The next ten slides showed the arrival of aid workers. Men and women of every age and race were shown picking the babies out of their rank beds; unpacking food parcels, tossing bedding in a human line stretching from

221

a truck to the door of the orphanage. A sweet-faced young girl sat on the floor with both arms wrapped tightly around the rocking torso of one of the vulpine adolescents Madeline had seen scavenging in the previous series. A bald, piano-mover of a man who reminded her of Patrick swilled and scrubbed the floor with disinfectant, his face a marriage of disgust and determination. And the babies, the babies – still with their ancient faces, still with the staring eyes that seemed to look two thousand yards past you, still covered with sores, but now at least clean, at least dry, at least approximating the human.

Flynn left the last slide on the wall. The pictures had worked: good had triumphed; basic humanity had responded to basic humanity; she saw them all – Flynn, the aid workers, UNHCR, the press corps – as heroes, while his lilting voice seduced her, coming softly from the darkness behind: 'What do you say, Madeline? A miracle, no?'

'Yes. It seems like a miracle.'

'Seems is the right word.' He snapped on the lights, startling her. 'I can't show you part three, but believe me, there is a part three. And four. And fuckin' five. We did our bit. We saw what was too horrific to believe and did something about it. We got the humanitarian agencies in there, we got money flowing, got our hands dirty. Some of those people you saw aren't aid workers, they're media. Journalists aren't aid workers, nor medics: not my job, we say. But if there's no one else to help, you help. If it's children, you help. If you reach the stage where you think reporting it can't do any fuckin' good, *you help*. You've got to do something to stop yourself rolling in the dirt and howling about your own pointless existence. The big bald guy swabbing down the floors? He's a BBC cameraman. When you see people pull together like that, it makes sense of the world, doesn't it? You think to yourself, maybe the Almighty's plan is to make these things happen just so as to trigger such goodness in others . . . A hare-brained scheme, some might say, to use those innocent babes as pawns in his demonstration of the triumph of good over evil, but then the kangaroo wouldn't win any design awards either . . .' The hairs on the back of Madeline's neck rose at the new edge in his voice; it was as if she could hear him whittling his knife behind her back. She stood up and turned her chair around to face him. He was packing up his bag, putting the projector away, waiting for her to speak.

'What do you mean by "there is a part three, and a part four" . . . ?'

'Professional objectivity is bullshit. It's always about identification, good and bad. Like I said, I can identify with the killers as well as the victims. I know I'd look for a way of killing someone who'd blown my home to pieces. I identify with those children as well as the despair of the people who have given up trying to help them.' He continued to pack his bag, avoiding her gaze. 'It's different on a battlefield; I've seen people wounded and not stopped to pick them up. You can't be half-Hemingway, half-Mother Theresa; you have to take the pictures and get them back to the desk. But in an orphanage everyone helps – you unfurl the blankets, mop the vomit, hold the IV bottle, do what you can.'

'And you did.'

'Yes. Me and many others. So you really want to know about part three . . .' He gazed at her questioningly for a long time. 'We're all complicit, you know? We all agree to act as if we believe we can do something. So we act. But two, three months after the photographs I showed you were taken, the food was gone, the beds were gone, the blankets and clothes and fucking disinfectant were gone and those kids were back licking the floor. We – the media – weren't back. Our story was over.'

Madeline lowered her eyes as his wretchedness washed over her. She heard him shut the clasp of his bag with a metallic snap.

'I've decided it's time to go back to work. Georgia says I should get your permission.'

223

'Do you need permission?'

'No. If I don't get back to work now I never will. Might as well kick my heels in Sierra Leone as Fulham. Pick up a bit of a tan . . .'

'You don't sound very motivated.'

'No? Well, maybe motivation isn't that important. Maybe it's a question of being somewhere else, anywhere else. Georgia's got this thing, you know? A fantasy travel file. She collects photos and articles about someplace – one place – she's longing to go. The thing is, she won't ever try to go there. Everyone should have a place like that.'

'Why Sierra Leone?'

'Why not Sierra Leone? It's as good a place as any to die.'

'Do you feel you are going to die, Flynn?'

'I've heard it happens to the best of us.' He flashed his regular disarming smile as Madeline continued to gaze at him with wide open, searching eyes. 'What I'm trying to tell you, Madeline, is that there are stories, images, that are worth anything. That are bigger than individual lives. You can't be in this business and not know the risk of what you're doing, even if you end up with a badly cropped snap on page eight, or five hundred words at the bottom of page twelve. When push comes to shove, your man has to decide if the story's good enough to die for.'

'What makes a story "good enough" to die for?'

Flynn shrugged. 'Big enough. Worthy enough. I don't want to die for a kitty up a tree. Some blokes I work with don't want to die in Africa. Bosnia, Kosovo were OK to die in, but Africa made them shudder.'

'Why do you think that is?'

'Maybe they couldn't identify with it as home.' Flynn's mouth twisted in an ironic grin. 'Now *you're* the kind of woman who would rather die in Africa than out on an oil rig in the middle of the North Sea. You'd say, the further away from home, the better. The more distant. The more noble.'

'What would *you* say?'

'I don't have a preference.'

'Not Rwanda?'

'I'm not going to die in Rwanda,' Flynn replied flatly.

'Would you go back to Rwanda?'

'No. Maybe.'

'I wonder why you didn't show me any slides from Rwanda,' Madeline deliberately thought aloud.

His tongue made a frustrated sound against his teeth. 'The *geography* doesn't matter. These are all *dying* places. When it comes to death, there's no room for cultural differences, or social or racial distinctions. It's what you might call the purest democratising process.'

The room seemed to be growing darker, the night seeping in through the windows and threatening the light within. Flynn was calm. He had been drained of game-playing.

'I have to go back to work or else . . . I need to go back to work.'

'Do you, Flynn?'

'I've been hiding at home for eight – nine? – months. It makes me feel like a coward.'

'You're not a coward. Would you tell me before you went away?'

He grinned. 'The way I'm feeling, I'd check with you before I took a crap.'

Madeline hesitated. She wanted him to feel safe, she wanted him to feel anchored, before he went 'somewhere else', somewhere she suspected would take him nearer to the clearing where Erik had died; yet she did not want to constrict him, nor suggest what was right or wrong. As if he could read her mind, as if for the first time there was an open and uncontaminated channel between them, he said what she knew he would say, although he put it in a way she had not expected:

'Somebody once said, I don't know who, but somebody once said: a ship in harbour is safe, but it's not what ships are built for.'

SIXTEEN

'Mum called about Christmas.' Georgia stood at the sink doing the washing up. 'She wants to know if we'll all go there for Christmas Day.'

'Jesus wept. It's only just November.'

'You know what she's like.'

'Tell her you and the children will go but I'll be working.'

'No. If you're home then we want to be with you. I'll ask them here. You aren't going to be working on Christmas Day, are you?'

'If it means not having to listen to your mother recite her three favourite poems after five glasses of fino sherry, you can count on me working.'

Georgia's voice lowered. 'For Christ's sake, Flynn, can't you respect the fact that she's my mother and our children's grandmother? After all these years, can't you accept her, even if she's different from you, even if she votes Tory and runs the local WI, and only buys British cars –' Flynn barked with laughter – 'can't you just respect her for *my* sake?'

'No. I cannot respect a woman who calls her grandson her "little soldier" and thinks A. E. Housman was the greatest poet who ever lived.'

'You're so bloody arrogant.'

'True. But that doesn't alter the fact that your mother's a bore. Go ahead and ask the old bag. Ask the whole lot of them. I'll find some way of amusing myself.'

'I bet you will.'

'If you sleep with dogs, you've got to put up with the fleas . . .'

'What the hell is that supposed to mean?' Georgia snapped. 'Are you calling me a dog?'

Flynn had meant quite the opposite; the slight had been directed at himself, but Georgia's defensiveness irritated him. Instead of replying, he shrugged.

'I'm sick of all of this, Flynn, sick of you being so nasty. What's the point of going to Sierra Leone? You don't have to travel a million miles to find misery – you've created it right here.' Georgia felt like shoving her face right in front of his as he sat at the table, blocking out everything from his vision except herself.

'Maybe I should offer it to the *Guardian* supplement. Portrait of a Marriage at 93 Munster Road.'

'You total bastard.'

Upstairs, Oliver crouched on the top step, listening intently. Beth came out of her room and stood white-faced behind her brother, worrying the skin around one thumbnail with her teeth. Below, their mother's voice rose in a crescendo.

'There's no point playing at being Mr Wonderful, being a sodding hero on one side of the world and such a one hundred per cent shit when you get home. I'd rather not have you here at all than have to pussyfoot around, holding my breath in case you combust. And you know what makes me angriest of all?'

The children could not hear their father's reply, only the low murmur of his voice. Whatever he said did not placate their mother.

'No. It's having to feel sorry for you. Having to pretend your bloody job is so bloody noble; constantly waiting in the wings

227

to hail the conquering hero. You know what? I'd be just as good at it as you are. It would be a relief to get away from all the domestic shit and leave it to someone else. I'd rather be dodging bullets and get my name on the front of a magazine than be a single parent for three-quarters of the year.' As soon as she said it she realised Flynn *had* been home for nearly three-quarters of that year. But she couldn't stop.

'Maybe you should try it. Strange that you never volunteered yourself for the front line during all those years on the foreign desk.'

'Maybe I will.' Words flew into her head and off her lips. 'Maybe I'd handle it better, too. Maybe I wouldn't be losing my nerve and feeling sorry for myself and seeing a goddamn shrink three times a week!'

As the kitchen door opened, Oliver shrank against the banister. Flynn looked up to see the ashen faces of his children. He climbed heavy-footed up the stairs and sat down next to his son, pulling Beth into the small space remaining on the top step and pressing his lips to the top of her fair head. The hall rang with the sound of slamming pots. 'My lambs, how many times have I told you not to eavesdrop?'

'We weren't, Dad,' Oliver said solemnly. 'It was too loud.'

Flynn nodded. 'Now listen to me, both of you. Your mother's only upset because I have to go away again. She doesn't think I should, but I have to.'

'Why?'

'The government has decided to increase our military presence in Sierra Leone, a country in Africa where the local people are fighting each other. I'm going to take pictures of the British soldiers arriving.'

'Why?'

'Good question.' Flynn smiled at his son. 'It's what I do, Ol. How else d'you think we pay your school fees?'

'I thought Granny paid our school fees.'

'Good point!' Flynn punched him playfully on the shoulder.

'But I have a job I've been neglecting and I need to get back to it. Besides, it's driving your mother mad having me under her feet all day. So I'm going to go away just for a little bit.'

'To Africa? Today?'

Flynn tensed as a wretched wail rose from the kitchen. 'I'll kip with a friend for a few nights before I go to Sierra Leone. Just to give Mum a breathing space. Trust me. It's the right thing for all of us. D'you understand?' Oliver nodded but his chin quivered. 'Good lad. And you, Bethie?'

'Are you and Mum splitting up?' Her voice was high and nervous. 'Are you leaving us?'

'Don't be silly. Wild horses couldn't keep me away from you two.'

'So we'll see you . . . ?'

'Not if I see you first.' He tweaked her nose and tried a grin. 'Now be *kind* to your mother. Try to understand how she's feeling and take care of yourselves for me, OK? Take care of Mum, too.'

'I don't see why you have to go. You didn't say anything; she was the one who was being a cow.'

'That's not true, Beth. I know you're growing up fast but there are plenty of things you're still too young to understand. I've made life difficult for Mum and now I have to try to put that right.'

'When are you coming back?'

'I won't be gone long. Let me see a smile. There now. That's better. I've got to chuck some things in a bag and get my gear ready.'

When Flynn had closed the door of the master bedroom, the children listened in silence to their mother's erratic, diminishing sobs. Oliver clutched his sister's hand in his own sweaty one. 'Beth; who is Dad seeing three times a week?'

'I'm not sure,' she whispered. 'I think some kind of doctor.'

'Is he sick?'

'He's the same as he's always been. It's Mum that changed.'

'Shouldn't we go and see her?'

'No,' Beth said firmly, pulling him to his feet. 'Let her calm down, like Dad said. I'll tell you what: let's play your football Monopoly, OK? I'll even let you buy Chelsea if I land on it. Come on; let's play in your room.'

Georgia did not raise her head when Flynn entered the kitchen twenty minutes later. Twisting the stem of an empty glass between her fingers, she stared down at the table and said, 'Please don't say anything. Let me explain first. I'm worried about you working but it came out wrong. I've been wanting to help so badly . . . and it hurts feeling shut out all the time. I didn't mean anything I said. I don't know why I lashed out like that; I just felt hurt. Something came over me . . .' She raised red-rimmed eyes to his as he stood in the open doorway with two bags slung over one shoulder, cameras on the other and a third grip held in his hand. For a moment she was silent, blinking at him in confusion, then she inhaled sharply, her heart beginning to thump hard against her ribs. 'You're not going already?'

'Not for a couple of days. I'll let you know when I've made some plans.'

'Plans? What kind of plans? Are you leaving me?'

'I'm leaving the house, Georgia,' he replied. 'I'm not leaving you. This isn't doing either of us any good. I need to be able to think and I need to try to work; see if I *can*. I know you feel hurt. That's my fault. I'm ashamed of myself for that, but right now I've got to get my head round other stuff. We'll talk when I'm back.'

'No. You can't leave. If you leave me, you have to leave for a real reason, a proper reason. Not because of what I said. It was a stupid, stupid tantrum; you *know* I didn't mean it. I love you. Just sit down, talk to me . . . *please*.'

'It wasn't what you said, Georgia. What you said was fine. But I need to be in another place, somewhere else. Alone.'

230

'Go tomorrow – don't leave like this. I don't think I can bear it.'

Flynn looked at her with an odd expression, and for a moment Georgia thought he would remain. Then a veil came slowly over his face and he shifted the strap on his shoulder. 'I'll call you, OK? When I get back.'

Oliver knelt next to the board, praying for a seven. He spat on the die in his fist, rattled them and rolled. 'I've got Chelsea!' he crowed. As the sound of their mother's anguished weeping rose from the floor below, the two children stared at each other in silence.

Three days later, Flynn stood in line at the British Airways desk. Despite his physical size he was unobtrusive amongst the smartly suited bankers and excited tourists in the check-in queues. A small boy, wearing a pale pink harness that kept him pegged within a yard of his harassed mother, clambered onto Flynn's baggage trolley. The photographer smiled at him and waggled his eyebrows and the little boy beamed back, then tugged at the strap of the camera case on top of Flynn's bags. Slowly the pile unbalanced and Flynn's flak jacket and combat helmet tumbled. The boy's mother swung round, saw the helmet rolling about the floor and yanked on the reins, glaring at Flynn with open suspicion. He restacked his trolley and waited patiently in the queue.

He felt calm for the first time since entering the tarpaulin tent on *Nepenthe*. This was a pattern he knew: the busy, civilian airport; then the flight, the breathing space alone with the newspapers and whisky that separated his two worlds. He was accustomed to a split-screen life, the journey being the transfer point between the two. Airports and planes allowed him the time to switch from one world to the other, his working life running constantly in fast forward while his domestic life was muted, put on pause.

He was glad he was going back to Africa. He felt the beginning of the old buzz, the liberating thrill of going back into action, back to old chums, the camaraderie of the press pack, the never-ending stories, the kick of living on his wits, being cunning and flexible, all on somebody else's expense account; not having to obey other people's rules, and not having to hurt anyone. Least of all his wife and children. The thought of them made his heart stretch. Once in Freetown, life in 93 Munster Road would be no more real than a dream on waking. He would not have time to think about Georgia or her mother or Christmas, or anything but the work. While on assignment, Flynn's London life seemed irrelevant and cloudy, not wired into the reality of human existence. For nearly nine months he had been held in that domestic blur, but now, as he handed over his ticket, he felt the familiar tangle of elation and tension.

The check-in clerk took Flynn's ticket without looking at him and asked, in a voice stagnant with boredom, 'Transit in Zurich; bags checked through to Freetown?'

Flynn leant against the counter. 'That's right.'

When she looked at his passport photo she glanced up and her expression brightened. 'Nice place, is it – Freetown?'

'Not after a nine-year war it isn't.'

Her tongue flicked over her lips. 'In that case, sooner you than me.' She extended the procedure of labelling his bags as long as she could, ignoring the impatient sighs of the couple behind. 'There's a chance I could get you an upgrade on the second leg . . . seeing you're so tall . . .'

He grinned.

She cleared her throat nervously. 'Have I seen you on telly? You look familiar.'

'A lot of people say that; I've just got a common face.'

'Excuse me,' the man behind Flynn barked, 'my flight's already boarding . . .'

The girl rolled her eyes at Flynn before she remembered

her customer-management training. 'I'm going as fast as I can, sir.'

'You could have fooled me,' the man said under his breath.

Flynn took his tickets with a wink.

Flynn touched down at Freetown airport and stepped into bedlam. He squinted as he emerged into the shattering light and was enveloped in a blast of heat. Nothing had changed. The chaos was still engulfing, but chaos was a minor element in a place of hallucinogenic violence, where the hacking off of human heads had become a routine business. When you landed in a place like Freetown you had to change your money, your religion and your mindset. Airport officials, at least half of them bogus, demanded documents and dashes in the name of visa fees while they shouted into defunct walkie-talkies. Flynn fought his way to the edge of the baggage carousel. Arriving passengers clambered onto it and raced like crazy hamsters to duck through the plastic flaps and rescue the bags which were being systematically looted. A mad drive to the ferry terminus in a clapped-out bus loaded with five times its legal passenger limit. What should have been a twenty-minute, fifty-cent ferry crossing from the airport to Freetown itself took him three hours and cost him ten bucks. Not that he cared.

Freetown, once a highly functioning colonial outpost of the British Empire, had disintegrated into a state of siege and decay. At the port Flynn, a good six inches taller than anyone else in the crowd, was pressed forward into the crush, while hawkers selling cigarettes, CDs, sunglasses and home-made rum tugged at his sleeve. Would-be porters tried to snatch his bags. 'Hotel? Hotel? Very nice hotel . . .'

Flynn grinned. There were no very nice hotels in Freetown. There had been one, a French resort some way out of town along the coast, but it was long closed. He knew where he was going and he could guess who he'd find there, which journalists' weathered faces would be lining the bar. And he knew what they'd say. 'Been here too long,' they'd say. 'Too many times,' he'd reply. And one of them, maybe even Flynn himself, would offer the predictable line, 'Never fear, the British are coming.' The British were already there and more on the way. That was why the hawkers were multiplying like rats: the troops and ever increasing NGO officials put a few drops of liquidity into the parched economy. The British were coming, a cease-fire of sorts had been agreed, but the atmosphere remained permanently twitchy, with the bizarre, jerky animation of a severed limb.

His head rang with noise. Eddie Grant declined to dance from a ghetto-blaster in a jacked-up, bullet-punctured truck, its wheels long stolen. The full volume concert of shouting, laughing, singing, bargaining, selling, flirting and fighting deafened him. He could pick out the different odours that mingled in the air: kerosene; carbolic soap; the stench of rotting vegetables rising from the gutters; animal waste; human waste. There were chickens everywhere, alive and dead, some swinging from the hands of brightly dressed women pushing their way to the market; some pecking at the debris that littered the dusty streets. He passed outdoor cafés, their stacks of fizzy drinks being guarded by children not yet in double figures. On the corner of a street that bore the small and oddly polite notice 'Mine', bitches suckled their litters next to mothers doing the same. He walked past identical pitiful houses, little more than sheets of corrugated iron patched with bits of tin, with calico curtains for doors and cardboard for curtains.

Flynn's passage to the hotel was robotic; it was the only way to handle the sensory flood. He could barely move in the enervating heat; unaccustomed to it, it temporarily drained him of curiosity, of any thought at all. No bad thing, that. He tried to begin each assignment with as few preconceptions as possible. The process was about going there; staying there; being there. Trying to understand and see more than your eyes saw.

Three children sat on the crumbling doorstep of the dilapidated hotel. Flynn stopped and returned their stares without speaking for a moment, thinking of Oliver and Beth. One tiny boy wearing nothing but ripped and grimy khaki shorts held out his hand, palm up. The trick in Africa was to reach the age of five, Flynn thought; if you could do that, maybe you'd have a fighting chance. Not much of one, not in Sierra Leone, but a chance of your life not trickling away like sand in an open hand. Flynn felt tears pricking behind his eyes. He reached into his bag and pulled out a packet of biscuits.

There was no lobby. He walked straight into the bar, as hot there as it had been outside. Two white men sat on one side of the bar, tilting into the feeble breeze of a small fan. On the other side the barman tried to catch his own share of air. Flynn dropped his bags behind them and draped an arm round the shoulders of both journalists.

'I need a room,' he said to the barman.

'Back again?'

'Bloody hell, Brennan. Trust you to find your way to this pit.'

'I need a beer and then I need a room.' Flynn sat down with his colleagues. 'So. What's going on?'

'The British are coming . . .'

The two correspondents began to talk with relief, as if a new arrival let them extend their minds the way they might stretch their legs to relieve an aching muscle. He could see the craziness in them and knew they could see it in him too, and that made him feel comfortable, like a fish back in water. They recounted many anecdotes, funny ones, bad ones and terrible ones. Flynn understood; it was the Scheherazade syndrome. Stories were a protection against death.

'I was thinking of heading upcountry. Bo; maybe Kenema. What's the situation in Makeni like?'

'Forget it, Flynn. OK, so they've signed a cease-fire, but if you're thinking of going to RUF HQ you're even madder than I thought. Don't whistle the wolf out of the forest, for Christ's sake.'

Flynn turned his face to the barman. 'How about that room? And make it one with a phone.'

The barman shook his head limply. 'No, boss, no phone; I can't give you a room with a phone . . . I only run the bar. Phones are . . .' He rubbed his fingers together.

Flynn addressed the Reuters man. 'Jim: what'll you charge me to use your sat phone?'

Jim smiled. 'I could let you have it for twelve bucks.'

The barman, suddenly self-appointed manager, tugged Flynn's sleeve. 'For ten dollars extra I give you a room with a phone.'

'Just make sure it works.' Flynn pulled out his wallet and paid the barman, who showed a sudden burst of energy as he left to prepare the room.

Jim looked after him. 'Poverty's a terrible thing; it reproduces itself. No work, no money, no electricity just leads to more sex, more babies, less money. Televisions; that's what Africa needs. Lots and lots of televisions.'

'I'll see you later. I've got to make a call.'

'You'll be lucky if the phone works. My rate's gone up to fifteen bucks, Brennan.'

Flynn did not want to linger with their cynicism. He was beginning to see things differently. Everything was familiar, the faces at the bar, the heat, the colours and smells, all the old ghosts, but he was able to face them calmly when he had feared he would not be able to. His colleagues had greeted him in the same old way; they had not seen a flashing danger sign smacked on his forehead, just the same old Brennan. Yet everything was different; he had found himself thinking not of Africa but of Georgia as he sat with his colleagues. He was looking for a connection to bridge his two worlds, but he did not know where that bridge might be found. Twenty feet away from them he turned back and took a picture of the two exhausted men draped over the bar.

*   *   *

Madeline was in bed, her knees pulled up to her chest, glasses on, studying a file of closely typed pages. Although she rarely made detailed notes on her clients, when Flynn had again failed to turn up for their session the day before she had spent the time making comprehensive notes of what he had told her over the previous ten weeks, as well as her own reactions. She was now re-reading the file for the third time in twenty-four hours, trying to find something she'd missed, checking and rechecking her instinctive reactions. She came back time and again to one of his first questions – what happens if you leave me? Beneath the bravado, Flynn had a horror of abandonment. In the early sessions she had recorded his candour but also his emotional reserve; regular flashes of self-deprecation masked what she now saw as a bedrock of self-confidence. Session after session he had demonstrated the essential conflict of the trauma-sufferer – between the will to deny, to banish the horror and atrocities and grief and guilt from his consciousness, and the will to proclaim, knowing that his ghosts would not sleep.

At the end of the session in which he had shown her the slides, she had been certain she – and he – were approaching a breakthrough. Sitting on the edge of the desk he had again taken her through the dream in which he saw Erik dead, but instead of starting in the bombed house, he had moved straight into the clearing, and instead of being unable to see in the dark, he had mentioned the light. In bed, Madeline searched her thoughts as if turning the pages of a book. Had he taken that short cut because the beginning – the house, the shelling, his son – didn't matter to him anymore? And why had the night in his dream become suddenly so bright?

Madeline had been surprised and wounded when he missed the following appointment. She had decided against calling him to ask him to explain the no-show, loath to make contact with him without being certain that she called for his sake rather than her own. Perhaps he had gone to Sierra Leone after all: *a ship in harbour is safe, but it's not what ships are built for*. As she stared sightlessly at the file on her knees she thought only of his personal safety. She was furious with herself for not cautioning him against going back to work. Trauma caused a personal fragmentation which ripped apart the complex system of self-protection that had guarded him from physical harm so far in his career. She should never have let him go without ensuring he had other systems in place.

Patrick was lying beside her with his eyes closed. She felt his hand on her thigh before it slipped down between her legs. For the past few weeks he had fallen into bed in a near narcoleptic state, physically and emotionally exhausted from his labour of love. The ten or fifteen minutes of physical sweetness he offered before sinking into sleep had not been enough for her. She had been hungry for more, yearning for the wipe-out sex to which Flynn had alluded. She had told herself that everything would get back to normal once the Cardinal was complete, but as she registered her resentment at Patrick's intrusion into her private thoughts, she realised that the distance she had put down to his preoccupation with the sculpture had been caused by her own preoccupation with Flynn.

'Patrick,' she said gently, 'I have to finish this. Is the light bothering you? I can work in the living room if you like.'

'No,' he mumbled, 'don't go. Don't work. Kiss me, Maddie?'

The uncertainty in his eyes made her miserable. With her heart full, Madeline tried to pull herself away from Flynn and transfer her desire to Patrick. She laid her glasses on the floor beside her bed and rose to open the curtains so that the bright lights of the City glittered at them from Tower Bridge. The building cranes that were a permanent feature of the skyline were already festooned with multicoloured lights like futuristic Christmas trees. Back in bed, she switched off the light and curled in to Patrick, nuzzling his neck before raising her lips

238

to his. When she kissed him he held her tight in his powerful arms, so tight that it hurt.

'Are you back with me, Maddie? It feels like you've been far away. I know I've been neglecting you. Don't ever let me treat you as second fiddle to my work. You'll always be first.'

'I know,' Madeline said, rubbing his cheek with her own. 'It's OK.'

'What's been keeping you awake? Is it still the Astra Four report?'

She could have told him lies, white lies at best, shoving aside the knowledge that there were no white lies, not in therapy, not in life. Or she could have tried the truth: *I am trying, Patrick, trying to live a decent life with you; I am trying to shake myself free of the past and look to a future with you. I am trying to love you with my whole heart.* Her thoughts swung to the e-mail from her godmother Patricia. *What held us together was all those shared memories, the triumphs and failures of two ordinary lives, woven together* . . . With a sense of barrenness she saw that she and Patrick did not have a shared past; they had managed to spend nearly a decade together leading close but always parallel lives. She did not know if she had any preserved past; she had shared it with no one and shut it away. She arched her back and shuddered.

Patrick held her in his arms and felt the tremble beneath her skin, and for an instant he convinced himself that it was desire. A ripple of sadness moved slowly through him. He wanted to make love to her to comfort her and to comfort himself, to erase the absence of her. Holding her by her forearms he lifted her on top of him. As her mouth lowered to meet his he gazed hungrily into her limpid green eyes. Madeline froze when the phone rang. With her dark hair tumbling around Patrick's face, she winced an apology and rolled over to pick up the phone. The line crackled and fizzed like a spitting cat.

'Hello?'

'Madeline? It's Flynn.'

For a second she did not answer. Then a cautious, 'Hello.'

'Did I wake you?'

'No.'

'I left a message, but I had to speak to you. I strong-armed your answer service.'

'Is it something that could wait until we meet?'

'No. I know this is breaking your rules but I need to talk to you. Would that be OK?'

Madeline glanced at Patrick. 'Just give me a minute.' She clicked the hold button and rose from bed.

'A client?'

Madeline nodded. 'Sorry. I'll take it downstairs.' She shrugged into the heavy green velvet dressing gown that Patrick had brought her from Venice, picked up the portable phone and went down to the studio.

'Hello, Flynn. Sorry to keep you waiting.'

His reply was soft and apologetic. 'I wanted to apologise for not turning up, not letting you know beforehand.'

'That's all right. Will you be there tomorrow?' Madeline opened the door out to the yard and stood leaning in the doorway, squinting up at the night sky.

'That's the thing, Madeline, I won't be. I'm in Freetown, waiting for the British task force.'

'I see. Thank you for letting me know.' Flynn was silent, but as she stood, shivering, she could hear his breath softly against her ear. 'Are you all right, Flynn? You sound . . .' He said something indistinct, then she heard his low chuckle.

'You'll have to repeat that – it's not a good line.'

'I said, I'm still breathing. It's an old joke I have with a chum. I'll explain it when I see you.'

The midnight sky was clear and cloudless, the stars beaming bright above her. Madeline could feel her heart pounding in her chest. He sounded contained and in control, if weary, but there was an intimate pulse in his voice – or was the intimate pulse in her? Madeline knew she should cut the call short, but the mellifluous rasp of his voice was so seductive, his tone so gentle as he continued, 'So that's my reply. I'm still breathing.'

'I'm glad to hear it,' Madeline said slowly. She was frightened for him in Freetown, knowing how dangerous Sierra Leone was, how dangerous for Flynn of all people. And shocked that he had gone without telling her. 'How long will you be there?'

'A week. Ten days tops,' he drawled. 'I should make the Monday session. If I'm stuck I'll call you again.'

'That will be fine.' Madeline's skin was electric, her heart pounding, *Doomdoomdoom*. 'OK. Goodnight, Flynn.'

'Maybe I'll call you again. I like talking to you on the phone: I don't have to see how cross I'm making you, I can just imagine it.'

'There's no need to call unless you need to cancel a session.'

'Right, boss. All being well I'll see you in a week.'

'Goodnight, Flynn.' *How could he go back there*, she wanted to yell at him. *How could he be so reckless?* 'Take care of yourself.'

'Madeline? There's something I need to tell you.'

'I think we should talk when you return.' She made an effort to sound firm.

'I know you do. Just listen . . . minute.'

The bad line caused a stagger between his words and her hearing what he said. It reminded her of therapeutic communication: the strain of listening so hard, not to miss a single inflection. The lag. Filling in the gaps. The broken statement. Beat. The intuition. I need Jillian, Madeline thought instantly: I need to see Jillian tomorrow.

'I'm lying on my back in a shite hotel in Freetown. There's stuff on the walls of this room you don't even want to know about. But I'm *alive*, you understand me? When I got here lots of stuff came back. The old ghosts came back, like I knew they would. But I'm doing what I'm meant to be

241

doing. We're kicking our heels waiting for the commandos to arrive tomorrow. I feel OK. I feel like I have a purpose. Like I'm being used for a purpose, as your man Shaw said, not just a selfish clod of ailments fretting that the world isn't struggling to make me happy.'

'It's good you're able to feel that, Flynn,' Madeline murmured.

'What? I can't hear you.'

'I said that's all good.'

'It's all good except for one thing.' His voice faded in and out and she strained to hear him. 'I've started waking up in the night . . . Not knowing . . . where . . . knowing who . . . I don't want to wake alone . . . strange places . . . alone . . . I don't want to wake up alone.'

'It's a long time since you've been on an assignment.'

'No. I couldn't put my finger on the reason until now. Tonight. But I know what it is. It's you.'

'Flynn,' Madeline stalled, hearing him clearly as she stared at the stars. She tried to stop thinking about him as a man in danger and think of him as a client. 'These feelings often emerge when clients are in the middle of intensive therapy. If the sessions are suddenly interrupted, the client may miss them more than they expected to.'

'I don't miss the sessions. I bloody hate the sessions.' She heard him laugh before the register of his voice dropped and softened. 'I miss *you*, Madeline. I want to wake up with you.'

Madeline did not immediately reply, other than her heart pounding so loudly she feared Flynn would hear it. *And I want to wake up with you. Doomdoomdoom.* No. OK. This was routine stuff. Behind the safety barrier of the telephone or the camera he again felt safe to engage intimately with his feelings. She cleared her throat. 'That's something we should address when you return. It would be better to discuss the issues you are raising face to face . . .'

242

The line crackled and spat. 'Shit. Call yourself a trauma therapist. This place is a disaster zone and you're talking about my "issues" . . . Don't work yourself into a lather, Madeline. Listen. I'm not sitting in a sordid hotel bedroom jerking myself off at the thought of you.'

His flash of irritation put her back on solid ground and she retorted, 'Hey, don't spoil it – I was enjoying the flattery.'

He chuckled softly. 'I miss you, Madeline. I'm not saying I want to make love to you. I do, don't get me wrong, but that's not what I'm trying to tell you. I'm making a bollocks of it but what I'm trying to say is, I go to sleep thinking about you. I fall asleep with you, feeling OK. You sleep with me. And I wake up alone, not knowing where I am, with nowhere to go.'

'Are you having the dream, Flynn? Are you dreaming about Erik?'

'I'm not dreaming at all,' he said tersely, 'but I'll make up a few. I'd hate you to think I'm getting better and lose interest. Will you hear what I'm saying? You bridge my lives, Madeline, link them together like they haven't been before. I wanted to tell you I'm grateful. I wanted to tell you that I see your face when I fall asleep and it's the face I need to imagine when I wake up. I couldn't go to sleep without telling you that.'

'Thank you.' Madeline had trouble speaking. 'We'll talk . . . when you get back. Next session . . . we'll talk.'

'That'll be grand. There's a lot I need to tell you.'

'Be careful, Flynn. Take care of yourself.'

'Since you've asked so nicely, I will.'

Madeline stood in the yard for several minutes, watching the moonlight caress the ghostly, half-finished bust of Cardinal Hume. She returned to the bedroom and made love to Patrick as if the man holding her, the man beside her and inside her, were Flynn.

SEVENTEEN

Jillian sat beside Madeline on a high, wooden chair. It was easier on her hip, and it made her more aware of how frequently Madeline's eyes sought the wide fields beyond the window. Half an hour after her arrival at the cottage, Jillian was playing it by ear, still uncertain whether Madeline's visit was purely social. With the intention of suspending all her supervisory work during the month of her recuperation, Jillian had called the builders in to redecorate her consulting room, and so had been obliged to show Madeline into the conservatory. She wished her old bones and new hip had been strong enough to take Madeline for a long tramp across the fields at the back of the house to the river; they would both have benefited from a lungful of sharp air.

Unprompted, Anna had brought a tray of tea and biscuits to the conservatory, which Madeline had refused, explaining that she and Patrick were going out to dinner with friends. They had chatted about Cardinal Hume; Madeline had asked about Jillian's great nieces and nephew; Jillian had assured her that her hip no longer caused pain, only occasional discomfort. Just as Jillian was beginning to fear that Madeline's visit to the hospital had jeopardised the professional contact between them, Madeline had told her about the phone call from Freetown.

'Jillian: I felt so awful about Patrick; lying upstairs, waiting for me to come back and make love to him. I felt like rushing to Westminster Cathedral and confessing.'

Instead, she's come to see me, Jillian thought. 'What on earth did you have to confess?'

'That I felt Flynn was a friend, someone I cared about. An intimate.'

'It doesn't surprise me you feel that way, Madeline,' Jillian said firmly. 'This is a man with whom you're working very intimately. A deeply troubled man in personal danger, whom you care for. He called and you listened. Why did that make you feel awful about Patrick?'

Madeline's hands twisted in her lap. 'I felt flattered. Not as his therapist. As a woman.'

'That doesn't surprise me either,' Jillian repeated. 'I would have felt flattered as a woman if any man said that to me.' She could sense the energy rippling through Madeline's discomfort. *At last*, she thought with satisfaction. *At last, we're going somewhere with this*. Jillian tried to keep her face devoid of expression as she posed an uncharacteristically direct question in as bland a voice as she could manage. 'Have you fallen in love with this man?'

Madeline blinked in surprise. 'Fallen in love?' she echoed slowly, her head inclined to one side. 'Fallen in *love*? I haven't thought about it like that.'

'Haven't you? It's the question I've been asking myself for some weeks now.'

Madeline was silent, gathering herself. 'If I said I *had* fallen in love with him, what would you say?'

It was unlike Madeline to test the ground before her, especially so clumsily, but Jillian answered honestly. 'I'd say, *lucky you*. I would feel envious. It's such a wonderful state to be in. But it sounds as if it's very difficult for you to admit the possibility of falling in love, Madeline.'

'It is. Yes. It is. Very difficult.' Madeline covered her eyes with one hand and spoke blindly. 'I don't remember what it would feel like to be in love. I know how powerful the erotic impulse is, but falling in love . . .'

Jillian was intrigued by her use of the conditional. 'Yes? Tell me about falling in love.'

'I would never fall in love with a client. I know the difference, however slim, between therapeutic love and romantic love.'

Jillian smiled at Madeline. 'Of course you do. It's an interesting subject . . . Of course, falling in love with a client doesn't mean making love to the client. But it does change the stage, and it does mean you have to be even more professionally and personally vigilant than you would naturally be.' As she pressed her hand into the small of her back to settle a twinge, Jillian thought how regularly and willingly objectivity was sacrificed on the altar of love. A parent's love was wilfully blind to the faults of an adored child, even when objective judgment might serve the child better. It seemed to her that in that case the power of love clearly outweighed the benefits of cool assessment. Might the same not be true for Madeline, that she should trust love rather than her much trumpeted objectivity, Jillian mused. Madeline had travelled far over the past ten years; not least her journey from the green fields of Somerset to the urban streets of SE1. The ground she had covered with the photographer also seemed a personal journey; Madeline was now looking for an authoritative signpost to follow, but Jillian could not point the way. She could only stand beside her at the crossroads.

'Flynn needs to be loved,' Madeline said abruptly, throwing her hair back off her shoulder. 'I feel, when I am with him, when I think about him, as lonely as he does. I identify very closely with him. I feel that *I* am standing alone, abandoned, in the dark. It is sometimes –' she closed her eyes and covered them with one hand in an expression of pain – 'unbearable. If I *let* myself fall in love with him, it might take away the distance between us.' Jillian did not need to speak; she let Madeline continue thinking aloud about Flynn's needs until she reached an end. 'I believe that if he knew I loved him, he would be able to forgive himself for leaving Erik at the checkpoint. He would be able to accept that others love him. His friends, his family, his wife.'

The risks would be great, Jillian thought, and she was not certain that Madeline had the experience to manage those risks. 'Do you feel the same way, Madeline? That if you knew he loved you . . .' Jillian paused, letting the obvious conclusion linger.

'That I might be able to let Patrick love me? No.' Madeline shook her head. 'It isn't the same. I thought I knew the rules, Jillian. I thought I had them all down pat, the rules of engagement and the rules of detachment. And now, the first time my heart is fully engaged, I come a cropper.'

'The first time your heart is fully engaged as a therapist, or the first time your heart is fully engaged as a woman?' Jillian asked sharply.

It was time for Madeline to recognise that she needed to stop putting her flaws as a therapist under the microscope and examine the wounds she had suffered and inflicted as a woman. That was her best chance of personal as well as professional fulfilment, and Jillian felt too tenderly towards the younger woman to see her throw that chance aside. Theirs had become a closely woven triangular relationship: as Flynn had brought Madeline to the edge of therapeutic boundaries, so Jillian now found herself willing to breach her own supervisory ones. When she taught, she repeatedly told her students that they should never 'get involved' with a client. There's plenty of space for sexuality in the therapeutic process, she told them, but there's no space at all for sexual intimacy. She told them not to get emotionally involved, because she knew it to be sound advice, essential for therapist as well as client. But like much good advice, sometimes it had to be disregarded. Jillian spoke warily, without knowing as she began quite how much she would tell Madeline.

'Many, if not most, if not even *all* therapists fall in love with their clients at some point in their careers. We fall in love professionally. There's nobody better at it, because it is an integral and necessary temptation of what we do. One should expect to be tempted. I know that many of our colleagues would not sanction what I am about to say, but to me, Madeline, the sin lies not in feeling tempted but in covering up your eyes to what lies in front of you.'

Madeline stared at her with such intensity that it was a moment before Jillian continued. 'I'd like to tell you about a personal experience, Madeline, which I think will have resonance for you. In my own working life, only once did I succumb to romantic temptation.' In her mind Jillian could still hear the bewilderment in her own supervisor's voice all those years ago: *one bloody fly hovers over the water, Jillian; just one, and you have to go and snap it up.*

'You fell in love with a client?'

Jillian nodded. 'It was almost thirty years ago . . . a lifetime. I was older than you are now. I had recently divorced, quite amicably. Before my divorce, before I was even fully aware of the problems in my marriage, I had taken on a client, a man a few years my junior. He was an academic, a wonderful man, deeply connected to his feelings, of great emotional as well as mental intellect. We worked well together over a couple of years. Around that time, I learnt that my husband had been serially unfaithful. I cannot pretend it broke my heart; we had been growing apart for some time. But it dealt a mighty blow to my ego. I found myself reassessing my client, comparing him constantly to my husband, in an increasingly favourable light. I justified this to myself by saying that our work together was nearly complete. I felt warranted in contemplating a post-therapy relationship. He had himself raised the possibility many times.'

Thirty years, but tears still came to Jillian's eyes when she thought about Ian. 'With hindsight, only with hindsight, as I did not sufficiently scrutinise my needs and desires at the time, I believe I felt *entitled* to take him for myself. I had been wounded and betrayed; here was a man whom I had restored and whom I admired and desired. He loved me; why shouldn't I love him in return? I ended the therapeutic engagement and embarked on a romantic one.'

Madeline's eyes remained on her supervisor's face when Jillian stopped talking. 'Jillian? Are you OK? You don't need to tell me anything . . .'

'But I do. I want to,' Jillian said firmly. 'It was an outright abuse of power. I made a mistake. I have thought about it for thirty years and no, I cannot think of a stupider, more reckless or more selfish decision than the one I took. One I regret bitterly to this day. Our professional relationship had lasted nearly three years, but I brought it to an abrupt halt well before its time. Our love affair, and very sweet it was for a time, very sweet to me, lasted only six months. In those six months I undid any good I had done and did him more harm than I could ever have imagined.'

'What happened to him?' Madeline asked, as Jillian had known she would.

'*That* I would prefer not to answer.' Ian's heartbreak and subsequent collapse were for Jillian alone to bear. 'I have not told you this story to attempt to alter your feelings and commitment to Flynn. You and I are not the same, not then nor now; I err from an excess of self-confidence in my abilities. I mistook the intimacy of our professional partnership for the intimacy of a romantic union.'

As Madeline leant towards her, Jillian brushed aside her silently offered sympathy and continued in a clear, strong voice. 'We offer our clients a shoulder to lean on and we expect them – encourage them – to put their full weight on us. But that weight can be an intolerable burden outside the sanctuary of the consulting room. Intolerable for the therapist, who needs support herself, and intolerable for the client, who must always carry the memory of their total exposure.'

As Jillian twisted in her chair she closed her eyes and stifled a groan. Madeline immediately leapt to fetch two cushions from the window seat. She knelt beside Jillian, rearranging the cushions until Jillian's face relaxed.

'Thank you, dear. It's eased.'

Madeline remained on her haunches at Jillian's side, looking up at the old lady. 'I shouldn't have come, Jillian. You must be exhausted. I'm so sorry.'

'I'm glad you came. You needed to. You are dealing with a man who has suffered a form of disintegration. Your task is to reintegrate him, but you cannot reintegrate him *through* you; you must restore him to himself. You will do that by letting him make his own journey towards the truth, however long it takes him. You know you have no map. You cannot even go with him, not all the way, not at his side. The healing process moves through stages of dependence, interdependence and independence,' Jillian struggled to continue, feeling her voice catch in her throat as the burn in her hip flared, 'but you must not, as I did, allow yourself to be lost in the middle.'

'No . . .'

Madeline's eyes had never left Jillian's, but her scrutiny was more comforting than unnerving; Jillian considered her clients fortunate to be the object of such attention. Madeline was committed and astute, but she was also damaged, and her ability to access that damage was the greatest gift she could offer her clients. Above all, Jillian wanted Madeline to trust herself and to trust love, as she did. That was what made her place one hand gently on Madeline's arm and continue.

'Madeline. My instinct is that with this man you need to let yourself fall in love, to gain the full arousal of all your instincts. Do not be afraid of love – it is your greatest asset. But you will need to be able to withdraw, and withdraw with a whole heart.

You will never be able to help this man if you feel depleted. Put your own heart under the microscope you use so well with others. Your love for him can be a constructive addition to the therapy rather than a violation, as mine was. Love him fearlessly and selflessly enough to create the supportive structure that allows him to heal himself: his fulfilment lies in him, just as yours lies within you. That would be my approach. It may not be yours. Do what feels right to you, but you will have to be strong, you will have to be clever and you will have to have courage. Great acts of healing involve great risk, and they always demand great courage.'

As the train rattled through the bleak November landscape, Madeline struggled with Jillian's advice. Fifteen years ago she *had* fallen in love with Hugh, she acknowledged reluctantly, and had believed herself happy in that sloppy state for several years. In less than one day, over a matter of hours, her heart had frozen. Even now she could not think of Hugh. She could not conjure his face or say his name without beads of sweat breaking out on her forehead in the damp chill of the train compartment.

Even the phrase 'fallen in love' made her angry. It contained one of the most destructive fallacies in the history of human thought: that love was as accidental and random as plunging head-first down a staircase. Not that romantic love was a condition you could approach rationally, any more than death was. It was impossible to look straight-on at either. You could merely snatch a quick, sideways glance at them, one quick sliding look and turn away – in case proper examination turned you to stone.

She had never made the mistake of falling in love with Patrick. Patrick was safe; Patrick was as solid and permanent and monumental as one of his own sculptures. She had flung herself into love with Hugh blindly, hurled herself down that precipitous staircase, closed her eyes and prayed it would pay off and that he would catch her as if he were some God-like being, not an ordinary mortal. She had never asked that of Patrick and he had never failed her. She had learnt to love him without the ludicrously loaded expectations of romance. He had even done her the service of declining her impulsive proposal of marriage two years earlier, recognising it as little more than innate good manners. Patrick had never done anything to loosen her grip on calm composure. He had kept her safe from the dangers that falling in love brought. Safe. What was it Flynn had said? That a ship in harbour was safe, but it was not what ships were built for.

Flynn. Madeline closed her eyes and pressed her flushed cheek against the window. She would look steadily at Flynn and her feelings for him, scrutinise them, meet them head-on – but it would wait until he came back. If Flynn came back.

A group of children were playing a game in the yard outside the hotel as Flynn walked out on his last morning in Freetown. Narrow your eyes and you might be anywhere in Africa, Flynn thought, anywhere in the world with kids. A rudely carved woman's head was mounted on a pole, a pipe stuck in her mouth. The children took turns to chuck sticks and stones at her, aiming to knock the head off the pole or the pipe out of her mouth. As he leant in the doorway smoking a cigarette Flynn watched a heavily pregnant woman shuffle, through the middle of the game, drying her tears with her headscarf. The instant Flynn lifted his camera the children abandoned Aunt Sally and started to whoop with delight, turning cartwheels, pulling faces, striking poses against the opposite wall which proclaimed in shaky white graffiti, 'Operation no living thing'.

Flynn moved down the street, passing wide-porched colonial houses, shaking the proffered hands of the children and giving them chewing gum, which was all he had left after nearly two weeks in Freetown. He spent much of the time after the arrival of the British task force visiting the Aberdeen Road Amputee Camp, talking each day to one particular man. Justus had been with his two daughters planting groundnuts under the bloated trunk of a baobab tree when the RUF rebel attacks had struck Freetown the year before. He had made the mistake of telling the twelve-year-old to run, and had had both his arms hacked off at the elbow, 'short-sleeve' style, as punishment. When he talked to Flynn, he used his prosthetic arm to draw his six-year-old daughter to his side, resting the two pincer fingers on her shoulder. She too had lost both her arms, from the elbow down. Flynn had spent several evenings at the Nayera beach bar, under the banner of a sign which said, 'France Cosmetics! Peau Claire and Soft Hair!' The walls and hoardings of Freetown were scattered with original frescos in the style of 1950s America. They would have merited an exhibition of retro art. Flynn's particular favourite was right by his hotel: a flamboyant painting of domestic bliss, emblazoned with the words, '"Electronics, radio receivers, disco lights, electric fans – You Name It! – 24f Wilberforce Place'. He had made friends with Sullay, the barkeeper, as well as Fatu, the most driven of the various prostitutes who hung about the beach bar. Just the night before they'd had their final confrontation when she once again thrust herself against him as he sat on a barstool.

'No, Fatu – I'm too poor . . .' He'd pulled out the linings of his pockets.

The other women had laughed and jostled about him.

Fatu waggled her hips. 'Bega-bega no can pik and chuz.'

Flynn took his cue from the cries of a market stallholder advertising her wares further down the street. 'Big market, I ge de big market, a ge de sweet sugar . . .'

'Fatu,' he pleaded, hoping to temper rejection with flattery, 'you ge de sweet sugar, but me hef wife . . .'

'Hef mohni na han?' Fatu taunted.

The women roared in one voice. 'Mohni na han, bak na grohn . . .'

Flynn had stayed in Freetown to attend the Sympathy Demonstration, when thousands of local demonstrators marched through the torn and tattered city to the National Stadium in support of the increased British military presence. Flynn began by walking beside the marchers, linking his arm with one old woman draped in a brilliantly coloured geometric print, who held a sign proclaiming, 'Keep the Candle Burning Great Britain!' The people of Freetown shuffled their support, hooting and hollering. Flynn took one shot of four proud young men carrying a banner abreast: 'Petty Traders Asso. Of Freetown thanks the British Government for sending its troops', and decided to leave.

By the time he had collected his bags from the hotel the march had dispersed peacefully. As he stepped into the taxi he tripped on an abandoned banner, already covered with tyre tracks and grime, which promised, 'De Wah Don Don!' He had no confidence that their optimism was right. Despite the cease-fire, it was still a place where you only had to put your hand into the embers and stir a little to relight it.

They drove through the city, under washing lines and crazily draped electricity cables, past people the colour of ebony, charcoal and liquid chocolate. This city used to be called the Athens of West Africa, Flynn thought, and closed his eyes. He wanted to be home. As the taxi swung crazily round the bend of the final hill towards the port, Flynn stuck an arm out to stop himself being catapulted into the driver's seat. He saw two homemade signs taped to the dashboard. 'No beutiful woman stays with man' and 'God never twist justice'. Flynn paid the driver double the rate, and climbed out, hoisting all his bags, wanting to leave Freetown on foot.

Ten minutes later he dumped his bags and wiped the sweat off his forehead. An old man was coming towards him, trying to push a ramshackle cart up the slope. The cart was heavily loaded, carrying possibly ten times the man's weight. Every time he reached the halfway point something fell off the cart, and when the old man stooped to pick the bundle up, the cart rattled back down the incline and tipped over, scattering the man's life in the gutter. Flynn stood still, watching the same thing happen three times, the old man never getting any closer to him.

He taught Flynn many lessons. That people kept moving, cease-fire or no. That all over Africa people were moving. Two million people had been displaced in Sierra Leone. Add to that the Rwandans, Congolese, Ugandans, Kosovans, Bosnians, Macedonians . . . A hundred and ten million peasants pushed off their land every year, worldwide, Flynn thought. That's globalisation: not McDonald's sodding Golden Arches. Flynn looked at the old man, restacking his cart at the bottom of the slope: Sisyphus, in the world of the Shades, right there on the edge of Freetown.

Sometimes it wasn't the commissioned shots that mattered, the British troops landing with all the banners and the bunting. Sometimes it was just the old man and his cart. Flynn put down his bags and took several pictures. He pulled three shirts from his bag and jogged down the hill to where the old man had stopped, leaning his frail weight against the cart. Flynn ripped his shirts into ribbons and wove the ramshackle collection of belongings together. He elbowed the old man out from between the handles and pushed the cart easily to the top of the hill.

Ten hours later, safe in the efficient arms of KLM, Flynn took the complimentary newspaper and learned of the assassination in Maputo of the journalist Carlos Cordoba.

The waiters rushed past like demented dodgem drivers, pushing trolleys of dim-sum which issued wreaths of enticing vapour, making the customers ever-more hungry as they attempted to flag them down.

Madeline tried to listen but was mesmerised by the piece of spiced seaweed that was stuck between the teeth of the woman opposite and missed the question entirely. She found herself running her tongue over her own teeth before making some bland and non-committal reply. Patrick had cajoled her into coming to lunch with an Italian couple he hadn't seen for a decade, claiming it would do her good to get out of the house and see someone new. Madeline had yearned for a solitary afternoon at the wharf, but she had been unable to reject Patrick's well-intended if clumsy efforts to 'bring her out of herself'. Now she privately accused him of having an ulterior motive: she had been brought along as a decoy to attract the woman's incessant flow of conversation and allow Patrick to catch up with Luca.

As Madeline offered advice on the best places to buy English cheese, and commiserated about the exorbitant cost of theatre seats, she asked herself what was wrong with her: why couldn't she smoothly switch gear, stop thinking about Jillian's story and let herself enjoy a normal and natural social activity like Sunday lunch in Chinatown? Luca's wife was perfectly pleasant; talkative, certainly, but a couple of months ago Madeline would have found her enthusiasm charming. Now, after an hour and a half of her company, she found the woman's preoccupation with squeezing the last drop out of a long weekend irritating, and had to stifle an impulse to be rude. This isn't me, she thought, feeling the slight pressure of Patrick's hand on her leg under the table and turning to give him an automatic smile.

'Are you all right?' he asked softly.

'Um-hmm, absolutely fine. The food's wonderful . . .'

Patrick's eyes flicked to her barely touched plate before refilling their glasses. When the waiter grumpily banged down another steamer of har gau, Patrick looked at Madeline pointedly.

'What?'

'Your mobile. I can hear it.'

'My what?' Madeline blinked.

'Your mobile. It must be in your handbag.'

'Oh. I didn't hear it.' Madeline reached down and pulled it out of her bag. 'You're right. I've missed a call.'

'You better go outside and call them back,' he said casually. 'Just in case.' As she rose to leave he explained, 'Madeline's always having to rush off to see some client or colleague. Mark my words: when she comes back she'll say she has to go, won't you, darling?'

Madeline waited out of sight for a few minutes before returning to the table to make her goodbyes. 'You were right,' she said as she pressed her lips to Patrick's ear, 'as ever. I'm so sorry to have to rush off. It's been so lovely meeting you both . . .'

'But that's so sad!' Beatrice exclaimed. 'You really have to work? Even on a Sunday?'

'Madeline's never off duty. I can't ever count on having her all to myself.'

EIGHTEEN

'Madeline?'

She could hear the crackle of a tannoy behind the voice she recognised instantly. 'Yes, Flynn.'

'I just got into Heathrow. I'm sorry I didn't call to say I was staying on in Freetown. I meant to, but, well, you know; other things got in the way.'

His apology for missing two further sessions without warning was embarrassed and stilted. Madeline had daily scanned the papers for news of renewed fighting in Sierra Leone. She felt a little wooden, his shyness passing to her. 'No problem. Will I see you Friday?'

'I was thinking maybe I'd come by now.'

'I, ah . . .' Madeline paused, her eyes on her open diary. 'I don't think I can do that, Flynn. Unless . . .'

'Unless?'

'Is it essential?'

'Christ no. Nothing that won't wait. To be honest you wouldn't want to see me. You know, when you get on a plane from a place like that they spray you with disinfectant – I'm stinking like a roach trap.'

Madeline smiled as she listened to him, holding the phone very close to her ear.

'So forget about it. I only called because if I leapt on the tube now I'd get to you with ten minutes left of the session. I'd pay for the whole thing . . .' He cleared his throat and the wistful note in his voice vanished. 'But I suppose you'll charge me anyway. Forget it. I'd rather get straight back home. It's nearly two weeks since I've seen Georgia and the kids.'

'That's a good idea. So I'll see you in two days. Friday.'

'Yeah, well . . .' Flynn didn't hang up. 'I spent a long time looking for presents to bring them, you know, something small, something that wouldn't break, something to show how much I'd missed them.'

He was holding her at arm's length, pointing to his family and letting her know that he regretted his impulsive declaration from Freetown. Madeline felt slighted. She wondered whether something had happened in Freetown that had made him shut down on her all over again, whether he had come too close to Rwanda.

'I'll look forward to hearing all about your trip on Friday. Maybe you'd bring some of the photographs you took.' As the word goodbye formed on her lips an idea flashed to the forefront of Madeline's mind. 'Flynn? Would you be willing to bring a camera when you come on Friday?'

'I could . . . why?'

'Just an idea. I'm still trying to understand how you use it.'

'You mean, to photograph you?' His voice was guarded.

'You can photograph whatever you like. The room, me, whatever's outside the window. Anything at all. Just tell me what you see as you do it.'

'OK. Maybe I can do that.'

A week before Georgia and the children had sat at breakfast looking at newspaper photographs of the Aberdeen peninsula on the coast of Freetown: five Royal Navy ships lying at anchor across the bay, everything neat and orderly and safe under sparkling tropical sunlight and British protection. They weren't

259

Flynn's photographs. They meant nothing at all. That Sunday Flynn had called to say he was on his way back to England, but when Georgia had asked him if he was coming *home*, he had stalled; said he'd sort things out. It was Wednesday afternoon and she had not heard a word from him.

It will be all right, she told herself firmly, pulling out of the car park; the important thing was that he had called and that he was safe. Everything else would be all right because it had to be; she would do whatever it took to make it so. She only needed to be patient. She headed for the restaurant where she had agreed to meet Suzie for lunch. They wouldn't talk about Flynn, she promised herself. They would have *fun*, as they'd agreed. They'd settled on a Wednesday because Suzie could take a longer lunch break and both boys had a football match and wouldn't need collecting until six-thirty. So plenty of time for fun, and Georgia could still do the weekly shop before picking up the children. Two hours later she let Suzie talk her into a third glass of wine.

'Zanzibar . . . that's where I'd like to go,' Suzie said. 'All by myself, just me and ten novels, all the books I never have time to read. No Roger, no kids . . .'

Georgia clinked her glass against Suzie's. 'To Zanzibar. But I thought we weren't going to talk about men or children or work.'

'I'm talking about fantasy. The absence of Roger and the kids was just a by-product.' Suzie waited for Georgia to laugh. When she was rewarded with only a faint smile she shoved her half-eaten crème brûlée to one side and rolled up her sleeves. 'OK. Cards on the table. Has he called?'

'Not since Sunday to say he was leaving Freetown.'

'And you feel . . . you feel . . . ?'

'I feel pretty wretched right now, Suze.' Georgia swirled the wine around in her glass. 'Beth blames me for Flynn being away. That's OK. She's thirteen; she has to blame someone. I can handle it. I miss him too, but I'm used to that. I just wish

I knew for certain he'd come back, that I'd be able to pull him in the front door and know we're all safe all under one roof; together.'

'He's going to come back. I know it. I have a gut feeling.'

'I know it too. I trust him,' Georgia said simply. 'I'm not going to lie to myself any more. I've stopped telling myself he's fine, just fine, and it will all blow over and be just like it was. Now I tell myself he's not fine, but he's going to get better. And if I'm hurt and lonely in the process, it isn't half as bad as what he's going through. I'm learning to be alone, Suze; but that doesn't mean I'm giving up. I want to be someone who can be counted on – by Flynn, by the children. I don't want to lie to anyone, I don't want to pretend it's all that simple.' Georgia could not tell Suzie that for the past few months she had approached her marriage as warily as she did an oncoming migraine, trying to freeze, to be as still as stone, not to move a muscle in case the fireworks exploded in her head. 'I have to face Beth and Ol and make them understand that, even if he doesn't come back, we'll make it. Because we will. I'm learning to let him be free, and I just have to believe that when he feels that, he'll know where I am, and he'll come back to us.'

Madeline stood in front of the bathroom mirror. The neckline of the black jersey dress she'd bought a year ago and never worn draped loosely at her shoulders but clung to her breasts. She was not certain she liked the effect.

As she looked at her reflection she questioned her impulsive suggestion that Flynn should bring his camera to the next session. She'd seen from his slides that he was drawn to images of introspection, where great emotion welled underneath. It had seemed absolutely right to bring that into the therapeutic arena. She bit her lower lip as she leant forward, searching her own face. *Great love involved great risks,* Jillian had said. And Jillian had done more than just say it; she had exposed her own pain for Madeline's sake, and it had liberated Madeline, given her the conviction that she could accept her love for Flynn and use it to help him. Suggesting that he take photographs during a session was a risk; Madeline did not know if she would be able to withstand his scrutiny.

Madeline leant closer to the mirror to stain her lips blood-red. They had accepted an invitation to a friend's preview: Toby was an installation artist Patrick had known for years, and was launching a new exhibition at a gallery close to the wharf. Patrick had been inclined to pass, but Madeline knew she had let Patrick down miserably at the Chinese dinner – not that he had complained – and for once she wanted to look the part of the sculptor's partner and enjoy it. She drew a violet kohl pencil under her lower lashes, deepened her green eyes with gunmetal shadow, then threw her head forward and sprayed her hair upside-down. When she tossed it back she stared at her reflection, wondering who she was.

Patrick appeared in the mirror. 'Your mother's on the phone.'

'Oh?' Madeline tried her hair in a twist, then let it fall in two heavy coils about her throat.

'Your mother's on the phone,' Patrick repeated, sliding his hands round her waist and clasping them over her stomach. 'I hear we're going to Florida for Christmas.'

'You agreed?' Madeline tipped her head back, arching her neck against his chest.

'Of course I agreed. You look like a gypsy,' Patrick growled, kissing her beneath her chin as she twisted her neck, and inching the fabric of her dress up over her thighs with the flat of his hands. 'Aren't you going to speak to her?'

Georgia Brennan drooped against her trolley in the queue at Sainsbury's, trying not to think about anything except what she would prepare for the children's supper. She gazed vacantly at her choices: the new shin pads for Oliver she'd bought next door chucked on top of a chicken, a bag of tomatoes, three boxes of cereal and an Indian meal-for-one. Two oak-leafed lettuces, which she had tossed in automatically because Flynn liked them, before she realised that Flynn wouldn't be there to eat them. That's great, she thought; I'm so pathetic that just looking at a lettuce makes me cry. She was trying to continue a normal routine for the children's sake, but each day was more of a struggle. The idea of roasting a chicken for dinner was too exhausting; fish fingers then. Beth would eat the salad, and would probably ask her again when Flynn was coming home, and she would try to look confident and assure them he'd be back any day now. I'm learning to let him be free, and I just have to believe that when he feels that, he'll know where we are and come back to us.

The repetition of this mantra sustained Georgia all the way to the school gates, where Beth waited in the rain with her friends. She rolled down the window and called in a cheerful voice, 'Come on, Beth – we'll be late for the boys! In the back, you know it's Ol's turn in front ... How was your day, darling?'

Beth grunted from the back seat. She had yet to forgive her mother for driving her father out of the house and had resolved not to extend so much as a smile until Flynn returned. Which Georgia understood. 'In that case, shall I tell you about *my* day?'

As she brought the car to a halt in front of the football ground, Georgia spotted Oliver and Luke Bushell, both caked in mud and blue with cold, so rapt in some imaginary game that they were unaware of her arrival. They were laughing helplessly, elbowing each other in the ribs and pulling faces. Georgia watched them, entranced; she could almost see them growing before her eyes. These moments of childhood delight were so transient; she could not recall those times in her own life and she knew that if she asked Ol, when she put him to bed that night, what he and Luke had been doing, what had been so all-consumingly funny, he would most probably shrug and say he didn't remember. But she would remember the delight on her son's face always; his joy was transforming and was transferred to her in one pure moment of recognition. How could Flynn leave, she thought; how could Flynn leave *that*?

'Mum, do you think we could possibly get home sometime in the next month?'

The horn summoned the boys, who tumbled into the car oblivious to the mud streaking the upholstery. Oliver turned towards her, beaming. 'We won, Mum; we one hundred per cent whipped.'

'That's fantastic, darling, well done. Well done to you too, Luke – put your seatbelt on would you? So what was the score?'

'Four nil. Banger scored the most amazing goal I have *ever*, ever seen. Ever. Mr Fletcher said it was poetry in motion. You should have been there, Mum. You should come watch.'

'Luke, could you get your filthy boots off my bag, please?'

Georgia looked in the rear-view mirror to see Beth's nose wrinkled in disdain. She could feel Luke's feet drumming against the small of her back, imagined the streaks of mud all over the rear of her seat and dismissed it. Washing the car was not a big deal; none of the so-called rules were a big deal. Let the boys have their moment of triumph unadulterated.

'Luke was cool too, he set up Banger's second goal, did this wicked bicycle kick from midfield.'

When Flynn calls I'll tell him about the game. I won't ask when he's coming home or cry or anything. I'll tell him about the game, put Ol on the phone, and tell him what a privilege it was to see them so happy. Thank God for football.

The traffic was heavy around Parson's Green; when the lights turned green Georgia inched forward round the corner, but they had turned red again by the time she reached the crossing. Georgia's foot rested on the brake.

Luke yelped, interrupting Oliver's blow-by-blow account of

the match. Georgia craned her neck to look over her shoulder. 'She pinched me!'

'Beth, for heaven's sake act your age!'

'Then tell him to get his stinking boots off my bag!'

Georgia looked straight ahead, watching for the green light. Her fingers tapped jauntily on the steering wheel, drumming in time with the song on the radio as she glanced again in the rear-view mirror, irritated by the mean expression on Beth's face. The sudden roar of an approaching car and the squeal of tyres on slick asphalt seemed remote, but Georgia's right leg instinctively stiffened on the brake pedal. For the briefest instant she was aware of a red car racing towards them, but the only thought she registered was surprise that it was travelling so fast in the rain. Too fast for anyone to do anything at all. With the whole world in slow motion she turned her head ninety degrees to look at Oliver and heard the crash of metal and shattering glass, Beth's hysterical scream and the crack of her own forehead hitting the steering wheel. Shaking violently Georgia lifted her head and began to scream herself. Oliver was slumped in the passenger seat. His eyes were closed and blood poured from his head. With one hand clapped across her mouth to stifle the sounds and another pressed against her son's head Georgia turned towards the back seat. Both Beth and Luke were staring in shock. Someone jerked open the driver's door and leant in. The voice on the radio babbled merrily: 'We're coming up to the seven o'clock news, but first here's Craig David to take us into the break.'

'Come on,' Patrick growled, taking Madeline's arm. 'He's coming our way. Let's get out of here before he asks us what we think.'

They were standing in the middle of the Moser-Mackay Gallery, only a few blocks from their home.

'Patrick,' Madeline hissed through teeth clenched in a smile, 'he's already seen us. And he's your *friend*. That's why we're here.'

'Fine. So we came; we saw; we can go. Just because I like the cretin doesn't mean I have to like his work . . . Toby!' He clapped the artist on the back. 'Madeline was just saying how much she loved the installation.'

'Really? That's great to hear. What in particular? Come on, I'll grab you a glass of something and we can discuss it. You don't mind if I steal her away for a moment, Patrick?'

Patrick rocked on his heels with a smile. 'Be my guest, Toby; be my guest.'

'I think the wall is extraordinary.' Madeline allowed herself to be led away with only a small but stabbing backward glance at her partner. 'Tell me about it.'

'It's a new ICI treatment called Priva-glass. Layers of glass are impregnated with millions of electrical particles, so that at the flick of a switch it turns from transparent to impenetrable. I saw it in my stockbroker's office and couldn't stop thinking about it.'

'Things must be going well; I didn't know you had a broker.' Madeline was intrigued by the glass because it made her think of Flynn. Obfuscation; sudden clarity. It amused her that Toby had 'discovered' the idea at his broker's and amused her more that he had done little other than install a vast sheet of it that sliced the gallery in half. The switch was on a timer. Every ten minutes the barrier 'wall' revealed the guests on the other side. One minute later they disappeared again. She held a sip of wine in her mouth and looked back at the wall, willing it to change. Where the hell had Patrick gone?

'It's that: is it there, or isn't it thing; you know what I mean, Madeline?' Toby topped up her glass. 'I knew *you'd* get it. What do we see, what do we merely imagine we see? It doesn't work so well with so many people here, because you don't get the effect of . . .'

The wall cleared as they strolled towards it, and on the

opposite side figures appeared from nowhere. Madeline stopped listening to Toby. Flynn stood ten feet away from her, deep in conversation, wearing the brown leather jacket he had worn when they had first met at the heliport. Keeping her eyes locked on Flynn in case he was a mirage, Madeline put a hand on the artist's arm. 'Toby, excuse me. I just need to find Patrick.'

'He's right behind you, talking to one of the gallery owners. Probably lining up a show of his own, the jammy bastard.'

'Excuse me.' Madeline spoke to him in a low voice. 'A client of mine's here, Patrick. . . . I need to leave. I can't meet him in this setting. I'll see you back at home, OK?'

'I'll come with you.'

'No, stay a bit. You should exhibit here. I'll just slip out.'

'Just come and meet Mel Moser before you go.' When he flung his arm lightly over her shoulders to draw her towards him, Madeline turned back to the screen. Flynn was looking at her through the glass. It darkened as she met his eyes. Abandoning Patrick she went straight for the gallery door, but Flynn was there before her, standing at the top of the open iron staircase that led to the street.

'Hello,' he said hesitantly.

'Hello, Flynn. I was just on my way out.'

'You were?' He leant against the doorway, blocking her path. 'Because of me? Through a glass darkly, hey?'

'Whenever I meet a client in a social setting it's better if I leave. That's the way it works.'

'You look incredible. That's a very pretty dress.' Flynn flicked his cigarette butt into the dark, keeping his eyes on her. 'It suits you. Tell you what; you don't have to leave, I was going anyway. I'm only here because Toby's the brother of a friend of mine and I had nothing better to do. I never dreamt I'd see you. Modern art, hey?'

'Well . . . if you're leaving anyway . . .'

'It's a crap show, don't you think?' Flynn jerked his head towards Patrick. 'So is that your husband?'

Madeline hesitated for only a second. 'No.'

Flynn lit another cigarette, his eyes on hers over the flame of his lighter. 'Aren't you going to ask me about my trip?'

'How was Sierra Leone?'

'When you land in Freetown you think you're going to go blind – there's such a downpour of light. It's hard to adjust.' Smoke coiled from his mouth as his eyes flicked over her face and past her. 'Madeline. Are you angry about what I said when I called you from Freetown?'

The wind whipped through the flimsy staircase. Madeline was shivering with cold and reached for the iron railing at her side. This conversation should *not* be happening here, she told herself, not outside the sanctuary of the consulting room. Yet she heard Jillian's voice ringing in her ears: *great risk, and great courage.*

'Angry?' she repeated. 'No. I've thought a great deal about it. It moved me enormously. You said you felt alone. You're not. I am there beside you, all the time, as far as I can go within the bounds of therapy. As far as you will let me.'

Flynn leant back against the railings, looking away from her into the street below. 'In Freetown, sometimes I felt like my old self, and then suddenly I'd lose my grip. I need you to fix it.'

'Flynn?' Madeline's teeth tugged once at her lower lip. 'Listen to me, Flynn. When someone has experienced a profound trauma, one that they have buried, or attempted to bury, for many years, they are no longer the person they were. You are no longer the man you were before you went to Rwanda. You may be trying to get back to where you were, who you were, and you may be able to do it, but *I* can't help you do that.' Madeline pulled her wrap more tightly around her shoulders, struggling to express what she felt. 'Because I believe that trauma changes people for ever. It doesn't heal over, the wound doesn't recover; you are always going to be knocking that scab off the instant it forms. Trauma becomes part of who you are. To live with it you are going to have to change the way you see the world. *Both* your worlds,' she added with conviction, 'both your lives. For a long time you have relied on a certain system of dealing with life – and death. And danger. It doesn't work anymore because there's been a kind of . . . rupture. I can't fix it; because the glue doesn't exist that will hold it. Flynn?'

He leant against the wall with a groan. When he turned his face to hers she could see the ache in his eyes. 'Tell me, Madeline: why is it that I want you so badly?'

'Because you believe that I can help you. I believe it too. I am certain of it. I think it's time we got going on integrating your life. When we next meet, on Friday, I think it's time we talked about Rwanda.'

Flynn put his hand on her arm. Madeline felt the solid weight and warmth of him through her sleeve. She knew she would be haunted by the kiss in his eyes; the offer made, silently declined; that one touch; the immediate ache of regret as she turned on her heel, back to the heat of the room where Patrick was waiting.

NINETEEN

Georgia smoked as she paced outside the hospital. Suzie had pressed a pack of cigarettes and a lighter into her hands when she'd come to the hospital to take Luke and Beth back to her house. Georgia was working her way through the pack and her phone list to find anyone who could get hold of Flynn. None of their friends knew where Flynn was, even whether he had yet returned from Sierra Leone. She drew another blank with each and every member of Flynn's family. Then she'd thought of the therapist. Finally reaching a human being at the paging service, she had begged and bullied and pleaded and screamed to get Madeline's home number. The answerphone gave a mobile number, which she scribbled down with shaking hands. She drew another cigarette from the pack and lit it from the butt of the last.

'Hello?'

'Dr Light?'

'Hello?' Madeline went back to the stairwell to drown out the noise of the party. 'Yes? This is Madeline Light.'

'It's Georgia Brennan – oh God . . .'

'Hello? Georgia?'

'It's Flynn.' There was no reply from the therapist. 'I need to find Flynn right away. Do you know where he is?' Georgia coughed, choking on the swallowed smoke. 'Where's my husband?'

'Mrs Brennan, has something happened? Is there a problem?'

'Just tell me where Flynn is!' Georgia screamed down the phone.

'I saw him twenty minutes ago, by chance. But he left. I don't know where he is now.'

'I have to find him.' Georgia's head pounded. 'Listen. I don't care about the confidentiality stuff. Just tell me where he's staying. I have to reach him.'

'Where's he staying? Mrs Brennan – Georgia – Flynn called me from the airport earlier today to discuss his next appointment. I had the impression he was on his way home.'

'"Home?" You don't know that he's left me?' Georgia asked dully. 'He didn't tell you?'

'Georgia. Are you in some sort of trouble? Flynn may still be outside; perhaps I can catch him . . .'

As Madeline searched in vain for Flynn in the street below, she heard the growing desperation in Georgia's voice and pressed the mobile tightly against her ear. 'There's been an accident. A car accident. I have to find Flynn now. My son – my *baby* . . .,' Georgia howled. 'I'm at the hospital. *Please* help me find Flynn. He has to be here. Didn't he give you a number, any number? Please help me . . .'

'Georgia. I'm sorry. The only number I have is your home number. If there's anything I can do – where are you? Shall I come to –'

Georgia hung up.

Madeline checked the last incoming number and called back. *The number you have called is engaged. We cannot connect you . . . Please try later.*

Madeline no longer needed to shut out the sounds of the party; everything around her had already been switched to mute. She had tried to assemble the composed front she had been trained to present to the grief-stricken and hysterical. She had been stunned by the information that Flynn had left his wife. But none of these things meant anything when she heard Georgia's cry: *my son, my baby . . .*

She began to walk towards home, staring blindly ahead to Tower Bridge, as glittery as the giant cranes of Astra Four. Home. She felt the sun beating hot down on her neck, felt the nauseating sting of rape fill her nostrils, the rust-stench of blood permanently mingled with the sweet spice of summer roses. Her stomach heaved. She could feel her long, loose cotton skirt tangling against her bare thighs like seaweed as she tried to run and went nowhere. She tried to run towards the fields, away from the house, into the golden countryside, but there was no country, no colour, only black and white and a terrible smear of red.

Jillian was already in bed when Patrick called, but as soon as he hung up she dialled the number of a local taxi firm and asked them to take her to London. Patrick had said there was nobody else she was willing to speak to.

It was barely ten days since Jillian had last seen Madeline, but when she arrived at Blake's Wharf and Patrick helped her down the spiral staircase to his studio, the fragile girl she saw curled up at one end of the big sofa was a different woman. There was no colour in her face, nor animation in her expression. Patrick put two glasses and a bottle of wine on the table in front of them and left them alone. Madeline did not touch the wine and she did not greet Jillian when Jillian sat close beside her. Her wide green eyes were fixed on the Hume wall, and when she spoke her voice was lifeless.

'It fell apart, Jillian. Poor Patrick. We were at a party. I left . . . Patrick came looking for me. I'd thrown up everywhere, over the bed, the floor . . . It was the terror in her voice that made me sick. It brought everything back. Everything. The train. That god-awful summer. How much I hate the country, the sodding soil and all the shit that comes out of it. I thought I was all right about Sam. Now I know I only chose my work to stay near him.'

'Most trauma specialists are drawn to the work because of their personal history, Madeline. You know that.'

Madeline waved Jillian's reassurance away with anger. 'Most trauma therapists don't come into the work as a result of killing their son.'

'You did not kill your son.'

'But I did not look after him.' Madeline stared at the wall. 'I did not prevent him from being killed. Ever since I started working with Flynn, everything has kept leading me back to Sam. I see that now. It was ten years, ten years to the week of Sam's death that Flynn turned up on my doorstep. Right after Astra Four, after I'd met him, I started having that dream again, trying to get away from the farm and the harvest and not being able to run. I can't get away from the farmhouse or that summer however hard I try, because I can't leave Sam – I can't abandon him again. I lost control with Flynn when he said he knew I didn't have children. I lost control, Jillian. Again and again. In his dream he runs with a small child, with his son, knowing he is trying to save him, but he can't hold him tight enough, he is slipping away . . .'

Madeline's face was blank, numbed by the anaesthesia of grief. 'Gradually, after years of missing him, I'd see something lovely – your daffodils in flower, a strip of sunlight on the Thames, and for a moment I could forget about Sam. There was a moment with Flynn, when he called me from Freetown, that I knew he had displaced Sam in my heart; I could not feel the ache for my dead baby. I felt Flynn in my heart. It was what you told me to do. You shouldn't have. You should have told me to cling to my grief with both hands, because when I let go of it, just for a moment, it lurks around the corner and slams into me. And now Flynn's son is dead. And now all I can think about is Sam.'

'Tell me about your life with Sam. Your life with Sam, and your life with Sam's father.' Jillian had heard Madeline's story many times during the first year of supervision. It was not a story you could forget, but Madeline needed to tell it again.

'You want me to tell you about Hugh? Fine. I can tell you about Hugh; that's the easy bit. I met Hugh a few months after my father's heart attack. I "fell in love" with Hugh, as you'd put it.' Her eyes snaked round accusingly. 'Everyone thought it was a bad idea; my mother told me to wait; said I was too young; Daddy's death too recent. But I was . . . *in love*, and I married him. I was pregnant six months later, not that happy about it. We'd moved to Hugh's farm in Somerset, and I missed London, I didn't like country life, and I didn't want a baby when I was only twenty-four. But Hugh was so damn sure it would be fine. He wanted an "heir", he said, someone to take over the farm when he retired. And it would give me something to do. I'd never seen myself as the maternal type.' Madeline's lip curled but then her face melted. 'But when Sam was born, I was so *happy*. He was the most beautiful baby. The sweetest, gentlest baby. His eyes . . . I felt I had known him all my life, that I had been waiting for him.' As her voice trailed away, Madeline twisted and untwisted the belt of her green dressing gown. 'He was lovely, that's all. I was very proud being his mother. When Sam started at the village nursery I needed to fill the hole in my day, and decided to train as a child psychotherapist, just part-time. I wanted to learn everything about children; I wanted to be the best mother I could be.

'And how were things with Sam's father?'

'I don't know. He wasn't important to me.'

Jillian opened her mouth to remind Madeline that she'd been in love with Hugh. It wasn't the right time. 'Tell me about the day Sam died.' Madeline shook her head in a tiny movement and closed her eyes.

'Madeline. Tell me about that day.'

'It was late July; nearly the end of term. Unbearably hot. Stifling. I'd been up half the night with him, he couldn't settle. He woke up snuffly, red-eyed. Hugh insisted it was a summer cold, but I knew it wasn't, I knew it was hay-fever. He was no more suited to living on a farm than I was. Hugh said I was over-protective, foisting my urban neuroses onto Sam, when Sam was a country boy born and bred. I had a lecture in Bristol that morning. Hugh and I had a fight about whether Sam should go to nursery or stay home. It was the start of the hay harvest. Hugh said he wouldn't be that busy, he had plenty of help. He said he could easily look after Sam at home, but I thought, Hugh's only going to haul him round the fields with him, and Sam's hay-fever would be better if he was at nursery rather than trailing about the farm after Hugh. That was what we *agreed* – that Hugh would take him to school. He promised me. I ran to catch the train. I didn't even say goodbye to Sam. I just ran out of the kitchen.'

'And caught the train.'

'Yes. I caught the train. I drove to the station. I had the windows down, and the rape . . .' Madeline flinched. 'It's the worst smell in the world. But I caught the train. And I went to the lecture. About halfway through, about eleven-thirty, I was called out to take a phone call. I knew it was something bad. The moment the lecturer said my name, I knew . . . My legs wouldn't work for a minute. It was Ned, the farm manager. He started talking about an accident, a terrible accident with the combine harvester. Almost before he said anything, I knew it was Sam. I prayed it was one of the farm workers, or Hugh; prayed that someone, *anyone*, had had an arm mangled. Just an arm. But I knew it was Sam. From the moment I woke him that morning he'd seemed so *vulnerable*. I knew it was Sam. On the train from Crewkerne I'd had a pain in my stomach, a stabbing pain.' Madeline inhaled sharply, and pulled her elbows tight in against her ribcage, straightening her back, so that when she exhaled, her breath came out with a gasp. 'I knew it was Sam.'

'Did Ned tell you what had happened?'

'Yes. He said Hugh had gone to hospital with the ambulance.'

'And you went to the hospital?'

She gave a tiny nod. 'I got back on the train. I was on that train forever. I wanted to get out and run but finally we got there. I couldn't drive. I was praying, kneeling on the floor of the taxi, praying. Somebody must have taken me to Sam's room, but I don't remember anyone. I was already alone. Hugh was in my way, between me and Sam. Sam was lying on a bed with the sheet pulled up to his neck. His eyes were closed. He looked so small. They didn't have to tell me he was dead. I knew he was dead. I knew he was dead on the train.'

'Do you know what happened while you were in Bristol? Do you know how the accident happened?'

Madeline looked straight through Jillian. 'Hugh was driving the combine. Sam was pulled under and crushed. He died on the way to hospital. There was an inquest. It was an accident. Modern combines have some sort of a cut-off switch, which might have stopped it. Ours didn't. It wasn't illegal, or negligent, they said; it was a "tragic accident". I didn't need an inquest. Sam was dead. That was all.'

Madeline's head dropped back to the cushion. 'How did you manage the aftermath, Madeline?'

'Aftermath? I'm still trying to manage the aftermath. Immediately after, the worst thing was Hugh.'

'He must have been in terrible pain.'

'I don't know what Hugh was in,' Madeline said coldly. 'I spent weeks avoiding him, pretending to be asleep when he got up, lying there rigid till his car pulled away. I remember thinking the only good thing about his being a farmer was that he had to work seven days a week. People were coming and going all the time. There was a lot of praying. Everyone prayed except me. I thought about it a few weeks ago when I saw Patrick praying for the first time. It reminded me of those people, the days after Sam died, before the funeral. Hugh's family – Christ, even his cousins . . . all of them sitting there with their eyes shut and hands clasped, rocking . . . After the first few weeks I spent a lot of time in Bristol. I stayed in the most expensive hotel as often as I could. I told Hugh I had to carry on with my course, but I didn't. I just lay on the hotel bed till I had to go home. Saturday mornings were the worst: Saturday mornings we'd always spent together. I can still hear Hugh saying, why don't we go to an antique market? Why don't we treat ourselves to something special?' Madeline closed her eyes again and Jillian wondered what visions she was seeing. 'Sam had only been dead six weeks.'

'Were you and Hugh ever able to comfort each other?'

'No. Never. That October I came back to London. I have never seen Hugh since. I don't even know if he's alive. I don't care if he's alive or not. He has nothing to do with me. I no longer think of him but—'

'You do not forgive him?'

'No.'

'Can you feel any sense of gratitude –' Jillian was conscious how very gently she needed to make the suggestion – 'that it was through Hugh that you came to know your son? That without him you would never have known the joy that Sam brought you?'

Madeline's gaze was stony. 'I would rather never have known either of them than had to suffer losing Sam. Do you know what it is like to sit holding your dead child in your arms and remain alive? Be expected to carry on living and feeling that your life is of value?' She shook her head. 'All that pain and rage, all that regret and self-reproach and searching for someone to blame, anyone to dump it on. The ache and ache and *ache* of it. Searching for any way at all

277

to turn off the pain. The sounds – the sound of crying and screaming, *my* screaming – it took me *so long* to get them out of my head, and last night, last night . . .'

'They came back?'

Madeline nodded. 'Everything came back. Running through the garden and driving to Crewkerne and being in the hospital and Sam's funeral, all at once, and the room swimming with the scent of roses, the roses and sweet peas that were all over Sam's coffin. And I didn't see Hugh's face but Flynn's . . . I thought of Georgia, what Georgia . . . Hugh's mother . . .' Madeline swallowed hard. 'At the funeral, Hugh's mother said something to me. She said children can't help but be careless with their own lives – they don't *know* how fragile life is. But parents know. We *know* it is our job, our most important, only job, to look after them. Keep them alive at the very least. How can I accept that I failed my child? How can I have ever pretended that I accepted it?'

'You never have accepted it, Madeline. I have never heard you say that you accept it.'

'Years ago you told me that grief was less a wound than an amputation. Learn to live without the limb, you said. But I *still* feel it. I still try to get up and walk and I fall over. I have *tried*, Jillian. I am trying all the time, trying to go on, to exist, to survive. But I feel as if my guts have been ripped out. And I'm so angry, so angry . . . I live in the belly of grief, I don't try to avoid it, but sometimes I think it's only the anger and grief and pain that flows through my veins that's keeping me alive . . .' As Madeline began to shake, as the tears began to fall silently from her closed lids down her pale cheeks, Jillian moved closer to her. She could feel the warmth of Madeline's body and hoped Madeline could feel hers. 'I didn't only lose Sam, I lost my whole relationship with him. All I'd known. The end cancelled all the rest. I can't imagine him. I see his crushed body under the sheet. Not my little boy running through the garden, all pot-belly and sway-back . . . Sam was so *young*.'

278

Madeline's fist hit the sofa again and again. 'I've lived twice as long without him as I did with him and I now feel all he ever did was die. He'd be fourteen. Fourteen. I won't ever know what he'd be like.'

Sobs shuddered through Madeline's body as Jillian embraced her, not to quell her tears but to share them. 'At Sam's funeral, the vicar said to me, "the child that can produce those tears won't ever be lost to you".' She began to shake as if in a seizure. 'It was a lie. An ignorant, platitudinous, fucking lie. I *still* want to put cream on the eczema on his arms; I still want to smell him, and hold him, and feel him, and lick him and taste him – I want it so badly I feel like an animal, I want to get on all fours and howl, and I cannot face the horror of not seeing him again,' Madeline banged her fist against her temples, 'I *cannot*, and I try to dream about him, I look for his face when I pass a playground, I pray for a hallucination, madness, *anything* that will just let me see him, just see him and let me love him again, to know and feel how much I loved him, just for a few seconds. When he was born, I held him for a moment and then the midwife said, we need to take him now . . . I begged her, just a minute, just a minute more . . . And then he was dead, and I was begging for just a year, a day, an hour – one single minute to look at him, just have the chance to love again . . .'

Jillian knew that the pain that was still pinning Madeline to her lost child had very nearly ruined her, but she began to see a glimmer of Madeline waking up after what had been a long and tormented sleep. She could feel her uncurling and, although she could not feel any certainty about the future, she knew that Flynn was as central to Madeline's recovery as she was to his.

'The chance to love again,' Jillian echoed softly, her eyes brimming as Madeline pulled herself up straight.

'When Flynn's wife called, everything in me, everything that makes up a person, emptied. I don't want to spend the rest of my life searching for Sam. But I can't stay with Patrick. I have never been fair to him. I have stayed with him – starved him – because I felt that level of companionship was all I deserved – more than I deserved; that I had no entitlement to more.'

'It sounds as if you now feel differently.' Jillian stroked her friend's cheek. Madeline looked exhausted as she dragged her hair back from her face and half sat up. 'I don't know whether Flynn's son is alive or dead. If he is dead, I want to try to stop them both being lost as a result. Flynn was very nearly lost already.'

Jillian had listened to Madeline as she might have listened to a daughter, but she had never had a child. She believed that Madeline's courage with her clients, which she had seen many times, was the only good that could be salvaged from the wreck of a young life. Had Madeline been her daughter, she would never have been able to leave her that night.

TWENTY

After leaving the gallery, Flynn crossed the Thames and walked through the dead streets of the City. He did not know where he was going, only that he needed to keep moving along the river. For two months he had told himself that if he could only see Madeline outside her consulting room, at home, browsing idly through magazines on her coffee table, watch her face flicker with irritation at some comment her husband made, hear her telling her child to turn off the computer that instant; if he could only see her as an ordinarily flawed woman, it would release the passionate hold she had on his heart and mind. Now he wished he had not seen the large man with the sculpted head drape his arm so intimately around her. It had not weakened her mystique.

It was well after dawn when he opened the door of his friend's flat to find Andy dozing in a chair in the hall. He staggered to his feet at Flynn's entrance.

'Christ, Flynn – where the fuck have you been? I've been waiting up all night. You've got to go to the hospital right away; there's been an accident.'

As Flynn stood without speaking, swaying from side to side, Andy shook him. 'Jesus, are you drunk? What's the matter with you?' He spoke carefully. 'Yesterday evening Georgia was involved in an accident. I'm going to drive you to the hospital, OK? Listen, Flynn: she's *OK*. I talked to her; she called me around midnight. She's OK, but we need to go now.' Andy searched his pockets for his keys. 'Flynn? Do you understand?'

'She's OK? You're sure?' The stubble on his chin gave Flynn's face a blue cast. 'Georgia's OK?'

Andy found his keys on the kitchen counter. 'She's fine. It's Oliver. Oliver's not so good . . .'

In the early hours the A&E reception area had a surreal vacancy, the near-empty seats like the benches of a deserted train station. A few people sat slumped, waiting. Only the duty nurse seemed truly alive. She began to type in answer to Andy's question. 'I've just come on duty . . . but let me check . . . Brennan . . . Is that a double "n"? Brennan . . . Here he is. Oliver. Is that your son?' Flynn nodded. 'He was brought in by ambulance yesterday at . . . seven twenty-five p.m.' She scanned the screen silently before indicating the chairs across from her desk. 'Yes. If you'd like to take a seat, someone will be here to talk to you as soon as possible.' When she lifted her head, compassion broke through her starched efficiency. 'Mr Brennan; you do know your son's all right?'

'He's not dead?'

'Dead? *No* . . . He was well enough to ask for food an hour ago.' She patted his shoulder. 'Your son's fine, Mr Brennan. He's booked for surgery later today, but I'm *sure* he'll be fine. I'll get a paediatrics nurse to take you to him.'

Andy stayed with both arms wrapped around his friend until the nurse arrived.

Their footsteps echoed in the endless corridors that connected A&E with the rest of the hospital. The nurse pointed Flynn towards a semi-curtained bed at the far end of the small ward and gave him a small shove. 'You see? He's sitting up. Your wife will be so happy you're here at last.'

Flynn watched his wife and son for several minutes without moving. Georgia was half sitting, half lying on one side of Oliver's bed, with her face in profile to Flynn. A bandage covered one of Oliver's eyes and half his face, and his skin was the colour of thin milk. Despite the cage under the sheets that partly obscured them, Flynn could see they were playing cards. A livid purple bruise embraced one of Georgia's eyes, but she was able to wink at Oliver as she swooped the deck off the bedclothes. 'Mum! That's three times in a row you've whipped me.'

'Sucker.'

'Why do you always win?'

'That's easy.' Georgia shuffled the deck expertly. 'It's because I always cheat.'

Looking at his wife and son, knowing he had arrived too late with too little to offer, Flynn felt the blowback of a mortar explosion, the sudden suck and back-blast that was more far-reaching than the bomb itself. He was not aware of making a sound, but Oliver's head rose sharply. 'Dad!'

Flynn approached hesitantly. 'What have you got under those blankets, Ol, a couple of goal posts?' His voice cracked and he looked away; he could not bring himself to meet the recrimination in his wife's eyes. He shuddered and began to weep when he felt Georgia move off the bed and envelop him with her slim but strong arms. She stood on tiptoe as he bent to hold her, rubbing her cheek against his wet face.

'Oh Flynn . . . thank God,' she whispered. 'Thank God you're here.' Flynn smoothed her hair away from her face and pressed his lips to her temple, not trusting himself to speak as she clung to him. 'Ol's got a broken leg. Three separate fractures. They're going to do more X-rays in a minute, but they think it will have to be pinned. His head . . . last night . . . last night . . . there's something I have to tell you . . .'

'Shh, darling, shh.' Flynn rocked her then held her slightly away from him to look at her face. 'Are you all right, Georgia?'

She nodded and smiled. 'I am now. Apart from the panda impersonation.'

Flynn sat beside his son. 'And you, Ol?'

'I'm OK, Dad. My head hurts a bit. The doctor said it must be made of rock.'

'Full of rocks more like.'

When the orderlies who came to take Oliver to Radiology explained that she could not go with them, Georgia supervised their every move. Fragile, washed out, yet ferociously protective, she watched them wheel her son away with her arms akimbo and her lips set into a tight smile so that Oliver would not see her downcast. Once Oliver was out of sight she sank down on the bed with her eyes closed and Flynn sat beside her waiting for her to speak. His heart caught as he looked down at her face; one eyelid was swollen and multicoloured, the other a pale, translucent violet. When Georgia spoke she was calm, but it was the calm that partners exhaustion.

'We weren't even moving. We were at a red light. When I saw the car coming up behind it didn't cross my mind that it could hurt us. I watched it coming at us. I *must* have thought something, that the driver was stupid or not in control, but I don't remember feeling afraid. It hit us, I looked at Oliver and thought he was dead.' Flynn lay down and wrapped his arms about her, holding her as hard as he dared. 'Bethie was screaming with her hands over her face, Luke was staring at Oliver and I couldn't move at all. I was absolutely useless. I didn't even try. I thought, maybe we're all dead, and that's why I can't move. I didn't move until the ambulance came. Ol was unconscious. I sat next to him praying that if he was in a coma and was going to die, then God would let me die too. And right when I thought that, Ol opened his eyes for a second and looked straight at me.' Georgia could feel Flynn's tears trickling down her neck and put her hand against his cheek. 'It was all very clear, Flynn, like someone had switched on the light and I knew exactly what I had to do and dying –

any of us dying – went straight out of my head.' Her voice was a little breathless and very quiet. 'If he hadn't had his seatbelt on . . .'

'But he did.'

'If I'd been paying attention, been more careful.'

'You were stopped at the lights.'

'I should have put the handbrake on.'

'Nobody puts the handbrake on at a red light.'

Georgia took his face between her hands and made him look at her. 'Flynn. I'd just had lunch with Suzie. I'd had three glasses of wine.'

'It was a shunt, sweetheart, d'you hear me? You could have had three bottles of wine and it wouldn't have been your fault.'

'All I wanted was to find you.'

'Jesus, Georgia; you must have cursed me to hell and back.'

'Cursed you?' Georgia's eyes opened wide, making her wince. 'I didn't curse you – I wanted you. I needed you so much, and I knew that I would find you, however long it took, and that you would come and that Oliver would be OK so long as we were both here. I'd been so frightened since you left and all at once I could hear your voice in my head; I kept asking you, *are we going to get out of this Flynn, are we going to be OK*, and I could feel you with me, saying, *I'm here. Yes, Georgia, we'll handle this, I know we will*. As soon as I spoke to Andy I felt such a rush of strength and instinct; like some kind of wild animal.'

'My lioness,' Flynn said, his lips against her throat.

'Only because I knew you were coming and I was sure I could survive anything until you arrived. The doctor came to tell me that Oliver had woken up and his head scans were fine, but he was hungry . . .' Her bubble of laughter took them both by surprise. 'And now you're here, and Oliver's going to be fine.'

'Let's hear what your man says about his leg now, OK

Georgia? If they have to pin it . . . just don't be too optimistic.'
Flynn's voice faltered. 'I don't want you to be disappointed.'

'No. Don't worry about that,' Georgia said. 'I told you, I
know that he's going to be fine. I *know* it.'

Ever since they had met, Flynn had been charmed, if secretly
dismissive, of what he saw as Georgia's illogical and wholly
feminine inconsistencies. Now he could see something else
beneath them, a conviction and resilience that humbled him.
Her strength came from the boots up.

Late that night, Flynn insisted that Georgia went home to Beth
while he stayed with Oliver. As he watched his son sleeping he
wondered how Georgia had been able to confront what she
had most dreaded. He had belittled much of her fear for the
fragility of her children's safe existence as irrational maternal
dread. For most of his life Flynn had been confident that he
knew about risk and was able to assess it. He had felt himself
accustomed to walking abreast with fear and suffering and
death, but he had never expected to confront them on the
domestic side he had cordoned off. His split-screen life was
disintegrating. His heart ached for Georgia and he marvelled
that she had not shown the anger she was entitled to feel. She
had let her fear give her purpose, then set it aside. Flynn both
admired and envied her. Even now, in the middle of the night,
with Oliver sleeping soundly beside him, he could not switch
off the fear pumping through him.

He tried to focus on the tasks that lay ahead of him. Talk
to the doctors; deal with the car. Talk to the police. Make
sure that his family was safe and could not slip through
his careless hands. Stay with Oliver. Spend time with Beth.
Convince Georgia that she would not be left alone again, that
he was always beside her and that he loved her. He wanted
Georgia to know that with the same certainty with which
she had known that Oliver would recover. Phone Madeline.
See Madeline. His throat tightened. Do something about the

286

fact that he was in love with Madeline. Do something about it.

It was dusk on a midwinter Friday; the time of day, the time of year when the light can trick the eyes. Flynn had talked at length about the accident and his feelings arising from it. Madeline knew that Oliver was in plaster to the groin but a career with Chelsea Football Club had not been ruled out. As soon as he entered the room she had seen that he carried a camera, but neither of them had referred to it, and there had been no mention of their meeting at the gallery.

Flynn's eyes moved restlessly about the room; his fingers tapped his knee, as if he were impatient for something to happen. 'I know what you're going to say.'

'You do? That's good, because I don't.' Madeline's voice was rough around the edges.

'Ah, come on! You're thinking, how do I connect my son's accident with all the deaths I've seen, and with the dream about carrying him out of the shelling. Aren't you?'

'How do you connect them?'

'I don't. That's just it. Georgia and Ol were in an accident. Erik wasn't killed by accident. Plenty of people are, but not on a front line, not in Rwanda, not in Sierra Leone, not in the Congo. People are deliberately killed there.'

'Does that make a difference to how you feel about it?'

'I can't stop a traffic accident, some machine going out of control.' The blood pounded in Madeline's ears, almost drowning out the sound of his voice. 'I can't do anything about something I can't see round the corner. But in a combat zone you know the risks, when you can assess them, however large . . .' He shrugged. 'Now what about these photographs?'

Madeline inhaled deeply; she felt too ragged for the photo session. 'There's time for that later, Flynn. I'm interested in the distinction you made just now . . . I'd like to stay on that for a while.'

'Because you think I'm saying I could have prevented Erik's death. You're right. I could have. After Georgia's accident . . . I had another dream . . . about Erik, but different from the regular one.' He studied one shoe, still for a moment, but then grew increasingly restless. His hands didn't stop moving, rubbing an ear, flicking at imaginary dust on his sweater, jiggling the foot that rested on his knee. 'I should have told you I'd moved out the house.'

'It's entirely up to you what you tell me and what you choose not to.'

'If I'd told you, she wouldn't have given you such a rough time.'

She didn't give me a rough time. Madeline waited, three, four, five beats, then asked him gently, 'Do you know why you didn't tell me that you had left home?'

'I don't know why I do anything . . .' He thought for a moment, and then spoke quickly, so quickly that he wouldn't be able to take anything back. 'I'll tell you what I *think*. I think I didn't tell you because you are private, private to me; you, and my time with you belongs to me, not to anyone else. And I think that *you* are the jumping-off point into my working life, not my home life. That's what I'm here for, isn't it, to sort that out?'

'You are still managing to hold those two worlds separate?'

'No,' he said softly. 'No. Not since Sierra Leone.'

Her heart was filled with what he had told her on the phone from Freetown and the expression in his eyes when he had left the gallery. It felt an age ago. 'When you go on assignment, Flynn, when do you leave "home"? Is it when you close the front door, or when you board the plane, or when you first hear the mortar shells?'

'By the time I hear the mortar shells I'm generally praying I was *back* at home.' *She wished he'd stop smiling at her; she wished he'd stop looking at her altogether. Just his look made the fine hairs rise all over her skin.* 'No; I guess it's at

288

the outgoing airport. On the way to the airport. Maybe even on my doorstep.'

'And this has always worked for you?'

'It used to. Like you said at the gallery, it's not working any more.'

Madeline could not read Flynn's face; he seemed to be weighing up two alternatives.

'When I work,' he began slowly, 'the most important thing to me is to be inside my subject and still to remain outside them.' Madeline nodded. 'I didn't get to the hospital till Thursday morning. I was out of my mind. I couldn't think about what might have happened. I couldn't stand what they'd lived through. When I realised they needed me and weren't ready to kick my arse out the door for not being there before, I knew I didn't deserve it, but right then, in the hospital, that didn't matter. I just felt lucky to be wanted like that. I felt closer than I've ever felt to my family. That we were inseparable. But now . . .' Flynn's straight dark eyebrows pulled down in genuine bewilderment. 'I love my son. I maybe love my son more than anything on earth. I love Georgia too. More than love her. But right now I do not feel connected to them. I do not feel that we are living in the same world.'

'Does this sense of not living in the same world apply only to your immediate family,' Madeline asked, 'or do you feel that *no one* lives in the same world?'

'Ah . . . she narrows in on the key issue with the inevitability of death itself . . .' There was resignation in his voice. 'You know what I feel, Madeline. You and I are in the same world. Nobody else. But with you, that being inside and outside thing doesn't work for me: I can't be inside you. I can't get under your skin – I know nothing at all about you apart from what I can see in those sad eyes of yours. That's why I want to get on with these pictures. I don't know if you're real or if I've made you up.'

Sad eyes? My God, do I have sad eyes? Resting her chin in

289

one cupped palm, Madeline struggled to work out whether she should permit the photo session or not. Maybe his eagerness to photograph her was provoked by the desire to connect his life and his dream world. Maybe, maybe. And maybe her own arousal, the fizz of semi-sexual fermentation that she felt was anticipatory fear, not thrill, fear at what she might reveal as the subject of such intimate examination. She could not assess the risk, but she was willing to take it for both their sakes.

'Go ahead. Photograph whatever you want.'

Flynn checked the light monitor, fractionally adjusting the shutter speed and focus settings. He held the camera to his eye and observed her through the lens. The room was darkening rapidly. Madeline felt excited and nervous with possibility. She had always believed that she was in control of her image and chose how she wanted to appear, and the notion of being Flynn's raw material was profoundly unsettling.

He lowered the camera and smiled. 'You don't have to sit there like a deer caught in the headlights, you know. You can talk, move . . . just carry on as normal.'

'You mean, forget you're here?' she smiled back. 'That isn't part of my normal method with a client.'

'You do your thing, I'll do mine.'

Great risk, she thought, and astonishment of heart. The proof of her integrity was not her ability to control the situation and protect herself, but their mutual capacity to trust. 'Flynn. You said earlier that you'd had a different dream about Erik.'

He was leaning against the corner wall some six feet away from her, and she had turned her head and shoulders to follow him, seeing his mouth but not his eyes. She was aware of each faint click of the camera. 'Yep. Last night I slept in the chair next to Ol. I couldn't stop thinking about Erik – I think I was *trying* to think about Erik, trying to go over it again. Sometimes I can bring the dream on, you know? So, I was expecting the nightmare, *wanting* to have it.'

Wanting to have it, last night, after the accident? Madeline leant towards him, resting an elbow on the arm of the chair. *Click*. And the dream had shifted. She waited; patient; still.

'Sure enough, I had the same dream, until the end of it.'

'Tell me from the beginning.'

As Flynn moved about the room talking, looking at her through the lens, Madeline became aware of several things: first, that she felt he was stalking her. The safety of her consulting room had been invaded; the space was too small, too contained, it was too easy to be cornered and there was no place to hide. She understood what had made Flynn pace the room in their earlier sessions. As the camera gave Flynn control and confidence, it stripped them away from her. That was all right, she tried to reason with herself; she had deliberately suggested this to put him in his natural environment, with the necessary, if risky, correlation that she would be taken out of hers. And, second, she realised, that in contrast to his manner during the original account of his dream, Flynn spoke calmly and steadily – whether because the camera distanced him from the intensity of his feelings, letting him wear a professional mask, or whether because it gave him control back, she did not yet know. Madeline's curiosity heightened as she listened to him.

'I am in the same building, yes . . . I hear the shelling and incoming fire. I know I have to get out of there or the whole thing will blow. I start looking for the way out.' He moved to the desk behind her and switched on the lamp. As Madeline craned her neck to keep her eyes on him, he took another photograph. 'On my way to where I think the door is, I trip over something, and pick it up. It's Oliver, small; the age he was when I was in Rwanda.'

'How old is he?'

'He's three – maybe four. I take him with me. It's the same

291

dream, Madeline.' *Click*. 'Just the same dream as always. But at the end—'

'Could we go back to when you are trying to leave the house?'

He groaned impatiently, lowered the camera to argue with her, looking momentarily belligerent, but then his face softened. 'OK. Sure. I pick up Ol, and think, what the hell is he doing here? He shouldn't be here. I start running, holding him as tight as I can, and it's hard to run, there's a lot of mud, sticky red mud, clinging to my legs and slowing me down, I'm covered in it. I'm thinking maybe it's better to turn back, go back to the house, but it's too exposed, and we keep on . . .'

'What's happening to Oliver?' *Red mud. He had never said red mud before. Had he? Had he? Madeline searched her memory. Red. Was it blood? Was he trying to run through blood?*

Flynn shrugged. 'He's tight in my arms.'

'You have him held securely?'

'Yes . . .' he echoed slowly, 'I have him held securely . . . he's not slipping. Last night, he wasn't slipping. He was held up close, here.' Flynn patted his chest above his heart. 'I hadn't realised that. Before, it was always hard for me to keep hold of him. I guess that's because he was lying next to me safe and sound?'

'Perhaps.' *Or was it that Flynn's grasp on his memory was again sound?*

'We stumble into the clearing, backwards.'

'How do you feel?'

'I'm shitting myself with fear. Just like always. I shouldn't have come, shouldn't have brought him there. All my blood's in my head; my chest's so swollen it could burst. It's pumping. Drumming in my ears. I can't get my breath. I turn round and look about me and I see the bodies, hacked apart, hundreds of them, you can't begin to count them – it's pointless to try. It's like one of those wooden puzzles – you can't tell which limb belongs to which body. It's silent, like a tableau from a play. The fear is eating me up.' A shudder passed straight over his body as Flynn stood at the window, one hand holding the blind open a crack, the other holding on to the camera. He continued in a muted, hesitant voice. 'But then the dream changes.'

'What do you see, Flynn?' Madeline held her breath.

'I see the little Tutsi boy. He's tiny. He's alive, squatting next to his mother. She's ripped open. The little boy's staring at us with one hand in his mother's guts. There are flies crawling up his arm. He lifts his hand to his mouth. He's going to put his hand in his mouth. The smell. I can't get the smell out of my mouth. My own guts are all twisted. I want to empty everything in my body.'

The room darkened. *Madeline could see the scene Flynn depicted, she could hear the buzz of the flies and feel the summer sun beating, beating down relentlessly on her head.* Flynn swung abruptly back to face her with a tight smile on his face and the promise of revelation in his eyes. 'But I *don't* see Erik. He's *not there*. And we don't get shot. I want to get away from the women and the little boy, get out of there before I suffocate, before I choke on my own sick, so I turn round towards the ravine. It's full of water flowing really fast – but, and this is weird, Madeline, crazy – there are chunks of ice in it, great ice floes. The bank we're standing on is hot – in brilliant sunshine – but the river's full of ice. I hold Ol tighter and start to cross the river, leaping from one ice floe to another and, as I look up at the opposite bank, I see Erik. Just standing there. He's smiling but shaking his head, waving me back, telling me to go back, and I think, you stupid fucker, I can't go back to that, it's safer on your side, and all the while I'm trying to think what the hell to do, the river's carrying us downstream. Maybe there's something waiting on his side, something I don't know about, something more dangerous than where we've come from. Then . . . then . . .' Madeline was unaware that the fingers of both her hands were spread open over her face. 'I look over my shoulder, back where we've come from, to check if it's safe . . .' Flynn tipped his head to one side and took another picture. His arm dropped to his side, holding the camera limply.

'And I see *you*. I see you, Madeline, on the bank, back where I've come from. I don't know what Erik wants. He wants me to do something: maybe get you and the boy. I stare at you, and the way you're holding yourself – you're kind of sheltering yourself; there's something exposed but at the same time proud about the way you're standing. But you're on the *wrong* bank. The dangerous bank.'

'Do you go back across the river?'

'To rescue you?' Flynn smiled gently. 'I hope I do. I woke up midstream. I hope I don't leave you there. I'd like to get back to that dream. See what happens.'

'Believe me, so would I!' Madeline laughed. The dream lifted a heart that for two days had felt leaden. She did not laugh at the idea of Flynn either rescuing her or abandoning her. She laughed with sheer delight at what the altered dream suggested: Flynn was approaching consciousness, integrating his present with the memory he had denied. Flynn gazed at her. He raised the camera to his eye, took a photograph, looked at her again and took another. Then he closed his eyes. He seemed in shock.

'Flynn? What is it?'

She could not read the sudden emotion that washed over his face. 'You look exactly the same,' he murmured. 'Just then, you looked *exactly* as you looked in my dream.'

'How did I look in your dream?'

'Vibrant. Proud. It astonished me.'

Madness, blindness and astonishment of heart. There was a talismanic quality in their silent communication in that moment. The transfer between them was so startlingly clear; it had no discernible joins or barriers, but was as seamless as a river flowing into the sea, as seamless as falling in love. She

294

longed to touch him, simply to lay a hand on his cheek and feel the warmth of his skin, but she did not need to touch him and she did not need to use words. Her eyes spoke for her, proclaiming her delight and pride.

'Madeline. Am I dreaming Erik's alive to pretend it didn't happen? To forget?'

She leant towards him.

TWENTY-ONE

Winter had seized London with a sudden and vice-like grip, but the snug of Flynn's darkroom remained immune, as warm as the womb. The room had long ago lost the persistent chemical sting it had held when Flynn developed his own photographs but now it again lingered in the air. He filled the developing trays, strung up the two rolls of Tryex black-and-white film and examined the small negatives of Madeline with an eyeglass. He selected five prints to develop in full size, one by one, entirely absorbed in his work. Through the wash and fume of the developing fluid, Madeline's image emerged mistily. Her face was frozen, her gaze intense, a hundred questions posed in her eyes. Flynn remembered why he had elected to stop developing his own work a few years back. He had too often seen the faces of those he had loved emerge in the faces of his subjects, or seen his own face floating there.

He clipped the first print up above the worktop, next to the wooden sign he had pinched from a mortuary in Kosovo which bore the inscription: '*Hic locus est ubi mors gaudet succurrere vitae.*'

He worked steadily, trying to ignore an image that flashed against the backdrop of his dark memory. In early February of 1994 he had been shooting the devastation caused by a single mortar bomb in the market square of Sarajevo. An old woman had tugged his arm and asked him why he bothered to take pictures that wouldn't make it into a newspaper. He had argued with her, insisting that it would make a difference, that even if the war had been going on for a year, even if it went on for another year, it *would* be brought to an end; that world opinion *would* intervene. He had held forth for several minutes, determined to convince her not only of the service of the media, but of his own validity, that the right photograph could deliver as forceful a message as a punch between the eyeballs, an image that resonated long after you had closed your eyes or turned the page. He remembered what he had told her as he battled the desire to weep: 'What we hear, we forget,' he had insisted, 'but what we see, we remember.' Even at the time he had cringed at his arrogance. The old lady had remained dubious. She had been right; newspapers and television stations across the world excised the goriest visual reports of Sarajevo in deference to their viewers' vulnerability. There was an irony in protecting one group of people from the obscenity inflicted on another.

Surrounded by Madeline's face, her voice filled his head. He had put down his camera and asked her if the dream that Erik was alive was an attempt to forget Erik's death. 'People dream to save their lives,' she had told him. 'We dream to remember, and to connect divergent aspects of life, to make *sense* of the incomprehensible, not to try to forget it.' He shook the fluid off another print. Madeline's hands covered her face; her lynx-like eyes were only partly visible through her splayed fingers. He had hoped to capture something of the mask she assumed as a therapist, but the artifice of the pose was glaring; instead of seeming masked, she appeared coquettish. The photograph did not ring true.

There was a gentle tap at the door. 'Dad? Can I come in?'
'Hold on a second, Bethie . . . OK.'
Beth slid into the room, closing the door quickly behind

her. She stood close to her father, leaning into his chair in the dim light, shifting her weight from hip to hip. He slipped an arm about her waist, still studying the failed photograph of Madeline.

'Olly's coming home tomorrow, isn't he?'

'Now –' amusement lit Flynn's face – 'if I didn't know better, I'd say you were missing him . . .'

Beth punched him gently on the shoulder. 'It doesn't feel the same without him.'

'I know,' he said, giving her a squeeze, 'but it will all be back to normal in a few days. We'll have to help him get about, so don't let me catch you kicking his crutches from under him.'

'Who's that woman, Dad?'

'She's called Madeline Light. She's my psychotherapist.'

'You're not sick, are you?'

'I'm not exactly sick, Bethie, but it's like being sick. I need help to get over some problems.'

'Does she help you?'

'Very much.'

'What kind of problems do you have?'

'Let's sit down and I'll try to explain.' Flynn led her gently to the threadbare sofa. 'I've seen some terrible things in my work, Beth, acts of wretched inhumanity; it's my job to photograph them so that other people can see them too.'

'Why should other people want to see them?'

'That's a good question. Often they don't want to. But I believe they need to be seen so they can be stopped. You wouldn't watch somebody suffering and do nothing about it, would you?' Beth shook her head. 'That's good; that's what people are all about. But if you didn't know, then you wouldn't be able to do anything about it. I believe that most people are essentially good and won't tolerate the suffering of others. So long as they know about it. It's my job to let them know . . .'

'OK. I get that.'

'But sometimes, Beth, what I see is too disturbing for me to

298

live with. Sometimes it's been difficult to come home and be a proper dad to you, and a proper husband to your mum. Sometimes I can't stop thinking about those people and places I've left behind. Sometimes I want to go back to them.'

'I heard Mum and Suzie talking about it; Mum said sometimes journalists who cover wars get addicted to their work because of an adrenalin rush.'

'She may be right, sometimes. It's a common old saw about war correspondents, but personally I don't buy it. It *is* a perk of the job, Bethie, that feeling of being *keenly* alive, alive in a way that maybe nobody else has ever been; but the addiction is overstated. I'll tell you one thing I know for certain: the Countryside Alliance are talking through their bollocks when they say the fox enjoys the thrill of the hunt. I've had a few moments lying in a surrounded bunker and trying to work up the nerve to run across the plain, and it isn't a kick. The kick comes when you know you got away with it, not when you're crouching there witless.'

'So are you always frightened?'

'Pretty much. Some people aren't; maybe they don't feel fear the way normal people do, or believe they are just born survivors. In my experience, the ones who are really in it for the adrenalin kick just burn out.' *Or get whacked*, he added silently.

'Martin says he's never afraid: not about auditions or exams or anything else. He just feels excited.'

Flynn smiled. Martin was becoming an increasingly strong presence in Munster Road.

'Martin's always asking me about your job. He thinks it's really cool . . .' A scowl settled on Beth's face. 'I don't see why Mum's being such a cow when you have to live with all that, being scared and having people shoot at you and everything. Sometimes she doesn't care about anyone except herself.'

'That's not true. Beth. Look at me. You're wrong. Your mother has a huge and – *stalwart* heart. She's one of the bravest people I've ever known, sixteen hours a day, week

299

in week out, and she doesn't make a song and dance about it. You must never forget that what happens here, in our family, is just as important as anything that happens in the outside world. And here, your mother runs the show, and I don't know anybody who'd make a better job of it. She loves us ferociously. And she's been working very hard to help me come back.'

'Then why have you been so angry with her?'

'I'm not angry with Mum. I'm angry with myself.'

'So why can't you sit down and talk normally? Why are you always fighting?'

'*Another* good question. Let's see if I can come up with an answer . . .' Flynn scratched his head theatrically. 'Sometimes people fall into a rhythm. It can be a whole group of people, like tribes within a country, or just a couple of individuals. When a country has been at war for a very long time, there's a *culture* of war there. Fighting and suspicion is sort of addictive; and revenge is instinctive. Men and women can fall into that pattern, too; even when they love each other, they might have a culture of fighting. Maybe the anger I've been feeling with myself, about things that aren't to do with your mother, or you children, maybe it gets spread around, so she's angry back. Mum and I need to find a new way to talk. We're trying to do that. Sometimes she feels, quite rightly, that I am a stranger. It's *hard* to sit down and talk to a stranger. It's hard to trust them.'

'But you talk to that woman all the time. You talk to her three times a week and she's a stranger, isn't she?'

'It's very complicated, darling . . .'

'I'm not a baby.'

'Beth. You're not a baby, but what I want to explain is difficult; it's difficult for grown-ups, even people in their forties and fifties.' He rubbed his head. 'Your mother would make a better fist of this than I will. OK. I hope that one day when you're older, *when you're a very great deal older –*' Flynn dug his elbow into his daughter's ribs – 'you fall in love and get married, as your mother and I did. And I hope you have a very happy marriage. But loving someone isn't a thing that you do once and it stays the same for ever. It isn't just about having fun and being happy. Loving someone is hard work. If you work very hard at it, it is the happiest thing of all, just like being absorbed in a job you love is a great happiness. Love is a delicate thing. We can't treat it like a bandage we hoick out of the medicine cabinet and slap on whenever we're feeling a bit sore. And that's why I can't count on your mother to make me better all by herself. It isn't possible, and it isn't fair.' His eyebrows drew together. 'Am I making any sense or talking rubbish?'

Beth smiled. 'I think you are talking rubbish.'

'Wise girl. You must take after my side of the family.'

Beth's eyes moved slowly over the photographs of Madeline hanging above Flynn's desk and rested on the wooden sign.

'What does that say, the Latin thing up there?'

'It says, "*Hic locus est ubi mors gaudet succurrere vitae*".'

'I *can* read, Dad,' Beth groaned. 'What does it mean?'

'If you'd worked harder on your Latin you'd have the pleasure of knowing that yourself,' Flynn retorted. 'It means, "This is the place where death rejoices to teach those who live".'

Beth looked at it blankly. 'Are you and Mum going to get divorced?'

Flynn's gaze also remained fixed on the inscription. 'I don't know, Bethie,' he said, 'but with all my heart I hope not.'

'Does Mum want to?'

'I don't think so. If it's worrying you, you should ask her. It's always better to talk about your worries rather than keeping them to yourself. Which is why you're smart to come and talk to me like this.' Pulling her close, Flynn kissed the top of her head. 'Whatever happens, there's nothing more important to your mother and me than you and Oliver.'

When Beth left him he returned to his work. A smile of

satisfaction spread across his face as Madeline's delighted expression appeared slowly in the developing tray. As he was lifting it out he heard the expected second light tap at the door.

'Come in, Georgia.'

'I don't want to disturb you . . .' she began nervously, leaning against the door she had closed behind her.

'You're not.' Flynn stood up, hanging the photograph to dry, studying it closely.

'Beth told me you were developing prints of your therapist.'

'I thought she might. Come and have a look.'

Georgia moved forward hesitantly, her arms wrapped around her as if she wore a straitjacket. There were now four ten-by-eights fluttering in the breeze of the drying machine. Georgia was silent as she registered the other woman's introspective beauty.

'You've never taken portraits like that of me,' she said finally.

'Then I should. I don't think you've ever asked me to.'

'And she did?'

Flynn considered the photographs before answering thoughtfully, 'No, come to think of it, she didn't. She asked me to bring in the camera as a way of understanding how I use it.'

He heard Georgia's uneven breath behind him before she asked, 'Are you having an affair with her?'

'With my therapist?' Flynn said. 'No. Of course not.'

'Would you like to?' Georgia pointed at the photograph of Madeline, cat's eyes masked by a lattice of fingers. 'You couldn't have taken that picture unless you were attracted to her. It's as plain as day.'

'Is it?' Flynn leant forward, studying the photograph curiously. 'Personally, I don't think much of that one.'

'Just tell me, Flynn. I can cope with anything if I know the truth.'

302

Flynn considered her statement; for a long time he had felt certain that not knowing the truth was a far more sustainable way of coping. Early on in a relationship truth was almost always alluring, even when unpleasant, but the later it came, the greater the risk it would be cataclysmic. Flynn was not sure that he had the ability to tell Georgia his true feelings for Madeline in a way that she could accept without threat; he was not sure he could make sense of them himself. He could not tell Georgia that while Oliver was unconscious, while she was searching for him, he had met Madeline and wordlessly offered his heart to her and that his offer had been declined as he had known it would be. He could not tell Georgia that watching her playing cards in the hospital had bound him to her with such a powerful cord that he could never leave her. He could not tell her, without her feeling that he had made a compromise she could not tolerate, that he felt he loved Madeline in a way that he could never love her, but that yet he chose her with a whole heart. He could not tell her that he needed Madeline still to bring him back safely to her.

Georgia mistook his silence for confirmation. 'I came in here,' she said quietly, 'because Beth told me I had to reassure you that I loved you and didn't want to divorce you. She said you didn't want a divorce and that it was only me. But I only need to look at these prints and I can see everything that you haven't been able to tell me . . .'

'What do you see?'

'That she's in love with you.' Georgia's finger moved along the photographs as she translated them. 'Here, she's serious. Then suddenly she's flirtatious – why? What had you said? And look at that. Have you ever seen a woman look happier? Why? Had you told her you were in love with her? Did she tell you she was in love with you?'

Flynn swung round on the seat and grabbed her by both wrists. 'Stop it, Georgia. Stop acting like an adolescent,' he ordered in a voice rough with emotion. 'I'm not having an affair with her and I don't want to have an affair with her. She means more to me than that.'

Georgia backed away from him when he released her wrists. She sat on the sofa, numb with shock. 'She means more than that?' she breathed. '*More* than that?'

'Yes. She's helped me understand something about love that I didn't know or couldn't accept. She's let me face my own horrors and stood beside me. Ever since I came back from Rwanda, I've only been half here; part of me's still stuck there.'

'I know that,' Georgia whispered, 'because of Erik van der Hoeven, because of his death, but you'd never talk about it . . .'

'I couldn't. On Astra Four, it came back to me in a flood. I couldn't stop thinking about it. I felt I was dying. Madeline, this woman —' he jabbed at her photograph — 'has let me believe that I can somehow face that part of my life and still continue, that life's worth continuing. That I can come out of the ashes. That's all I'm trying to do.'

'Oh God, Flynn. Why couldn't you have come to me? Why didn't you trust me to understand, when I love you so much?'

'I didn't want you to know. I wanted something that was safe and clean and straight; I didn't want to infect my home. You asked so many questions, making me remember what I didn't want to remember and couldn't express. I've wasted a lot of time. I wasted years, trying to find a way of changing what happened, living with the dead.'

'And she brought you back to life?'

Flynn smiled at his wife sadly. 'I don't know, sweetheart. I'm not there yet. I'm trying . . . it's a start. I know one thing; I don't want to be the cause of your unhappiness.' He spoke as if he recognised how delicate and fragile was the promise he held out to her, as if even the acknowledgement of his wish might jeopardise its fulfilment. 'As for Madeline . . .' Flynn continued hesitantly, '. . . I cherish the time I spend in her room. It's like this room. It gives me a separate place, lets me think about things differently. You shouldn't feel threatened by it.'

Georgia released her breath in a slow sigh. 'All right. Maybe I should be down on my knees thanking her. I don't quite feel ready for that. I can't help wishing she wasn't quite so beautiful.'

'Give me time, Georgia. Trust me a little bit longer. This isn't going to be easy, not for any of us.'

When the door closed he raised his eyes to the best print: Madeline's face radiant in the gloom of the darkroom. The moment when she had unexpectedly laughed, when her complicated, impenetrable expression had been suddenly illuminated by that embracing smile, had moved him so violently he had had to close his eyes. 'Ah Nepenthe,' he murmured aloud, 'you won't leave me now, not when I need you most . . . you won't leave me now, will you?' He turned off the solitary desk light and, with a mixture of dread and elation, stretched out on the sofa and closed his eyes, squeezing down hard on the sponge of his memory . . .

For a town that had been home to mass murder for several weeks, Kigali was oddly quiet on the evening Flynn arrived, the evening of 13 May 1994. He had flown in over the small landlocked country, admiring the steeply terraced slopes and lush rainforest through the small window before the military plane prepared to land. The outskirts of Kigali, once famed for its infrastructure of orderly, well-maintained roads, were now wretched. The streets were pitted with holes, burnt-out cars had been left smouldering in the road and abandoned shacks were open to the temperate breeze. Some signs of normal life remained in the lush and heavily cultivated countryside: on the way from the airport they passed a few brightly dressed

305

women with babies strapped to their backs and old men in suits wobbling precariously on ancient bicycles. One man was trying to ride while balancing a battered armchair behind him. Two young children, barely old enough to walk, herded a few cows up the hill, listlessly kicking up the red dirt beneath their feet.

Other markers along the route were more shocking. The roadside was sporadically dotted with corpses rotting in the sun. Small children wandered aimlessly along the streets, whether orphaned, abandoned for their own safety or in order that their parents might travel more lightly and swiftly, the occupants of the UN car could only speculate. Flynn sat listening to the shocked exclamations of his fellow passengers, two aid workers and two official UN observers, breathing in the mingled scents of the earth, eucalyptus and charcoal fires, all of which failed to mask the dominant stench of putrefaction.

As they approached the town, the clutches of straggling civilians were replaced by disorderly groups of soldiers, who stared at them with suspicion. Their driver crawled slowly down the road, his terrified eyes glancing right and left, and came to a halt at the first road block. It was manned by perhaps seven or eight men and three women, yelling and waving machetes in the air, beer bottles littering the ground around them. For twenty minutes the five Westerners insisted, calmly, that they were not friends of the RPF rebels, nor Tutsi supporters, nor enemies of the Rwandan state. They were simply there to help. This was only the first of four blocks set up by the Interhamwe militia, and it took Flynn's party another two hours to pass some three miles into the centre of town and reach the shabby but still standing Hôtel des Diplomates where their driver stopped. Any hope of reaching their original destination, the Hôtel des Milles Collines, was abandoned; the hotel and its Tutsi refugees were under siege, and although the Ghanaian blue-caps of the UN were so far managing to hold off the Interhamwe, the situation was presented as more than precarious by their driver. He sat shaking his head, refusing to move, begging them to get out.

Entering the terraced bar of the Hôtel des Diplomates, Flynn spotted a friendly face seated at the bar, a Ghanaian journalist called Kofi Ampofu who worked for Reuters. He was deep in conversation with a young red-headed man who seemed vaguely familiar.

'Kofi!' Flynn called. '*Eleagbea?*'

The two men had become friends when Flynn had spent a month with the Ewes in the north of Ghana; Kofi had come from Accra to join him. Ever since, the two men had adopted the standard Ewe greeting: *Eleagbea?* How are you, or literally, *Are you alive?* It seemed to Flynn a particularly fitting salute that evening.

The big man turned with a grin and drew Flynn into an embrace, slapping his back with one hand while the other held him tight. '*E mele gborgborm*, Flynn, *e mele gborgborm . . .*' *Well, I'm still breathing.* 'Which is more than can be said for a lot of the people in this hell hole. Take a seat, old friend . . . I was hoping you might turn up, like a bad penny. And, as always, you turn up too late. That's the problem with you Brits, always too late. You know Erik van der Hoeven?' Flynn nodded at the young Dutchman, recognising him as one of the more recent recruits into what Kofi had years ago labelled the Africa Club, a collection of journalists who, try as they might, couldn't seem to get the continent out of their blood. They'd met in Mogadishu eight months earlier – that was it, when Erik had been a stringer for *De Volkskrant*, feeling his way on the periphery of the veteran press pack.

Over the next few hours, many drinks and a pack of Marlboro Lights, Kofi briefed the other two men on the situation. 'Make no mistakes, my friends, this is not a typical African civil war. This is a planned, efficient genocide.' Four thousand Tutsis had been massacred in one day in the Kigali suburb of Kacyiru; those Tutsis and Hutu moderates who

307

remained holed up in Kigali faced the choice between fleeing to supposed havens that held no real promise of safety, or staying hidden in the vain hope that the genocide would exhaust itself. Kofi told tales of barbarism that had not yet found their way into the world's press, of men forced to kill their own children, youngsters who had had their hands and feet removed so they could not crawl away or shield their eyes from the disembowelling of their parents and grandparents. He told them of the people denied sanctuary at the UN building, who had begged for the relative mercy of a UN bullet in the back of the head. Parents who tossed their tiny babies over the razor wire into the arms of the horrified soldiers.

Kofi's face was hollowed and drawn. He talked of death by machete, known locally as the *panga*, death by the *masu*, the heavily studded club that had become an alternative execution weapon of choice for the Hutu militia. He acknowledged the awful appropriateness of the Hutu Power's abusive term 'cockroaches' for the hunted Tutsi minority. 'They are running, like roaches scuttle when you turn on the kitchen light. *Phfitt, phfitt* . . .' His hands shot up, fingers spread wide, in a gesture of sudden disappearance. 'But you know where they run? They run to church . . . and there they get butchered. A short cut to the burial service.' Kofi shrugged and gave a tight, ironic smile that sat uneasily on his broad, open face.

Erik slammed down his glass. 'What are we doing sitting here? You and I –' at this point he had grabbed Kofi's great fist in his own pale, freckled one and banged them together hard on the bar – 'are here for a reason. There is one question to answer: how can so many people, so many human beings, be so quickly persuaded to kill their friends and neighbours?'

Flynn glanced at Kofi and saw his own thought reflected in the veteran's face. There was a second, even more difficult question that needed to be answered: how could so many people allow themselves to be killed, without apparent protest, without even a glimmer of resistance? If Kofi was right, and Flynn had had many opportunities to test the Ghanaian's judgement, the Tutsis had flocked to churches and there prepared themselves for death on the instruction of their priests. Barely even a rock had been thrown back against the grenades and automatic fire.

Kofi sighed with an extended low whistle that sounded like the air leaving a highly pressurised tyre. 'I can't answer your question, my young friend. I've had enough. Enough time here for me.'

Flynn's mouth lifted into a half smile. 'That's the problem with you Ghanaians. No staying power.'

Kofi tossed back his head and released a one-syllabled shout of laughter. 'Believe me, Flynn, my friend, I would stay, but it would be signing my own death warrant. Annie's having a baby next week. I don't fear even the Interhamwe as much as I fear what she'll do to me if I don't go home.'

'Ah, women . . .' Flynn nodded in empathy.

'Annie says if I keep going on the road next time I come home, she'll say, "No thank you, no deliveries today," and shut the door in my face. And a new baby! Well, a new baby . . .' He rubbed his hands together, his deeply hollowed eyes shining with delight.

'How many is that now, Kofi?'

'This will be our fourth. We have three beautiful girls.'

'You have a photograph?' Flynn asked unnecessarily.

Kofi rifled through his wallet with pleasure, pulling out some crumpled snaps and offering them to Flynn. A congratulation session ensued, while Erik looked on with a mixture of impatience and disbelief and Flynn ordered another round of beers. At some mysteriously predetermined point the chat stopped and Flynn began to cadge contacts, scratching down the names of UN officials and UNAMIR officers, as well as those of local drivers and interpreters who might be trustworthy, and might work, whether for moral or financial motivation.

At the end, Kofi dropped his voice to a whisper. 'You should try to join up with one of the RPA units – get close to Kagame; he's a man of integrity. I met him a few years ago. You are safer with either army than you are with civilians. I've got two small leads you can follow.' His eyes flicked around the room nervously, his voice now barely audible. Flynn and Erik leant in close on either side. 'There's a Tutsi family, hoping to leave Kigali tonight or tomorrow; women and children. Their men are either with Kagame or dead. They have been hiding in an orphanage. I met the nun who has been sheltering them this afternoon.' He shunted a heavily folded piece of paper along the bar to Flynn. 'I advised her to keep them there, but they are convinced their only hope is meeting up with some priest in Gitarama.' He sighed again, shaking his big head with defeat. 'Go and see them; tell them it's safer to wait. The RPF is growing stronger every day, and maybe the UN . . .' He shrugged. 'Talk to the sisters. Tell them to keep the family there. Whatever you do, don't go with them. You'll never get through a road block if you travel with a Tutsi. You might not get through alone. They don't like us here.'

'Kofi, they don't like us anywhere.' Flynn nodded once and shoved the paper into a pocket without looking at it, his eyes fixed on a small lizard that ran up the wall behind the bar. 'And the other story?'

'Kibeho. There's been widespread slaughter all round there. There's a shrine to the Virgin Mary at the top of the hill above Kibeho, a shrine with a history of miracles and apparitions. The people say the statue of the Virgin sometimes sheds blood. They say she foretold the genocide. Witnesses had visions, heard voices, years ago, of the Virgin saying she saw rivers of blood.' Kofi drained his glass. 'Several people have told me the Kibeho Virgin is weeping again. Only a few days ago, they saw blood tears. It might make a good photograph. And now

I'm going to bed. And tomorrow morning I'm getting out. Be careful, careful, huh?'

'Give my love to Annie.'

Flynn nursed his drink for a few minutes. Marian apparitions were the stuff of his childhood, the monks at school holding out the tantalising promise that if he only prayed hard enough and purely enough, the Virgin would speak to him directly in answer to his prayers. He signalled for another beer. The Virgin had not yet spoken to him directly, however hard he had prayed; the Virgin had not done a whole hell of a lot for her own son, in his hour of need, and was unlikely to break the habit of an eternal lifetime. He'd stick with the refugees. Flynn dragged deeply on his cigarette and rubbed his thumb contemplatively across his lips. He had forgotten about Erik until the young man spoke in a low and serious voice.

'We'll go together, OK? It's better to travel together, right?'

Flynn studied the Dutchman dispassionately. He didn't know him well enough, barely knew him at all, and he distrusted Erik's youth and the brand of knee-jerk, finger-on-the-trigger journalistic idealism that the young man had already evidenced that night. Erik looked steadily back at him through unblinking, startlingly blue eyes. 'Sure,' Flynn agreed softly. 'It's better to travel together. But we won't go tonight. I don't want to try anything at night. I need to check out the place, and we have to find an interpreter, unless you are fluent in Kinyarwanda.'

'And if the family have already left by tomorrow?' Erik whispered urgently.

'Then they've left,' Flynn shrugged. 'Do you think they are the only family in hiding in Kigali? I dare say we'll be able to rustle up a few more if we try hard enough.' His own cynicism tasted bitter in his mouth, but it was natural for Flynn to counter enthusiasm with caution, and impulse with reason.

Feeling he had slapped Erik down a little too hard, Flynn turned the conversation to Erik himself, and what had brought him to Kigali for AP. As the two men talked into the night, Flynn gained an insight into the Dutchman's fervency: he wanted to make his mark, and he wanted to be where the action was. Two simple desires had propelled him into the bar of the Hôtel des Diplomates. The more they talked, the more Flynn liked him and found his optimism refreshing, if likely to be short-lived.

When Erik went to his room, Flynn sat up trying to pump the hotel's night manager, an understandably edgy Hutu who professed to know nothing about anything. A stack of dollars and a few packs of Marlboro persuaded him to pull out a city map and ring several areas in red. Flynn pocketed it along with the paper Kofi had given him and went to bed. Stripping off his clothes, and prepared to brave the mosquitoes momentarily, he opened the window and leant out. The stench that hung in the air like a vapour cloud was unforgettable: damp, cloying, sickly sweet. Immediately it filled his nostrils and clung to the back of his throat with the texture of a spider's web, making him gag as it coated his throat and lungs with the odour of a charnel house.

The next morning Erik and Flynn worked swiftly, using the sat-phone to contact some of the names Kofi had given them. Most land and electrical lines in Kigali had failed, and it was impossible to reach many of the names on their list, but by superhuman persuasive effort they had managed to arrange a liaison with a woman attached to the Catholic mission and a major from UNAMIR, who had agreed to lend them a Land-Rover and escort them to the orphanage.

At three they set off, the blue-capped, armed soldier driving, with Flynn at his side and Erik talking earnestly to the Belgian lay nun in the rear. Two more UNAMIR soldiers travelled behind in an armoured vehicle. They passed in convoy through the road blocks, prompting only shouting, the brandishing of AK-47s and machetes and stares of hatred, and made their way to a previously well-off and pleasant suburb on the outskirts of Kigali, a mile or so before the tarmac road dissolved into the red-dirt track that led to Gitarama. The street spoke of sudden abandonment: broken windows were left unmended, bits of ransacked furniture littered doorways and vegetables rotted in the gutter.

The major turned off the engine and looked at Flynn wearily. 'I can't come in with you. We will wait here, but we cannot wait long.' He climbed down from the Land-Rover and glanced around him at the group of young men loitering malevolently along the walls of the compound. The two soldiers behind left their jeep and simultaneously cocked their guns as Flynn, Erik and the young Belgian woman made their way to the entrance. The major's eyes shifted between the door of the orphanage and a man sharpening the blade of his machete. His colleagues stood, feet apart and braced, berets tipped rakishly over one eye and their British-issue SLR assault rifles held tightly across their chests.

In less than ten minutes the two journalists and the young woman emerged, Flynn and Erik talking heatedly, the woman shaking her head at the major. 'They've gone,' she said quickly, in a quiet voice. 'Early this morning. The sister is frightened; she needs your help. These people,' her eyes flicked nervously to the young men watching them, 'have been threatening her. They say they will kill her and all the babies. She has sixty orphans there. Sixty. They need to be evacuated now.'

The officer squinted up at the sun pouring from the heavens. 'Evacuated? Where? There's nothing I can do. Nothing. I'm not allowed . . . there are three of us . . .' His shoulders rose and sagged before he looked questioningly at Flynn.

'We need to borrow the Land-Rover—' Flynn began.

The major cut him short. 'No. That's not possible.'

Flynn laid a hand on his arm and led him aside. 'These people, these women and children, left last night. Maybe they were killed twenty yards down that road,' his eyes narrowed as he looked down the dirt track, 'but maybe not. We want to find out, one way or another. We can't go on foot.'

'It's suicide to go at all.' Jerking his head at the watching men, the UNAMIR officer asked, 'D'you think they're just sunbathing out here? D'you think they'll just wave you off? You know what they feel about Gitarama, these Hutus? Kagame comes from Nyaratovu, just by Gitarama. That's his hometown, and now his army is advancing on Kigali bent on wiping this lot out. You think they are going to let two foreign journalists amble down that road?'

'They won't do anything so long as you are here. You need to talk to the sister. Just let me take the Land-Rover. That's all I ask.' Flynn could see a momentary flash of indecision in the man's exhausted face. 'You aren't responsible for us.'

'But I am for the vehicle. I am responsible for whatever happens here in the next ten minutes. We've got no people – I can't protect you . . .'

'I know that. Forget about us.'

The two men looked at each other in a moment of understanding before the officer nodded curtly. 'Take it and get out. Wait until I've called some more troops over and talked to these – killers.' He spat copiously and with precision into the dirt. 'If you find the family, dead or alive, don't try to bring them back. Don't come back yourselves. Head north, somehow. Towards Gisenyi, that's where the RPA is coming from. Shit, I don't need people like you screwing things up. There's another "official" checkpoint a mile down the track; there may be more after that, we don't know. It changes every day, every hour. Tell them you are expected by the UNAMIR force in Gitarama. They might believe you; they might decide to kill you. If they don't kill you for the Land-Rover first.'

He approached the dozen or so young men whose faces had taken on a hard, set look and spoke to them calmly, flanked by his two soldiers. Pulling out a radio, he called for support and nodded at Flynn and Erik, who climbed into the car.

'You really think we can go?' Erik asked nervously.

'You don't have to, Erik. Stay with UNAMIR. You'll get a good story there. Go back and talk with the sister.'

'No,' Erik said firmly, 'I will go with you. Otherwise I won't know what happened.'

Flynn reversed ten feet, and pulled out, one hand raised in a salute.

Kofi had warned Flynn that the Kigali–Kibuye route, on which Gitarama stood as the halfway marker, was a mass of hairpin switchbacks, dotted with rocks among the red dirt; it could easily take them as much as three hours to cover the thirty-five miles to Gitarama. Flynn drove slowly, watching for signs of the women and children, any mark in the dust that might indicate they had abandoned the road and made their way through the trees, which would have been the sensible option. Why, he asked himself, did he assume that a terrified group of fleeing women and children might have taken the sensible option when he himself had not? Erik's nervousness seemed to have evaporated; he was singing, in a beautiful bass, in Dutch.

Flynn had no idea what he sang, but the bizarre incongruity of the situation made him smile. He slowed to a crawl as he spotted the haphazard barriers ahead. 'Shit, shit, *shit*,' he muttered under his breath. He fired a string of instructions as they inched their way towards the checkpoint, cursing himself for not rehearsing Erik before they'd set off. 'Say nothing about anything. These guys don't look like Interhamwe, but shit knows who they are. Probably they're FAR. *We are not heading north*, we're stopping in Gitarama. Joining the UN station, returning the Land-Rover, then leaving the country. Don't say *anything* unless they separate us, and then say

315

exactly what I've just told you. You work for Associated Press, I'm a freelancer, you don't know who I'm working for. You barely know me from Adam. All you know is I'm a freelance photographer, I'm Irish and an arsehole. All I know about you is you work for AP, you're Dutch and an arsehole. We were lent the truck by UNAMIR; we are expected tonight by UNAMIR in Gitarama.'

Beads of sweat broke out on Erik's unlined forehead. 'Flynn, I have a bad feeling . . . maybe we should go back to Kigali. Maybe just reverse . . .'

'Don't be a fuckin' eejut,' Flynn snapped back. 'We so much as stop, let alone reverse, they'll blow our brains all over the fucking dirt.' Staring straight ahead, Flynn reached behind him and fumbled with his bag, rearranging it so that a carton of cigarettes and the last bottle of the hotel's whisky protruded from the top.

He halted at the barrier and leant out of the window. A heavily armed and uniformed soldier shoved his face mere inches from Flynn's and started yelling, sending a lavish spray of spittle flying all over his cheek. Flynn did not appear to object at all.

All this Flynn remembered clearly as he lay in the dark on his much-loved sofa. He could see the lizard frozen above the bar before it darted ten inches up the wall. He could see the photograph of Kofi's three pretty daughters clearly, pink ribbons in their hair, and he could see the UNAMIR officer gobbing in the dirt outside the orphanage. He remembered how his saliva had created a red pool, which he had immediately scuffed over with the toe of one highly polished boot. It was the events that occurred later that day – after the swooping clouds had massed and rippled down from the mountains, after they had passed, mystifyingly smoothly, through the checkpoint manned by soldiers of the FAR – it was the four or five hours after that, and what had happened some dusty

316

ten miles further down the road, that were so difficult to bring to the surface. When they slowly bubbled up, he could feel the flood waters rising and the walls of the dam straining with the effort of holding them back.

TWENTY-TWO

Madeline pressed two fingers at each side of her neck, below her jawbone, and felt her pulse throbbing below them.

'I don't know if I can do this, Patrick.' They were standing in the yard in front of the Cardinal, their breath turning to mist in the chilly evening air. Madeline had her coat on. 'I don't know if I can.'

'You can. It will be all right.'

'I . . .' Madeline shook her head. 'I can't.'

Patrick placed his heavy hands on her shoulders and turned her to face him, looking at her with a haunting sadness in his eyes. 'Yes you can. You must. You need to end this to begin something else. It's time, Maddie.'

She followed him back inside and watched him shrugging into his coat and fishing the car keys out of the pocket.

'You don't have to take me.'

'I know I don't. But it's on my way. I have to go to the cathedral. I need to see the chapel at night again. And it's starting to rain.' Patrick scraped the key along the old wooden table. His voice was gruff. 'If you like, if you finish early, you can call me on the mobile and I'll come and pick you up. Or else I'll see you back here.'

*   *   *

Rowley's on Jermyn Street was an odd, anonymous place to meet anyone after ten years. Madeline forced herself to scan the room for her former husband. 'I'm meeting a Mr Cowan,' she said flatly. The waitress led her to the back of the room and round a corner to a small alcove. He was on his feet, his brown hair speckled with grey. He smiled hesitantly.

'Madeline.' Hugh pulled a chair out for her with his habitual, old-fashioned courtesy. She sat without greeting him. 'I've, umm . . . ordered a bottle of wine.'

Her eyes strayed to the empty tumbler on the tablecloth before him. She felt nauseous at the thought of food or drink.

'How are you?'

'Fine,' Madeline replied, 'I'm doing fine.'

'I shouldn't have picked this place.' The forgotten yet familiar timbre of his voice made Madeline's flesh shrink.

Hugh glanced at the other diners, tugging at the shirt collar that seemed too tight for him. 'Who comes to Mayfair for steak and chips?'

Madeline did not reply. 'When you called me,' Hugh began again, 'I was, well . . . shocked.'

'I can imagine.' She had been shocked herself, shocked that she had even suggested seeing Hugh to Patrick, shocked when Patrick had called her mother, and more shocked when Patrick had got Hugh's phone number from her former in-laws and handed it to her without comment. The initial idea had been hers, but it had taken Patrick and Rachel Light's combined effort to bring her to this point. Reluctantly she raised her eyes to his. He seemed a total stranger. 'I'm sorry about that.'

'No, no, not at all. I am very glad you called. I would never have had the guts. I've thought about it often. I saw your name in a paper once. You'd been involved with some disaster, a debriefing, I don't know the right word . . .'

'That's what I do.'

319

'Yes; so I gathered. Well,' Hugh lowered his head, 'I wanted to call you then . . .'

'But you didn't.'

'No.' Hugh lit a cigarette and inhaled deeply. 'I didn't think you'd want to speak to me. After all this time.'

'No . . .' Madeline sipped the wine the waitress poured. She held the liquid in her mouth for several slow seconds before she could bring herself to swallow. 'How's the farm?'

'The farm? I sold it. I put it on the market a couple of months after you left. Didn't you know?'

'No. That must have been very hard for you.'

Hugh's mouth twisted. 'Losing the farm? No. That wasn't the hard part. I never cared about it as much as you thought I did. How could I when you hated it? But we're not here to talk about the farm, are we? Are we, Madeline?' It sounded as if his question were genuine. Madeline's queasiness surged as he leant forward. She could smell him. He was wearing the same aftershave. 'Aren't we here to talk about Sam?'

At the mention of her son's name she tried to conjure the image of her little boy's sleeping face. 'I didn't hate the farm, Hugh. I just had no place there. Sam gave me a place. When he wasn't there I had to go.'

Hugh waved away the hovering waitress and leant halfway across the table, dropping his voice to a whisper. 'Don't you think you could have told me? Don't you think you could have told me you were going, rather than having your mother call to say you never wanted to see me or speak to me again? I'd lost my son, too.'

Madeline heard the still-raw wound in Hugh's voice. 'I haven't come here to be told off, or to apologise. But I accept that I was wrong to walk out like that. And I should never have made my mother call. She hated it. She told me I was wrong. It didn't seem to matter at the time.'

'What else could have mattered?'

Madeline could not find the words to reply. She had wanted

320

to see him, she told herself numbly, to listen to him, not to talk. If she began to talk, she might say anything; she might tell him that it was only the force of her hatred for him that had kept her alive when Sam was dead. She did not feel that it mattered now how much or how little she told him. If he wanted to hear what she had really felt, so be it. He was welcome to know the deep chill she felt towards him. She began to speak in a precise, factual tone, keeping her eyes lowered, drawing the tines of a fork along the stiff white tablecloth.

'At the time I couldn't do anything except think about Sam being gone. I couldn't stand you talking. I couldn't bear lying next to you at night and listening to you weeping and talking about Sam. Do you realise how much you talked? You never closed your mouth. Everything you said made me hate you more. Your talking drove me mad. I longed for you to leave the house so I could have silence. I wanted the house as quiet as a tomb.'

Hugh looked shocked. 'I wanted it full of noise. I missed the sound of Sam's football banging against the kitchen door, you singing along with the radio, completely out of tune . . .'

Her jaw clenched. 'You kept pushing in, talking about antique markets . . .'

'I wanted to find a way *out*; I wanted to let you know that we could look ahead, there was a future, we could have other children . . .'

For the first time, Madeline looked directly at him. 'Other children?' she said bitterly. '*Other* children? Sam was my *life*. I know it was an accident, I always accepted that, but that didn't matter. You were driving the combine. You were meant to be looking after him. I trusted you. He was still my little baby.' Madeline realised that he didn't know what had happened to her, whether she had found a way to replace Sam. 'He still is my little baby, my only baby. From the second I walked into that hospital – no, before – the second I heard Ned's voice –

I hated you. I told you to take him to the nursery as soon as I left. I told you. You promised.'

Hugh tried to take her hand but she pulled it free. 'That's not the way it was. You don't remember, do you, Madeline? You told me to keep him at home and not take him to school. You said he'd only pick up more germs from the other children, so *not* to take him. *That's* what we fought about that morning, Madeline: I said I didn't want him under my feet all day, not during the harvest, and you told me it was high time I looked after him. That was what made it so awful.'

'That's not true,' Madeline said automatically, knowing it was. 'It can't be.'

'It is true,' Hugh said with quiet insistence. 'It's the first thing you said to me in the hospital – you said very quietly, how could you let him get under your feet? You didn't shout, or scream. You didn't even cry. But you looked insane. I kept trying to tell you how it had happened – the accident. You wouldn't listen.'

'Tell me now. Tell me how it happened.'

'What's the point?' Hugh shook his head at her silent entreaty. He rubbed his eyes as if he would poke them out and spoke with effort. 'All right. We were short-staffed. I was doing three men's jobs. That's not an excuse, it's just the way it was. Sam was sitting on the fence watching. I told him to stay put. He'd done it a hundred times. I told him not to budge and sent Ned to get something.'

When he paused and stared down at the table Madeline asked sharply, 'What? What did you ask Ned to get?'

'My lunch box. My lunch box and a few cans of beer.' He looked up at her. 'It was hot.'

Madeline swallowed the lump in her throat. 'Where was Rob?'

'Rob was on the other side of the field. Sam waved at me. I waved back. I looked down at the controls and put the combine into reverse. I saw nothing and heard nothing until

Rob started pounding on the side of the door and I switched the engine off. That was how it happened, Madeline. *That was how it happened*. Sam must have jumped off the fence and run behind me. I couldn't see him. I couldn't hear him. A spike snagged his jeans and pulled him under. That's what the inquiry said.'

Madeline was staring at him but she did not see him.

'Yes. It was my *fault*. I was driving. I will never stop knowing that it was my fault, but, my Christ, believe me I couldn't help it. He wouldn't stay inside, he'd sat on the fence a *hundred times before* watching me. How was I to know he'd jump off that one day?'

Hugh's eyes were rimmed with red. Madeline sat opposite, her face implacable, but some frozen block within her began to thaw. 'I know it was an accident, Hugh,' she said flatly. 'You don't have to persuade me of that. I read the report.' She handed the hovering waitress their menus. 'We're not eating. Could you just leave us alone for a while?' The waitress backed off, intimidated by the expression in Madeline's eyes.

Hugh wiped his eyes with a starched napkin. 'Are you married, Madeline?'

'No.'

'I am. I have a wife. Two stepdaughters. I manage my father-in-law's farm.'

Madeline gave a tiny dismissive shrug. 'I'm sorry if I sound cruel, Hugh, but I don't really want to know. I'm glad you've gone on with your life,' she shrugged, 'but it doesn't concern me any longer.'

'I want you to hear this. Nearly every Sunday, I have lunch with my mother- and father-in-law, my wife and our two little girls. It's a tradition, you know? We meet, we have a sherry or a gin while the roast is in the oven, and either my wife or my mother-in-law frets about how the potatoes won't crisp up by the time the meat's done, and my father-in-law and I are playing with the girls, and telling them stories . . . And there's always a point, every bloody Sunday, when I see you. I see you just before Sam's funeral, coming down our front stairs, wearing that shroud-like black dress, and I see you throw yourself into your mother's arms at the bottom of the steps with that terrible wail. I can still hear it, Madeline, I'll never get the sound out of my head. It was the first real sound you'd made. And still you didn't speak. All I could hear was that awful noise. And I still sit there, for a moment, every single Sunday, knowing I caused a woman's heart to split wide open.'

Madeline looked away.

'That night . . .' He drew a sharp breath and swallowed hard. 'The night of Sam's funeral. All of us there, sitting round the fire. God knows who lit a fire in late July, but we huddled around it, and you were sitting in my mother's old chair and your mother was there, standing at your side, I can see her stroking your hair, and you had those two friends from Bristol –'

'You hated them.'

'Yes, damn right I hated them: they took you away from me, Madeline; they took you further away every time you went there. But I didn't hate them that night; I was too busy hating myself. And worrying about you. You stood up, in that awful dress, and you walked across the room and opened the front door. I was right behind you. You walked across the lawn with me maybe ten feet behind. I looked back at the house and saw a row of faces watching from the window. When I looked back to you, you were on your knees. You howled. You howled like an animal. I've never heard anything so chilling in my life.'

Madeline twisted the stem of her wine glass back and forth between her fingers as she looked at him. 'My son was dead.'

'*My son too!* But I had a wife to care for, a wife I loved. I couldn't stand to see you in that pain.'

324

Her thoughts turned to Georgia. Perhaps there was some crucial difference between fathers and mothers, that while a man could always drag himself to look to the broader horizon, merely the fear of the loss of a child was all-erasing for a woman. Madeline looked at him sadly. 'I'm sorry, Hugh, I don't remember that. I don't remember you. I don't remember anyone being there.'

'In a way, we weren't there at all.' Hugh took her hand. This time it lay limp; she did not withdraw it. 'What made you call me now, Madeline? What is it you want to know about me? Say to me?'

She tapped her glass distractedly with one fingernail. 'I don't want to know anything – I mean not about you. I'm sorry. I need to ask you a favour. It isn't easy for me . . . or for you. I need to know . . . I want you to tell me . . . I want you to tell me what you saw when you came down from the combine.'

Hugh shook his head slightly. 'I've told you before. You made me tell you again and again.'

'Yes. But I can't remember. I need to know.' She pulled her hand from his and held them in her lap, looking at Hugh's ashen face.

'Rob banged on the door. When I switched off the engine Rob was yelling; I couldn't make out what he was saying. He kept pointing to the back of the combine. I went round. The tracks were up to Sam's waist. His eyes were open, on mine. He was very white. I knelt next to him and held his hand. He didn't look frightened but he didn't say a word. I said, we'll get you out of there, Sam, I promise . . . or something like that. His eyes fluttered. I thought he was dying in front of me. I can see those black lashes – just like yours – fluttering. Rob was back in the cab, starting up the engine. Then Sam opened his eyes and this sound came out . . .' Hugh stared down at the table, folding and refolding his napkin, pressing down hard on the creases of each fold. 'It wasn't a scream or a moan. He gave this kind of . . . *Oouff*, like the air was going out of him, as if he was surprised. *Boouuff* . . . But he wasn't dead then, I knew that. By the time we'd got the combine off him, we could see he'd been crushed. But he wasn't dead and he wasn't in pain. When he died, in the ambulance, he never made a sound. He never opened his eyes.'

'That's enough,' Madeline said, and drained her glass. 'Thank you for telling me.'

'Madeline, do you have someone . . . someone you love?'

'Yes.'

'But you're not married?'

'We live together. I was never cut out for marriage.'

'You?' Hugh looked at her in disbelief. 'You were more cut out for it than anyone I've ever known. Do you remember what it was like, Madeline? When we first married, before we had Sam? And *after* we had Sam?'

Madeline, who felt that the evening had now resolved all that she had intended it to resolve, glanced towards the door.

'You were the light of my world and everything in it. There was nothing on the surface of the earth but you. I wasn't surprised, like you were, when you got pregnant with Sam – Christ, we made love all the time, everywhere. It would have been worrying if you hadn't got pregnant, after all that.'

Hugh's voice shot up, nearly cracking, and Madeline felt her chest constrict. She craned her neck and asked the waitress for a glass of water, wanting to be gone, wanting to be out of the ghastly place, knowing she couldn't leave without hearing what Hugh had to say, knowing she couldn't sit there, straight-backed, and listen, without a glass or cigarette to play with. She clasped her hands and rested her chin on them. Right. Say this is a session, she told herself; put the other stuff in the corner of your mind for later; cut it off and listen. *Christ*. Hugh looked so wistful. She couldn't pretend he was a client.

'I'd drive the Land-Rover back from the top field and you'd

be at the door, in some long, drifty skirt that clung about your legs. It didn't matter how filthy I was. You used to say you liked that better. We made love on the kitchen floor, on the stairs, in the barn. Sometimes I'd stay out with the lads thinking if I kept away a little longer you'd be even happier to see me . . . but I could never keep myself away as long as I wanted to. I couldn't keep myself away from you. And then, in the morning, I'd drag myself back into the Land-Rover, barely able to drive, barely able to keep my eyes open because we'd been up all night. Sometimes I thought, this is the way to go – crash the car into the ditch and die thinking about making love to you. Deep in the smell of you. I loved you so much. We loved each other so much.'

Madeline stared at him silently over her entwined fingers. She could remember clearly enough; how often they had lain in bed at night with the damp sheets twisted tightly around their ankles and joked about bondage. She remembered it all, but had sealed the memory into a vacuum and did not want Hugh to pierce it.

Hugh's cheeks reddened and he shook his head. 'I'm sorry. Stupid of me to say that. Crass. Bloody crass. I've never had much skill when it comes to knowing what to say and what not to. Especially to you. Madeline,' his eyes were lowered, 'I just wanted to tell you that as far as I'm concerned our marriage was *based* on something. I know it was all lost with Sam. That morning I had a bright-eyed son and a passionate wife who loved me – even if she loved her child more.' As Madeline frowned he continued quickly, with a sweeping gesture, 'Oh, God yes, I knew Sam had far more than half your heart. I never resented it; I counted myself lucky to be part of it and keep some of you. But twelve hours later, I had no son and was looking at a woman with no light in her eyes.'

He fiddled with a cigarette, taking three tries to light it, still not meeting her gaze. 'I'm sorry for what I did. I'm sorry that Sam died and that I couldn't hold you together afterwards.

327

I'm sorry we lost everything we had. I'm sorry all the life was crushed out of you.'

Madeline stood up, compensating for the weakness in her legs by laying her palms flat on the table. For the first time since Sam's death, she felt a flutter, faint but distinct, of compassion towards Hugh.

'Hugh; did you want more children of your own?'

'Yes. Very much. My wife couldn't. She had a hysterectomy after her second daughter.'

Madeline nodded. 'I have to leave now. I'm grateful to you for telling me how you felt. It does help. A great deal. It helps me see Sam again . . .' Her voice broke and Hugh half-rose from his seat. She raised a hand to stop him. 'I have to go, Hugh. Maybe we'll meet sometime. I don't know. I wish you and your family all the best in the world. With my whole heart. But this is enough for me, do you understand? This is enough.' She touched her lips fleetingly to his cheek, certain she would never see him again and relieved that she had been able to find something for him in what she had seen as a dry reservoir in her heart.

Madeline sheltered under the awning of the restaurant for several minutes. She thought of Sam without pain but the longing remained. She thought of Sam as a spirit angel, a presence in her life who might have been there forever but had stayed only briefly. Her pursuit of him had brought her back in touch with her own feelings, feelings she had thought she did not want to recognise. She stepped out and tilted her face up to the cleansing rain.

Patrick had told Madeline that he wanted to look at the chapel of St Gregory and St Augustine at night. It had not been important to him to see it that night. It had not been important to him to see it at all; he knew the chapel and the setting for the bust as well as he knew his own yard. Besides, the bust was complete; only the final polishing remained. He had merely wanted an excuse to take Madeline to meet her ex-husband and an excuse to drive her back home. He had been tempted to wait outside like an obedient hound but knew he had no right to stand guard. He had driven on to the cathedral and waited in the Chapel of St Patrick and the Irish Saints, where Madeline had lit a candle for him. He had already stuffed ten pounds in the box to clear her debt.

He studied the marble inlay above the altar as he thought about her. Over the previous eight years he had told her many times that he was too old for her, that she was frittering away her youth on him, and to his great relief each time she had quashed his reservations. He found them harder to still. Every female image he had sculpted since meeting her held something of Madeline. He had knowingly attributed each feminine form with her grace, her containment, her kindness, her breadth of heart. Now he was watching Madeline unfold and move away from him, which was what he had wanted and what he had dreaded for a long time.

Be wary of your wishes, wary of your prayers, he told himself as he sat hunched on the simple wooden pew. He loved her more than he'd loved any woman, but he knew that he had been merely a caretaker, and he did not want to consign her to that for eternity. She should leave him, but she could only leave him if he left all the doors wide open.

Patrick made an irregular confession to a Portuguese priest, joined in the communion Mass, then sat in the rain on the cathedral steps, waiting for her call. His ancient greatcoat was soaked by the downpour and he had not bothered to change his shabby trainers before they'd left the wharf. The glancing double-takes of people leaving the cathedral told him that he looked like a tramp. Tempted to hold his hand out, Patrick smiled at them, his mobile phone held loosely in his open palm.

*   *   *

329

Madeline called at nine thirty-five and asked him to pick her up on the corner of St James's. Ten minutes later she leapt in, soaked to the skin and shivering. He waited for her to speak about Hugh and her son as the windscreen wipers pulsed their rhythmic battle against the pebbles of rain. When she spoke, she stared straight ahead. 'Patrick. I've fallen in love with one of my clients.'

TWENTY-THREE

Her emergency bleeper vibrated in the pocket of her jeans. Madeline hated breaking the rhythm of a session, particularly this one, and glanced at it with irritation.

'Excuse me, Flynn; I have to answer this.'

Madeline and Patrick had talked well into the night after returning from Jermyn Street. Madeline had been tempted to postpone all her appointments the following day, but she had kept her engagement with the combat veterans' group, and had spent the intervening time before five o'clock looking out of the window, preparing to take Flynn towards what she felt would be the final stage of the process. *Just don't say you love me: she pleaded with him silently when he arrived; say anything at all but that.*

From the anteroom she dialled back the number on her pager. 'John? It's Madeline Light.'

'Madeline, great. Thanks for getting back so fast. Any chance you can come over right away? There's been an incident here. One of the homeless badly beaten up by some fascist bastards. I've got some very distressed witnesses . . .'

Madeline glanced at her watch as she listened to the details. 'I'm really sorry, John, I'm in session. It may be a couple of hours before I can get to you – I can't give you a firm time. I can give you the numbers of some other therapists . . .'

'No, Madeline. I want you. I'll just try to hold the fort till you get here.'

When Madeline stepped back into the room and closed the door behind her the angle of Flynn's neck told her what he would never have revealed verbally. He was sitting in his chair, absolutely still. His head was bowed. One hand covered his face. He seemed to be thinking very hard, shrouded in despair. Madeline wanted to put her arms around him and dry his tears against her cheek, but returned to her seat. 'Flynn?'

'Ach, Madeline. I'm not what you think. I haven't –' he spoke through his hand and it was hard for her to hear him – 'I haven't . . . been straight.'

'Tell me how you haven't been straight, Flynn.' Her eyes shone with support but Flynn could not see them.

When he lowered his hand Madeline knew that in her short absence he had revisited the road to Gitarama; she could see the tracks of the journey in his eyes. 'I didn't tell you the truth. I wasn't trying to lie. I told you what I wanted to have happened, what I've told myself had happened; but it wasn't the truth . . .'

His breathing was loud and irregular and he again covered his face with his hands, rubbing them up and down, up and down. Then he continued. Madeline sat silently, aware of nothing but him. The ever-present noise of traffic from the street vanished, even the birds ceased to sing as Flynn told her about the journey to the hotel, the session in the bar with Kofi and Erik, and all that had happened up until the checkpoint.

'I could feel how violently he didn't want to go on. It was too late to turn back. Besides, I felt OK about it once I realised they were FAR soldiers.'

'FAR?'

'The official Rwandan army; the Hutu government army.'

'That made you feel OK?'

'An army is an army, everywhere; they have systems, there's a protocol, however mad. Like I told you, you just have to be a grey man. So when I saw the FAR boys, I thought, OK, I can do this. We'll get through no problem, I told Erik, we'll be grand.'

After waiting a few moments, Madeline prompted gently, 'But that was the point where you were turned back?'

'No. It was just as I predicted. Those guys knew things were falling apart. They wanted to get the hell out of there and they weren't thinking about us, they were thinking about Kagame and the RPA, the so-called rebel army. By that stage most of the FAR soldiers were on the point of deserting and running for the hills themselves. They did their bit of sabre-rattling, but their hearts weren't in it. They took some money, some booze, a carton of smokes. Erik's torch. But they didn't even strip down the car. We were through and out the other side in thirty minutes tops.'

'And you felt . . . ?'

Flynn sat up and flung both arms out. 'King of the fuckin' heap. You get a surge when you go through a place like that. Your muscles are like twisted steel, and as you go through, you think, *fuck*, are they going to take us out now, hit us in the arse? Then suddenly you know you're through, free as the breeze, they've turned their backs on you, and it's like *whoosh* . . . like levelling out at the bottom of a roller-coaster. And, don't forget, my judgement had been given a seal of approval,' Flynn added with heavy irony. 'Erik, the new boy, had been wrong, and my gut instincts were right. I pulled away and told him so: I said, sometimes you just have to keep your nerve, and *ease* your way through things. Don't give up so fast; don't let them turn you back till the last minute.'

'And Erik? How did Erik react?'

'Ah, he was good then. A trooper. He got the same kick I did – relief, exhilaration. We were back on the road – we were going somewhere, anywhere. I don't think either of us

333

honestly expected to find the refugees. Just because the FAR boys had been soft on us didn't mean they'd hand out candy to Tutsi women and children. And it was triumph enough to have got out of Kigali. At that moment I just wanted to get to Gitarama before dark. If we found the family, OK; if we didn't, that was OK too.' A shadow passed over his face.

'Did you find them, Flynn?'

'Oh yes. We found them all right. About ten miles further down the road. It was getting dark, not late, but the clouds were coming in low. Erik spotted marks in the dirt where the ground was all scuffed up at the edge of the track. They disappeared into some bushes. He was all for leaping out, but I didn't want to get out of the vehicle; anyone could have left those tracks. I was the boss. We went on, inching the Land-Rover forward, searching for signs of life, listening so hard you think your ears will burst. Either side of the road there were patches of cultivated land – plots of manioc, corn, broken up with sorghum. Thick vegetation.' He sat with his head in his hands, mumbling so that Madeline had to strain to hear him. 'Maybe fifty yards after we'd seen the footprints there was a break in the road, a tiny track leading down to a small settlement. Just a shack with a corrugated roof, a couple of mud huts. I turned down it and we pulled the Land-Rover up as close as we could get, a hundred yards from the first shelter. I looked up and saw these great, dark clouds above us, rolling in at speed. It's something biblical, when those African clouds barrel in. I knew we should get the hell out of there.'

Flynn shivered and sat up. His elbows rested on the armrests of his chair; his chin rested on the tips of his folded hands, as if in prayer, and his eyes were raised, fixed on the ceiling. He swallowed frequently as he led her step by stumbling step along the path of his memory. 'There wasn't a soul there. Erik went one way, I went another, checking the huts. The stench . . .' His nostrils flared as he grimaced. 'I made for the shack, the one with the tin roof, and had to put my shoulder to the door.

When it gave way . . . I can't describe the smell. Like a mixture of jam and shite and rotting meat, so strong, you puke. I nearly lost my balance. I staggered and put my hand down to stop myself falling. Flashed my torch around. I was standing on a body. There were seven or eight butchered people in there. I must have yelled because Erik came running. He looked like a ghost in the torchlight. His skin was like paper, his eyes so blue. He was jabbering, said we had to go back to the car and get the hell out of there. He had his jacket pulled up over his mouth and nose, and all I could see was his eyes. I refused to leave. Point-blank.'

'Why?'

'The facts were before us, at our feet. That's where the story was. It was obvious they weren't the family we were looking for, but they might still be around, maybe close by. It was worth checking out. At that moment I wanted to find them more than anything. It was a family, you know?'

'How did you know the bodies weren't the family you were looking for?'

He lowered his eyes to her face and for a moment or two struggled to speak. 'They had been dead a while, maybe over a week. The bodies were alive with maggots. All men. We knew our family was only women and small children: three women, four children, the sister had said.'

'And then?'

'We walked into the scrub behind the settlement.' He drew in a long breath. 'I don't know how long or how far we'd walked when we both heard something. We were walking together, side by side, twigs snapping under our feet, when I heard something different, a muffled whimper, like a puppy. We pushed our way through into a clearing and there they were.'

'The family?'

'Yes. They were squatting on the ground. When I shone the torch in the face of one of the women, her eyes flipped

335

backwards so you could only see the whites; they sort of flipped *inwards* as she fell back into some sort of fit. They all started hooting and moaning. I couldn't stand the noise, the night was so quiet, and they were jabbering, and all these sodding birds started squawking, and I thought, *They'll fucking hear us in Kigali.*' He was shaking his head, but it was more of a flinching spasm than a gesture of denial. 'One of the women didn't have a hand. Just a stump coated with dried blood. The sister at the mission must have bandaged it, it was properly done, but the sister hadn't mentioned it to us.' Flynn looked bewildered by this omission, but he continued his story, his voice throbbing with emotion. 'And then Erik . . . *Erik* . . . took control. He was . . . unbelievable. He started talking very softly, tried German, then French. I stood there, shaking in my boots, thinking what the fuck is he telling them, but the women stopped their noise and hushed the children and it was quiet again, apart from Erik. He got down on his haunches next to them. They were all crowded together, around the woman who'd passed out. One woman spoke French. The sister had told us one of them was the wife of a doctor, an educated woman, the one who knew the Gitarama priest and felt she could trust him. Erik kept talking to her, asking their names, how they'd got that far, and she talked to the other woman, the one without a hand, and then he looked up at me and told me to see if there was any way I could get the Land-Rover in closer.

'The way we'd come was too dense, but on the other side of the clearing the ground dropped off, sharp, down to a river bank. I found a kind of miserable little track looping back, looping round from where we'd come. There was a slim chance of getting the Land-Rover down there, not into the clearing itself, but at least closer. I checked out the opposite bank. It fell away to a kind of ravine, with barely a puddle of water in it. I wondered if it wouldn't be better to cross, try to help them cross, but we didn't know what we'd find on the other

336

side and the last thing I wanted was to abandon the wheels. I wanted to get the fuck out of there . . . leave them to it. But sometimes there's no one else; you have to do something.' His face twisted.

'I came back and told Erik about the second track we'd missed in the dusk. It was getting so dark that I didn't know if I'd be able to find it without the headlights, and I didn't want to have to use the lights. I suggested we carry them back, it wouldn't take too long, but the women wouldn't leave the children and they wouldn't let us take the children away from them. I said we could carry two each, but one of the women was still out cold. I thought she'd died of fright but Erik said no, it was just the shock. I told him to do it, he could get the Land-Rover while I stayed with them, and Erik just looked up at me with this big, big smile and asked me how good my French was. I felt like an eejut, thinking, how the hell is it that I can speak Latin, can translate any goddamn Latin text, negotiate in Italian, and I can't bloody speak French?'

He stared at Madeline accusingly, as if this injustice were her doing. She was finding it hard to breathe in the small room, hard to stop the tears that had welled up behind her eyes, and hard not to look away from Flynn, not to look away from the sight of the burden he carried and was about to lay at her feet. 'What did you do then, Flynn?'

'I went back to the Land-Rover. I clapped my hand over the torch, saw straight through my glowing red hand, saw the veins and the dark shadow of the bones, all the way back to the Land-Rover. I climbed in and sat shaking in the dark. I could hear my teeth chattering and I looked down at my hands and they were shaking and shaking . . . I couldn't get my hand into the pocket of my jeans. I had to get out again to get the key out of my pocket. I couldn't go back like that, trembling like a leaf. I sat there in the driving seat, lit a smoke, took a few drags, maybe three . . . Then the noise started.'

Flynn choked and tears began to fall down his cheeks, his

eyes screwed tight, seeing his own story, far away from the safe haven of Madeline's room. Madeline's hand covered her mouth and her heart pounded dully, muffled, against her ribcage. *Doomdoomdoom*. Flynn began to speak again.

'Shouting and yelling and screaming like I never heard in my life. I couldn't move. I had the key in the ignition, my hand frozen on it, and I couldn't move, couldn't turn it. Wouldn't. I sat there listening in the dark. Screaming and crazy yelling. I heard Erik shouting out, shouting in French, and Dutch, then in English, I heard him call my name, yell it out loud. *He* wasn't screaming; he shouted my name clearly. And I sat in the Land-Rover, listening in the dark.'

Madeline's skin shivered over her flesh with the involuntary powerful shudder that ripples a horse's flank. She sat across from him, gripping the arms of her chair with white knuckles. She felt derailed by his account, blinded by the vision he had thrown onto the white wall of her room. Any gesture of comfort, of consolation now might stop his tears, but would also halt what had at last become a narrative. If he did not complete it, he might be left forever in that savage clearing.

After several long minutes, Flynn's sobs subsided. 'It started to pour. Torrential rain. I listened. I imagined what was happening. I thought I don't want to die, please God don't let me die in this pit of a place, not cowering in the dark in the driving seat of a UN Land-Rover. I don't know how long I sat there. It felt like I sat there all through the night, but the screaming stopped. I could hear men singing; it rose out of the night, wild singing. I thought, they'll come along this path, back towards the road. I got out of the Land-Rover. I didn't have trouble moving *then*. I crawled to the shack and lay down on the floor. It was quiet there, apart from the rain. So dark and still, like everything had been smothered with a blanket. I waited until the morning, listening to the rain on the corrugated roof.'

338

'Flynn . . .' Madeline could hardly bring herself to voice what she needed to ask. 'I can't imagine . . . it's terrible. In the shack. You felt . . . ?'

'I felt safe. Safe with the dead. It was where I should be.'

'And in the morning?'

'Everything was beautiful. Like nothing had happened. The morning had that perfect, golden light; no clouds, just sunlight bathing the place. I went back to the clearing.'

Revulsion was written broadly across his face, but his voice was steadier. 'The first thing I saw was the little boy, Ol's age, alive. Squatting next to the others, kind of playing. The bodies of the women and the other three kids were all together, tangled together. One of the . . . one of the children had his skull split like you'd crack a coconut. His head was lying in the woman's lap, the woman who'd been unconscious when I left, his brains spilt into her lap. Maybe she never came round. The other little boy was squatting on his heels, sucking his fingers, and they were red and covered in –' Flynn broke off. 'He froze when I came into the clearing. He looked at me with an awful dead stare. I've seen children look like that a hundred times . . . I saw Erik over at the side. His throat was slit. He wasn't meant to be there. None of them should have been there. Those women weren't responsible for the situation they were in. They didn't know why they had to take their children and hide in the bush till someone eviscerated them. But Erik . . . I felt furious with him. It was so idiotic. There was an absurdity about it, his big grin and blue eyes, and his dick standing up. It didn't seem real.'

We're all wired to avoid horror, what cannot be stomached, Madeline thought. *How natural to try to register that awful tableau as a farcical nightmare and file it away with the unreal. How could any man lie on the dead all night and in the morning accept that as real? She was aware of another tug in her stomach, a desperate, aching tug that she could not still.* 'And the little boy, Flynn? What did you do with the little boy?'

'Do?' He looked at her blankly. 'I must have spoken to him, I don't know. I stripped off my clothes and I walked down to the ravine to wash.'

'You washed in the river?' Madeline was uncertain whether Flynn was still in the factual account or whether he had slipped back into his dream. The boundary between the two was so very thin.

'Yes, I washed myself,' he said flatly, before an expression of such shame flooded his face that Madeline again gripped the arms of her chair. 'I'd shat myself in the Land-Rover. I'd been lying in my own shit all night, that and the blood and brains and guts of those poor bastards. I was covered with it. So I washed. Then I picked up the boy.'

'How did he seem, Flynn?'

'Limp. He didn't move; didn't make a sound. But I was damn glad he was there, glad there was somebody to do something for, something that stopped me thinking about myself. I put him on the seat next to me and we drove back to Kigali. I had to get out of the country. I couldn't go on to Gitarama.'

It struck Madeline that it might have been easier for him to go on to Gitarama, where no one knew about him, or Erik, or the Tutsi family. 'What about the road blocks?'

'The FAR soldiers had vanished. The first road block we came to was a UN checkpoint they'd set up that morning. I told them I was taking the kid back to the orphanage and returning their motor.'

Madeline tried to imagine what the UN patrol had seen: the huge, rangy journalist in sodden, filth-splattered clothes with one tiny, stupefied child beside him. 'And then?'

'I took the boy to the orphanage. The same two UNAMIR soldiers were still there, on patrol. I tried to tell the Belgian sister what had happened: "*Ils sont morts*," I said. "*Toute la famille est mort. Et mon ami – le Hollandais – est mort.*" *Le Hollandais.* She changed to English pretty damn quick. I couldn't stop shaking. I asked her to hear my confession. She said she couldn't because she wouldn't be able to understand enough. She understood what I'd done. She understood well enough,' he repeated. 'I spewed it out, anyway, before she could shut the door on me. She was very gentle; very kind. She took the child's hand and she laid her other palm, like this,' Flynn raised his own hand to his cheek, 'and she said something . . . she said, with her eyes on me, "Thank you. We will care for this little one, this lonely one." I wanted her to take my hand and lead me away. I didn't deserve such kindness from anyone.'

Madeline could feel her heart crack for the sister, the child, Erik. Flynn. Most of all for Flynn. He needed to end his story. 'And then?' she breathed.

'I went to the UN headquarters,' Flynn continued, 'and handed over the Land-Rover. I told them where to find Erik and the Tutsis. I asked them to help me get out of the country. I'd given up on the weeping Kibeho Virgin. I didn't believe in miracles in the first place.'

'And you left Rwanda?'

'Yes. They got me to Nairobi that night.'

'Why Nairobi?'

'I needed to go to Erik's office, tell his people so they could recover his body.'

'How did you feel, talking to Erik's colleagues?' Flynn gazed back at her mutely.

'Flynn? Was it difficult for you to talk to them?'

'No. Because I didn't tell them what happened. I told them I'd been following him, coming along the next day and I'd found him. That was all I said. There wasn't exactly anyone about,' he added bitterly, 'anyone left to call me a liar, or write up the story, was there?'

'Did you stay in Nairobi?'

'Till I could stomach going home.'

'Did you talk to anyone about that night, about what had happened?'

341

'No. I didn't talk to anyone. I cried in front of people, but lots of people were crying about Rwanda. I didn't talk to anyone. Except –' his face clouded – 'I had an argument with one feller, an Australian cameraman.'

'And you told him what had happened?'

'Jesus, no. *I didn't tell anyone.* He was just in a bar. I spent most of those few days in a bar, crying when I'd drunk enough – or when I hadn't. He said he didn't understand how Rwanda could have fucked me up so badly. He said that "kind of killing" was predictable in Africa. He used a phrase I can't stomach. He said the continent was riddled with "endemic violence" and hatred, and that it wasn't a war we Westerners could identify with. We need dead white people and dead white babies in order "to get our juices flowing".'

'Did you answer him?'

Flynn made a rough sound in his throat. 'Yes, I answered him. I broke his nose.'

'And when you left Nairobi?'

'I flew home.'

'To London?'

'Yes. I was violently sick at Heathrow. There was so much *stuff*, cafeterias groaning with food, so many people, all so clean and busy. I couldn't take it in, keep it down. Then I went back to Georgia and the children.'

'Do you recall how you felt when you came home to your family?'

'I didn't want them to look at me. I thought if they looked closely enough they'd see everything. I remember sitting on the bed a few days after I'd got back, staring at the stuff in my bag. The boots I'd worn had red dust in all the cracks; that dust got everywhere. Georgia offered to clean them, unpack for me. I couldn't let her touch them. I sat there holding them and told her to fuck off.' Flynn covered his face again. 'Maybe it was dirt, but I think it was blood – dried blood.

I must have spent a week scrubbing myself raw; scrubbing everything, the boots, everything. At the end of that week I threw it all out.'

Except for what he had seen and what he had experienced; what he felt he had not done that he could have done. Those had been burnt into his memory and sealed off. Madeline struggled to say something that wasn't prescriptive or conclusive or banal. She could feel Flynn's exhaustion; how depleting the effort of telling his story had been for him. 'I am filled with admiration for your courage . . .'

'My courage?' he challenged. '*Courage*? I told you, I crapped myself.'

'Let's talk about what you might have done.'

Flynn spoke quickly; he had spent over six years rehearsing alternative scenarios. 'I could have forced us all to stay together. We could have all gone back to the Land-Rover together. The Interhamwe came from the other side, across the ravine.'

'You didn't know that. One of the women was unconscious; another injured. It seems very sensible to try to bring the Land-Rover closer to the family and leave together. That was what you planned.'

'That was what *Erik* planned. Erik took control. I let him take control.'

'That must have been hard for you.'

'If it had been harder, if I'd resisted, maybe this wouldn't have happened.'

'But you agreed with him on the best way to get everyone out?'

'I suppose I did.' Flynn sounded bitter; he did not want her to wrench the blame away from him.

'And so, following the plan, you went back to the Land-Rover and then you heard screaming.'

'Maybe I sat in the Land-Rover for half an hour first, twiddling my thumbs, and all the while . . .' He gave up.

343

'How long did it take you to get from the clearing back to the Land-Rover, in the dark, shielding your torch?'

He shrugged. 'I wasn't looking at my watch. Twenty minutes?'

'And in the Land-Rover, you said you were shaking so much you couldn't get your hand in your pocket to get the key. You got out, got the key, got back in and steadied yourself to be able to drive. You smoked a cigarette – three, four drags? And then heard screaming. I don't think you were dawdling, Flynn.'

'I was in the driving seat, God damn it! *I* was the experienced hack, *I* was the guy who was meant to be in control . . .'

He had taken control at the heliport on the way out to Astra Four, taken control at the orphanage, taken control at the FAR checkpoint; he had wrested control of their first real session by kissing her. Her instincts told her it had always been a defining issue for him. *And the dream – the dream about Erik on the far frozen bank. . . . She'd thought the far bank, where Erik stood, represented death, but the Interhamwe killers had come from that side; Flynn had been right to fear it on both counts.*

'You must despise me. That was why I didn't want to tell you. Of all people, I didn't want you to despise me.'

'I don't despise you, Flynn,' Madeline said with passion, 'but you feel you should despise yourself. Can you tell me what you think you should have done, hearing the screaming, in the driving seat, in control?'

'Maybe the sound of the car engine alone would have scared them off.'

'Is that possible?'

'Maybe. I didn't even try.'

'Imagine you had. Imagine you had started the engine and driven back along a path you didn't know and couldn't really see. That would still leave you some way from the clearing. Imagine the screaming continued while you were driving. What would your next step have been?'

'Maybe I could have talked my way out of it,' he said

falteringly. 'Maybe I could have negotiated, persuaded them to spare the Tutsis, flattered them, dropped a few hints about our UN friends – bought time. Bought them off. That worked in other situations in Rwanda; cash saved a lot of lives. *I don't know.* Maybe I might have been able to do something.'

Maybe I might have been able to do something. Madeline knew very well what that 'maybe' felt like. *Maybe if I'd stayed home with Sam. Maybe if I'd got back sooner.* She knew his self-image as a man who could solve anything, blag his way round any obstacle; it would be very hard for him to admit that there was a situation in which he was powerless.

'You might have been killed alongside them.'

'For sure.' He gave her a weary smile. 'I thought about it for years and I still don't know what might have happened. I never will.'

'No, Flynn, you never will. You are going to have to carry on living with that uncertainty. But there is one thing you need to accept, need to know, and I think you *do* know: there's nothing that you could have done, no possible action you could have taken, or action you failed to take, that absolves the perpetrators of responsibility for murdering Erik and those women and children.'

At first Flynn did not make any gesture of acceptance or dismissal. Then he said slowly, his eyes steady on hers, 'I'm not sure that doing nothing isn't as criminal as doing something wrong. I'm not sure. It's a crime in France, you know? The crime of non-assistance.'

All Madeline's conscious mind was focused on Flynn, but one deep part of her heart still dwelt on Sam. *For ten years she had swung between two versions of reality: one that Sam's death was her fault because she had failed to preserve his life; the other that took her entirely out of the frame and charged Hugh with sole responsibility for keeping Sam at the farm, neglecting him and crushing him.*

'Flynn, I'm wondering about something. I'd like to check if it makes any sense to you. Understandably, you hate the feeling that you lost control; you still want to take responsibility for everything that happened. There were many people involved in what happened that night. The woman – the doctor's wife who spoke French and wanted to get to Gitarama – insisted on going against the advice of the Belgian sister, your friend Kofi and the UN officials. She made a decision and acted on it. She persuaded others to go with her, to follow her decision. Erik made choices and decisions too; he decided to go with you and he persuaded you to go along with his plan. Whoever killed them also took decisions, perhaps on the orders of others, equally culpable. Can you allow Erik to take some responsibility for his actions, and his choices? Can you allow all those people their own responsibility?'

'The children? You include the children?'

Madeline's throat tightened. 'No, I don't,' she said fervently. 'I think young children are reckless with their lives, because they do not understand how precarious life is. It's our duty to protect them until they learn that lesson. I'm sure the Tutsi women believed they were protecting those children, as did Erik. And as did *you*, Flynn. You *did* protect the little boy. You took him back with you. That wasn't non-assistance.'

'No, but he was probably sliced into pieces a couple of days later. I didn't hang around to find out.' After a pause he said abruptly, 'I was asked to go back to Rwanda, later that year, to visit the refugee camps. I didn't go.'

'Why was that?'

'I kept looking at the footage that had come out of the camps. The genocide didn't get much attention, but the refugee crisis did. When cholera broke out, it got full-scale cover. One night I was watching telly, and the camera panned over Kibumba camp, the bodies stacked on pallets like piles of firewood. I punched the air, sitting there in front of the box. It felt like victory. Georgia looked at me like I'd finally tipped over the edge. Which, in a way, I had.'

'What made you feel victorious?'

'The camps, that one in particular, were known to be full of the Interhamwe. I thought maybe the scum who'd slit Erik's throat had met divine justice. I prayed they were there. I believed in God again.'

What was it Flynn had said to her, early on, when he had referred to the cholera epidemic – God's terrible answer to the Hutus. *Madeline could hear his voice, then artificially jocular: sometimes you've got to have the walls of Jericho come tumblin' down.*

'I couldn't go back, not feeling like that. I would have been gloating. I wasn't fit to work.'

'You believed you were unfit to photograph the camps?'

'Yes. I'd lost my objectivity.'

But not your professional ethics, not your compassion, and not your self-knowledge, Madeline thought privately.

It was a quarter past six. More than time to stop. She was so terribly weary. Madeline hesitated.

347

TWENTY-FOUR

She did not know that she had the physical strength to continue, but in some ways exhaustion cleared her mind. There were so many ways in which she had tried to position Flynn as a heroic saviour; her ballast on *Nepenthe*, the wounded hero she could save through therapy – and so save herself. The dream hero in her life, when she had been looking so hard to find one. Flynn had failed his own test, but as she had listened to his moment of failure, her respect for him had not been diminished. She wanted to help him unravel what lay within his dreams, to catch the feet of the vanishing figure before it disappeared for ever.

'Your recurrent dream, Flynn. You are carrying Oliver, then experience being shot through him . . .'

'I suppose Ol's there because I'm frightened I'll fail my family the way I failed the Tutsi family. Like I failed Erik.'

'Ol's presence in the dream may have other interpretations.' Madeline was wary of suggesting too much. The recurrence in his dream of the two figures – the child and Erik, dead – was a sign of Flynn's continuing close identification with them; the bullet passing through the child into him might indicate how thin Flynn's personal boundaries had become. To her, the child now represented many things: the small child he had seen picking at his mother's entrails; Erik as a young, innocent version of himself, whom he felt obligated to protect. And above all, Flynn himself; his own vulnerability and compassion, which also needed protection. Madeline thought rapidly, a myriad connections flashing through her mind. The images were cloudy and confused. Guilt over his own survival hung over the dream like a cloud – all his choices; his resentment of finding the child at his feet; the burden of carrying it when he could hardly move himself; his shock that the child had not stopped the bullet from piercing him. She felt that she needed to take a chance, to touch the shadow that hung over him and contradict his own feelings. 'What would have happened to your family had you been killed alongside Erik?'

Flynn held up his hand in warning. 'Oh no, Madeline . . . if you're suggesting that I hid in some virtuous attempt to safeguard my family, I'll have none of that. I hid because I was scared to death. It was nothing but cowardice.'

'I think you hid to save your life,' Madeline replied simply. 'And I think that this dream is reminding you to continue saving your life. For yourself and your family. I don't call that cowardice.'

'Why do I keep having it?'

'I'm not sure anyone yet understands the full purpose of dreams, but they seem to help us to integrate experience; they let us try out different scenarios that might help with our daily lives. In your dream, I do think there's a clear message about survival. You are a survivor in the dream.' Madeline stopped; she had realised that she was using personal pronouns far more than she would normally do – she was uniting her own experience with Flynn's. *Except that my dream doesn't change positively; my dream has no progression.* I am always running away. She cleared her throat. 'You did alter the sequence of events in the dream, didn't you?'

Flynn's face was uneasy; she could see him struggling to hold onto the darkness of his original dream. Madeline understood the desire to grip onto grief; if you released it for a moment it would come back with such a vengeance it would knock you flat.

'You mean,' he fumbled, 'that you come into the dream?'

'That too,' she acknowledged, but her own presence was the least interesting aspect to her at that moment. She reined in her eagerness to lead him. 'Look again at the dream you had after the accident, how it diverged from the original version. You told me that when you come out of the house, carrying Oliver, you can hardly walk for the red mud sticking to you.'

'That's the colour of the earth in Rwanda. Like a bloodstain.' He let out a heavy sigh.

Madeline nodded, remembering how he had been white with plaster dust in the original account of the dream and that it had made her think of Patrick. The second version anchored him in Rwanda, an indication of his approaching conscious acceptance of the trauma.

The light in the consulting room had grown starker as night fell, one lamp pinpointing her desk in a pool of light but leaving both of them in the shadow. As Flynn opened up she felt the distance between them reduce as tangibly as if he were physically approaching her.

'I'm holding Oliver tight as we come into the clearing.' He flinched, the muscles around his mouth working as his breath grew shallow. 'Bodies everywhere, too many limbs . . .'

'When you come into the clearing, this time, there are many bodies, is that right?'

'Hundreds. You can't work out where one stops and the next starts.'

'Isn't that a change from the original dream?'

Flynn was puzzled. 'Maybe. Maybe in the original dream I just see the seven bodies. That night, I saw all of them, all the dead I'd seen in Rwanda, maybe all the dead I've ever seen, all of them heaped together . . .'

'And you feel . . . ?'

'Fear. Fear and revulsion. Disgust from the stench of it –'
even as he spoke Flynn's breathing became more rapid – 'Oh
God, the *reek* of it . . .'

His voice washed over her like an incoming tide. Madeline
scanned her memory, trying to recall if Flynn had mentioned
the smell in his original account of the dream: he had not. He
had been in the clearing, the bodies were newly butchered. She
believed the second version had returned him to his night with
the dead. 'And then?' she said softly.

'It changes,' his voice lightened. As he described the icy river,
Madeline's eyes never left his face. She did not hear the traffic
outside, or the front door of the building slamming, or Jack
and Michael's voices rising up from the street. 'Erik's on the
far bank.'

'Does Erik speak to you?'

Flynn shook his head. 'Not really, but I know what he's
saying, he's telling me to go back.'

'When he tells you to go back, you feel . . . ?'

'Pissed off. It's better where he is, safer, and I think . . .'
Flynn stopped short, staring at his hands.

'Flynn? You think . . . ?'

He lifted his eyes to her face, and said numbly, 'It isn't better
where he is. He's telling me not to come over. It's too cold on
that side of the river and . . . he's dead. That's why I don't
hear him. He's smiling and he's waving, but I don't hear him;
I know he's dead. He's telling me not to cross. Is that right?'

'Go on, Flynn,' Madeline urged, unaware of the warmth and
encouragement that rang in her voice.

'I see you. Erik's telling me to go back and get you, you and
the Tutsi boy. And I feel OK. For a moment there, I feel . . .
grand.'

Madeline's face was radiant. 'It's an extraordinary dream.'

'Extraordinary,' he echoed, gazing at her with yearning. 'The
best dream I've ever had. I wish it wasn't a dream.'

Flynn stood up slowly and, as he did, Madeline leant

351

back two inches in her chair, less in apprehension than in preparation. *My Christ – I still want him to kiss me,* she thought; *right now I am longing for him to kiss me.* He did not approach her. He walked to the back of the room by the door and stood looking at the painting on the wall. She waited with her heart full of love for him. 'I like this,' he said softly, 'it's nice.' He leant closer to the watercolour and Madeline waited. 'We're getting to the end, aren't we, Madeline? You're getting ready to leave me.'

She allowed herself to smile while his back was turned, longing to correct him and say that he was preparing to leave her, that she would never leave him, but she knew this did not need to be said. Flynn continued to address the painting with his hands thrust deep in the rear pockets of his jeans. 'I could have another dream, you know. I could change this. I could have a dream where Erik's dead on the ground and I drop the child, and I kill you, kill my way out of the whole business . . . I could have that dream, Madeline, couldn't I?'

Madeline looked at his back, her eyes as clear as green glass and warm as liquid molasses, tempted to tell him that if he had that dream, it would certainly tell her he was ready to stop.

'It wasn't the fuckin' horror of that night that was driving me crazy. The thing I couldn't live with, what made me long to be with Erik, go over to his side, was the idea that I'd got away with it. I wanted to pay a price.'

'You have paid a price.'

He shook his head, one finger now tracing the line of colour along the edge of the painting. 'And you don't know what that price is.'

'You're right,' she acknowledged at once. 'I don't know. Tell me what price you've paid.'

'I don't get to rescue you,' Flynn said in a low voice. 'I don't get to rescue you, do I? I don't even get to know you. I only get to fall in love with you. I get to know that I have to tell you about the road to Gitarama, that night in the shed; that if I don't tell you I might as well be dead. I get to show somebody who I really am, all the sick and the shite and the shame of it; I get to do that in order to save my own life. And as soon as I do it, I know that's the end. I don't get to have my life back and get to love you, do I? You take me into this new place, this new world, and I see wonder, and I see things I've never seen before . . .'

There was a long pause.

'What do you see?' Madeline asked gently.

'Hope?' At that moment he turned back to face her, studying her face, searching for some imperfection, some defect of compassion or understanding that might sever the skein of enchantment she had unintentionally wrapped about him. He did not find it. 'And all the time I know that once I go through there, you'll close the door behind me. I love you, Madeline. You're the ideal woman, the dream woman, the perfect girl I told you I tried to imagine on the road back to Kigali. So I get to meet her in the flesh. And the price I pay is that I feel all that, and because of what you've done, I know that you're like Georgia's secret place for me – the place you know about and long for but never get to visit.'

He was preparing, Madeline thought, and she needed to do the same. 'It sounds like we should talk about bringing our sessions to a close.'

'I'm not ready to stop. I'm not ready to be without you.' He flung himself back in his chair. 'So, say the sessions come to a close. We can still meet as friends? Once in a while?'

'No, Flynn, we can't.' Madeline strained to hear Flynn and her own heart, but listen to her professional voice. The ending had been raised; it had to be addressed. *She would not be able to bear seeing him as a friend.* 'It sounds easy and natural; we have grown so close. But we cannot meet as friends. It isn't time to part yet, but it will be very soon and that will be hard for both of us. You are important to me. You always will be.

If I agreed to meet you socially, I could be of no future use to you.'

Before he replied, she saw the protective mask of flippancy settle back on his face, and for the first time felt grateful for it.

'So what?' he grunted. 'You've been bloody useless so far. If it means you can't be my therapist any more, then I'll find someone else. You can refer me.' She did not speak, nor take her eyes from his. 'OK. So we don't meet socially. If you leave me, I'll find a reason to come back. I'll schedule a major breakdown.'

Madeline smiled. 'Flynn: I won't leave you. Not until you're ready to end our sessions, not until we both agree that you're ready to stop. Even then, I won't leave you. I will always be here. But I can only be *here*, on the other side of this room. That is *my* limit. This has been a searching few months for both of us. I'm very moved by what you've said tonight. I'm also very proud.'

'I'm over my time, aren't I?'

'Yes.'

'You want me to go?'

'No.' Madeline did not attempt to conceal what she felt.

'In Freetown, I had this idea about you and me. I thought we could offer ourselves up as a team. To Médicins Sans Frontières or some group like that. They must need counsellors and photographers . . . Nepenthe . . .'

'What makes you think of *Nepenthe*?'

'That's what I call you. Nepenthe. But it's the wrong name, I see that now. You know the origin of the word?'

Madeline did. 'Tell me.'

'It's the opiate Homer describes as a remedy for grief and heartbreak. It induces forgetfulness. But you've let me remember.'

'You let yourself remember. I simply gave you the space to do so. But it reminds me of something I've been meaning to ask you. What do you think triggered your seeing Erik on *Nepenthe*?' She knew how memories remained intact, ready to be recalled and reactivated even after six years. After more than six years.

'I thought it was the smell in the tent,' Madeline leant forward, 'but it wasn't that. It was you. It was the way you trusted me. And I let you down. I felt such a coward. I'd got there by pretending to be responsible for you and I abandoned you. In the captain's room, I felt your eyes on me and I was frightened again. I felt you'd open everything up. You looked at me and saw straight through me. You brought Erik back to me.'

'It was time for you, Flynn. You'd been in pain too long. I'm glad I was there.'

'I'm glad too.' His brows furrowed again as he searched her face, a bewildered expression shadowing his eyes. Abruptly he waved a dismissive hand. 'I have to go, Madeline. I have to get back home. And I won't be here next week. I'm going to a refugee camp in Kosovo. It might be a few days, maybe the whole week . . . it depends what comes up.'

'I'll be here. I won't be expecting you, but I will be here.'

'I want to bring one of the prints that I took.'

Madeline's eyes stayed on him. 'Just let me know when you're back.'

Madeline turned off the light and sat alone for a moment in the gloom. It was not a time for conceit or vanity; she had witnessed Flynn's redemption with humility and gratitude. She had seen him as a man who had hit rock-bottom, a man who knew, as she knew, what rock-bottom was like. Madeline was certain that Georgia knew it too; Georgia had provided Flynn with an effective membrane against trauma for years. She hoped the knowledge would bind them closer together. They would not live at rock-bottom, but they would share a knowledge of it forever, in some locked and central space of their hearts. And in the process of bringing Flynn back to the clearing, Madeline had looked at her own heart, and found herself taking a step back, like an artist gazing with amazement at his own work. She buttoned her coat right up to her chin and set off for John's night shelter.

The relentless rain had forced Patrick and his assistant to move the Cardinal inside to complete the arduous stage of polishing the marble. The bust stood on its turntable in the middle of the studio, and for the past fortnight Patrick had slowly worked away at the surface with a riffler, gradually erasing the scars caused by two months of chiselling. When Madeline came home late that night he was perched on the edge of the stool, rubbing the Cardinal's neck with a small pad impregnated with industrial diamond grains, his tiny, circular movements polishing the creases in the slack throat to take every inch of marble to a highly reflective finish. Madeline stood with both arms draped loosely around Patrick's neck, her cheek pressed lightly against the back of his bald head.

'It's the best work you've ever done.'

He grunted dismissively, but Madeline knew he was proud of the piece. His thumbs had reddened patches where the abrasive pads had stripped the skin off them; they would be raw by Christmas. Madeline walked around the bust, letting her fingers trail over the features that Patrick had carved with such infinite care. 'He's simply . . . grand,' she said. 'Every inch of him.'

'Hume had a rare face.'

Although Patrick was not looking at her, bent close to his subject and seemingly engrossed in his work, Madeline felt the full force of his concentration on her. 'Does my talking disturb you?'

'Not if my working doesn't disturb your talking.'

'I'd like to talk about us.' Patrick glanced up at her from under bushy eyebrows. 'I think,' she continued gently, 'that it's time for me to move out. Not now, but sometime over the next few months. Unless you'd rather I went now?'

'I don't want you to go at all.' He shoved his stool back a foot, regarding her with a firm set to his chin. 'You said nothing was going to happen with this man, your client. If you're in love with him, so be it. It doesn't mean you have to move out.'

While they had talked about her falling in love with a client, Madeline had told him next to nothing about Flynn; the confidentiality of the therapy room prohibited her from discussing any client with anyone other than her supervisor. Still caressing the marble bust, Madeline shook her head. It wasn't fair to Patrick to keep so much from him. 'It's only partly because of my client. He's a strange man, Patrick, a difficult man. There are ways in which he reminds me of you. He's a good man. He's passionate about his work, committed; a man of great integrity.' She looked at him steadily over the top of the Cardinal's head. 'But he's been badly damaged by an experience he had several years ago. He's haunted by it and has been lonely for a long time. Something within him broke. Working with him, I recognised how I'd sliced my heart in half when Sam died. I *am* in love with him, but that really isn't important. My work with him is nearly complete.' She smiled wistfully. 'Like you and Basil here. I won't see him after our sessions are over.'

'I don't see why you shouldn't,' Patrick said gruffly. 'If you love him. I imagine he's in love with you?'

'No; he may think he is, but he's not.'

Patrick picked up the polishing pad and looked at it closely. 'Then he's an arse.'

Madeline smiled gently. 'I want you to understand that for all the work I did, all the help I had in the years after Sam's death, however much I grieved for him and told myself that I had come to terms with it, I hadn't. I've been half alive and half dead. In deference to Sam.' Her deep, magnetic eyes were fixed on him unblinking. 'The living half of me has *always* been with you. I love you so very much. I love you with all my heart . . . but it's only been half a heart.'

'Come here,' he instructed brusquely. She moved to stand between his knees as he took her face in his hands, tilting it to one side and then the other, one grazed thumb rubbing away a stray tear from her cheekbone. 'How many times have I told you I'm too old for you?'

He felt her body stiffen. 'Your age has nothing to do with it.'

'I know.' He drew her face to his. 'I *know*. But I've watched you, all the time over these eight years, and I've seen the compromises you make.'

'You were never a compromise. Never.'

'I know that too. I knew from the day you moved in, like a bird with a broken wing. I know you loved me as much as you could. I know how hard you've tried to love me, but the bottom line is it was never enough. So I've been expecting this. It's been enough for me. It was precisely what I wanted, but it was never enough for you, Maddie.'

'It was,' she sobbed, tipping her forehead to meet his. 'It was.'

'I am an old man –'

'Will you stop saying that?'

'I am,' he said firmly, 'old, and set in my ways, and I want to be left in peace to do my work. That's really what I live for. You have been a lovely presence in this place, Maddie, a lovely presence and an inspiration. My perfect muse. But I've always known that you would go your own way when the time was right. I've always known I was a caretaker.'

'Is that why you wouldn't marry me when I asked you?'

He smiled wryly. 'I'm not the marrying kind, kid.'

'Too damn footloose and fancy-free?' She smiled back at him, their lips inches apart.

'That's right. Too damn young, too.' As her eyes filled with tears she nuzzled her face in his neck and inhaled the dusty, sweaty scent of him.

Patrick closed his eyes. He felt her tears on his neck and imagined his life without her. He had not been truthful with Madeline; he had not been expecting the moment calmly. He had been dreading it with all his heart for years and had listened to each word with increasing pain. Now he took her firmly by the shoulders and pushed her away. 'I've been thinking about taking a trip to Carrara around Christmas. See some old friends. So if you want this place to yourself for a bit, you've got it.' He gave her a little shake. 'You stay as long as you like and you go when you like. But I have one condition.'

The canter of her eyebrows arched like the Bridge of Sighs. 'Which is?'

'That you leave me and Basil in peace for the next hour.'

As she walked slowly up the spiral staircase, Madeline bent her head to keep Patrick within her sight. He picked up the diamond pad and, if Madeline had not known him better, he would have seemed utterly absorbed the Cardinal's jawbone.

Patrick waited until he heard her turn on the bath above him and then poured himself a large whisky. He flung up the huge window and stepped out onto the concrete terrace abutting the Thames. Madeline would go and he would never love another woman as he had loved her. He doubted he would ever love again. His back ached dully and his shoulders slackened with the realisation that he had surrendered Madeline's soft and steady presence in his life without a fight. If he had only married her two years ago . . . Patrick shook his head. The bitter and unfamiliar sting of jealousy had sat in his mouth ever since she had told him about the client. The rush of possessiveness had taken him by surprise. He had battled to summon some form of genuine largesse but he had failed. He prayed that Madeline would not turn from him to her client.

He could give her up for her own sake, but he could not feign the generosity of spirit to hand her over to another man. 'Stupid old fool,' he muttered to himself as tears fell silently down his weathered cheeks and turned icy in the cold night air.

TWENTY-FIVE

In deference to the cast on Oliver's leg, the Brennans had been allocated front row seats. Oliver sat between his parents, two of the most benevolent critics in what was a most generous audience.

'*Dad*,' Oliver hissed, 'did you bring your mobile? Can I play Snake? I'll put it on mute.'

Flynn shook his head and stretched his arm behind Oliver to reach Georgia's shoulder. She turned her head and gave him a radiant smile.

'*Dad* . . . please.'

'No.'

Georgia took Oliver's hand with her left and entwined her right arm with Flynn's across the back of the seat as the curtain rose.

'She's *word perfect*,' Flynn whispered. 'Don't worry. She'll be grand . . .'

'I know,' Georgia said. 'I know.'

The audience roared when the curtain dropped. When the nurse came shyly on to take her bow, she received a standing ovation.

*   *   *

Two suitcases lay open on their bed. Madeline stared at the shirt she had tried twice to fold, shook it out and tried again as Patrick tossed clothes from the wardrobe. Her third attempt was no better. She placed the crumpled shirt in the suitcase, smoothed it with her hand and picked up the next.

'Maddie.'

'I'll get your stuff from the bathroom, OK?'

Patrick caught her wrist as she turned to leave. He had been about to tell her to leave it, that he'd be better off packing for himself. 'Would you do the rest of the shirts for me? I've never been able to fold a shirt.'

Madeline nodded. 'Yes. Of course . . .'

Patrick moved about the bedroom, looking for anything to chuck in the pile so he would not have to stop still to watch her. He had very few possessions. He put a scrap of paper on the bed beside her. 'That's my number. Where I'll be.' He was going back to the Massa Carrara, the Kingdom of the Moon. He wanted to see the light raking across the jagged marble teeth of the Apennines. That, and playing chess, and drinking grappa in the Bar Anarchista would be his only chance of taking Madeline off his mind.

'I'll call you.'

'You do that.' Patrick shoved a washbag into the side of the suitcase. Madeline zipped it up. 'Are you sure six shirts are enough?' She looked at Patrick as he stood in front of the glass wall. 'You have my mother's number in Florida?' He tapped his breast pocket. 'You'll call me? Christmas Eve? Christmas Day?'

Patrick nodded with a grunt. 'There's something I need to show you. In the studio.'

Madeline smiled. She had been waiting for the final unveiling of the Cardinal. Patrick went down the stairs before her but she stepped ahead as he lingered at the foot. She pulled the dustsheet off the bust.

'It's *so damn good.*'

When Patrick didn't answer, Madeline glanced over her shoulder. He stood at the windows with his back to her.

'It isn't the bust I want you to see. Come over here, by the light.'

Curious, Madeline joined him. Patrick held a small carving, some ten to twelve inches high, fashioned from a dark wood. He turned it over in his hands.

'What's that?'

'Your Christmas present.'

Madeline leant against the window and held the base of the figure gently in both hands. 'It's for me?'

He had carved a slender young woman in the traditional sway-backed pose of a medieval Madonna, long-necked, her bearing graceful and contemplative. In her arms she bore a sleeping child. She drew him tightly to her, her cheek resting gently on the top of the child's head. Madeline began to tremble with an overwhelming rush of conflicting emotions – grief and gratitude, tenderness and a near ferocious love for Patrick, mingled with the awful poignancy of his final gift. When she closed her eyes with a stifled sob and clutched the statue to her, Patrick enfolded her in his arms and rocked her gently, as he would a child.

The white poinsettia that the combat veteran trauma group had presented as a Christmas gift only that morning already looked sick. When Madeline hesitantly touched one pallid, papery bloom it dropped to her desk. She didn't know what to do with it; it would die in the wharf as quickly as it would in her office. Patrick had left and she had booked her departure to Tampa only four days later. With a slow smile she decided on its future home. She'd bequeath it to Jack Zabinsky at their 'office' drinks that evening. He'd already given her a bottle of perfume with a gift-card reading, *Wear this for our first date in January 2001*. The wilting poinsettia would be an apt reply.

363

There was a sharp rap at her door before Flynn came in and threw himself into his regular chair.

'Is that smell you or that thing?' he asked abruptly, leaning forward and sniffing loudly. 'I've never seen flowers in here before.'

'No.' Madeline looked at the scentless flowers, lost for a moment in thought, then back to him. 'How are you, Flynn? How was Kosovo?'

'It was grand. I'm grand.' He spoke strongly, but she was aware of an edginess below the easy confidence that she had not seen in several weeks.

'The refugee camp was grand?'

'Yes. I brought some pictures to show you.'

'I'd love to see them.'

She waited for him to bring them out but he seemed absorbed in a minute examination of the sole of his shoe. When he spoke there was a low throb in his voice. 'Madeline, tell me: is this the end? Is this the end of my time with you?'

Her mouth tightened as her heart tugged within her. She watched him picking at the leather on his shoe, aware that he could not raise his eyes to her face until she answered him. 'Does it seem to be the end for you, Flynn? Do *you* feel that?'

He nodded.

She exhaled silently, letting all the breath leave her body, slammed with rejection. *Was this how Patrick had felt? That it was right, but too soon, too soon; it would always be too soon?* 'If you feel it's the right time, then I'm sure it is the right time.'

'I don't want to say it came to me in a dream,' he growled, 'because that sounds full of shite. But I had another dream. Right after our last session. The night before I went to Kosovo.' Flynn rubbed his chin, his hand rasping against the blue shadow. He spoke hurriedly. 'I was back at the ravine, but I was alone, you know, just me, no bodies, no Oliver, nothing;

364

just me looking across the river. There was no water, no ice, nothing. Just a dry river bed. And I stand there waiting for something to happen, but I can't think why I'm there, or what it is I'm waiting for. I'm kicking my heels. Bored. One minute there's nobody on the other side, then the next time I look, Erik's there, leaning up against a tree. So I wave at him. I shout out to him.'

'What do you shout?'

'Well, that's a funny thing. I don't know what I shout, but I notice it isn't my voice doing the shouting. It's my mouth, but it's *your* voice, Madeline. It's your voice that comes out.'

'I see . . . how does that make you feel?'

'I'm speaking with a woman's voice, for Christ's sake,' he said sharply. 'How do you think I feel?'

Madeline stopped herself from smiling. 'That's upsetting for you?'

'No. It's fine.' He was impatient to tell her what had happened next. 'I kind of do a double-take, but it's fine. Erik and I are chatting, like we're sitting in a pub over a couple of beers, not saying much . . .'

'And this is your voice, now?'

Flynn shook his head vigorously. '*No.* All the time it's your voice. Until I say, I hear *myself* say that I've got to go now; I've got other stuff to do.'

'Do you leave the dream then?'

Flynn stared hard at her, his shadowy eyes piercing clean through her. 'I start to leave. Then I look back, and Erik's leaving too, he's walking away, and I cup my hands to my mouth, like this, and shout, bringing him back, I shout out, "Is this a dream, Erik? Tell me." But I know it makes no difference if it's a dream or not.'

Madeline's skin tingled with anticipation. Something triggered in the back of her mind, some familiar echo of what Flynn was saying. *Is this a dream? Tell me.* An echo from an earlier session? From another client? A case study? She couldn't place the phrase. 'Does he reply?'

'He walks away without looking back. I think: tell me, you miserable fucker, just tell me – yes or no. And then you're there, standing where Erik was.'

'OK.'

Flynn stood up. 'No, it's not OK. People popping up in your head like targets on an FBI shooting range is very far from OK.'

'Do you speak to me?'

'Absolutely I speak to you. I ask you the same question. "Am I dreaming, Madeline? Is this a dream? Tell me."'

'And?'

His stare gathered intensity, drilling into her. 'You don't say anything for a minute. You sigh and sort of shudder . . . ripple. You close your eyes and you run your hands down your body. I feel – ah . . .' He closed his eyes briefly.

'How do you feel, looking at me?'

'I feel unbearably sad. It's . . . it's erotic, watching you, but it makes me feel sad. I feel like a voyeur. You're on the other side of the bank.'

'What is it that makes you feel sad?'

'You're on the other side of the bank, the wrong side,' he repeated. 'You're with Erik. And you look so *sad*. You're shimmering with sadness. So far away . . . I keep asking you the same question.'

'Is this a dream?'

He nodded impatiently. ' "Is this a dream, Madeline? Am I dreaming, Madeline?" And then all at once . . .'

'Yes?'

'You smile at me.' He stared at her in astonishment. 'Just like you're doing now. You light up with the most beautiful, unearthly smile I've ever seen. And you say, you say . . .' *Madeline knew what she said to him, she could hear the words ringing clearly, long before he told her.* '. . . You say, "Go away now, Flynn; this isn't for you." That's it. That's all.

366

Now just you tell me in the name of Jesus what the hell that's all about.' Spent, he slumped back in the chair, looking at her so accusingly that Madeline wanted to laugh.

'Tell me the mood of the dream.'

'I'd say it was happy, except it's too sad. When I woke up I thought I'd just said goodbye to you.'

And so you come in here and do precisely that, Madeline reflected.

Flynn hadn't finished. 'And I was crying like a baby.'

'Have you ever had a dream in which you ask that question before? "Am I dreaming?"'

'No.'

'And when you woke up, you decided it was time to end our sessions?'

'Christ, no. I felt you'd gone away, that's all. Left me. I felt I'd left you there. I felt sad. I felt lost.'

'It *is* sad,' Madeline agreed seriously, admiring the subtlety of his thought, the flicking between her leaving him and his abandoning her, 'it will be very sad for both of us, and the mixture of happiness and sadness in your dream is what I feel about our sessions coming to an end. I think you've prepared yourself very well for this. You question the reality of the dream within the dream itself. It's a sign of coming up to the surface, coming up to full consciousness. You are turning away from the ravine, from Erik; it's no longer filled with bodies, or blood or ice. All the death images that crowded your dreams have gone. You are not frightened looking at the ravine now, are you?'

'No.'

'And you are in control, in the dream, aren't you?'

'Yes . . .' he said slowly.

'So?' Madeline's eyes were shining.

'You told me once that dreams were indications of the state of mind of the dreamer, pointing the direction that the dreamer wanted to move in.'

367

'They can be, yes, a sort of barometer.'

'But you're wrong –' Flynn's eyes narrowed – 'because I don't want to stop seeing you.'

'You're taking it too literally. When you came in, you stated, "This is the end of my time with you." Whether you welcome that or not, I think it is something you feel strongly. It is your decision. If you don't feel ready to go, I certainly won't encourage you to. But if you do then I rejoice for you.'

'But I'm so aroused, watching you on the other bank. So sexually aroused. It frightens me.'

'Eroticism is a key part of dreams, a key part of life.'

'But I can't have it, can I?' His eyes flashed up at her for a second and back down. 'I can't have that with you, can I?'

'No; we can't have that kind of relationship.'

'I know what happens in here, in this room, is set apart from the rest of my life.' He sighed heavily. 'But sometimes, you know, it's tempting to fantasise a little bit.'

'Yes; it is tempting.'

Flynn crossed the room to take his customary guard at the window and prised open the blinds. 'I told Georgia about the dream; and you. Because she asked me why I was crying. I told her everything. It just all . . .' He shrugged. 'I wish I hadn't hurt her so much. I wish we could go forward without that lurking behind us. She says it's OK. I really don't know why she still loves me.' He let the blind snap and turned to her. 'I feel so damned lucky.'

'I'm glad. Recovery from trauma takes place most powerfully within the context of loving and supportive relationships.'

'Don't talk like a textbook.' She smiled, for once accepting the criticism with grace. 'Not now. Is it meant to be frightening?'

Madeline nodded. 'Yes, Flynn. It's very frightening to commit yourself to life again.'

'I don't want to say goodbye to Erik. I don't want to lose him.'

368

'You won't. You will continue to mourn him.'

'Will I still see him in my dreams?'

'Probably.' Madeline leant towards him. 'Does that worry you?'

'No. I don't want to spend the rest of my life thinking about that night, but I don't want to bury it. Or Erik.'

'You won't.'

'I don't want to stop seeing him alive. He's been my companion for nearly seven years. I've been sleeping on his grave. I want to be able to see him when I miss him.'

Madeline's teeth clenched with the effort of repressing the sob that rose within her chest as she felt Flynn's profound attachment to his own mourning. *She would give anything, everything if she could only trick herself into dreaming of Sam – Sam laughing and waving – be able to summon him at will.* She tucked her chin down and focused on the limp petals on her desk. Flynn's voice continued to resonate behind her.

'So you think I'll still see him?'

'I think so. At least for a while.'

'If I choose to go now, if we stop this evening, can it be a sort of trial separation?'

Madeline put a hand to her lips as she took time to word her reply. 'We can't have a trial separation, Flynn. I believe the work we have done together has reached a conclusion. I don't think you need me any more. Your own courage and compassion have enabled you to deal with what you were not previously able to confront,' she said finally. 'That doesn't mean that the symptoms you were suffering might not recur: as I told you when we started, there is no "cure" for trauma. If you need to see me again, professionally, always feel able to contact me. But you should leave this room believing that won't happen.'

In the grey light, Flynn looked at her sadly and went back to his chair. He picked up his case and pulled out two photographs, passing the first one to her wordlessly. It showed a movement during a football match. Two of the players were missing an arm, two had bandaged heads, yet all four were rushing towards a man who leant heavily on one crutch, waving the other in the air in triumph. 'This was the winning goal?' Madeline asked as she looked up at Flynn. The photograph sang with the elation and exhilaration spread wide across the faces of the triumphant players. It glowed with humanity, a ringing affirmation of life. Her voice wavered as she said, 'Now I understand why you called Kosovo grand.'

'I've never covered a soccer match before.' Slowly he slid the other print on top. Madeline looked down at her own face laughing back at her. 'I'd like you to keep them.'

Madeline sat motionless, holding her image loosely on her lap, seeing her own delight as tangible and vigorous as the football players'. She could not speak.

'You don't like it?' Flynn asked in a halting voice. 'Jesus, there isn't a woman on earth who ever likes a picture of herself. It's beautiful, Madeline. It's the best portrait I've ever taken. Do you remember when I took it?' Still she couldn't respond. 'Say something. Anything.'

Madeline met his demanding stare through a mist of tears which she made no attempt to hide. 'Thank you.'

It was Flynn's empathy with his subjects that gave his work such power. And, Madeline thought, his capacity to love. This was how he would be judged, on the manifest intention of his entire life, not the single incident of failure on the road to Gitarama. He had presented her with an image of connection between their two hearts, and she saw herself transformed. She knew that the strength of that love would remain even when she no longer shared his company. She would be able to laugh and rejoice and be carefree without it being a betrayal of Sam, and for that alone she would never forget him.

'Tell me one last thing, Madeline. I have one last question.'

'If I can answer it, I will.' She looked at him steadily.

'Will I still be able to see *you* when I want to? Will I be able to summon you to my dreams?'

'I don't know the answer to that.'

Flynn stood abruptly and slung his bag over his shoulder. 'Then I'd best be home before I make a complete arse of myself. Don't say goodbye: don't say the word. In fact, don't say anything. And if you think you've seen the back of me . . . don't count on it.'

He stood for a moment gazing at her, then walked out without turning round.

Madeline strained to hear his footsteps all the way down the stairs. She sat like a statue, one hand limply holding the two photographs, listening to his slow tread, waiting for the slam of the front door and the echo of his steps taking him across the street, away from her. *Madness and blindness and astonishment of heart.* It was far from a curse. She stepped into the reception hall and pulled a volume from the bookcase, flipping through it to find the section that had echoed in her memory.

> '*Merlyn,*' said the King, '*it makes no difference whether you are a dream or not so long as you are here. Sit down and talk to me for a while, if you can. Tell me the reason for this visit. Say you have come to save us from this war.*'

Madeline closed the book.

Standing on the kerb opposite her office, Flynn gazed up. His eyes were narrowed, intent on catching a final glimpse of her silhouetted against the window. He stayed, still watching, long after he knew she would not come. The visceral memories of the road to Gitarama remained, but they would no longer set the persistent rhythm of his life. He had learned that it was possible to encounter a true love and be wholly transformed

371

by that encounter, without the requirement of sexual fulfilment or even steady companionship. Not a day would pass when he would not think of Erik. Not a day would pass when he would not think of Madeline, but gradually her image would pale and her voice would fade to a faint but persistent echo at the back of his mind, as she withdrew like a slow retiring wave from the beaches of his heart. Flynn turned up the collar of his jacket against the wind and headed for home.

ACKNOWLEDGEMENTS

I would like to thank the following for their support, assistance, advice and expertise: Ross Appleyard, George Avery, Peter Bailey, John Ballance, Carole Blake, Georgina Brown, Elizabeth Capewell, Toby Farrell, Ginny Iliff, Tina Jenkins, Martin Jennings, Gerry Jonkman, Julia Kreitman, Guy Leech, Allan Little, Tom and Eleanor Mead, Buchi Mseteka, Janos Nyiri, Susie Orbach, Hannington Osodo, Paul Rees – and all his team at Centurian Risk Services, particularly Mick, John and Rob – James Runcie, Dr. Gordon Turnbull, Bill Scott-Kerr and Erik Westerink.

I have drawn information, inspiration and great benefit from many books and essays on trauma therapy, but I must express my admiration and appreciation of the following in particular: numerous papers and research studies by Dr. Bessel van der Kolk, *Trauma and Recovery* by Judith Lewis Hermann and *Trauma and Dreams*, edited by Deirdre Barrett. Philp Gourevitch's outstanding book *We Wish To Inform You That Tomorrow We Will Be Killed With Our Families* has contributed enormously to my understanding of the Rwandan genocide. The work of photographers Tom Stoddart, James Natchwey, Don McCullin and Sebastiao Salgado, to name but a few, has had a powerful impact on me, as it has on many others. I am indebted to them.

It needs to be added that any errors of fact – or implausibilities – are entirely my responsibility.

The HarperCollins team has been worth its weight in gold: my warm thanks to Lynne Drew, Rachel Hore, Nick Sayers, Maxine Hitchcock and Fiona McIntosh.

The continuing support and enthusiasm of my very special agent Joanna Frank has been invaluable; my thanks to her and to her colleagues at A.P.Watt, especially Linda Shaughnessy and Vicky Longley.

There is one person without whose inspiration I would never have begun this novel; without her patient and insightful explanations I would have never have finished it: my sister Christine Mead.